An ICEBERG'S GIFT

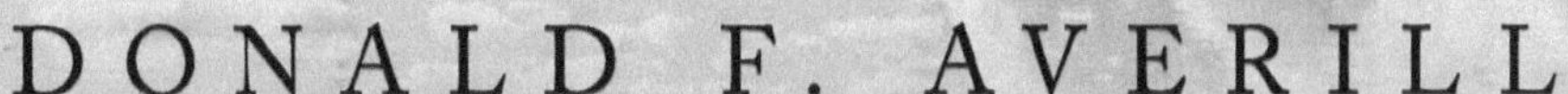

DONALD F. AVERILL

INK START MEDIA
265 Eastchester Dr Ste 133 #102
High Point NC 27262

An ICEBERG'S GIFT

DONALD F. AVERILL

C H A P T E R   1

FISHERMEN'S FIND

Brothers Luka and Rolan Ivanov struggled to rise from under their quilts the first Thursday morning of April. They had stayed up late playing cards with some neighbors who were celebrating their teenage son's birthday party and their twentieth wedding anniversary. All party-goers had exceeded their limit of alcohol. Some celebrants arrived already happy, but not willing to pass up offers of more celebratory beverages. On the way home, the tipsy brothers hadn't noticed the night air was cooler than normal, their sweaters and warm glow providing immunity to the cold. April was still clinging to the last signs of the gloomy days of winter, but this was not unusual for Eastern Siberia.

When the alarm clock sounded at 5:00 a.m., the young men stumbled around their bedroom, eyes half-open, struggling to get their clothes on. Luka said, "I feel like staying in bed all day, Rolan." He stood in his ragged, gray underwear and stretched, touching the ceiling. "Oh, my neck is stiff." He flopped down on the bed, pulled on a pair of socks and slipped on his shoes. He moved his head from side to side stretching his tight neck muscles. As his eyes began to focus more clearly, he realized he was wearing Rolan's shoes. He kicked them off and away from his bed.

"You make my neck sore, Luka! You just put on my socks and shoes and you don't even have your pants on. Can you not tell the difference between black and brown? Your socks are black, mine are brown, remember? Are you still drunk?"

Luka squinted at his feet, wiggled his toes, and said, "The light was too dim for me to tell the difference. I was wondering why my shoes felt funny. Give me a break. Today I am slow to wake up; I drank too much last night. Be nice to your older brother."

1

"I drank too, but I think not as much as you. Did you see that birthday kid? He puked twice, maybe three times, during his celebration. I'll bet the balcony below will need a fire hose to clean it up. You can keep my socks on, but I want my shoes. I think you need to have your eyes checked; maybe you need glasses. I hope you stay awake when you pilot our boat. If you hit something, that stupid Dimitri might stop us to see if you are drunk."

Luka replied, "You are sometimes crazy. I do not need glasses." He tossed the shoes to his brother.

Rolan shook his head and replied, "Keep the socks on. I will not wear them after they have been on your dirty feet."

"I washed my feet last night before we played cards; they are not dirty. Stop your bitching."

"I bet you washed them in a mud puddle. I will wear your socks today. After breakfast we will try to beat the Golokovs out of the harbor. Leonid and his father leave their marina berth around 6:00 a.m. So, hurry up, who knows what riches we may find out in the ocean."

"If we find some diamonds or gold, I will buy you enough socks so you will only wear each pair one day; then throw them away. We will save on soap." Luka grinned as he watched Rolan put on shoes, then jammed his feet into his own shoes after pulling up and buttoning his pants.

The Ivanov brothers set out from Provideniya, for their favorite fishing site along the coast of Siberia on the western edge of the Bering Sea, at 5:45 a.m. They had been quiet while eating breakfast to avoid waking their parents and sister. Wearing mariner's jackets over their heavy sweaters, they sucked the cool harbor air into their lungs, trying to remove the last vestiges of hangovers from their bodies as they drove the dilapidated family pickup to the dock along wet foggy streets.

Their boat, Maligin V, nine and one-half meters from bow to stern, was named after the original Maligin, a famous USSR icebreaker. The young men, both over six-feet tall, called their weathered old boat Maligin V as a joke. The V was for victory, not the Roman numeral. A naval relic from the Second World War, their dark-gray boat's original name was no name at all, but a military number, which they had obscured with light-gray marine paint. It looked like a bandage on the hull.

The Maligin V could have served as a lifeboat on the famous ship; it was about the right size. Ivan, their father, had added a deck and wheelhouse to the front third of the old boat. Now the boys did all the fishing and took care of the antiquated craft. They had rebuilt the engine and added blocks of Styrofoam under the deck to prevent the Maligin V from sinking if a hole were ever gouged through the hull. Eventually, the brothers were going to repaint the boat in a bright color. Luka wanted red, but Rolan, more conservative than his brother, wanted green; thus, the boat had not been repainted. Arina, their younger sister, had suggested they flip a coin. The small areas they had painted to cover the old military numbers looked odd.

The sun began to slowly burn away the morning fog along the coast early in the morning, but in the fjord where the harbor was located, the sun's rays wouldn't be striking the streets and buildings until after 9:00 a.m. Then, the slight morning breeze would help the sun clear the last traces of fog from the inlet. Moving the Maligin V away from the pier, Luka and Rolan headed slowly toward deeper water to avoid striking objects hidden in the fog, which was denser over water than in the city. As an assist to harbor navigation, the horns of the starboard buoys sounded at a higher pitch than those of the port buoys. A few hundred meters out of the fjord, the air began to clear, and Luka turned the Maligin V to port and headed along the coast. They didn't notice any other fishing boats either ahead or behind them.

As they cruised northward at about fifteen knots, Rolan watched for the shoreline to appear out of the fog. He could hear the faint sound of waves crashing against the rocks on his left. He yelled, "I can still hear the waves, Luka, bear to starboard." The two young men traveled thirty-five to forty minutes to arrive at their favorite fishing area. The ocean swells were running a about a meter high as they worked their way along the coast. They made sure no one had followed them before they started pulling in the catch that would supply the family market. After an hour's fishing, they stowed their gear and made their way toward two rocky islets, today's destination for exploratory activities.

Their home port, Provideniya, population slightly less than 2,000, had been built to service cargo transports and warships on the eastern end of the Northern Sea Route through polar waters. Over two decades ago, the town's population had reached nearly 6,000 inhabitants, but economic and world conditions had changed dramatically; the military had almost completely withdrawn, except for a token force to act as police and tourist monitors. The plans for the town had been forgotten, lost in bureaucratic nightmares when the USSR broke up, but tourism from Alaska allowed the population to stabilize during the 1990s. Tourists normally flew in from Nome, Alaska, 160 kilometers directly east of the city.

Rolan, two years younger than his brother, was twenty-three. They looked as if they were twins, and their mother said they looked like younger versions of their father. Both young men had tried boxing to earn money but being struck on their square jaw and prominent nose was no joke, so they retired from the ring after five fights, each having four wins and one loss. They studied engineering for two years at the local technical school before dropping out. Luka had taken English courses each year in school, but Rolan had taken technical classes instead. He didn't foresee that English was going to be of any benefit to his future. They were not going to be academicians; they wanted more adventure than pencils and paper had to offer. But the young men were not quitters, they just hadn't found their niches.

Their sister, Arina, had just turned twenty, and was attending the same technical school, following in her brothers' footsteps. According to the instructors, Arina was significantly more academically talented than her brothers, although they had been above average students. Her questions in class stimulated her professors to prepare better, more sophisticated lectures.

While her brothers were out fishing, Arina was home studying celestial navigation, dark matter, and the curvature of space. She loved cosmology. Arina was not only smart, but without a doubt she was the best looking female Caucasian in Provideniya. Several young men from military families had admired Arina, but she had set her sights very high; she didn't want anything to prevent her from reaching her goal. Arina wanted to study astronomy in America, but her parents considered her idea foolhardy; how would she ever get to America? But her brothers encouraged her, even if, in their eyes, her goal seemed a bit whimsical. Rolan and Luka discussed Arina's dream often when at sea, and before long, they realized America should also be their destination, but they needed money to follow their dreams.

Unbeknownst to the rest of the Ivanov family, the brothers did very little fishing. They had found a spot where, in less than an hour, they could catch enough fish for several days' use at home and their parents' fish market/diner. With the fish packed on ice, Rolan and Luka transformed into treasure hunters, starting off each day with the hope of finding something valuable. They called themselves entrepreneurs, but most everyone in Provideniya considered them a couple of clowns; and that is how they wanted to appear. They had made a pact to keep what they were doing a secret from everyone, including their family. Hidden in the back of their minds was their most recent and greatest desire—a way to leave Russia and go to the United States; the land of opportunity—but that required self-sponsorship. If Arina found a way to go to the USA, they were going too, if at all possible. They were on constant watch for opportunities to exploit.

They turned the boat out to sea as they put away the fishing gear. They had changed their minds about visiting the islet area and instead, were going to visit Mirokov, a small island about five kilometers off the coast. They hoped to find some precious mineral deposits on one of the islands within ten kilometers of the continental shore.

One day when Rolan and Luka were at the pier working on the Maligin V, an elderly fisherman, dressed in tattered clothing, sporting a ragged beard, and smelling like alcohol, had told them a story. Perhaps it was anecdotal, perhaps fictitious, it dealt with a bear hunter finding diamonds on Mirokov, a rugged chunk of rock with little vegetation. During the summer it was a roosting place for seabirds. As they approached the island from the southeast, a Russian patrol boat bore down on their position.

Rolan idled the engine when Luka yelled, "Hey! It's Dimitri. Let's talk to him. Maybe he can tell us something interesting."

The twenty-meter patrol boat, labeled P-432, coasted up to the Maligin V. When the craft were five meters apart, one of the uniformed sailors tossed Luka a rope so he could pull the boats together. When the smaller boat bumped the patrol boat, Luka and Rolan looked up to see Captain Dimitri Ulisnilov, in his black uniform, standing three-meters above them, with his hands on his hips, his eyes scanning the Maligin V's deck.

Luka frowned and said, "What are you looking for, Captain?"

"Where are your life vests, Ivanovs? You know you should be wearing them at all times in these waters, especially now."

Rolan replied, "Why is that? Has something happened?"

"In the last week, several small ice floes have been reported by cargo ships. Most of the pack ice has melted in the warmer water and the recent sunshine, but not all. It should all be gone by the end of the month and the water will be clear of ice in June. If you don't put on your survival gear, I will cite you for not following the rules, and I will notify your parents. I am sure they will not be pleased. I will wait while you put them on."

Rolan picked up his bright orange vest, put it on, and tossed another one to Luka.

Dimitri relaxed and scanned the Maligin V. "How is fishing today?"

Luka answered, "Good. We are low on ice, but we should be able to get back to Provideniya before what we have melts."

"We saw a small berg a few kilometers back. If you need some ice, chip off some. Have you got some piolets?"

Luka replied, "No, we didn't bring any ice axes with us, just fishing gear. Well, we have a hammer, in case we get mad at our engine," he smiled.

"Well, I'll let you borrow one from the Navy. You can return it next time you see us." Dimitri motioned to one of the young seamen who scurried off, returning with an ice ax. The seaman handed it to Dimitri and saluted. Dimitri tossed the ax to Luka, and said, "Do not lose that. It will not do any good on the ocean bottom."

"Thank you, Captain. We will not lose it and we will remember your generosity. Do you want to inspect our catch, sir?"

Dimitri replied, "That won't be necessary. My best wishes to your parents. How's that pretty sister of yours? Has she a boyfriend yet?"

"Arina is fine, thanks. She's too smart for the scum in Provideniya. We wouldn't let any of them lick her boots. She has her sights set on becoming an astronomer." Rolan smiled and waved to Dimitri, tossing the line back to the patrol boat.

As the boats drifted apart, Dimitri yelled, "Does she want to study in Moscow? I know some people that would take her in."

Luka yelled back, "No, she wants to go to America, to New Mexico or Texas, maybe California or Arizona, someplace warm where she can stay out all night and look at stars without wearing a coat."

Dimitri threw his head back and started laughing, "Tell her good luck!" Still laughing, the captain saluted the boys as the patrol boat pulled away and headed southeast into open water.

Luka pushed the throttle forward and the bow slid through the cold water heading northwest. Rolan went below and checked the ice situation. There was enough to keep the fish cold for a few more hours, but not the whole day; just as Luka had told Dimitri. They would have to get more ice if they wanted to explore all afternoon.

Rolan went back on deck and joined Luka. As they skirted the northern extreme of Mirokov, the brothers began watching the horizon for ice. Occasionally, Luka would scan with his binoculars as they chugged along, but he didn't see anything for nearly 20 minutes. "There!" Luka shouted as he pointed to the north.

Rolan squinted, sighting down Luka's extended arm. He couldn't see anything out of the ordinary, just blue-green ocean water extending to the horizon. He reached out for the binoculars, still on a cord around Luka's neck.

"Let me take the cord from my neck! I don't need you to garrote me, little brother."

"You are such a pansy, Luka."

Once Rolan had the glasses, he scanned the horizon, stopped, and refocused the lenses.

"Your eyes are very bad, Luka. I had to change the focus quite a bit."

"My eyes aren't bad; your eyes are bad. So, do you see the ice?"

"Yeah. It's about 2,000 meters from us. Should be plenty of clean ice for us to chip off. I hope we can get close enough, so we don't have to row over to it. Maybe we can find a place to dock and just step onto the ice. Change our heading and we'll be there in a few minutes."

As the fishing boat approached the small ice floe, the frozen water grew in size. The bluish-white mass jutted four-to-five meters above the sea. The area of the ice looked to be about ten or more times the area of the boat's deck. Luka piloted the boat, circling the floating body, and found what he was looking for, a small indentation where he could place the bow very close to the ice.

Rolan jumped from the boat to the ice, almost falling into the ice-cold water, but he was able to steady himself. He crouched down, pulled an old railroad spike from his pocket and pounded it into the ice. Luka tossed him a line and he secured the Maligin V. Rolan stood up, his eyes nearly two meters from the ice, and scanned what he could see of the surface, then he climbed to the highest point and visually checked the frozen body in all directions.

Luka yelled, "See anything?"

Rolan replied, "Maybe. Something is trapped in the ice. I'll have to chip away some of the floe so we can see what it is. Toss me that ice ax."

Luka responded, "I'm going to add another rope to secure us and join you. I'll bring the ax and a bag for ice to spread over the fish."

While Rolan waited, he broke away some of the solid with the hammer. He didn't want to damage whatever was entrapped, so he hadn't made much progress before Luka climbed up beside him.

Luka handed Rolan the ax and squinted, looking into the ice, "What do you think it is?"

"I don't know, maybe it's an alien spaceship. Do you remember the American film, The Thing? We have to be careful, whatever it is. It might eat us. Then Mom and Dad wouldn't have fresh fish to sell, and who would keep the wolves away from Arina?" Rolan laughed a little nervously, wondering what he had discovered. Maybe it was just a piece of wood.

Luka replied, "That story took place in the Antarctic, not the Arctic."

"Maybe there were two beings from space; in case one didn't make it through the atmosphere, the other one would—you know, a backup."

"Come on, Rolan, get serious. There are no aliens. Stars are too far apart for civilizations to make physical contact. Just ask Arina, she knows all about that shit."

Rolan broke away several large chunks of ice and Luka hit them with the hammer, smashing them into smaller pieces so they would easily fit into the burlap bag. When it was full, he dragged it back to the boat, dumped it over the fish, and returned. After emptying the second bag of ice over the fish, Luka left it on the boat and joined his brother.

"Hey, Luka, it looks like a skid of a small airplane, but it's still attached to something. I can't budge it, but the bottom is up."

Luka started laughing, "Keep digging, maybe there's a plane attached. We could fly our fish to market instead of using that old slow boat, and then fly with Arina to America."

"You are too funny, Luka. If you have to pee, do it here to melt some ice." Rolan laughed, "Just do not splash on me."

The young men chipped away at the ice for over an hour before resting. They went back to the Maligin V and ate sandwiches. Finished with lunch, they put on dry gloves, and went back to the skid, which was completely exposed. They worked another thirty minutes before Rolan said, "This is going to take a long time, Luka, maybe weeks. I've been thinking, let's tow the whole thing into that hidden inlet. The sun and the salt water will melt the ice and we can help it along by knocking chunks off with axes."

"Damn. That is a good idea. We can attach a line to the ice so our discovery will not float away. You are not as dumb as Arina says you are, Rolan."

"Da, and we can use that camouflage netting to help hold the ice against the shore. It didn't work for catching fish. It is good that we saved it. If we start towing, it's going to take several hours to get it to the inlet. I hope Dimitri doesn't show up; what will we do then?"

Luka responded, "Let's cover the skid with some loose ice so it isn't obvious. Okay? If we see Dimitri, we'll say we wanted to beach the ice so it would be easier to manage. We'll tell him we will come back for more ice every day we fish. We won't have to haul ice from Provideniya, just on the return trip. It will be more economical that way. We will be saving fuel. He will like that."

Fifteen minutes later, with the iceberg in tow, the little boat was laboring, but the small floe was gradually moving shoreward. In another hour, Rolan, in the pilothouse, yelled to Luka, who was watching the tow lines, "I can see where the inlet is located; we'll be there in another half-hour. We are going to have to use our extra fuel to get back home."

"That extra twenty-liters of gas should be enough to get us back to the dock, even if we run dry getting the ice in the inlet. I have not seen any sign of Dimitri. I think we are safe, and lucky. Hey, Rolan, do you think the ice will go through the inlet without hitting bottom? Remember, most of it is under water."

Rolan thought a couple of seconds and said, "I think we'll be all right; the inlet is fairly deep." When Maligin V entered the narrow waterway, the large chunk of ice glanced off the inlet wall on the starboard side of the boat and moved to the center of the rock-walled opening when Rolan gunned the engine. The ice barge cleared the subsurface rocks and was towed into the arctic lagoon accessed through the hidden inlet. They called it the hidden inlet because from several hundred meters offshore, the rocky shore cliffs appeared to be continuous. The channel of water leading inland couldn't be seen unless the observer was nearly at the opening to the small circular bay or looking down from the air.

When the mass of ice, now hidden from ocean vessels, struck bottom in the lagoon, the portion above water was about five meters from shore. Rolan and Luka stripped their boat of all the rope they had and tied the mass to the shoreline, and then stretched the camouflage netting over the top so it wouldn't be noticed easily from the air. When they had determined everything was considered, they boarded Maligin V and started home.

On the way back, Luka said, "What if that skid is something someone pushed off a ship as a piece of junk?"

Rolan didn't have to think about it, all he said was, "We will see, won't we?"

CHAPTER 2

SECRETS

Maligin V chugged into the busy dock about dinner time. There was one small cargo ship being unloaded and Dimitri's patrol boat was being refueled farther down the pier. The catch of two other fishing boats, one of which was the Golokovs', was being transferred to trucks. As the Maligin V passed by the Golokovs' boat, red-haired Leonid waved. A few people were buying fish directly from the fishermen, but the Ivanovs' fish was for their family market and home use.

As they approached the end of the wharf, their battered, old, green pickup looked lonely, but when Arina stepped out and waved, the sun seemed to shine brighter. When their boat bumped up against the wharf, Luka tossed a line to Arina, who tied off the Maligin V to one of the wooden pilings.

"How's our pretty sister?" Luka looked up at Arina and grinned.

"Do not always say the same thing, Luka. Sometimes you should say lovely, or beautiful," Arina laughed and tossed her silky-blond hair back from her rosy cheeks. "How many fish did you get today? You were gone for a long time; two hours longer than normal. I was going to ask Captain Dimitri to search for you."

Rolan jumped from the boat to the wharf, gave Arina a hug, and responded with, "We got enough fish for the market. Arina, please do not ever send Dimitri after us. We do not want him to know what we are doing."

Arina reached out and pinched Rolan's cheek. "Sooo, you are doing something secret? You must tell me."

Rolan pulled back from her nipping fingers and said, "If I tell you now, it will not be secret anymore, will it? You'll tell Mama and Papa and then all their friends will know, and the whole adventure will be spoiled. After dinner, when mother and father have gone to bed, we will let you know our little secret. Okay?"

"But you know that is torture. Must I wait four hours?"

Luka joined the others and gave Arina a hug. "Your wait of four hours will be worth it. You will be very excited, I'm sure."

"Oh, Luka, tell me!"

"Four hours, dear sister. You will have to wait. Think of spaceships. I have a question for you."

"Your secret has to do with spaceships? Oh! You can be so frustrating!"

The three siblings loaded the fish into the truck and Arina drove to the market. After the fish were transferred, they went home for dinner. During their meal, Luka and Rolan asked Arina about space travel. A lively discussion ensued, that included their parents, Ivan and Sofiya. After dinner, they played cards for a couple of hours. Sofiya had made dessert, a vanilla cake with thick white frosting. Ivan began to yawn and said to Sofiya, "We must go to bed. We have to prepare the new catch tomorrow. It cannot go to waste. You youngsters can stay up and talk all you like, just not too loud, and no drinking. I know how many Ochakovo bottles are in the refrigerator. Good night."

Arina, trying not to show her excitement about the upcoming revelation, said, "Okay, no beer tonight. Good night, Papa, Mama."

Luka and Rolan were gathering up the cards and both said, "Good night."

Rolan folded down the leaves of the black lacquered wooden table and placed it against the wall. Luka put Sofiya's treasured blue vase, containing artificial white and yellow flowers, back in its location on the table, and placed the deck of cards next to it.

Arina couldn't hold back any longer. She grabbed Luka's arm and said, "Okay, tell me!" She was trembling and bouncing from one foot to the other.

Luka looked down the hallway to see if their parents' bedroom door was shut and whispered, "Relax, Arina. Let's go in your bedroom and close the door."

Rolan followed with, "Wait for me, I am getting more tea."

When Rolan entered the bedroom, Arina was sitting on the edge of the bed with her arms wrapped around her pillow. "Please, no more waiting. Tell me your secret," she begged. Arina's fingers were dug into her pillow, as she anticipated hearing Rolan tell her the long awaited mystery. Since, at dinner, they had talked about space travel, she expected Rolan and Luka to tell her that alien bodies had been discovered frozen in polar ice. But Rolan and Luka were always playing tricks, so she had doubts about believing what they were going to tell her.

Luka sat down at her desk beside her computer, smiled, and said, "We think we found an airplane."

Her eyes opened wide. "What? You think you found an airplane? You do not even know? How could you not know? I don't get it. What was all the talk about spacecraft?"

Rolan explained, "The spacecraft talk was a diversion. The plane is frozen in ice."

"Frozen in ice? What ice?" Arina frowned. "Come on, Rolan, no jokes."

"It is not a joke. We towed the floating ice to an inlet and tied it to the shore. We have to wait for it to melt. The airplane is upside down with only one skid visible. We chipped about 100 kilos of the floe away so we could tell what it was. That is why we were so late returning to Provideniya today."

"Oh! It is not a fighter-jet. How big is it?"

"We do not know, but not too big." Rolan raised his hands up and exhaled. "Can you think of a way to melt the ice faster than with the sun and the ocean water?"

Arina thought for a moment and said, "What about your bilge pump? Can you rig it to pump ocean water over the ice? The salt in it will speed up melting the frozen water. How big is this ice, anyway?"

Rolan rubbed his chin and answered, "About twice the size of our house. What do you think, Luka?"

Luka rolled his eyes around, rubbed his forehead, and said, "Da. That is about right."

Arina held out her hands toward Luka and asked, "Can you hand me that tablet and a pencil, please." As soon as she had the pencil, she said, "How far into the ice is this airplane?"

"Wait, Arina." Rolan wanted to stop Arina from wasting her time. "We don't know for sure if there is a plane attached to the skid. It might just be a piece of junk someone threw off a ship long ago."

Arina looked at her brothers and lectured. "If the ice is an iceberg, the thing in the ice didn't come from a ship, it had to come from a glacier. I do not know of any glaciers that calve into the Arctic Ocean. The nearest glaciers are along the southern coast of Alaska. When ice falls from a glacier into the ocean, it becomes an iceberg, but they float south, not north. I think what you have found is from pack ice. The arctic ice has been melting for many years, so a piece of pack ice has floated south, and you found it. You might be correct though; the object could have been thrown off a ship, maybe a cargo ship or an icebreaker."

Rolan looked at Luka and exclaimed, "She's right! The ice did not come from a glacier, so the thing we found might be from a ship; but if it is a plane, it is most likely one that crashed on the arctic ice. I wonder how long ago."

Luka responded, "Good thinking, Arina. You are very smart! I think we have found an airplane in pack ice. Maybe we can fix it and fly to the United States. You will study astronomy just like you want."

"Let's not get ahead of ourselves, my brothers. We have a lot of ice to melt in order to discover what is entombed. Let's go to bed now, and tomorrow I will go fishing with you. I will think about what we need to take with us. Your secret has tired my brain. Good night."

As the boys left Arina's bedroom, Rolan hesitated at the door and said, "Remember, do not say anything to Mama and Papa."

Arina put on her pajamas, brushed her teeth, and slid under the covers. The cold sheets warmed quickly from the heat of her body. She tossed and turned, trying to subdue her imaginative thoughts and recognize only reality. What Rolan and Luka found surrounded by frozen water might be nothing of value, but if the object is an airplane, how exciting. Her dreams of going to the United States might actually take place in the not too distant future. She fluffed up her pillow, cradled her head, looked up at the ceiling, and imagined what the sky looked like in California. Orion would be magnificent, his belt dazzling. After thinking for nearly an hour about the ice, and what they might find encased, Arina drifted off to sleep.

She was awakened at 6:12 a.m. when she smelled coffee and heard the voices of her family coming from the kitchen. Everyone else was up. She blinked a few times and rubbed sleepers from her eyes.

Dressing quickly, she combed her hair, put on heavy socks and slippers, and joined the family at the breakfast table.

Sofiya smiled, "Good morning, Arina. Did you sleep well?"

Before Arina could answer, Rolan contributed, "I heard her talking in her sleep. She was telling some boys to go away; she had other things to do today."

Luka commented, "I heard her fart. It was very loud. It woke me up and I laughed."

"Oh, shut up, Luka. You are the one who has loud farts; you know it, too." Arina shook her table knife at Luka. "How would you like to be stabbed?"

"Do not stab my clean shirt, you will get butter on it," Luka smiled.

Rolan couldn't be left out. As he began to laugh, he said, "The noise woke me up, too, but I thought it was a sonic boom. I imagined one of our fighters must have passed over Provideniya during the night."

"Mama!" Arina was getting irritated.

"Look, you guys, that is enough about farting. I am still eating my breakfast." Ivan was holding his fork ready to poke it into someone. They all knew he was not joking; it had happened before. Each of them had been stuck with a fork, their hands had a few tiny scars as exhibits of his handiwork.

Sofiya asked, "Anybody want eggs? You may each have only one, we are almost out."

Sofiya and Ivan left for the store before Luka and Arina finished eating. Rolan was collecting all the hoses, tubing, and connecters he could find and tossing them into the back of the truck. While Luka made lunches, Arina sat at the table doing some calculations. She looked up occasionally to ask Luka questions about the chunk of ice and what he thought the temperature of the water was in the inlet. The door banged when Rolan came back into the house.

"Are you two ready to sail? Let us see if we have an airplane or a spaceship."

Arina looked up from her numbers and said, "Rolan, you say the cutest things. Have you got extra gas for the bilge pump?"

"I do, sister dear. I have a twenty-liter can filled to the top. Will we need more rope?"

She replied, "You probably already saw the thirty-meter piece in the truck. We'll take it."

Luka raised a bag of lunches above his head, grinned, and said, "Let us go smelting!"

"Luka! What a terrible joke!" Arina laughed and said, "Let us melt some ice."

With the Maligin V's diesel engine purring, they headed out of the harbor, turned northwest, followed the coast for about an hour, and pulled into the hidden inlet. The brothers expected to see more of the airplane exposed following more than twelve hours of melting, but little had changed from the day before. Luka guided the boat up to the floating ice, Rolan jumped onto it, and secured the boat. Arina was looking at the ice with her mouth open.

"Oh! It's bigger than I thought." She jumped onto the ice and climbed to the top to see the exposed skid under the netting. She crouched down, shielded her eyes from the glare of the sun, and tried to look into the mass of ice, but could only see a dark object without definition. It could be a plane, or maybe just debris thrown from a ship.

Rolan looked questioningly at Arina, "What are your orders, ma'am?"

"Okay. We have to connect a hose from the pump input to the ocean water. Then, connect the output hose to the top of the ice, start the bilge motor, and watch what happens. I hope we will see the ice melting away from the object at a significant rate. We might be able to use the ocean water like a knife, if we have a fine spray, and cut or melt away the ice in large pieces. We can use the ice ax to create a waterway for the melted ice to flow to the inlet water. Get the warmest water possible, so put the input hose as far from the ice as it will reach, and if possible, place it in a sunny spot."

"Luka, run the hose to the ice from the pump. I will get the other one. Let us do it!"

Arina watched Rolan uncoil the hose he had brought from home and attach it to the pump input. She filled the pump gas tank and watched her brothers get the hoses in position. When they were ready, they signaled with a wave and she started the pump.

Arina joined Luka at the top of the ice floe and watched the ocean water begin to melt the ice around the metal strut to the skid. It only took a couple of minutes before the water began to turn gritty; sand and dirt were coming from the hose.

Arina turned and yelled, "Rolan! Raise the intake hose up, it is picking up junk from underneath the water. Wait! I have an idea." She got in the boat, grabbed a life preserver and ran to Rolan. "Here, tie this to the end of the hose—near the opening. It will keep the hose off the bottom." Rolan did as Arina asked. They looked back at Luka and watched for about thirty seconds.

Luka waved and yelled, "Now the water is clear." Arina volunteered to keep an eye on the pump; every fifteen minutes pouring more gasoline in the tank to keep it full. Luka and Rolan directed the ocean water around the strut and chipped ice away from the ever enlarging cavity. When the cavity was about a meter and a half deep, they could see a partially painted surface. Rolan tapped on it and said, "It is made of wood. It might be the fuselage of a plane, but it must be very old; modern planes are made of aluminum alloys."

Luka remarked, "It could not be older than World War One." He could see water accumulating in the cavity, approaching where Rolan's feet were placed, so Luka chipped a groove into the ice to make a pathway for the cold, diluted ocean water to spill from the ice back into the sea.

C H A P T E R 3
THE WRECK

"If we only had some driftwood." Arina was looking around and commented as they sat on the shore eating lunch, "We could boil ocean water and melt the ice much faster."

"How much ice do you think we have removed in three hours?" The others could hear frustration in Rolan's question.

Luka replied, "I am thinking maybe fifty kilos." He tossed a rock at the ice and watched it ricochet off into the water. "We need hot water and a nozzle on the hose. My fingers are really cold and my arms are very tired. I am going for a little hike, up there." He pointed to the top of the rock surrounding the inlet.

"Okay, brother, but don't be gone too long. We will be melting ice even longer if you do not help."

"Da. I will return in thirty minutes; maybe longer if I find something I have to carry." He laughed, "Do not bother to send the dogs looking for me."

Arina and Rolan watched Luka start climbing the steep rocky incline and saw him disappear over the top. They talked for a moment, and then paddled their rowboat to Maligin V. Rolan climbed aboard, got the hammer and a railroad spike, and returned to the floe. As the cold inlet water was being pumped over the ice, Rolan and Arina began chipping large chunks from it. Roland made holes in the solid, and Arina, using the ice ax, knocked out the bridges between the holes. When a good-sized chunk of material was isolated, looking like a toadstool, Rolan broke it away using his hammer.

They were working on their fourth icy mushroom when a loud scraping noise drew their attention away from chipping. Arina looked back at the hill where Luka had gone and watched something sliding down the rocks, coming to a stop about fifteen meters away from the narrow beach where they had eaten.

18

Arina heard Luka yell, "I am back! I found some wood!"

Luka struggled with the wreckage he had found, skidding it across the rocks. "It is part of an old rowboat. I bought it from some children for one ruble." He held up his right index finger.

Arina said, "You did not."

"You are right, I bought it from an old man with a beard. I paid him two rubles. I offered him another fifty kopecks, but he refused. He said I would need the money for the bus fare. He knew the boat wouldn't float."

Rolan started laughing and commented, "Good one, Luka."

Arina was also laughing and said, "Did you guys really hear me fart?"

Rolan replied, "No, we just said that so Mom and Dad would think everything was normal. We didn't want them to think we were doing anything strange. Besides, you are too beautiful to fart very loud."

Arina threw a piece of ice at Rolan and said, "I wish I had a sister so we could gang up on you guys. Two against one is not fair." She looked at the large ice floe and shook her head. "Let's get to work. Do we have a metal can so we can heat the water?"

Luka pointed at the Maligin V and said, "In the bow under the top deck there is a twenty-liter can. It is empty, a spare for extra diesel. Rolan, toss me the ice ax. I'll break up the wood and start a fire."

"Hey, Luka, put rocks down so the can sits above the fire." Rolan laughed and continued, "Do not put the lid on the can!"

"Geez, Rolan, do you think I am an idiot!"

Arina started laughing, "He is right, Rolan, one idiot should not suggest another is an idiot!"

It took twenty-five minutes to get the first half-can of water to near boiling, but after that, with the fire burning robustly, each portion of hot water was ready after fifteen minutes. After three hours of work, the second skid and much of the forward fuselage were exposed. Arina kept the bilge pump fuel tank full and the fire burning at a constant rate, but they were running out of wood. The old rowboat's remnants had contributed significantly toward liberating the entombed aircraft. That old wooden shell had performed its final duty. It had helped save an old airplane from sinking into the frigid depths of the Arctic Ocean, to be lost forever.

One last portion of water was being heated as the final sliver of wood was consumed by fire. The boys were still breaking off chunks of ice, and they were getting larger each time. After the last of the hot water was exhausted, Arina asked Rolan to look through an exposed corner of the cockpit window and peer inside the cabin.

Rolan broke off another large chunk of ice and pushed it into the water before sliding down, headfirst, into the deep recess they had created adjacent to the cockpit. He arrested his position with the ice ax but couldn't quite see into the plane. He called out to Luka, "Lower me down so I can get a better look into the plane." Luka grabbed hold of Rolan's ankles, braced himself, and lowered his six foot five brother into the depression.

Rolan rubbed the cockpit glass and squinted as he put his face to the window. He was very quiet; no jokes were being expressed. He was seriously analyzing the indistinct images.

"What is in there, Rolan?" asked Arina.

"I think there is a dead man—strapped in his seat. It is hard to see, there is ice everywhere. Do you want to see?"

"No, I will wait until we get the plane out of the ice. Do you think it will smell bad?"

"Maybe. I wonder how long he has been frozen. His body is black. Pull me up, Luka."

Luka bent his knees and lifted. When Rolan's legs were above the ice, Luka grabbed Rolan's left hand and pulled his slightly taller brother from the cavity. "Is he an American, Rolan?"

"I could not tell; it is difficult to see inside. Maybe Canadian—or maybe not a man."

Arina was looking at her watch and commented, "We should go now—get a few fish and be back home for dinner. We do not want Mom and Pop to worry. They might send someone like Dimitri to look for us if we are late."

"Good thinking, Arina. You guys dismantle the bilge pump and I will cover the plane with the camouflage net." After Rolan spread the netting over the top of the floe, he checked the ropes attaching the ice to land. One of the tie-downs was loose, so he secured the rope to another location; the other skid—a little closer to land.

Arina and Luka were waiting for him in the rowboat. They had the pump, hoses, hand tools, and the empty twenty-liter can ready to be transferred to the Maligin V. As the big boat left the inlet, Luka made ready two fishing poles. When they arrived at the wharf, they had three large salmon to take home.

That night the Ivanov family went to bed early; everyone was tired. Luka and Rolan talked for a few minutes before retiring. They had been quiet during dinner, trying to think of a way to get more firewood. They came up with the same idea. In the morning, as soon as their parents left for the fish market, Arina and the boys drove to the old military base. It had been sixteen years since the barracks had been occupied; the government had let the base go to seed. They tried to find someone in charge, but the run-down buildings were deserted. Several of the smaller buildings had fallen over in the fierce winter winds and needed to be cleaned up; the young Ivanovs were only too happy to oblige.

The pickup was loaded to capacity with wood of all sizes and shapes and driven to the Maligin V. While the boys transferred the wood to the boat, Arina found another twenty liter can for heating water. They left the wharf at nine o'clock, two hours later than usual, and headed for the hidden inlet and the plane, which, in spite of all their effort, remained more than half entombed in ice.

They had been traveling for about thirty minutes, wishing they had a faster boat, eager to free the plane from the ice, when Rolan noticed a boat coming toward them at high speed. "Luka, we have company!" He pointed about fifteen degrees to starboard.

Luka picked up the binoculars and focused on the ship. "Damn, it is Captain Dimitri. What are we going to tell him about the wood?"

Arina stood up and looked toward the patrol boat. "Do not worry, I will handle him." She looked at Luka, fluttered her eyelids, removed her life preserver and red sweatshirt, and smiled.

Luka gave a wolf-whistle and said, "That will do it."

Rolan, smiling, commented, "Arina, don't get your undershirt wet, those sailors might attack us to get to you. Luka and I will have to throw them overboard and then go to their rescue."

The patrol boat coasted up next to the fishing boat. Three sailors and Captain Dimitri looked down from three meters above the Maligin V. "Arina, where is your life preserver? Your brothers are wearing theirs."

"Oh! I am sorry Captain Dimitri. I took it off for a few minutes to move around more freely." She bent over to accentuate her butt, picked up the red-orange preserver, and slipped it on over her T-shirt. She could see the sailors' eyes were staring at her sexy body, imagining what was under her skimpy T-shirt.

"You look very nice today, Arina. What is all the wood for, if I may ask?"

Arina walked over beside the pile of wood, struck a sexy pose, and said, "We want to prepare some smoked salmon. We are going to make a smoke house; we cannot burn things near the fish market or on the wharf. It would be too dangerous to others."

"Be careful with the fire, I wouldn't want you to get injured," Dimitri smiled. "Also, don't burn any rocks." He began laughing and said, "Goodbye for now." He motioned to the sailors saying, "Get back to your posts, the entertainment is over."

Arina said, "Goodbye," and waved as the patrol boat pulled away heading southeast. When the patrol boat was out of range, Arina uttered, "What a dumb-ass. He is a bigger idiot than you guys are." She started laughing, removed the preserver, put her sweatshirt back on and then donned the life preserver.

Luka grinned and responded, "Thank you, Arina. It is comforting to know you rank us above Dimitri. Your explanation for the wood was very convincing—good job. Dimitri forgot all about the ice ax he loaned us. Maybe we will return it next time he comes by—if we have finished with it. Head for the inlet."

A half-hour later they were tied up to the ice as close to the beach as possible. While the boys were throwing the wood ashore, Arina used the life boat and moved the metal cans and bilge pump to the beach. She gathered some more rocks and prepared another site for heating water. It took Rolan and Luka fifteen minutes to empty the boat of wood. They went ashore and prepared firewood from the planks and laminated wood wallboard. Arina started two fires, and while the water was heating, she removed the camouflage net that disguised the part of the airplane they had uncovered. She noticed the cavity they had created the day before was about half full of water. "Rolan, we need to pump out the water from around the cabin of the aircraft. Quite a bit of ice melted since yesterday. I think the ice is rising in the water, too. The top is melting faster than the bottom."

Luka was listening and said, "What happens when we free the plane from the ice? It is upside down. It will sink into the water if we don't have something to make it float."

Rolan wondered, too. "Da, Arina. Maybe we build a raft?"

Arina didn't answer the boys; she was guessing the weight of the plane, and how much water would have to be displaced to keep the plane afloat. She quickly estimated it would take about a dozen empty twenty liter cans to float the plane, and that might not be enough. She decided to have Rolan and Luka replace the skids with wheels, turn the plane right-side-up and pull it ashore assisted by the boat. She was going to have to get more rope, some pulleys, and wheels that would fit the struts that held the skids. She would explain her plan as they continued to expose more of the plane. She knew Rolan and Luka would come up with the necessary materials from the military base.

Rolan said, "You are very quiet, Arina. What do you think? Have you a solution to the problem?"

"Da, I will tell you as we melt the ice."

The first few twenty liter portions of hot water were used to enlarge the cavity to access the cabin. Arina had arranged the bilge pump to force ocean water over the ice covering the left wing, which was tilted up at about a thirty degree angle. While Arina heated the water, Rolan and Luka broke away ever larger portions of ice with the ice ax and hammer. By the time they sat down for lunch, the cabin door was almost ready to be opened, and nearly one third of the left wing was exposed. About a quarter of the wood supply had been burned to heat the ocean water, but much of the plane had been exposed.

Rolan drank the last of his tea, stood, and put on his gloves. "I am going to free the pilot, I hope he does not smell bad." He picked up one of the twenty liter cans, half-full of nearly boiling water, and headed toward the cockpit. Arina quickly swallowed the last of her sandwich, jumped to her feet, and followed him. Luka watched his brother and sister climbing on the ice from the rowboat, noting that the angle of the exposed wing seemed to have changed during the morning's activities.

"Arina, jump up and down on the ice. See if it moves."

Luka watched, but couldn't detect any motion. He yelled, "Both of you jump, but together." As soon as Rolan added his weight, the ice began to rock very slightly, just enough so Arina could feel it. Luka was just testing to see how stable the ice floe was, he worried that the ice might turn over with the plane still trapped. That would be a big problem.

Rolan resumed pouring hot water over the cabin door and was able to pull it open about half a meter. Until he could swing the door completely open, he couldn't access the cabin; he was just too big, and there was still ice inside.

CHAPTER 4

THE PILOT AND THE PLANE

Rolan thought to himself, "One more container of water should do it. I do not smell anything; that body must still be frozen solid." Rolan was passed a second can of hot water.

"Rolan, pour the water where the door is touching the ice."

"Hold your yaks, Luka. I know where to put the water. As soon as I get the door open, you will have to help me. I will cut the pilot loose, take him out, and we can bury him. Just wait a few minutes."

"Sorry, brother, I forgot you had a brain. Arina thinks we are both idiots."

Rolan replied, laughing, "Well, I do not think you are an idiot—I think you are a moron."

"Thanks, Rolan. It is nice to know there are two in the family." Luka smiled, half-filled the empty can with ocean water and set it over the fire.

"Luka! Help me with this icicle, he is heavy."

Luka looked down into the cavity to see Rolan lifting the pilot, frozen in a sitting position. Luka, who was crouched at the top of the large pit, got his hands under the pilot's arms and lifted. As soon as the body was out of the hole, Arina joined the boys. Luka was trying to extricate a wallet from the man's left back pocket, but it was frozen in place. He was going to pour hot water over the wallet when Arina stopped him.

"No! You will ruin the information in the wallet. Pour the water on a rag and use it to unfreeze the wallet from what is remaining of his pants. You might have to cut his pocket open, too."

Rolan climbed out of the hole carrying a fur. Arina looked at it and said, "Oh! It's a frozen dog! The poor thing."

25

Rolan said, "He is Smokey. It says on the collar. He was below the pilot. Maybe the pilot was holding the dog when they crashed."

Luka was opening the pilot's wallet and said, "His name is Wallace K. Williams. He was born August 8, 1909. His wallet has twenty-eight dollars, not a rich man. He has a cheap watch; it stopped at nine minutes after four. I will see if he has a ring, maybe he had a wife." Luka cut off the glove on his left hand. The little finger broke off and was stuck to the glove. The black ring finger fell to the ice and a gold band came off, rolling toward the water. Luka grabbed it before it was lost.

Arina looked away from the body and said, "Put all the things in a bag. We will give them to the authorities in the United States. Maybe there are family members that would know of him. Was he a member of the armed forces?"

Luka removed a card from the wallet and stated, "He was a member of the Civil Air Patrol. There is a patch on his coat. See, it has a propeller with three blades."

Arina commented, "He might have been lost during the Second World War. He was about thirty-four or thirty-five years old, ran out of fuel, got trapped on the ice, and froze to death with his dog. We better bury him." She pointed up the hill behind them, "There is dirt up there. We cannot bury him here; there are only rocks."

Rolan and Luka carried the corpse up the slope about fifty meters where there was a small, nearly flat, terrace-like area where they could dig. Using the ice ax, Luka carved out a hole about a meter deep, in which they put the pilot and his dog. After filling in the grave with small rocks and dirt, they made a cross and pounded it into the ground. They covered the grave with big rocks and went back to the ice. Arina had nearly exposed half the wing. The fiber covering had nearly all disintegrated. The wing would have to be recovered. She had shifted her attention to the tail section. The tail wheel and half the stabilizer were exposed.

They sat down together to take a break. Rolan looked upset; he was very quiet.

Arina asked, "Rolan, are you bothered about the pilot?"

"No, something much more important."

Arina smiled and said, "The dog?"

Rolan didn't laugh. "No, there are only two seats in the airplane. It is too small for three people."

The enormity of Rolan's words struck Arina like a small bomb. She dropped to the ground. She looked up at Rolan, her smile gone. "Oh, no. Maybe we should not try to do this."

Luka had heard Rolan. He stepped next to Arina, and said, "I will stay, you and Rolan will go. I will find another way."

Arina sat on the ground crying, tears streaming down her cheeks. "But but we should all go together, one family."

"It is better this way, Arina. I will stay with mother and father until we can leave, too. I will do the fishing. Maybe I will find another, bigger plane. Can you tell me if there is a pilot training course at the technical school?"

"They got an old flight simulator after you and Roland finished your studies. I think it still works."

"Good. Then we will all learn to fly. Come on, we need some more hot water. We are making good progress at freeing the plane from the ice. You need to figure a way to turn it over without damaging it." Luka pulled Arina to her feet and wiped her face with his handkerchief and gave her a hug.

"Was that clean?" Arina quizzed and smiled.

"No, but I only used it twice." He folded the square of cotton material and stuffed it in his back pocket. "Maybe three times," he laughed.

Rolan was chipping away ice from around the stabilizer and rudder when Luka and Arina joined him on the floe with another can of hot water. Arina looked in the cabin to check how much room there was. She had to make sure the plane could only carry two people. Rolan was right, it would never carry three; especially since they were all so big.

She stepped back and looked over the entire structure of the plane. There was nothing but the skeleton of an airplane; the covering had decomposed over the years leaving a metal and wood framework that would have to be recovered before flying again. The entire structure would have to be inspected. Badly rusted and weak pieces would have to be replaced. This project was going to require a large amount of hard work, but she felt three people could do it, especially Ivanovs.

Disappointed, Arina felt like hitting something, but that wouldn't accomplish anything. She must melt some more ice before going back home. Tomorrow, they would bring some larger pieces of lumber and some wheels. She had an idea of how to turn the plane over. She took an empty can, half-filled it with water, and put it over the fire. While the water warmed, she began breaking away ice from around the engine. She had thought the propeller was broken or missing, but it was just concealed in ice and parallel to the wing; just as it had been when the engine stopped many years ago. They worked another hour before climbing back aboard Maligin V and heading home.

After dinner, Arina gave her brothers a list of things to get from the old military base. They needed more wood to burn, some stout wooden posts four to six meters long, and two pneumatic wheels approximately one-half meter in diameter. If they could find one, a pulley would also come in handy. Arina was going to stay home with her parents this evening, while the boys went to the military base and acquired the items on the list.

It was 7:15 p.m. when Rolan and Luka announced they were going to a friend's house to play cards and have some beer. They drove the pickup to the military base and started searching for the pulley and wheels, they already knew where the wood was located. As they drove slowly through the deserted streets, a man on a bicycle approached them. It was a guard, one of the few members of the military still in Provideniya. Luka recognized the man; it was Aleksey Karpov, a former classmate. They had been in the same mechanical drawing class three years ago. He was about twenty centimeters shorter than Luka, had a pleasant, square face, and light brown hair, cut very short. His eyebrows were bushy and needed a trim. Aleksey was dressed in dark-green pants, a khaki shirt, and black army boots. He put his foot on the running board and said, "I suggest you return home; this can be a dangerous place to be at night."

"Hi, Aleksey. Do you remember me? I'm Luka Ivanov, your old classmate. This is my brother, Rolan."

"Well, it is good to see you. I am grateful you let me copy your paper one time. How is your sister?"

"You know Arina?"

"Every young man in Provideniya has heard of Arina, but they are afraid her brothers will pound them into dust if they ask her out. Is that true?"

Rolan answered, "They know the score, Aleksey. We are like rabid dogs when it comes to protecting our sister. It would be a blood bath, the harbor would turn red." Rolan made a fist, shook it and grimaced, and then grinned.

"Aleksey, we are looking for some things for our smoke house. We need two wheels and a pulley. Have you any knowledge of where to find such things?"

"Sure, my friend. There is a cart at the loading platform beside the railroad tracks. It has some wheels, but they are flat. Do you have a bicycle pump?"

"We do. What about a pulley?"

"Over at the old machine shop. The floor is littered with stuff like that. I will show you."

Rolan got out of the passenger side, climbed in the bed of the truck and said, "Give me your bicycle and get in with Luka; you will ride with us."

Aleksey gave Luka directions to the machine shop and the men got out of the truck after a three minute drive. Aleksey pointed at the big gray building. "In there—take anything you like. Moscow and Putin won't care, they gave up on this place years ago. The equipment is turning to rust. The wheels are over there," he pointed at a long warehouse next to the railroad tracks, "on the other side. Hand me my bicycle, I have to make my rounds. Good luck, my friends."

"Thank you, Aleksey. We will see you another time." Luka stepped out of the truck and walked with Rolan about ten meters to the machine shop, where they found just what they needed. Three pulleys of different sizes and about thirty meters of six-millimeter-diameter steel cable were tossed in the pickup. Then they drove to the warehouse where they took two wheels off a package transfer cart. With the materials in the bed of the pickup, they headed to the old barracks and found the wood they needed. They tied the large beams to the side of the truck and drove back toward the dock. After transferring the supplies to the Maligin V, they stopped for a beer, and then returned home. They had been gone almost three hours.

Arina was sitting on the sofa talking to their mother, Sofiya, when the boys entered the house. Ivan was in the bathroom getting ready for bed.

"Are you drunk?" Sofiya asked.

Luka put his arm around his mom and kissed her cheek. "No. We are not drunk. Smell my breath." He opened his mouth, but Sofiya pushed him away, "Oh, you do smell like beer. I'm going to bed. We all have to work tomorrow. You better bring back more fish, not just salmon this time. Okay? And don't stay up too late."

Luka said, "Good night, Mother, see you in the morning." Rolan and Arina followed with "Good night." Luka sat down beside Arina. She looked at them and said, "Did you get the materials?"

"Yes, ma'am, and a few other things as well."

Arina said, "Take a look at my diagram. Do you think we can do this?" She flipped a couple of pages of her notebook and showed them her drawing.

Luka scratched his head and commented, "We have everything, except we need one more beam, we only have two."

"Can you get it after breakfast?"

"No problem, but it will take us about an hour. I will see you in the morning, I am tired."

Luka stood up, said good night, and went to bed.

Rolan sat for a minute with Arina. He told her what Aleksey Karpov had said about young men being afraid to ask her out, fearing that Rolan and Luka would beat them up.

"That is good to know, Rolan. I do not want to go out with anyone from Provideniya anyway. I am glad you scare them. I will marry an American someday."

CHAPTER 5

SECRETS REVEALED

The three novice archeologists left the confines of Provideniya Harbor in a thin fog, not needing the sounds of the buoys for guidance. As the Maligin V passed by the fifth buoy, Luka increased speed and in a long minute, they were in full sunshine, moving through deep blue-green water. They arrived at the inlet under bright sunlight, but the plane was still in the shadows of the steep walls of the plateau that rose nearly thirty-five meters above the water.

They could tell the ice was melting more rapidly now; much of the tail section was exposed, and most of the ice from around the engine had melted during the night. After the Ivanovs unloaded the military base materiel, Arina lit the fires and began heating water to begin freeing the other half of the trapped wing. Rolan and Luka were able to free the rudder from the ice by chipping away what little frozen water remained in contact with the tail surfaces.

"Did you notice the skin of the plane was fiber, Luka?"

"Yes, I discovered that yesterday when a small remnant of the plane's covering tore off with some ice. I was surprised; the skin of the plane was made of cloth, but it has almost entirely decomposed. Last night, I was going to ask you what we should do to recover the plane, but when Aleksey talked with us, I forgot about it. I thought you and Arina already knew about the fabric and did not think it was important. Will it be a problem?"

Rolan thought for a moment and replied, "We will have to get some waterproof glue and some fabric that will not deteriorate when glued and painted. It should not be a concern, but I am worried about the wood and metal surfaces. They look worse today than yesterday. We might have to replace some of the wing spars and the metal connections have all rusted badly. But I am not worried; we will figure it out."

"What are you guys talking about? Come help with the wing. We need to get it exposed so we can turn the plane over. Can you put on the wheels? You are wasting time. Remember, we have to take fish home for the market, so we must leave here early."

Luka answered, "Okay, Arina. Rolan will help with the wing and I will mount the wheels."

Arina yelled back to Luka, "When you finish with the wheels, take off the propeller. We do not want to damage it."

Working without a break and skipping lunch, by 2:00 p.m. the plane was ready to be moved from the ice to the shore. It took them nearly an hour to ready the cables, pulleys and beams so the plane could be righted. Rolan fed the cable through the highest pulley and attached one end to the fuselage in front of the rudder and the other end to the Maligin V. When Arina and Luka poured warm water where the plane was resting on the ice, Rolan pushed the throttle forward on the Maligin V's engine and the tail of the plane began to lift into the air.

Once the plane began to rise over the ice, Luka and Arina could hear tearing sounds, but they had to continue the procedure, the plane was now coming off the ice and the nose was starting to touch the water. Luka grabbed the end of the wing closest to him and pushed with all his strength. Arina signaled Rolan to back off on the throttle and the plane's nose and wingtip touched solid ground. Luka grabbed the rope attached to the tail and pulled, the bottom of the plane was moving toward the ground, one wheel touched and then the other. Rolan cut the engine and the plane settled onto the wheels, the nose came out of the water and the tail was coming toward the ground as Luka pulled the rope. The Maligin V acted like a slowly applied break, as the tail dropped, the boat was pulled back toward shore.

"We did it!" Arina screamed and gave a fist pump. "Good work you guys!"

Rolan and Luka both raised their fists into the air, shaking them with pride. Luka hugged Arina and said, "Not so loud, people in Provideniya will hear you and come to see what is going on." He grinned and yelled at Rolan, "Help us pull the plane away from the water and cover it with the camouflage net."

Arina had already begun to change the configuration of the pulley system and yelled to Rolan, "Stay in the boat, Rolan. We will use the boat to pull the plane farther away from the water." She showed Luka what to do, and in ten minutes, they signaled Rolan to move the boat forward. The plane slowly rolled a safe distance away from the water. After blocking the wheels, they put the beams on the ground under the plane and spread the netting over the wing and fuselage. They piled the remainder of the firewood haphazardly near the tail of the plane to help disguise it from air and satellite observations.

It was nearly 3:30 p.m. when they started back to Provideniya, stopping for an hour at their favorite spot to fish. Sofiya was going to be happy with the fish they were taking back to the market. The Maligin V reached the dock at 6:27 p.m. They took the fish to the store and were home in another forty-five minutes.

When Arina, Rolan, and Luka entered the living room and removed their jackets, they saw their parents sitting at the dining room table drinking tea.

Ivan issued an order, as if he were in the military, talking to a bunch of privates, "All of you, sit down. We have something to talk about."

Arina looked at her mother and smiled, but Sofiya looked like a statue, an inert piece of granite, and did not return the smile. Arina had seen this look before; her mother was pissed.

Ivan lay his hands on the table, made them into fists, gave Rolan and Luka a stern look, and said, "What is this talk about building a smoke house? We do not need a smoke house. What is going on?"

Rolan looked at Luka, who raised his eye brows, then looked back at his father, and said, "Who told you that?"

"Captain Dimitri Ulisnilov came by the market and asked about the progress on the smoke house. I told him I did not know. He said it was probably a surprise—he should not have asked."

Luka said, "We told Dimitri we were using the wood we had to build a smoke house. We could not tell him about our secret. He would ruin it, so we lied."

Sofiya looked at Luka and asked, "What is this secret you hide? What did you do with the wood? Did you sell it?"

Rolan replied, "No, we burned it—to melt ice."

Arina looked at Rolan and Luka and said, "Should I tell them?"

The brothers nodded and in unison, said, "Da."

"Well—Rolan and Luka found an airplane frozen in an ice floe. We have been melting the ice to free the airplane. Rolan and I are going to fly to America so I can study astronomy."

Ivan shook his head and said, "Of all the crazy things I have ever heard, this is the most outlandish. Are you all insane?"

Luka shook his head from side to side, gritted his teeth together, took a deep breath, and commented, "I knew we should not have told them."

Sofiya was grinning and started to laugh. "You found an airplane in an ice cube? Do you think we believe you? What are you really doing? Tell us."

Ivan suggested, "You are preparing something for our anniversary? Number twenty-seven is coming up in two months."

Arina smiled and said, "No, Papa. We really did find an airplane, well, Rolan and Luka found it. Rolan, where are those things from the body?"

Rolan went to his bedroom and came back carrying a small cloth bag. He untied the bag and emptied the contents on the table. "Papa, Mama, these things were on the pilot."

Ivan looked at the watch and the ring and said, "Did you take these from a tourist the other night when you went drinking?"

Luka bent over and hit his head on the table. He lifted his head and took a deep breath. "Let me try one more time. I will tell you the whole story. Please listen carefully and ask questions when I have finished. Okay?" Luka started telling the story. Sofiya got up and went in the kitchen to get dinner ready. Ivan leaned back in his chair and took a sip of tea.

Sofiya was stirring something on the stove and said, "Go ahead, I am listening."

Luka told the whole story, with Rolan and Arina adding additional information. When they finished the story, Ivan said, "So you buried this aviator with his dog. Do you think the United States Air Force is looking for him?"

Arina replied, "Papa, he died seventy years ago. No one is looking for him, his plane—or his dog. People that knew him are probably all dead, but we will give his things to the authorities when we get to the United States."

Sofiya said, "Dinner is almost ready. Can we all go in the airplane?"

No one answered her question. There was a pause in the conversation.

"So why did you keep this secret?" Stern-faced Ivan crossed his arms and sat back in his chair looking at his children.

Arina said, "We were afraid you and Mama would tell someone."

Sofiya brought a frying pan to the table, put a chicken breast on each plate, and then said, "So, you think we cannot keep secrets?"

Rolan said, "We did not want to chance telling anyone, they might let it slip accidently, of course."

Sofiya brought in a large plate of fresh vegetables, a loaf of bread, and sat down. "Your father and I have a secret for twenty-seven years. We never tell nobody."

Luka took a bite of chicken and grinned, "We are all adopted?"

Ivan scowled at Luka and raised his voice, "Listen to your mother! It is not funny."

"Sorry, Papa." Luka tried to pull his head back like a turtle, when threatened, would put his head under his shell.

Sofiya put her hands in her lap and looked at her children. "I was a member of the Olympic team until I started to grow. My specialty was the balance beam."

"Mama, why keep that a secret?" Arina asked.

"At that time, to be a good citizen, you were to do what the country wanted. The Olympic team doctors were to give me drugs to stop me from growing, but the drugs would make me sterile. I said no, but they insisted. I was to get the injections in two days. After practicing that day, I went outside and sat on a bench not knowing what to do. I was sitting there crying, and your father asked me what was wrong. I knew who he was, but he did not know who I was. He was an important member of the basketball team at that time, but he agreed with me that it was wrong for the doctors to do that. We went to dinner at the cafeteria and talked. He was so nice to me."

Arina looked at her father and he nodded. "I fell in love with Sofiya the first time I talked with her. She was beautiful, smart, and understood right from wrong. I walked her home and she agreed to see me the next day to talk some more. At the dormitory that night, I got a plan. We would run away together, somewhere far away, and change our names."

Sofiya continued the story. "When we met the next day, Ivan told me to take the train to Moscow and he would meet me. We were not to tell anyone or change what we did that day. We couldn't take any of our things, except some clothes and all the money we had. Your father rode on a truck to Moscow and met me at the train station."

Rolan, Luka, and Arina had been listening attentively. Luka asked, "What about your papers? I heard the athletes do not keep their papers; the officials have them."

Ivan smiled and said, "I took care of that. The night before we left, I asked a custodian if he would like to make some money, but I warned him, the job might be risky. He said he would do it because his job did not pay much. He was going to move away from the training village anyway. I told him I wanted Sofiya's and my papers from the administration building. He said that building was almost deserted at night, but he would have to have half payment before and half after he got the papers. How much was I going to pay him?"

Arina put her elbows on the table, placed her chin in her cupped hands, and quizzed, "How much, Papa?"

"You thought I would not have the money, yes?" He smiled at his children. "I gave him a gold ring I got at the European Basketball Championships. I had another from the Championships of the USSR. He would get that one when I got the papers. He agreed and put the ring in his pocket. He told me to meet him down the hall from my room before curfew. He knew where I lived."

Ivan sat back in his chair, shoulders back, and a gleam in his eyes. Luka, Rolan, and Arina could see that he was proud of himself. He continued, "The next morning, I waited until Sofiya came from her morning practice carrying her gym clothes. She was by herself, so I walked by and bumped into her. She dropped her bag and I crouched down, picked up the bag, and gave her papers to her. She pretended to not know me. It was perfect! I whispered to her that I would see her in Moscow; the address was with her papers."

Sofiya said, "Ivan, you did not just say you would see me at that address; you whispered that you loved me. Have you forgotten?"

Ivan looked down in his lap, his cheeks lightly flushed, "That was not important to our escape, Sofiya, but I did say that." He looked up, nodded, and grinned. "It was true."

Sofiya continued, "I boarded the train at noon and was in Moscow at 4:00 p.m. I waited in the station for about fifteen minutes. I was scared and very hungry, I did not eat breakfast for fear I would throw up on the train. I saw your father walking toward me and I ran to meet him. I remember crying; I did not know anyone in Moscow."

Tears were running down Arina's cheeks. "Oh, Mama. But you were strong to run away." She wiped her tears with her napkin and leaned back in her chair. "How did you get out of Moscow? Was anyone looking for you?"

"We went to the address your father had given me. It was in case we missed each other at the station. A friend of one of Ivan's uncles lived there. We ate and he asked us some questions. I did not know he was preparing new papers with new names for us. We stayed overnight, and in the morning, he gave us our new documents. My new name was Sofiya Rokotov and your father's was Ivan Ivanov."

Luka was shocked, his mouth fell open, and he looked at his father. "Ivanov is not our real name? What is your real name, Papa?"

"I am Ivan Ivanov, no other. Forget about those things, they are of no importance. We are all Ivanovs."

They all sat in silence for a moment. Rolan asked, "So how did you get to Provideniya?"

Sofiya spoke, "You are not eating. Your food is getting cold. Eat, and when we finish our meal, we will tell you about the trip to Vladivostok."

CHAPTER 6
TRANS-SIBERIA

Finished with dinner, Arina helped her mother with the dishes. The men retired to the living room, each with a beer.

Arina called out from the kitchen, "Papa, do not continue until we join you. I have to hear everything."

"All right. We will wait." Ivan took a sip of beer, looked at his boys, and said, "Now, tell me more about this airplane."

Rolan and Luka told Ivan again how they found the plane and towed it to the obscured inlet, secured the ice to land, and returned home. After confiding the secret to Arina, all three went to work removing the plane from the ice, getting it on the beach, and concealing it with the netting.

"Are you sure no one else knows of this?"

Luka answered, "The patrol boat is too big to enter the inlet and all fishing is done south of Provideniya, except for us. We have never seen any fishing boats to the north except for the native oomiaks."

"What about from above?" Ivan pointed toward the ceiling. "Airplanes and satellites?"

"The plane is very small. It would take two of them to be the size of a fighter jet, and it is just a skeleton. Unless someone knew what to look for, I do not think anyone will notice it and we covered the wing with the camouflage net. The wooden tail frame is standing above scattered pieces of wood on the ground."

Ivan quizzed, "What about American satellites? They can see a man from 100 miles above the earth."

Rolan smiled, "They would think it is a toy. They could turn it to gas with one rocket."

"How will you fly it to Alaska? None of you fly a plane." He paused and then said, "Is that another secret? Can you fly a plane?"

Luka replied, "No, Papa. We will take lessons at the technical institute. Arina knows one of the instructors that runs the flight simulator. One smile from her and he will melt."

Sofiya was standing in the doorway to the kitchen wiping her hands on a dish towel.

"She must be careful." Sofiya pursed her lips. "I have heard stories about professors taking advantage of their students."

"We go with her, Mama, Papa." Rolan assured his parents.

Sofiya and Arina came into the living room with some cakes and tea. They sat on the sofa and looked at the men. Sofiya said, "Where were we?"

Luka prompted, "You were to leave Moscow on the train." Sofiya nodded to Ivan, who took another drink of beer and said, "We waited two hours and bought third class tickets to Vladivostok. The train did not leave until midnight, so we shopped for some mugs and fruit."

Sofiya shook her shoulders, put her hand over her mouth, and smiled. She whispered into her hand, "I bought some candy and tea."

Rolan, Luka, and Arina laughed. Arina said, "You were an athlete and bought candy?"

Sofiya's big smile disappeared when she added, "We were not athletes; we left that life behind. We were just regular people on a trip across country."

Ivan turned to Sofiya and said, "Did we tell them about your hair?"

"Oh, I forget. I dyed my hair black for the picture on the new papers. When I looked in the mirror, I almost didn't recognize myself. The blond was gone. I was a different girl; I looked older. A week later, when we arrived in Vladivostok, I checked my hair. The blond was not showing yet. After a month, I dyed my hair again, but that time I used brown. I liked it better." Sofiya pulled several strands of hair so she could see it was now blond. She raised her shoulders and displayed an impish grin; the brown was gone; her hair was now grayish-blond.

Ivan took another swig of beer and continued, "We got on the train early and found our berths. We took two along the aisle, close to the toilet. I took the bottom and Sofiya took the top. She hopped up there very easily, I did not have to help her. We put our money in the box below my berth. That was the only thing of value we had, and not much of that. I was worried when I counted our money. When we arrived in Vladivostok, we would be broke."

"I met a nice lady from Beijing," Sofiya stated. "She could not speak Russian, just Chinese and a little English. We talked in English; Ivan and I knew a little English, and hand waving," Sofiya grinned as she moved her hands in the air. "I have forgotten her name, but she gave us things to eat. She was a real lifesaver. We said goodbye at Ulan Ude. She took a different train; south to Beijing."

Sofiya bit into a small cake and sipped her tea while Ivan continued, "When we reached Vladivostok, it was late at night on the seventh day of travel. We were so tired of that train, but happy to be getting to a place to start a new life where no one knew us. Unfortunately, we did not have enough money to stay in a hotel, but the temperature was mild from the ocean influence. We had on light jackets and I carried Sofiya's bag of things; she carried my small suitcase. It was not heavy. It only had some underwear and shirts inside. We walked and sat on a park bench until it was light. We had stayed near the train station on Aleutskaya Street. When the sun came up, we saw how beautiful the station was. I remember seeing a sign with 9,288 on it. That was the number of kilometers from Moscow. We hoped we would be safe from persecution."

Arina asked, "What did you do for money? Were you broke?"

Sofiya answered, "We had eleven Rubles; I kept them in my pocket. I was worried. We could not get money for playing basketball or walking on a balance beam. We had to find normal jobs. When walking along the waterfront, we found a restaurant. We did dishes for almost a week, and then Ivan found a job on a fishing boat. He was big and strong, just what the boat captain wanted. I began working as a waitress after learning what was on the menu and watching the other girls. I was pretty good at it, too."

Ivan said, "Sofiya was good for the restaurant, but men kept asking her out. She told them she was engaged. There was one skinny little man who told Sofiya he was a writer. Sofiya said he came to see her many times and ordered tea, nothing else. I came to see Sofiya one day and she introduced us. He never came back."

Ivan smiled, "I made a big fist when I met him. He got the idea. We had a small apartment not far from where we worked. After six months, we got married and started planning to move to another city, smaller than Vladivostok, but it had to be along the coast. I was a fisherman now."

"You had a beard then, Ivan. I remember it tickled when you kissed me." She smiled, "We had some good times though. We went to all the tourist attractions, museums, movie theaters, and took lots of walks, discussing possible places to move to. Ivan heard that the military base in Provideniya was declining; Moscow was making many changes. We went to the library to find out more about Provideniya. We did not know much about the East. Another month went by and I was going to have a baby. You, Luka."

"I have always wondered why I have a good feeling about Vladivostok." Luka laughed, "I tell good joke, yes?"

Sofiya tossed a napkin at him. He caught it and folded it on his lap.

Arina commented, "Maybe you are different. Maybe you are adopted." Everyone laughed.

Luka answered, "I will put snow down your neck, dear sister. Maybe a live mouse. Just wait."

Ivan continued with the story. "I heard of a ship going to Provideniya to pick up military equipment and transport it back to the western ports. The Finnish ship had been in Shanghai loading some cargo for Leningrad. Two of the crew had been injured and the captain needed some replacements. Sofiya and I went to the ship and talked with the captain. He said Sofiya could work in the galley and I could work as an ordinary seaman. We got hired, and two days later, we were on our way to Provideniya. The captain, Arvo Pihkala, was an interesting man. Sofiya and I were invited to his cabin for dinner one evening. He played chess and maintained a stamp collection. I almost won a game of chess, but he was too good. He was very knowledgeable. It was like we were attending a lecture at the university about world politics. He talked, and we listened. I remember Sofiya saying she wondered how many politicians had been ship captains."

"I remember being seasick on the way to Provideniya, but it might have been morning sickness; I was never really sure. I had never been on a big ship before, only airplanes traveling to competitions. We spent two weeks at sea. I was very happy to get back on land. I felt dirty. The ship was kind of stinky. When we arrived in Provideniya, I was shocked at how small it was. But Ivan and I found jobs at a fish market called Bering Sea Delicacies, owned by Svetlana and Valeri Marchenko."

"Marchenko? They owned the market we now have. Is that not right?" Luka asked.

Ivan replied, "You are correct. We had worked for Svetlana and Valeri for nearly two years, when the military decided to begin moving out of Provideniya. Their son, Serge, was in the military and was transferred to Leningrad, so they sold the business to us and moved back to the West to Novgorod, south of Leningrad. Svetlana said she did not like it here. We renamed the market Treasures of the Sea, added some tables and started serving dinners. Luka was just a baby then, but we worked hard and made the business work. Sofiya carried Luka on her back when she waited on the tables, but that did not last very long; he got too big."

Arina laughed and said, "You have always been a big baby, Luka."

"All right, Arina. Now you will have two mice down your neck."

Rolan asked, "How did you get the Maligin V, Papa? Was that part of the deal with Marchenko?"

"Nyet. They had a fairly nice eight-meter boat that was part of the deal, but we had trouble paying them, so I sold that boat to a navy man. I was lucky to find the Maligin V abandoned. No one claimed it, so I patched it up, repainted the interior, and we were back in business. It took us two more years to pay off Marchenko. About that time, Rolan came along to join his older brother. When you were five and Luka was seven, I took you out fishing. After you caught your first fish, you were on the hook. You boys wanted to go fishing all the time. I did not let you go alone until you were big enough to properly handle the boat. I think you were thirteen and fifteen then. At first you did not do very well, but after a few months, you were bringing back more fish than I could."

There was a pause in the conversation as the siblings thought about what their parents had told them. They never realized what their parents experienced in their twenties.

Arina spoke first after looking at Sofiya and Ivan, "We should never have thought you could not keep our secret. We are all embarrassed for not having shared our plan with you."

Sofiya smiled and said, "But look at what you know now. You are trying to do something similar to what we did. I think there is an expression that history repeats itself. Your father and I will do anything we can to help you." She laughed a bit nervously, "Just be careful, we do not want to lose you. We love you all so much. And do not forget to do some fishing."

Ivan looked at his watch, yawned, and stood, "I'm getting another beer." He took a couple of steps, turned around and said, "What is next?"

Arina replied, "Rolan and Luka have to take the engine apart, remove rust, put in new oil and test it. I think the engine will run on regular gasoline, but I will check at the technical institute." She grinned, "Professor Karpov should know, he is almost as old as that engine. I will start recovering the surface of the plane. Luka, can you get me some light-weight canvas from the military base? Oh, and some marine paint?"

"That will be easy. I have been thinking about patching, too. If we tear the new skin, we will have to fix it. We will need some paint remover and some waterproof glue. Let me ask you a question. How are we going to get the plane in the air? It is stuck in the inlet—no place to go; no runway."

"I know. Have you got any ideas, Rolan?"

"Only one, but I do not think it will work, pontoons. Can we make pontoons? We could drop them once in the air, but they might be too heavy; the plane is very small."

Ivan was standing in the kitchen doorway, leaning against the door jamb holding a bottle of beer. "I have idea. Maybe too difficult."

There was a hush as everyone watched Ivan cross the living room floor and drop into his big overstuffed chair, trying not to spill his beer.

Arina could not stand the silence. "What is your idea, Papa?"

CHAPTER 7
IVAN'S IDEA

Ivan took several swallows of beer and said two words, "Aircraft carrier." There was a stunned silence.

Arina's mind had jumped ahead and she said, "What a wonderful idea, Papa. We can put the airplane on the boat and take it to the ice, roll it onto the ice and take off. The early ice should be very smooth; will it not be?"

The boys grasped the idea quickly, too. Rolan said, "Yes. We can roll the plane off the boat using wooden ramps. Luka can pull the ramps back onto the boat and hide them in the inlet. No one will ever know how we took off with no skis, pontoons, or airport."

Luka added, "What a good plan! I believe it will work, as long as Dimitri does not see us."

"Now, we have a plan! Thank you, Papa." Arina moved to her father and kissed him on the forehead.

Sofiya asked, "But what about Luka? You are leaving him behind?"

Arina answered, "Luka volunteered to stay and fish, but I have been thinking. After Rolan and I get to Alaska, we will see if the Americans can help get you all out of Russia. We must make up a code, in case someone reads our mail."

Sofiya walked over beside Ivan, patted his shoulder, and said, "Come to bed. We have to work tomorrow. Let the young people figure out the plan. The less we know, the better." She pulled Ivan from his chair. As they went down the hall, they both said, "Good night."

Luka grinned and said, "Thanks for the bedtime story. Good night."

Arina and Rolan added, "Good night, Mama, Papa."

44

Luka dropped Arina and Rolan off at the technical institute at 8:00 a.m. He continued on to the military base to get some canvas, glue, and paint. Aleksey was getting ready to leave the base, night watch being over. Luka stepped on the brakes and asked Aleksey if he knew where the canvas covers for the army trucks were. Aleksey didn't ask what Luka wanted the cover for; he was tired and only wanted to go home to bed.

"Over there." Aleksey pointed at a large dark-green building. "The old motor pool. See you later, Luka. Just don't make a mess." Aleksey laughed and started peddling his bike and suddenly stopped and turned around. "Hey, Luka. The day watchman is in Japan on vacation. You will not be interrupted." Aleksey waved and peddled off.

Luka yelled at him, "Thanks, Aleksey. I owe you a beer." Luka relaxed and drove to the old motor pool structure. The doors were all shut but not locked. Luka slid one of the big doors to the side and began surveying the interior. An old diesel troop truck was sitting in the corner with one wheel missing, as well as the engine. Luka climbed on the back of the truck and looked under the torn canvas cover. It was loaded with a dozen new covers in plastic wrap, several boxes of motor oil, and four used truck tires. Luka helped himself to four covers, to be sure there was enough canvas, and a wooden box half-full of motor oil: twelve one-liter containers.

He spent another fifteen minutes looking for paint but wasn't successful. He sat in the truck thinking and realized there might be paint at the old wharf and dry dock area. All he found at the dry dock was heavy timber used to support the hulls of ships when they were out of the water. The only place remaining to be investigated was at the end of the pier, a small red building with a rusty metal roof. Luka didn't think he would find anything in the structure; it looked to be an office. He drove down the pier, the platform boards rattling under his wheels. If the pier collapsed, he would have to swim about a hundred yards, and the truck and contents would be lost. Luka had the door ajar in case he had to jump from the truck to save his life.

He parked the truck next to the red shack and climbed out, being careful where he placed his feet. The door on the building was locked. He turned the doorknob and shook the door; it looked as if the lock would fail if it were persuaded. He lunged at the door, his shoulder striking mid-door. The door burst open; the security hinge torn from the doorjamb. There was a rush of fumes through the open door. If he had been smoking, the little building would have exploded. Luka let the air clear for a minute before he entered. The building was packed with solvents and paints, just what he wanted. Alcohols, ketones, and mineral spirits were arranged along one wall and twenty-liter cans of paint were stacked waist-high covering two-thirds of the floor.

Luka put about five liters of solvents and a dozen one-liter containers of gray, brown, and black paint in the back of the truck, shut the building door as best he could, and started driving away from the paint shed. He suddenly stopped the pickup and started to back up. Luka had an idea. He moved the truck to about ten meters from the building and set the brake. He reentered the shed and grabbed a box of stencils off a shelf. He shut the door again, got in the truck, and drove off the rickety pier. As he passed the base checkpoint, he was satisfied with his acquisitions, and happy to be off the military base. He was always nervous when near anything military. When he reached the Maligin V, Luka loaded the government donations into the boat. After waiting for about fifteen minutes, he drove back to the technical institute to look for Arina and Rolan. He thought, "What is taking them so long?"

The secretary at the administrative office wasn't much help. She had no idea what a flight simulator was, nor if one existed at the technical institute. She was a new hire.

Luka asked, "Do you know where I might find Professor Karpov?"

She smiled, looked at a directory on her desk, ran her finger down a list of names, and said, "Building 4, office A-1." She pointed down the hall and said, "Second building over from here; this is Building 2."

"Thank you." Luka smiled and strode down the dimly lit hallway and out the door. He passed Building 3 and entered Building 4. The hallway smelled somewhat like the little shack on the pier. Someone had been painting or perhaps polishing floors. Luka watched the numbers on the office doors, descending from A-7 as he continued down the hall. The last door on the right was open; it was labeled A-1, Karpov's office.

"Yes?" A deep baritone voice emanated from a heavy gray beard under a large nose adorned with a pair of wire-rimmed glasses partly concealed by bushy eyebrows. The piercing blue eyes scanned Luka from head to toe. His bald head didn't move.

"I'm looking for my sister, Arina Ivanov."

"You must be Luka. She told me you might come by. Arina and your brother are in the flight simulator room upstairs; room 2A-6. Stairs are behind you on the left. You look much like your brother; you could be twins. I wish I were forty years younger; I would have enjoyed spending time with your sister. Such a smart young woman. I believe she knows as much about cosmology as I do. I hope she does well in her studies in Moscow."

Luka thanked the professor and made his way up the stairs. He walked the length of the hall before arriving at room 2A-6. Simulator was painted on the door. He turned the knob and entered the nearly pitch-black room. As his eyes adjusted, he could see a bluish-glow coming from behind a partition. He could hear Rolan and Arina talking and a robot-sounding voice saying, "Pull up! Increase air speed. Go around."

Luka stepped around the partition and saw the silhouette of Rolan's head and shoulders against the large display screen. Rolan was seated in the pilot's chair. Arina and the instructor were standing somewhat behind Rolan, their eyes fixed on the 180 degree screen.

The instructor said, "This time, descend more slowly, Rolan. Okay, you are lined up. Start your descent."

The robotic voice said, "On the glide path—more power— wheels on the ground, cut power."

Arina nearly shouted, "You did it! Good job, Rolan. I am very nervous, but I want to try."

Rolan needed a shoehorn to get out of the pilot's chair, the simulator was primarily for jet pilot training, little room was present for someone over six feet tall, and no room for a copilot sitting beside the student pilot. Rolan noticed Luka as he extricated himself from the seat. "Hi, Luka. This is Nikoli Gamov, our instructor. Professor Gamov, this is our brother Luka."

Gamov shook hands with Luka and said, "I am not professor yet, just instructor, but professor sounds good." He smiled and said, "Do you want also to fly?"

"Nyet. But I have an interest in history of early airplanes. When a cloth covered airplane got damaged, how was it repaired?"

"Several methods, depending on kind of fabric. I have book with instructions. I will loan it but remember to bring back. It is part of my collection."

"No problem, I will return it in a few days—as soon as I read it. Thank you."

Gamov said, "I will get it for you." He left the room.

Rolan slapped Luka on the back and said, "Good story. Good thinking."

The brothers watched Arina take off, climb to 3,000 meters, fly a circle around the airport, and land the plane. She had carried out the maneuvers flawlessly. Luka and Rolan applauded as she parked the airplane next to the simulated terminal.

Rolan commented, "You are our pilot, Arina. You are very good."

Gamov returned with the book and handed it to Luka. "Keep as long as you like. But bring it back when finished, okay?"

"I will return it before long. Do you have simulations of propeller aircraft? I would like to try a simulation—see what it feels like."

"Yes. We have simulations of old biplanes, but I must load the tape. This is an old system; no DVD available."

"That would be great. I would like to see how to take off and land a biplane. It would be almost same as a single wing, correct?" Luka wanted to get Arina familiar with a propeller type plane, not a jet like she had already tried, and he was curious to see if he could do the simulation without crashing.

"I will show you how to load the programs. You can try any of them." Gamov smiled and said, "Just do not crash the big planes, they are very costly." Everyone laughed. He opened a drawer in a wooden filing cabinet and selected a box containing a reel of magnetic tape. Gamov loaded the biplane program and showed the Ivanovs the drawer full of tapes, each labelled with a different model of airplane. Gamov said they could stay as long as they wanted, but to press the off button when finished. He excused himself; he had to assist another class.

Luka tried the simulation first but was a little clumsy at the controls. He was so cramped in the pilot's seat; he could not relax and crashed the plane when trying to land. "I wonder how much I owe the government for that old plane?" he joked.

Arina said, "Not much, Luka. It was imaginary. Let me try next." Arina was getting serious, she seemed to enjoy simulated flying, and if it was anything like flying a real plane, her mastery of the controls could mean the difference between life and death for Rolan and herself. Arina spent nearly an hour on the simulator before Rolan insisted that he be given a chance. He needed to know how to operate the controls, too, in case he had to take over for Arina on their flight to Alaska.

Rolan flew the simulator for a half hour before he landed and said, "I'm hungry. Let's go eat lunch with the flight attendants. I saw a brunette that has great legs. She might be American; her name is Samantha."

Arina and Luka laughed at Rolan's joking and Arina said, "All right, press the off button. We will come back another time to get more practice. We will eat on the boat on the way to the inlet."

CHAPTER 8
REPAIRS

Luka drove the truck with Arina sandwiched between her brothers. It was a tight fit having all three in the narrow seat of the old pickup. Arina knew what she was in for when she got in beside Luka. Rolan and Luka always moved as closely together as possible, squeezing their sister until she elbowed Rolan and pinched him under his arm where it was sensitive. She had always threatened to use a needle to poke them, but she never had one available. They knew she would carry out her threat if she weren't in a good mood.

They stopped at the market and went inside. It only took a few minutes for Sofiya to prepare them some sandwiches, dried apricots, and an insulated bottle of hot tea. They told Sofiya and Ivan what they had planned for the afternoon and got back in the pickup. Arina climbed in back holding the paper bag containing the food. Luka had grabbed several paper cups as he left the market.

With the truck parked at Maligin V's berth on the wharf, they boarded the boat, cast off the lines, and set out for the inlet. Arina began going through Luka's acquisitions as they pulled out of the harbor and pointed the boat northwest.

She held up the box of stencils and asked, "What are these for?" Arina was looking at him expecting an immediate answer.

Luka said, "Could I please have a sandwich?" Grinning, he looked back at her and said, "I had a bright idea; see what you think. We should put up a sign from the military, warning trespassers to leave the installation immediately or they will be penalized severely. This is a special military project, not to be revealed to anyone."

Arina grinned, "That idea just earned you a sandwich, and some apricots. What a good idea, Luka! How did you think of that? Have you been eating some brain food?"

Luka smiled, "I ate the same breakfast as you this morning. Maybe I should do that more often." He thought a moment, laughed, and then said, "No, I do not want to grow breasts."

Arina punched him in the stomach. "If you were not so big, I would push you over the side. The cold water would make everything shrivel. You would not be so proud of yourself." Arina continued looking through the cans of solvents and paint. "Did you bring that book Gamov loaned you?"

"Sure. Want to read it? It is not very thick. There is a general procedure in the front, followed by minor alterations of procedure for different materials. I think I know how to fix our airplane, but we will have to test the solvents. Oh! We have no glue."

Arina responded, shaking her head, "You are just like papa. Mother sends him out to get things for apple pies and he brings back everything but the apples."

Luka laughed, "I don't like apple pie. Maybe father feels the same. We have plenty of time to get glue. Rolan and I have to take the motor apart, reassemble it, and get it running. Without the motor, we will have to use rubber bands. They do not function well in cold weather."

Arina moved to the back of the boat, and as she watched the small wake dissipating, she muttered, "You are both crazy, but you are my favorite brothers." She smiled, sure that Luka and Rolan had heard what she said. She scanned the water behind the boat, hoping her dreams of studying in the United States were not going to vanish like the boat's turbulent wake merging with calm ocean water, disappearing forever. So many things had to be done in secrecy; one slip-up might doom the trip to Alaska, voiding her chances of ever studying what she loved. She pushed the possibility of failure to the back of her mind, turned to Luka, and said, "I will make the sign, you and Rolan work on the engine. We will do the covering later."

Luka asked, "You have been staring off the stern of the boat for nearly half-an-hour, what have you been thinking about?"

Arina looked at the coastline and recognized the rocky cliffs sheltering the inlet. "Oh, nothing."

The ice floe had shrunk to one quarter of its original size. Rolan commented when they arrived near the plane, "I think I will tow that big ice chunk out to sea, it is just in our way."

Arina and Luka went ashore after transferring the repair materials to the rowboat.

Rolan yelled at Luka, "Throw the two ropes on the ice to me, I will get rid of that chunk of ice." Rolan caught the ropes and secured them to the stern of the Maligin V, waved at Luka and Arina and yelled, "I will return in thirty minutes, do not send the fleet after me."

Arina laughed and waved at Rolan as the ice began moving toward the center of the inlet. Arina checked her watch, it was 1:33 p.m. She applied some sunscreen and started collecting wood for the sign. She bent down to pick a board up and the piece of wood moved.

Startled, she stepped back and looked up. Luka was holding the other end of the board. "Luka! You scared me! I almost wet my pants!"

"Arina, you have been lost in thought ever since we left Provideniya. You have something on your mind, do you not?" Luka watched Arina walk slowly toward him. She began to cry. He dropped the board and put his arms around her. "What is it, my sister? Are you ill? I am sorry I scared you. I thought you would pull on the board—I would let you have it."

Arina wiped her tears on Luka's sweater and said, "I am worried that our plan will not work and we might die trying to get out of Russia this way. I want all of us to get out of here and have a better life in America. What will happen to mother, father, and you, if Rolan and I go to Alaska?"

"Do not worry about that. We can always say we did not know of your silly plan. But I do not think anyone will know you are gone for a long time. We will make sure everyone knows that you and Rolan have gone to study in Moscow. Once someone finds out you are gone, but not in Moscow, all of us will be gone. You will figure out a way to get us to Alaska, I am confident." Luka gave Arina a hug and said, "Get back to work, Rolan will be back soon. We must show some progress." Luka picked up the board and handed it to Arina. When she grabbed the board, Luka pulled on it, and then released his hold. Smiling, he turned around to get some boards to hold up the netting around the engine and Arina swatted him in the butt with the piece of wood.

"I wish there was a nail in that board. You are a big devil, but I love you."

Luka had raised the netting above the engine and was dismantling the airplane's power supply when the Maligin V could be heard entering the inlet. Arina looked at her watch, it read 2:07 p.m. Rolan had been gone for a little more than thirty minutes. He beached the boat and jumped off, getting his feet wet. He sat down, removed his shoes, wrung out his socks, and lay them in the sun to dry. He stepped into his shoes, but didn't lace them, and joined Luka at the nose of the plane. He talked for a minute and then yelled to Arina, "What was my time?"

Arina replied, "You were gone thirty-four minutes, Rolan. Your estimate was not bad."

About fifteen minutes after Rolan returned, they were startled by a loud boom. Arina looked at Rolan and Luka and said, "What was that?" Two more explosions were heard, a few seconds between the rumbling noises that echoed off the walls of the inlet.

Luka answered, "Sounds like a gun, Arina—maybe six-centimeter cannon fire. I will take a look from up above." He pointed toward the top of the rocks and began to climb up the steep hill. When Luka returned from above, he said, "It was the patrol boat, about two kilometers out. They must have shot something in the water; maybe just practicing."

Rolan volunteered an explanation. "I think Captain Dimitri was killing that iceberg remnant. I am thinking we should have kept it here. Now we will have to bring ice with us to keep the fish cold. Too late now, but if we fish only on the way back, we will not need any ice."

Arina had constructed a panel about half the size of a door and was trying to find a spot on the rocky beach where two posts could be driven to hold the sign. She scanned the rocks for ten minutes before giving up the search. The ground was just too rocky. "Luka, did you bring a paint brush?"

"Uh, nyet. Just use a rag. Dip and rub—it need not be pretty— just military looking."

Arina thought for a few seconds, selected a can of gray paint, pried off the lid, and eyed Rolan's socks, then began to smile. She thought, "No, I better not use his sock for a paint brush. I do not want to argue with Rolan." She rowed the few meters to the Maligin V and found a rag in a compartment near the engine. "This should work." She smeared paint over the entire surface of the sign and resealed the can. The other colors were black and brown. The letters would have to be in black. She thought for a minute about the wording for the sign. She suddenly grinned, nodded, and said, "Aha! I have it."

Rolan heard Arina but wasn't sure of what she had said. "What did you say?"

She raised her voice and said, "Oh, nothing. I was just thinking out loud."

"Okay. Do not think so loud," Rolan laughed.

Arina returned to the wood pile and selected several boards, but they were not of the correct length for supporting the sign. She wanted to build a triangular structure, similar to an artist's easel, but to hold the sign on the ground. She dropped the boards and walked over to Luka and Rolan. "Do we have a saw, and where is it?"

Luka answered, "Yes—at home."

Arina frowned, a little frustrated. "I knew it! Never at hand when you need it."

Luka replied, "Better make a list. Rolan and I will need some things, too. We have to clean the rust out of the engine. We will have to sand and refinish the propeller, too—maybe you can start working on that. There is sandpaper in the toolbox."

Arina looked around but didn't see Rolan. "Where is Rolan? Was he not working with you?"

"I told him to take care of business. He was getting very smelly."

Arina smiled and watched Luka for about a minute when Rolan returned. Arina said, "Feel better?"

Rolan grinned and said, "Yes, and I think I smell better. Have you finished the sign?"

"Nyet. I need a saw to cut the wood. I am waiting for the paint to dry. Then I will do the letters."

"I put a saw on the Maligin V, in the long box in the bow. I will get it."

Rolan removed his shoes and waded to the boat, climbed on board, and returned with a carpenter's handsaw and a small paint brush. "Luka did not know I put the saw there, but it was too big for the toolbox." He put his shoes on and went back to help Luka.

"Thank you, Rolan. Did you get your feet wet?" Arina laughed as she walked back to the sign. She cut the wood and made two triangles of the same size, one meter on an edge, and nailed the sign to one edge of each triangle. She placed the sign high enough on the beach so the tides couldn't wash it away. She touched the paint; it was almost dry, just a little tacky. Arina looked at the sign and realized it needed to be weighted down to prevent it from being blown over by the wind. The only rocks of any size were high up on the hill where Luka had gone to check on the gunfire.

It seemed to Arina that it took forever to get to the rocks, and when she got there, the rocks were much too big. They had looked the right size from below. She continued climbing to the top of the hill, stood up and looked out to sea. Arina saw the patrol boat and dropped to the ground, hoping no one had seen her. The boat was coming toward the cliffs. She raised her head enough to see the boat and gave a sigh of relief when the military craft turned to the south and picked up speed.

She scanned the area, but no loose rocks could be seen, so she walked toward a shallow depression about sixty meters farther inland that appeared to be covered with shrubs. As she approached the dent in the landscape, the shrubs became a clump of trees, none of which stood higher than perhaps seven or eight meters. She began to notice wildflowers becoming more numerous and varied in color, the whites and yellows predominated, with an occasional blossom of blue or purple petals. The delicate flowers waved back and forth in the slight breeze like little pendulums, each requesting Arina to look at me.

The grove reminded Arina of an old book she had seen in the library several times as a child; the purple flowers were the illuminated letters beginning the first paragraph of each chapter, the whites and yellows were the other letters, and the blues were the punctuation. Beneath the trees were low-lying shrubs and berry bushes. The beauty of the miniature forest prompted Arina's memory of a story about a secret garden. That book seemed mystical to a youngster, but the story the wildflowers in Siberia told was different each year, the colors changed, and some disappeared, never to return.

Still no rocks were evident, but she noticed holes in the dirt; homes of evrazhka, arctic ground squirrels. She walked the periphery of the wooded region and finally found several rocks for weights to keep her sign from blowing over. With a five-kilo rock in each hand, she started back. As she neared the edge of the wildflowers, she saw a small yellowish-brown squirrel ducking into its ground burrow. It was time for the squirrels to be emerging from their six months of hibernation. In another month, many baby squirrels would be evident, and also foxes, hunting for the burrowers.

With some difficulty, Arina made it down the hill to the sign. She slipped and slid a bit descending the steep rocky incline but didn't have to drop the rocks to maintain her balance.

She believed she must have inherited at least some of her mother's ability to maintain equilibrium on the balance beam. She was so proud when she thought about her mother being a champion gymnast many years ago but having to give it up after all the hard work. Arina hoped if she had to make a big decision in the future, she would be as strong as her mother had been when young.

The gray paint had finally dried, so Arina started painting letters on the warning sign. When finished, the message wasn't as neat as she would have liked, but it could pass for something the military had produced. At first glance, it looked official. Holding a small can of paint and the brush provided by Rolan, she stood back to admire her work. Rolan and Luka joined her to see what she had produced. Rolan stood next to Arina and put his arm on her shoulder; Luka stood on her other side and put his arm around her waist.

Rolan read the sign, "Warning: Military Test Site 051. You are trespassing. Leave immediately. Do not divulge anything about this area. Severe penalties will result. Army General Anton Lupenikov."

Luka smiled and then frowned, "How did you decide on the number 051, and who is Lupenikov?"

Arina grinned. "That was easy, the United States has a restricted base in Nevada called Area 51. There are rumors that the government tests advanced aircraft there. Lupenikov is the name of a custodian at the technical school. He is a nice old man. I gave him a higher rank."

Rolan laughed, "That is very funny, Arina. We test old, worn-out aircraft here."

Luka added, "The sign looks good. It adds significance to the area, but I hope no one ever reads it."

CHAPTER 9
FAIRBANKS

Nearly two time zones to the East, in a different country, where a different language was the norm, the Newcomb family was getting ready for another day of passenger and mail delivery. The planes Dan and his father, Henry, flew as Alaskan bush pilots were capable of carrying six people, not limited to two as was the plane being reborn in Siberia.

Fairbanks, Alaska, about 700 miles due east of Provideniya, was exhibiting signs of spring days and more fair weather flying time for the Newcombs. Henry, or Hank, and son, pilots and general handymen for Conley, Newcomb, and Son, a small appliance and general fixit shop, flew their Cessna 185s nearly every day in April, delivering just about anything to locations within 250 miles of Fairbanks. Max Conley was Hank's brother-in-law, Dan's uncle. Jean Conley, Max's sister and Dan's mother, had passed away from cancer when Dan was fourteen, more than a decade ago.

Hank had disappeared on a hunting trip in the back country and was presumed dead when Dan was seventeen. Dan lived with Uncle Max, Aunt Mona, and their sons, Duke and Earl, until he joined the army and served in Afghanistan. Wounded, he returned to the states and spent time recuperating in the nation's capital. When able to travel, and curious about the lower forty-eight, Dan thumbed his way from one truck stop to the next, moving west, until he reached Oregon. There he accepted a job as a cabin-sitter in the woods south of Multnomah Falls, near Interstate-84 and the foothills of Mt. Hood.

After rescuing Ann Olson, a nursing student at the University of Washington, from kidnappers in Oregon, Dan learned to fly and adopted Nomah, a German shepherd puppy. Although Dan and Ann had become close, she returned to Boise, Idaho, and married a high school classmate. Five-months after accepting the job in Oregon, Dan returned to Alaska with Nomah, and began working with his uncle Max. Not long after he began working with his uncle, Dan resurrected a wrecked Cessna 185 airplane and started transporting passengers and freight within a two hour radius of Fairbanks. He occasionally flew farther under special circumstances.

Dan rescued a pilot and his passenger, an Emergency Medical Technician (EMT), when their plane crashed during landing on an ice-covered lake north of Fairbanks. The pilot had been shot. Dan was surprised to discover the EMT was Ann Olson. After Ann's divorce and the death of her father, Ann, the baby, and Ann's mother, Beverly, had decided to begin a new life in Alaska after moving from Boise, Idaho. Ann had hoped to see Dan again, but when she did, she found that Dan was engaged to another woman, Lisa Zorn.

Dan flew Ann to the Alaska pipeline, Station 6, for a medical visit, and during their return, the plane was shot at. Dan landed, went after the shooter, and discovered the culprit was his father, Henry Newcomb, long believed dead. Dan's and Henry's reunion was confusing to both men. Somehow, Hank had lost two years from his memory as he traipsed through Northern Alaska and the Canadian Yukon. It was difficult to believe Dan's father was alive and hadn't contacted any family member in nearly seven years. Dan asked Hank to come home with him, so Dan, Ann, Nomah, and Hank returned to Fairbanks. Hank had grown tired of the loneliness and harsh conditions and was prepared to face the consequences of his actions.

Lisa took a job with an architectural firm in Portland, Oregon, and within a month, began an intimate relationship with a coworker. When Dan found out, he severed all ties with Lisa, and before long, asked Ann to dinner. Dan discovered that his father had been seeing Beverly for about a month. At the restaurant, while the Olsons and the Newcombs were waiting for their table, Lisa reappeared with her grandmother. Dan introduced Ann to Lisa as his fiancée. Dan's presentation of Ann as his fiancée was a pleasant surprise to Ann, and during dinner, she told Dan she would marry him. They planned to be married at Christmas.

Beverly and Hank came up with the idea for Ann, Larry Daniel, and Beverly to move to Fairbanks from Anchorage. Ann, primarily assigned to the area near Fairbanks, would make shorter medical flights than from Anchorage, and both Dan and Hank could fly her to all sites where medical attention was requested. If a physician was needed, they could fly a patient to the hospital in Fairbanks. As the Newcombs' reputation for dependable flight service grew, they signed an agreement with the US Postal Service to deliver mail on a regular basis to locations as far north as sixty-eight degrees, and as far west as Wales, on the western coast of the Seward Peninsula, across the Bering Strait from the Russian Federation.

Beverly, Ann, and Larry were flown to Fairbanks on a Saturday towards the end of September. Dan and Hank were able to pack all of the Olsons' belongings in their two six-seat planes. Nomah was left in Fairbanks for the afternoon when the move was being made. Hank had rented a duplex, the Newcombs were to live in one side and the Olsons in the other, until after the marriages. The duplex was located about halfway between the shop for Conley, Newcomb, and Son, and their private airfield, which they were renting from Stu Graves, a former customer and gold miner. The house was furnished, but only the bare necessities were present. Sunday was spent stocking the refrigerators, buying firewood, and some furniture, including things for Larry. Larry's first birthday was celebrated on Sunday, the last day of September.

On Monday, Dan had to make deliveries to Ft. Yukon and Chalkyitsik, then he dropped off two passengers to Circle, before heading back to Fairbanks. The trip took nearly four hours. While Dan was flying, Ann was at the high school helping administer flu shots to students, faculty, and other staff members.

Ann was sitting with a school nurse eating lunch when they were joined by a tall young man who introduced himself as Roy Riggins, a high school teacher.

Ann smiled and replied, "I'm Ann Olson and this is Sarah Hamilton. I'm an EMT and Sarah is a nurse." Ann put down her fork and inquired, "What do you teach, Mr. Riggins?"

"You can call me Roy, or Rigs. That's my nickname from high school days. I teach math and physics, and help with football," he smiled, and then said, "when I don't have too much homework to grade. I know Sarah, I've seen her around the school. She gave me a flu shot last year. It didn't hurt at all, until the next day." Rigs laughed and noted that Ann's ring-finger was bare. They talked for a few minutes about high school classes they had taken, Rigs paying special attention to Ann.

Dan had told Ann about Rigs, but she had never met him. She remembered that Rigs had helped Dan recover a wrecked airplane which had allowed Dan to finish rebuilding Glacier Phoenix, Dan's plane. Ann held back a smile, wanting to tease Rigs like she would Dan. She had seen Rigs' eyes search for a ring on her left hand. Ann quizzed, "You must have played football: a tight end, or a defensive lineman?"

Rigs sat up straighter and answered, "A little of both. So, you know about football. What did you do in high school? I'll bet you were a cheerleader. Good looking girls are usually cheerleaders, aren't they?"

Ann smiled and said, "Thanks, but I wasn't too interested in high school—I cut a lot of classes. That made it difficult to get into college; my grades weren't very good."

Rigs looked at his watch, stood up, and said, "I've got to get to class; a one o'clock. It was nice meeting you Ann. Say, Ann, would you like to go for a drink after school? Maybe some pizza?"

Ann didn't answer immediately, she had seen Dan walking toward them. She waved at Dan and smiled at Rigs. "Thanks for the offer, but my fiancé would probably object. There he is, over there." She pointed at Dan as he approached the cafeteria table.

"Hi, Rigs. I see you've met my fiancée." Dan moved behind Ann, put his hands on her shoulders, leaned down, and kissed her cheek. "How's my girl?"

"I'm fine. Rigs was just hitting on me." She started laughing, "He wants me to have a drink with him after school."

Rigs looked down at his hands, wishing he had a book to hide behind, as his face turned slightly pink. He looked at Dan. "We haven't talked since we brought that plane back. I didn't know you and Ann were engaged, Dan, honestly. What happened to Lisa?"

"She wasn't really serious, so we called it off."

Rig's face lit up. "Is Lisa available now?"

"I guess. But I wouldn't recommend her to any of my friends. That includes you, Rigs."

"Well, I've got to get to class. See you later. Bye, Ann. You are quite a tease. Bye, Sarah."

Dan replied, "We'll have you over for dinner before long. Maybe we can fix you up. See ya."

Ann had stood up and grabbed Dan's arm to get his attention. "Can you give me a ride home? We're finished here."

"Sure. Do you need a ride, Sarah?"

"No but thank you. I've got my pickup."

"Okay. Do you know when classes are over this afternoon?"

"Uh-huh, three-thirty. My son gets home at four."

"Thanks. I want to call Rigs later today, after classes. See you. Take care."

On the way home, Ann asked about Rigs. "What's with Rigs' hair? Did he have it bleached?"

"Yep. My buddy, Simmy, over at the pizza shop, told me Rigs is letting it grow out, so now it's two-tone. It looks a bit strange, the outer part blond and the roots brown. You think he would cut off all the blond, maybe shave his head and let the brown grow back. But he has always done some wacky things. I think he's starved for attention, not many students take math and physics. There aren't any women teachers his age, either. We're going to watch for someone to hook him up."

Ann laughed, "Are we?"

"Let's help him out. He never was too great at dating. Rigs has to be pushed. I was a bit surprised he was hitting on you. Come on, we see lots of people, we should be able to find someone for him. I'm going to ask him to take a ride with me out west to Galena on Saturday. Dad and I are going to expand our delivery service for the winter. I need to look for a place to stay, and Rigs said he'd fly with me sometime. He's never been in a small plane. I think he's a little afraid to ride with Nomah and me."

"He's in for a real treat." Ann smiled, "I hope he doesn't get air-sick."

Dan replied, "I think he'll be okay. I'll take some barf-bags just in case. I need to find a cheap place to live, maybe a room in someone's house. Dad and I will alternate living in Galena two or three days a week. If I'm there, Dad will fly cargo to me, and I'll deliver it. That way we don't have long hauls to make. We're going to try it over the holidays and see how it goes, just during November and December."

Ann frowned, grabbed Dan's arm, stopped walking, and stared into his eyes. "You won't be gone for Christmas, will you? I want us all to be together for Christmas. It might be the first Christmas Larry will remember."

Dan put his arm around Ann and said, "Don't worry, honey, we'll figure something out so we can all be together. Remember, Galena is only about two hours from Fairbanks."

"Yes, but what about the weather? You guys can't be flying if there's a whiteout."

"That's right. We'll watch the weather reports, so we don't get marooned away from Fairbanks at Christmas. We can make all our Santa Claus deliveries a few days before the twenty-fifth."

"Well, okay." Ann started walking again and said, "Say, Rigs is kind of handsome, if it weren't for his hair. Maybe you're right, he needs some help finding a girlfriend. All the female teachers here are married or too old. I'll check out the hospitals. Maybe I can find a nurse here or in Anchorage."

Dan smiled and said jokingly, "So, you think he's better looking than I am?"

Ann wanted to laugh, but she fought to keep a deadpan expression, and said, "There's a good plastic surgeon in Anchorage. He has done wonders with accident victims—hiding scars, things like that." Both Ann and Dan were ready to tease each other whenever they could, especially at unexpected times. Ann thought this was a great opportunity.

They got into the pickup and fastened their seat belts. Dan tilted his head back and looked into his visor mirror to observe the scar on his chin. Pretending to be concerned with his appearance, he was going to go along with Ann's suggestion until he had her convinced he was worried, then he would start laughing. "Maybe I should have my scar fixed, what do you think?"

"Well, I kind of like your scar. In the dark I can tell where your mouth is by feeling for the scar."

"Ann, my mouth is right below my nose. You don't need to feel for the scar. I think I'll have it fixed. It shouldn't cost more than a couple thousand, should it?" They continued the discussion all the way home.

They were approaching the house when Ann leaned against Dan and said, "I don't want you to do anything to your appearance, I like you just the way you are."

"Oh, I get it. You are thinking of having some plastic surgery done. I was thinking you wanted me to have something done. I think you are perfect. You just wanted a compliment, didn't you? You are so sneaky."

Ann turned her head and looked at Dan saying, "How did this get started?"

Dan took his foot off the gas, the truck slowing for the turn off the street. As they pulled into their driveway, Dan started laughing. "Got you! You were thinking I was serious about surgery. I have been joking ever since we left the school."

Ann slugged him in the bicep and said, "You rat! I can't tell if you are serious or not. You are such a good liar."

Dan smiled, "I get that from my dad."

"You blame your dad? That is your trait, my dear." Ann kissed Dan on the cheek, opened the door, dropped to the ground, and slammed the door.

Dan lowered the passenger side window and said, "I have to take the truck back to the store. Dad might need it this afternoon. We'll be home around six o'clock. See you for dinner." Dan watched Ann walk to her front door, admiring her efficient, slightly sexy, stride. He waved as he backed out into the street. He saw Ann wave back as she entered her side of the duplex.

Dan worked on a snow-blower until four o'clock; it needed an overhaul. The owner had neglected the filters and rust had gotten into the engine. He took a coffee break and decided to call Rigs. He wiped the grime from his fingers and dialed. Rigs answered on the fourth ring.

"Yeah?"

"Hey, Rigs, how about flying to Galena with me on Saturday? I have to go there on business. I could use the company—Nomah doesn't say anything, he just sleeps and looks out the window. It's kind of boring alone. I can show you some of Alaska from the air; it's beautiful."

"Ah—."

"So, you're afraid to fly with me? I haven't had an accident yet."

"Yeah, but you've only been flying for two years or so."

"That's all right. I'll find someone else. Maybe I can get Simmy to go."

"I don't think so. I saw him the other day and he said he has to work this weekend. He has to put in orders for supplies. Pizza is getting more popular as the temperature drops. I wanted to drive to Anchorage before the weather gets too crappy though. I'll tell you what. If I go with you to Galena, will you fly me to Anchorage on Sunday? I need to go shopping for clothes. I can't find what I want here."

"It's a deal. Pick me up at my place around 9:00 a.m. I won't have the truck, Dad's going to be using it."

"Okay, Dan. See you Saturday."

"Thanks, Rigs. Later."

CHAPTER 10
GALENA

Friday night Dan talked further with Hank about establishing the cargo and mail-drop center in Galena and went to bed about midnight. The next thing he heard was the honk of a horn. He threw back the covers and took a look out the window. Rigs was leaning out of his jeep, looking up at Dan's bedroom window. Rigs waved and Dan motioned for Rigs to come to the front door.

Dan pulled on his pants, grabbed the nearest shirt, a red-and-black plaid; the one he had tossed over the back of a chair two nights ago, put on his watch, and headed downstairs to the front door.

Nomah was waiting beside the door to see who was visiting. Dan instructed Nomah to go in the kitchen, but Nomah wanted out. Rigs stepped aside for Nomah and then entered the house and followed Dan into the kitchen. "I figured you'd be ready and waiting for me, Dan." Rigs smiled as he leaned against the refrigerator.

"That was my idea—last night, but I talked with Dad until midnight and couldn't go to sleep. I was thinking about a location in Galena."

"Oh. You've been there before?"

"Nope—that's the problem. I don't want to get over-committed moneywise to a location that will eat our assumed profits. You know what I mean?"

"Uh-huh. Remember, I teach math. Got any coffee?"

"Could you make it? I've got to finish dressing. Dad will be up in a few minutes. He likes coffee strong and black. He's used to making it over a fire out in the woods. One mug of his coffee and it's like an explosion; you're up all day—naps are impossible."

Rigs looked around, saw the coffee, the filters, and the coffee maker on the counter. "Okay. Want me to fry you some eggs, and make some toast?" He said that sarcastically, but Dan didn't reply, he was already upstairs. Rigs prepared for twelve cups of coffee, flipped the maker on, and went toward the front door when he heard scratching. He let Nomah in and went back to the kitchen. Nomah was watching Rigs from the living room.

Hank entered the kitchen from the hallway, scratching his head, blinking his eyes, and rubbing his face. When he saw Rigs, he quizzed, "Who are you?"

Rigs turned and looked toward the voice. "Oh. Hi, Mr. Newcomb. I'm Roy Riggins." Rigs took two steps, leaned forward, and extended his hand. "I played ball with Dan. I teach math at the high school. Dan asked me to ride with him to Galena."

The two men shook hands and Hank said, "You helped Dan recover that airplane, didn't you?"

"That's right. Seems like that was a long time ago. The coffee's almost ready. Dan said you like it strong—it'll be that, for sure. If you reheat it, don't boil off much of the water, the coffee will crystallize. I like it strong, too. I take it straight. Those creamers disguise the taste, but sometimes I put sugar in it; just a little bit."

Hank pulled out a chair and sat down as Dan reappeared, fully clothed. "You didn't make toast and eggs, Rigs?" Dan laughed, "Just kidding. I'll fry some eggs and make some toast. Want some, Dad?"

"No thanks, I'll get my own. You guys better get going. It's getting colder today—probably won't get above freezing. Make sure you take some warm clothes. If you have to land out in the boonies, you want to keep warm. Got a heavy coat or parka, Roy?"

Rigs glanced at Dan and back at Hank. "Yeah. I've got a parka and gloves in my jeep. The plane's cabin is heated, right?"

Dan chuckled, "Don't worry, Rigs. We just have to be prepared for emergencies. We have the plane stocked with food and supplies—just in case we go down. We've never needed that stuff—yet," he smiled. "I checked the battery operated radio, flares, and dog food yesterday."

"Nomah is going, too?"

"Uh-huh. He almost always flies with me, he loves to fly." Nomah walked into the kitchen and barked. Rigs flinched and then reached out to Nomah, who was wagging his tail and looking at Dan. "You want to fly today, boy?" Nomah barked again and walked toward the front door. "Okay, just a minute." Dan stuffed a piece of toast in his mouth and quickly gobbled up two fried eggs, liberally coated with pepper and ketchup. He drank the rest of his coffee, checked his shirt pocket for antacids, and carried his dishes to the sink, rubbed his hands together, and said, "Let's go, Rigs." Dan checked his pants for his wallet and keys, slipped on his parka, and went to the door. "Bye, Dad. We'll be back about three this afternoon."

Rigs turned and shook hands with Hank. "It was nice meeting you, Mr. Newcomb."

Hank smiled, "Glad to have met you, Mr. Riggins."

Dan held the door open and Rigs followed Nomah to the jeep. Dan shut the door and exhaled into the cold morning air, the vapor revealing the low temperature. Five minutes later they were at the private airstrip. Dan slid open the big door to the Quonset building. Rigs drove his jeep in and parked.

Dan pointed toward the corner behind the jeep. "See that pile of bags on top of the trash can? Pick up a handful and bring them out to the plane. Also, look in that metal box and see if there's any mail for Galena. It should be marked, wrapped in paper, and rubber-banded." Dan watched Rigs open the box and look in. Rigs extracted an envelope, turned, and waved it in the air for Dan to see.

"Okay, got it. There's just one envelope."

They pushed the door shut, locked it, and walked to Glacier Phoenix, Dan's plane. Nomah was boosted into the cabin, where he sat in the front passenger seat, watching Dan and Rigs do the preflight walk around.

Rigs commented, "Didn't your dad say the plane was ready to go?"

Dan smiled and replied, "He did, but I always check the plane before I take off. That way there is no one to blame but myself if something goes wrong. Would you blame your dad if your car ran out of gas?"

"I see what you mean. What are we looking for?"

"It's hard to say, but anything that's loose, worn, bent, or doesn't feel right."

Rigs followed Dan around the plane, listening to Dan explain what he was doing and looking for. "You do this every day?"

"Before every flight, sometimes several times a day. Preflight might save my life and my plane someday." Dan ended up at the pilot side and opened the cabin. "Go around, or under, Rigs. We're ready to lift off. You have those bags?"

"Uh-huh. You think I'll need them? I've never been carsick."

"Ever flown in a small plane before?"

"Nope, but I was in a Boeing 747 once."

Dan smiled and said, "This is way different, but you might be all right. Just don't think about it, but I sure don't want to smell barf for two hours. If you feel something coming on, use the bags. Keep them in your lap."

Dan climbed in and moved Nomah to the seat behind him so Rigs could get in. He started the engine, began taxiing downwind, turned into the slight wind, and said, "Fasten your seatbelt." He looked at Rigs, who nodded. "Ready, Nomah?"

Nomah barked and Rigs gave a thumbs up, as he tightened his seatbelt and put the barf bags in his lap. Dan smiled, began increasing engine speed, and ten seconds later the plane left the ground heading almost due west. Glacier Phoenix climbed to 3,000 feet and leveled off. Dan heard a sigh from Rigs and looked at him. Rigs smiled and held up the barf bags showing Dan he had them ready, if necessary.

"Hey, Rigs. Who is that letter addressed to?"

Rigs opened his parka and pulled the letter out, looking at the name and address. "It says Chyler Skyze, CAP, Galena, AK. It's from The University of Washington Medical Center. What kind of a name is Chyler?"

"I'm guessing it's for a woman. I think there's an actress with the name Chyler. That reminds me, Ann and I are on the lookout for a woman for you. Maybe this Chyler person is someone you ought to get to know. CAP could stand for Civil Air Patrol. She might be a pilot. Better be careful, Rigs, she might fly off with you."

"Hah! What are the chances of that? Maybe the letter is an acceptance to medical school, or maybe she teaches math and physics. That would be great. We could talk about aerodynamics." Rigs looked at Dan and laughed. "Just kidding, but she could be over fifty. I'd have to bail out if that's the case."

"Well, we don't read the mail, we just deliver it. We may never find out what's in that letter. Hey, strange things can happen. Remember, Ann and I got together after I rescued Nate Burke and her when they had to land on that frozen lake. I never thought I'd see her again after she went back to Boise from Oregon and married that jerk. But now, we're going to get married. What's cool is her mom and my dad are going to get married, too. Geez, Rigs, I just realized, I'll be marrying my sister."

"Hmm. Maybe you need to get married first—you and Ann wouldn't be brother and sister until after they get married. Course, there's no real relationship—except by marriage. I wonder if there's a law for that."

Dan reflected for a moment and said, "I doubt if Alaska has ever had a law to cover our situation, but maybe I should ask a lawyer about it—just in case. Nah, nobody would care."

They flew in silence for about ten minutes before Rigs said, "I heard something the other day about your dad. One of the football players said your dad was on probation for killing two men when we were in high school."

"I don't know about any probation, but he did kill two hunters. He flew them into a mountain, but he was able to get out of the wreck and make it down from altitude. He almost died of exposure, but he made it out of the mountains with a broken leg. That's why he limps. I guess I should have told you about that."

"No, it's none of my business. I'm sure he was forced into it. He's a good man—just like you."

"Thanks, Rigs. You're a good friend. Who was talking about my dad?"

"It was Tobe Linton. James Linton is a lawyer. He must have read about the case somehow."

"Well, I didn't know about the probation. I think Dad just wants to forget about it. But just so you know, those hunters told Dad they would kill me if he didn't do what they wanted. He was worried about me and any of my friends that might get hurt. He didn't have any other option but to try to get rid of them."

"Hmm. I should thank your dad. I might have been killed too."

"No, Rigs. Don't say anything. Dad wants to put it behind him. Please don't say anything. Okay?"

"All right, but just remember, I've got your back."

Twenty minutes later, they landed at the Galena airstrip, on the north bank of the Yukon River. The airstrip had been shared with the Air Force during the Cold War. Dan taxied past a number of private planes, stopped at the old F-16 hanger, the largest building at the airport, and cut his engine.

"Rigs, when you open the door, Nomah will jump out. Don't let him knock you down, take your time getting out."

As soon as Rigs cracked the door, Nomah forced his way out onto the tarmac and quickly circled the plane twice, tail wagging. He sat on the ground and waited for Dan and Rigs to join him. They proceeded to the hanger and entered through a thick, metal-clad door. Dan instructed Nomah to sit beside the door outside the building. A young man about Dan's age, wearing a yellow T-shirt and gray overalls, walking rapidly across the hanger toward the men's room, asked, "Can I help you?"

"We're looking for the Civil Air Patrol office."

The man pointed to the back right corner of the building, said, "Over there," and continued walking across the concrete floor.

Dan said, "Thanks."

The workman, now nearly running, yelled back toward a Cessna that had the cowling removed, "Be right back, Sid. I've got to make a deposit. It's an emergency."

Dan and Rigs laughed and stood inside the door for a few seconds letting their eyes adjust to the dimly lit, but relatively warm hanger. Heaters with fans blowing were hanging from the high ceilings, causing a low pitch rumbling noise, as if students were stomping their feet in the bleachers at a football game. Rigs started walking toward the back of the hanger, Dan following. Rigs unzipped his parka and pulled the letter from an inside pocket. He knocked on the door and a male voice said, "Come in."

Rigs turned the knob, stepped in, and held the door for Dan to join him. Rigs watched Dan looking back at the plane being serviced and wondered what had gotten Dan's attention.

Two men and a woman were standing in front of a wall map

talking. One of the men looked toward Dan and Rigs and said, "What can we help you with."

Rigs answered, "I've got some mail for Chyler Skyze." He held up the envelope and the woman looked away from the map to see who had said her name.

"I'm Chyler. Where's it from?"

Rigs replied, "Seattle." He took a couple of steps toward the young lady.

The woman, about five-seven, looked to be in her mid-twenties, had dark-brown, short, curly hair. From the left, Rigs saw that she was very pretty, but his opinion changed abruptly when she turned to face him. The right side of her face was scarred. The obvious deformity was a wide scar below her eye extending down her cheek to her jaw and another scar, much smaller, ran from her hair line to the center of her right eyebrow, which was bisected by scar tissue. She reached out and Rigs handed her the letter. She smiled, but her face was contorted—the left side was smiling, but the right side seemed almost paralyzed, only a tiny movement of her cheek was evident. Rigs wondered how she had become disfigured.

"I'm Roy Riggins. This ugly devil is Dan Newcomb." Rigs pointed at Dan. "Dan flew me here from Fairbanks so I could deliver this letter to you. I hope it's something you've been waiting for."

"Thank you, Mr. Riggins. It is very important. It's a letter from a surgeon in Seattle. I've got an appointment to get my face repaired. The doctor thinks he can fix the scars and the muscles underneath. Early next year, I should look almost normal, maybe with the help of some makeup. The bear that did this is dead, courtesy of my uncle's hunting friends. Uncle Jack gave me a bearskin rug not long after the animal attacked us last year."

C H A P T E R   1 1

RETURN FLIGHT TO FAIRBANKS

Chyler stepped toward Dan and extended her hand. "I've heard of you, Mr. Newcomb. You're a little younger looking than I had expected."

Dan shook hands with Chyler, smiled, and said, "Maybe you're thinking of my dad, Hank Newcomb. He's been a bush pilot for about twenty-five years—ever since I was a baby."

"No, I don't think so. Surely your father didn't serve in Afghanistan."

Dan was racking his brain trying to figure out how Chyler had heard of him. It suddenly occurred to him that they knew someone in common, but whom? With heightened curiosity, he asked, "So, how did you hear about me? Have you been to Fairbanks in the last year, or did you go to high school about the time I did? You must know someone I know."

"Lisa invited me to your wedding, but when you backed out, she told me it was off."

Dan was astonished. "What? I didn't back out of the wedding. You better ask Lisa to tell you the truth."

Rigs was listening and said, "Well, there's another reason you couldn't recommend Lisa to me, Dan. She's a liar, too."

Chyler frowned and commented, "I'll have to ask her what happened, if you don't want to talk about it. But you didn't fly to Galena just to deliver this letter, did you? What is your real reason for coming here?"

"Oh, I should have told you that a few minutes ago. I need to find a place to stay in Galena. Dad and I are expanding our delivery territory—clear to Nome. We want to rent a room for two or three days a week. Dad will deliver mail and freight to me and I will fly it to the destination. After a week or two, we will switch positions so one of us is not away from Fairbanks all the time."

Chyler nodded, "I understand. I have an idea but let me read this letter first." She picked up a pair of scissors, trimmed off the end of the envelope, pulled out the letter, and began to read. She smiled and pumped her fist. "Yes!" She looked up at the ceiling and mouthed the words, "Thank you."

Rigs quizzed, "Good news?"

"Fantastic news!" Chyler responded happily, "My surgery starts next Wednesday in Seattle!" Her mood suddenly changed from elation to concern. "I have to get my clothes and money, find a ride to Anchorage, and then fly to Seattle."

Rigs inquired, "Is one of the planes outside yours?"

"Unfortunately, no. I just fly the CAP plane when necessary."

Rigs looked at Dan. Dan nodded and gave Rigs a thumbs up, knowing what Rigs was going to tell Chyler.

"You can fly to Fairbanks with us today, if you like. There's a plane that leaves Fairbanks for Seattle every couple of days. You won't have to go to Anchorage to catch a flight, and you can stay with my mother for a day or two if you can't get an immediate flight."

"That would be so nice of you, but you don't even know me."

"We'll get to know you on the flight back to Fairbanks. Dan and I have about talked each other out, so a new voice in the cabin would be a luxury."

"That should be fun. There aren't many people around here to talk to, except fellow pilots I talk shop with, but they are my parent's age. I think I can help you here in Galena. I mentioned my Uncle Jack. He lives in a two story house, but only uses the bottom floor. There is an outside stairway to the second floor. I think he would let you use the top floor while you are in Galena—that's where I've been staying. You would be doing me a favor, too. He needs someone to talk to; he doesn't get out much because of his artificial legs." Her eyes widened in anticipation of Dan saying he would agree to that.

Dan asked, "But where will you live if I'm in your place?"

"Oh, that's not a problem. I'll be gone for at least two months, maybe longer. When I return, we'll find you another place. What do you say?"

"That sounds good to me, Chyler. I won't have to search for a place to stay. Thanks for the offer. Can you leave your job here now? I'd like to meet your uncle."

"Sure, I was just here to talk over the plans for December and January. They knew I might be having some work done on my face in October and November."

Dan spoke up, "It's nice to know you have such a good relationship with your co-members."

"Yeah, we have a good bunch of volunteers in the CAP. We'll take my car. Just a minute and we'll go visit with my uncle."

Dan and Rigs watched as Chyler talked to the two men at the map, gave them a hug, and said goodbye.

As Chyler rejoined Dan and Rigs, Dan smiled and said, "You need to meet the third member of our group."

Chyler frowned. She wasn't sure she heard Dan correctly. "Someone else is with you? Did one of you bring a girl friend?"

Rigs grinned and commented, "No, more like a boyfriend. He's outside." Rigs beckoned with his right arm, "Come on, you need to meet him. Dan will introduce you."

Both Dan and Rigs believed they would be retracing their route to the front of the hanger, but Chyler led the two men out the back door. She looked around but didn't see anyone. "You said there was another person with you?"

Dan answered, "We left him by the front door. Just a second." He put his fingers to his mouth and whistled. Dan and Rigs smiled as they watched Chyler straighten up, a little surprised, when Nomah rounded the corner of the hanger and ran toward the threesome.

"Oh! You have a dog! My God, he's so pretty, and so big." When Chyler dropped to one knee, Dan gave two short whistles and Nomah gave Chyler a kiss. She leaned back to avoid Nomah's tongue, and then leaned forward to give Nomah a big hug. "Thank you, Nomah."

Chyler looked up at Dan and asked, "Does your dog like to fly?"

"Oh, yeah. Nomah loves being in the plane. He's disappointed when we're not flying. He watches the ground and sleeps when we're in the air. He's my co-pilot most of the time."

They walked toward an irregular line of cars, passing the first two. Chyler said, "Here we are." Chyler had stopped at the third car; a large gray SUV, pulled her keys from her pocket, and opened the doors. Dan opened the door to the cluttered back seat. "Just toss that stuff behind the seat in the back. I'll clean it out when I get back from Seattle."

Dan moved several books, a pair of boots, a pillow, and two blankets out of the way and ushered Nomah into the car. Dan climbed in and pulled the door shut. Rigs slid in front with Chyler. Dan saw Rigs look back at him with a trace of a smile as the car began to move. Dan winked at Rigs. Dan thought maybe they wouldn't have to look any further for a girl for Rigs. A couple of minutes later, they pulled into the driveway of a two-story white house, built on stilts, about six-feet above the ground. It was within walking distance of the airstrip, less than half a mile away, and a hundred yards from the river which tended to flood the town during the spring thaw. Ice dams blocked river water and flooded the town, but not the elevated airstrip.

Chyler parked, slid out of the driver's seat, and moved toward the front door. "Come meet my uncle. I'll tell him our plans." She rapped twice on the door. Not waiting for a "Come in," she turned the knob and entered. Rigs and Dan hesitated and then followed Chyler inside. Dan told Nomah to wait on the porch.

Uncle Jack, wearing a red, green, and yellow plaid shirt, was sitting in an overstuffed, light-brown chair with a thick, black blanket over his legs. It was warm in the house, probably near seventy-five degrees. Chyler leaned down and gave her uncle a hug and kissed the top of his balding head. He smiled and reached up to smooth what little gray hair remained on top. He looked to be in his sixties.

"Who have you got there, kiddo, two new boyfriends?"

Chyler grinned and turned toward Rigs and Dan. "Maybe, Uncle Jack, but I just met them. The one on the right is Dan Newcomb—he's a pilot, and the other gentleman is Roy Riggins. I don't know what he does." She looked questioningly at Rigs.

"I teach high school math and physics, sir." Rigs grinned. I'm the one looking for a girlfriend. Dan is engaged."

"Well, gentlemen, what can I do for you? Did you come to visit, or do some business?"

Chyler explained the situation as Jack listened quietly with his chin in his right hand between his thumb and index finger. When Chyler finished, Jack looked at Dan and said, "You honest?"

"Yes, sir. But I'm not alone—my dog, Nomah, stays with me."

Jack leaned forward and looked around, "Where's the dog? Is he housebroken?"

Dan answered, "Yes, sir. He's outside; can I bring him in?"

Chyler said, "I'll get him." She opened the door and spoke to Nomah. He entered the room and sat beside Dan, looking at Jack.

"Now that is a dog! Here, boy." Jack reached out and Nomah walked toward Jack and smelled the blanket. Then he put his front paws on the arm of the chair to let Jack pet him. "You're a very smart boy, Nomah. You can tell I don't have my legs on, can't you?" Jack flipped back the blanket so everyone could see that Jack's legs had been amputated below the knee.

Dan asked, "How did you lose your legs, sir, an accident?"

"You could say that. It was a 300 pound black bear, much larger than normal, the same one that clawed Chyler. He paid for it with his life. He tried to eat us, but we ended up eating him. His skin's on the floor upstairs—nice looking bear now. You'll see him when you move in. He's kind of thin now." Jack laughed and slapped his thighs with both hands.

Chyler said, "I'll show you the rooms upstairs." She smiled and continued, "I don't think any of my underwear is on exhibit."

Rigs grinned, "I wouldn't mind, especially if it's pink or black."

"Hey, Chyler, just a minute. I've got to put my legs on. I want to see that bear again." He pointed at Dan and said, "Can you help me with my legs?"

"Sure, I've done that before in the Walter Reed Hospital. Quite a few servicemen have lost limbs in Afghanistan—some were my friends."

Chyler was already helping. Dan assisted, and then helped Jack get out of his chair.

Rigs asked, "Where's your coat?"

"Don't need a coat, son. It's above freezing today," Jack smiled.

Jack worked his way down the steps and around the corner to the flight of stairs going up to the second floor. Nomah bounded up the steps, with Chyler and Dan close behind. They waited on the landing for Jack and Rigs. Jack climbed the steps, with some difficulty, and Rigs followed, just in case the older gentleman fell.

Chyler started packing two suitcases, while Jack showed Dan the apartment and handed him a set of keys.

"If you hear me pounding on my ceiling, I need some help—but it shouldn't happen very often. I'm nearly self-sufficient. Only my occasional blunders cause me any trouble. I would like you to help me get groceries though, bread and such. I've still got some meat in the freezer—bear meat." Jack laughed. "I asked the doctors if I could have my legs—they might be good eatin', but they said no."

Chyler responded, "You did not! Don't let that old man pull your leg, Dan."

"I learn quickly, Chyler. I once met a trucker named Billy who had a sense of humor like Jack's. He was short, too," Dan laughed. Rigs smiled. Dan had told Rigs about Billy giving him a lift to Bellingham.

Jack and Chyler laughed. Jack responded, "We're going to get along fine, Dan." Jack put his arm around Dan's shoulders and patted him on the back.

Chyler finished packing, sat down for a moment to think if she had everything, and the men went out on the landing. Nomah descended the steps first, followed by the men. Rigs and Dan teamed up to carry Jack down the stairs. Chyler came out with her suitcases, locked the door, and pushed her hair back. Rigs ran up the stairs, grabbed the larger suitcase, and followed Chyler down the steps.

After Chyler's belongings were in the SUV, she gave her uncle a big hug, told him to raid her refrigerator, and said goodbye. Rigs shook hands with Jack, saying it was a pleasure to have met him. Dan shook hands and told Jack he would see him in about a week, but he wasn't sure of his schedule yet. Nomah, not to be outdone, walked up to Jack, sat down and raised his right paw. Jack shook hands with Nomah, Nomah turned, ran for the car, and climbed into the back seat with Dan. As they drove away, Dan put his window down, and told Nomah to bark.

Jack smiled when he heard the bark, waved goodbye, and watched his niece and her new friends drive away. He was looking forward to some man-talk with Dan. Jack grabbed the railing and pulled his way up to the front door, gave one last look to see if he could catch sight of Chyler's car moving down the road, but she was gone. He went inside, sat in his chair, and took off his legs, leaned back, and pressed resume to continue watching the John Wayne western.

C H A P T E R   1 2

PASSENGER TO FAIRBANKS

It was noon in Galena when Glacier Phoenix was loaded with their passenger and a small package to be delivered to Tofty, Alaska, which was about twenty miles west of the Eureka Creek landing strip. Tofty was a little out of the way from the direct route to Fairbanks, but Dan calculated it would add only fifteen to twenty minutes, at most a half-hour, to their trip, so he agreed to transport the package to nearby Eureka; the map indicated Tofty was a ghost town.

Chyler looked at the package on the floor of the cabin at Rig's feet. "The package has drugs in it, Dan. Mrs. Milnar is probably waiting for the package. She's a diabetic. It's nice of you to deliver it to Eureka. She'll get it in another day. It must have come from Nome."

"I guess I'll get to know the people out here as I begin deliveries."

Nomah was sitting beside Dan in the front. Rigs and Chyler were behind them. Rigs looked at Chyler as they left the ground and ascended to 3,000 feet. He could see a few tears in her eyes and reached into his pocket for his handkerchief. Chyler dried her eyes and said, "I always cry a little when I leave family behind. I don't think I'll ever get over it."

Rigs replied, "I wouldn't even try. It shows how much you love your family."

Chyler smiled, squeezed Rig's arm, and said, "Thank you." Then she leaned forward and spoke to Dan. "How is your son?"

Dan frowned and replied, "You mean my fiancée's little boy. He's not mine, but when Ann and I get married, I plan on adopting him. He's doing great. Lisa must have told you he was mine."

Chyler replied, "Lisa told me that was one of the reason's she didn't want to marry you, since you had a kid with another woman, and you were never married."

Dan shook his head, unable to believe that Lisa was spreading so much garbage about him, when she had been the one that ruined their relationship. He told Chyler what had happened. It was entirely Lisa's fault he had broken off their engagement. But now that time had passed, he realized the marriage wouldn't have lasted.

Chyler sat quietly, listening to Dan tell his version of the story. The more she heard from Dan, the stronger her conclusion was that Lisa had lied to her. Chyler wanted to meet Ann.

"What does Ann do for a living?"

Dan smiled and said, "Ann is an EMT and a very good one. I sometimes fly her to her patients. She wanted to be a nurse, but her ex-husband put a stop to that, so she is temporarily an EMT. She needs one more semester of classes to complete her training. If you have any hesitancy about your surgery, Ann can probably allay your fears."

"What does she do about the baby when she's taking care of people?"

Dan smiled and replied, "Her mom, Beverly, babysits for her. You'll have to meet Ann, Beverly, and Larry Daniel. I call him LD for lethal dose. I really love that little guy—he makes me laugh. By the way, my dad and Beverly are getting married, too. I think you'll like my dad; Hank's also a bush pilot. He's been one for more than two decades."

"What does he fly?"

"A Cessna 185, same as this one, but his was never wrecked."

"This plane was wrecked? I can't tell. You did a great job of rebuilding it; it looks almost new."

"Thanks. Rigs helped with the restoration. He and two other friends of ours helped me get another wreck out of the forest about thirteen miles north of Minto. It took four of us two days to get that hulk back to Fairbanks. I got needed parts and we sold some of the instruments. We actually made a profit."

Rigs laughed, "I left a roll of toilet paper for the bears. We worked hard, but we also had a good time—telling jokes and kidding each other."

Chyler smiled and replied, "I'll bet you guys were drunk half the time. No wonder it took two days to retrieve the plane."

Rigs replied, "You're wrong, Chyler. Most of the time we were dead serious, and we didn't do any drinking. We all had jobs to get back to the day after we returned to Fairbanks. We were an exceptional team; we knew Dan wasn't out there to mess around, his future depended on bringing back that plane."

"That's right, and they helped me rebuild this plane. Of my three buddies, Rigs is the only one that has flown in it though. I'm going to fly him to Anchorage tomorrow. We'll check on flights to Seattle. Maybe we can take you to Anchorage."

Chyler scanned the cabin and said, "I'm impressed." Then she leaned back and closed her eyes, listening to the hum of the engine.

Rigs was impressed, too. He looked at Chyler, imagining how she would look after surgery to remove the scars. If the doctor could make the right side of her face look anything like the unmarked left side, he knew she would be happy. Whatever happened with the surgery, he wanted to get to know her better. She was the type of woman he had been looking for, strong, independent, smart, and possessing a good sense of humor. He hoped they would form a friendship that might develop into something more.

"We'll be landing in Eureka in about ten minutes," Dan announced. Dan expected a reaction from the seat behind him, but there wasn't a peep. He twisted in his seat and took a quick glance to the rear. Rigs motioned that Chyler was asleep. He put his finger up against his lips. Dan nodded and was quiet for nearly all of the ten minutes, but had to say, "Check your seatbelts, we're landing," a few seconds before he lined up with the airstrip.

Chyler opened her eyes and looked down to check her belt, then glanced at Rigs, who was watching her. "What?"

"Nothing—I was checking your belt, you were asleep." He smiled.

"No I wasn't. I heard everything Dan said. I was listening to the motor and went to my quiet place, evaluating you two gentlemen."

Rigs smiled and quizzed, "How was our evaluation?"

Chyler didn't answer until after they were on the ground and taxiing toward several cars parked adjacent to the center of the runway. Behind the cars was a windsock hanging from a pole, but it was limp.

"After that flight and landing, Dan gets an A, maybe an A+. I'm still working on your evaluation, but so far, it's pretty good," Chyler smiled.

"I hope I at least get a C," Rigs grinned.

"I'll let you know when the evaluation is complete, but it might take some time."

"Oh, great! I hope you give me a chance to do some extra credit."

"Well, maybe we can work something out to our mutual advantage. Let's get out and stretch our legs. How far are we from Fairbanks?"

Rigs looked out to see Dan and Nomah walking toward the cars. Dan was carrying the package for Mrs. Milnar.

"I'll have to ask Dan; I've never been here before."

As Dan approached the cars, the passenger door on a white pickup opened and a middle-aged woman got out. She was wearing a parka to keep warm, and was walking toward Dan, but watching Nomah.

"I'm Emma Milnar. Is that package for me?"

Nomah moved toward the woman, she suddenly stopped, and put her hands in her pockets.

"Don't worry about Nomah, he's big, but he's just a baby. Yes, the package is for you. We flew it here from Galena, on our way to Fairbanks." Dan held out the package to Mrs. Milnar. She accepted it with both hands and looked at her address.

"Oh, my! It should have come from Fairbanks; it's much closer— only eighty-seven miles. And what is your name, young man?"

"I'm Dan Newcomb." He removed his glove to shake hands with Emma. "Pleased to meet you. Have you been waiting long for the package?"

"Not too long, only about ten days, but I drove here today. It has my insulin and glucose test strips in it; I hope the insulin didn't freeze."

"Not since we've had it. Just the last two hours."

"Hello, Emma!" Chyler and Rigs had joined Dan and Emma by the lady's pickup.

Emma frowned, then suddenly realized it was Chyler. "Chyler! What brings you way out here? It's so nice to see you again. I should have recognized you immediately. I haven't seen you since that one time in Fairbanks, and you were bandaged."

Chyler and Emma hugged each other and Chyler introduced Rigs. "Emma, this is my new friend, Roy Riggins. Roy, this is my old friend Mrs. Emma Milnar. She lives with her nephew, Alex, in a ghost town called Tofty."

Emma laughed, "We don't really live in the town, or what's left of it; we have a cabin outside of Tofty near Patterson Creek. We're miners and raise dogs, but not as big as Nomah—he's a giant compared to our dogs—they're sled dogs, used by mushers in the Iditarod race. Our dogs can run for hours and can live in the snow."

Rigs was curious, "Where did you and Chyler meet, Mrs. Milnar?"

"We met in the hospital at Fairbanks. I was in there with a kidney infection and Chyler was recovering from a bear attack, along with her uncle Jack. Say, Chyler, how is Jack doing? Has he learned to get around with those artificial legs?"

"Oh, he can get around, but those prostheses are not very good. His insurance wouldn't pay for the good ones. Dan is going to watch out for him while I'm gone."

"Where are you going, dear?" Emma questioned.

"To Seattle to have surgery on my face. The damage from that black bear's sharp claws is going to be fixed, at least I hope. Then I won't look so awful. I don't expect to look the same on both sides, but I'll have a better chance of finding a nice man; don't you think?"

"Well, your face doesn't tell what is on the inside, Chyler. That's the important part." She looked at Rigs and Dan hoping for some support.

Rigs confirmed what Emma had said, and Dan said, "Being attractive helps start a relationship, but the inside cements it, making it a long-term deal. I know of an attractive   package, but I wouldn't want what's on the inside. It's kind of like using pretty wrapping paper on a sack of garbage, if you know what I mean."

Chyler started laughing. "I believe I know who you are talking about, Dan. You sure put that in colorful language." She turned to Emma and said, "On my way back to Galena, I'll try to stop and say hello. Is there a good place to land near your cabin—somewhere level for a quarter-mile?"

"I don't think so, Chyler, but I can meet you here. We have a ham radio—call me from Eureka; I'll drive over here."

"Okay, Emma, we'd better go now. Good luck. I'll see you when I have a new face." Emma and Chyler hugged. Dan and Rigs also gave Emma a hug and said goodbye.

Thirty-five minutes later, Glacier Phoenix landed at the Newcombs' landing strip in Fairbanks. Rigs called his mother from the Quonset hut, but there was no answer. He didn't want to take home a surprise guest because he didn't know what his mom had planned. He explained to Dan and then suggested, "Would you call the Olsons to see if they could put up a house guest? I think it might help Chyler if she talked with Ann about her surgery. We don't have to go to Anchorage tomorrow, unless we can get Chyler on a flight to Seattle. We could keep her entertained for a day or two. She hasn't seen the whole city yet. I could take her to dinner. What do you think?"

"Let me call Ann. I'd better ask her what she thinks. I like your idea though. Put Chyler's luggage into your jeep while I call Ann."

Rigs wrestled the two suitcases into the back of his jeep and had Nomah jump into one of the back seats. Rigs watched as Dan hung up the phone, gave him the thumbs up, pulled the Quonset door closed, and snapped the padlock shut.

Dan locked the plane, anchored the wing, chocked the wheels, and climbed in the back of the jeep with Nomah. Chyler and Rigs got in the front and they drove to the duplex. When they arrived, everyone was outside, even Larry Daniel. He was bundled up in a little parka, two sizes too big, hardly allowing him to move, but he couldn't fall over, the parka acted like a tripod.

Dan started laughing when he saw LD, and Nomah wanted to get out of the car as fast as possible. Nomah was so excited when he saw everyone, his entire body was shaking. As Rigs opened his door, Nomah jumped out and ran around to say hello to everyone, but he was careful with LD so not to tip him over. Nomah tried to lick LD's face, but Ann pushed against Nomah and said, "No, Nomah!"

Dan whistled and Nomah heeled, tail wagging. Dan introduced Chyler to everyone, and afterward, they all went into the Olsons' half of the duplex. Rigs and Dan carried in Chyler's suitcases and placed them next to the sofa bed, where Dan had assumed Chyler would sleep.

Beverly immediately asked the new arrivals, "Have you eaten since breakfast?"

Rigs answered as soon as he heard the word eaten, "No ma'am."

Chyler laughed, as did Ann and Dan.

Dan asked, "What's for lunch?" Before Bev could reply, Dan looked at Chyler and Rigs and said, "I'm sorry, I completely forgot about food on the plane. We could have eaten sandwiches on the way back from Galena. They're only about twelve-hours old." He grinned.

Bev answered, "Pizza and beer—or coffee, or a cold drink—." She looked around at the company, and then added, "I also have hot-chocolate."

Rigs spoke first, "Pizza and beer, Mrs. Olson, I think I love you."

Dan chuckled and said, "Rigs, you say that to all the ladies."

C H A P T E R   1 3
FLIGHT TO ANCHORAGE

It took Dan about fifteen minutes to get pizza from Simmy's after Ann called in the order. When Dan got back with the pizza, the others had consumed the day-old pizza Bev had warmed in the microwave. When he came through the front door, Dan found the group sitting around the dining table chatting. He put the pizza on the table, put his coat on the back of a chair, and said, "What have I missed, any new gossip?"

Ann said, "Chyler was just about to tell us where her parents are." There was an expectant hush.

Chyler looked around at all the faces, smiled, and said, "My mom and dad are in Chile. After Dad finishes his project there, they're going to Australia. Oh, Dad's name is James, and Mom's is Chelsea. They should be back by Christmas. I hope. I don't want to send them pictures of my new face, I want them to see it in person."

Rigs had assumed they would be nearby, especially since Chyler was going to have surgery. He had expected her parents to be in Seattle. He asked, "What does your dad do?"

"He assembles observatory domes for astronomical telescopes. Mom takes photos as the domes are erected, just in case there are insurance problems later on. She creates two photo albums at each location, one for the family, and one for the company. Theirs is for fun and memories, and the other is technical for advertising and insurance purposes. They've been in seven countries in the last three years, over fifteen different countries since Dad started working for Galactic Domes, Inc. The company's head office is in Australia."

Ann commented, "I'll bet they like the warm weather in the southern hemisphere while we freeze in Alaska."

Chyler grinned, and then said, "It's ironic; they have to go to high altitudes to install the domes. It's cold up there, too, similar to the Alaskan winter. Mom originally thought she was going to visit warm places in the southern hemisphere, but most of the time they're at 8,000 to 10,000 feet. In Chile, the Andes rise to 22,000 feet, but they're not near the top of the peaks. They learned early on when they traveled to far off places, they had to pack both summer and winter clothing."

Rigs was watching Chyler with great interest. He put his right elbow on the table and rested his chin in his palm. "So, how did you happen to come to Alaska, Chyler?"

"Well, one of Galactic Domes' factories is in Ohio, where we used to live. Dad had always worked in construction and he applied for a job with Galactic. They asked if he would mind travelling. He said no, after he checked with mom." She grinned, and said, "That's when they arranged for me to stay with Uncle Jack, after I was twenty-one, two years ago. Before that, I used to stay home with mom.

One day this spring, Uncle Jack and I went on a snowmobile trip and encountered a black bear. We're still not sure why it attacked us, maybe it was just hungry. It came at me first, and Uncle Jack saved me, but suffered severe bites to his lower legs. He fought the bear with a knife, his wounds got infected, and the doctors had to amputate his legs below the knees. I really believed he was going to die before I could get him to a hospital. In a way, I was lucky, I just got scars."

Rigs suggested, "You are both heroes; each of you saved the other."

Bev stood up and began to clean off the table. "All right, everyone, I'm sure Chyler doesn't want to answer your questions all afternoon. What would you like to do, Chyler?"

"I need to find out when I can fly to Seattle. Could we do that first? Then I can relax a bit."

Bev looked at Dan. He nodded, went to the phone, and called for flight information. It only took a minute, and he put down the phone. "There's a flight from Anchorage to Seattle at noon tomorrow. Rigs and I can fly you there in the morning." He looked at Ann and said, "Do you want to come with us?"

Ann thought for a few seconds and answered, "No, I need to spend more time with LD. Last week I was flying all over the place, and I didn't have much time with him. Pretty soon he will think his grandma is his mommy. I don't want him to get confused, and I don't want to miss his words other than mama and dada. About three weeks ago, LD started walking while holding on to the sofa, but I missed it. Mom told me about it. I almost cried."

"Yes, Ann is right. Larry calls me mama, too," Beverly added. "I've been trying to tell him to say mema for me and mama for Ann, but maybe he will call me something else before long. Baby talk will go away when he learns real words." Bev paused, smiled, and then followed with, "We have to be careful not to cuss, or he will be talking like a logger or a truck driver before long. I don't want him to talk like me." Everyone laughed.

Dan said, "He calls me dada. I've been wondering when we will tell him I'm not his father, but it probably won't come up for a few years. That will give me time to think of a good answer. He calls my dad Nah. I wonder where that comes from."

Rigs volunteered, "Maybe he's telling Hank no."

Hank said, "When I've been watching him, most of the time I hear funny sounds along with some drooling. Maybe he's repeating what I say."

Dan laughed. "Dad, you don't talk when you drool."

When the laughing stopped, Hank said, "You say some funny stuff, son. I thought what I said was funny, but you topped me."

Dan's cell phone rang. He stood up and fished it out of his pocket. "Hello?" There was a pause as Dan put his phone on speaker.

A female voice inquired, "Can you fly me to Anchorage tomorrow?"

"As a matter of fact, Lisa, I'll be going there tomorrow on business. We'll be leaving at 8:30 a.m. I'll have to charge you a fifty dollar passenger fee." Dan grinned.

"That's all right. I didn't think it would be free. Is someone else going, besides Nomah?"

"Yes, Roy Riggins and an old friend of yours, Chyler Skyze."

There was a pregnant pause, and then, "Chyler is here in Fairbanks? Can I talk to her?"

"Sure, here she is." Dan handed the phone to Chyler and pointed out the speaker phone button, which Chyler ignored.

"Hi, Lisa."

"Hi. Did you tell them what I told you?"

"Yes."

"I'm sorry I lied to you. I should have told you the truth. It was my fault that Dan and I broke up. I just didn't want my friends to know. Will you forgive me?"

"I'll have to think about it, Lisa. What you said might have prevented me from getting to know some really nice people. Right now, I'm not sure what to do. I considered you to be my friend, but if you treat people that way, I'm not sure I want you as a friend."

Lisa commented, "I would like to be your friend."

Chyler replied, "We can talk about this tomorrow on the way to Anchorage."

"Okay. Why are you going to Anchorage, Chyler?"

"I'm going to Seattle for surgery on my face. A bear and I had a disagreement, and it won."

"Oh, my God! You are so pretty. I hope it can be fixed."

"My doctor says he can fix the scars, but he isn't sure about the muscles. He will have to examine me before he knows. I'm getting more apprehensive as the day for surgery nears. Why are you going to Anchorage?"

"I have to pick up my grandfather. He just got back from heart surgery in Portland. I'm going to drive him home."

"Don't you have a chauffeur? Couldn't he drive you there and back?"

"Hah! Grandma fired him. One day he asked me to ride in the front with him, and then he put his hand on my thigh. Talk about being uncomfortable! It was scary. God, he's fifty-three years old, Chyler! I had him stop the car and I got out. I called Grandma, and he got the ax. She's looking for a new driver, this time a woman."

"Hang on for a second, Dan just wrote me a note." Chyler read the note and said, "We will be leaving Dan's airstrip at 8:30 a.m. so have someone drive you there. We don't want to, but if you are late, we will leave without you. I have to be at the Anchorage airport at least an hour before takeoff, and it will take us two hours to get there."

"I understand, anything else?"

"Oh, Dan just gave me another note. You should pay him in cash. Rigs and Dan will be going shopping after they drop us off."

"Okay, that's fine with me. See you tomorrow morning. We'll talk. Bye, Chyler."

"Bye." Chyler gave the phone back to Dan, grinned, and said, "Shall we have her sit in the back seat with Nomah?"

Rigs commented, "You mean you want the dogs to sit together? I think she should sit by herself so no one gets contaminated."

Dan spoke up, "I know you guys are just being funny, but I think Rigs and I will sit up front and you gals can sit behind us, with Nomah in the back." He looked at Chyler and said, "That way, you and Lisa can mend fences, or whatever you want to do. Do you think that will work?"

Chyler replied, "That'll work. We'll have a lot to talk about. You guys can wear earphones." She smiled and said, "Nomah can listen from the back and give you a report later."

Chyler, Ann, LD, and Beverly came over to the Newcombs' at 7:30 Sunday morning. Rigs showed up about ten minutes later and they had breakfast together. Chyler was a little nervous, so she didn't eat much, just a piece of toast, orange juice, and a sip of coffee. As her new friends finished eating, to keep busy, she transferred dirty dishes from the sink to the dishwasher.

When Chyler was out of earshot, Dan stood next to Rigs and said, "I want you to get the fifty dollars from Lisa and give it to Chyler. Tell her whatever you like—maybe that you want her to have some extra spending money. Don't let Lisa see what is going on. Maybe you can go to the ticket counter with Chyler. When she gets her ticket, give her the money."

"Thanks, Dan. You're a good man. I'll remember this. I'll pay you back." They shook hands.

"No you won't. I just want to help you both—grease the gears a little. Ann and I think you guys were made for each other. I hope it works out."

"Thanks, Dan. I really like her."

Mrs. Cornell, Lisa's grandmother, dropped Lisa off at the landing strip right on time. Lisa had a small suitcase containing some extra clothes and carried two small blankets to help keep her grandfather warm on the way back to Fairbanks. Lisa approached Dan and gave him a fifty dollar bill.

Dan accepted the money and stuck it in his jacket pocket. Rigs was helping load the luggage, so he wasn't able to take the payment from Lisa. Dan put Nomah into the plane first, then helped Lisa and Chyler in. Rigs and Dan did a walk-around, and Glacier Phoenix took to the air heading for Anchorage right on schedule.

As the plane was climbing to about 3,000 feet, Dan slipped the fifty to Rigs. Glacier Phoenix maintained altitude above the George Parks Highway, Route 3, never straying too far from the road. Dan knew where landing strips were near the highway, having made the trip a number of times. He had never had any trouble, but in case he had to set the plane down for servicing, he knew exactly where he was at all times. The Alaska Railroad and the highway followed the same route through the mountain passes.

Rigs occasionally glanced back at the women to make sure they weren't knifing or clawing each other, but he could see they were having a civil conversation. He reached in his pocket to be sure the fifty dollars Dan had given him after liftoff was still there. Rigs had to make sure it wasn't his grocery list, so he looked at the paper and saw the number fifty in the corner. As he adjusted his position so he could survey the ground below, he looked at the time and realized they had been in the air for nearly an hour.

Dan poked Rigs and said, "Look to the right at those mountains, the biggest one is Mt. McKinley, or Denali; 22,000 feet high. From here it doesn't look like much, but this plane can only fly a little over halfway to the top."

Rigs asked, "How far away are we now?"

"About sixty-five miles, at an altitude of around 5,000 feet. I climbed a little so you could see the mountain better. It's impressive, isn't it?"

"Sure is. Before you mentioned Denali, I was looking at the railroad below us. There's a train travelling parallel to the highway. It looks like a tiny toy. The cars on the highway look like little bugs, almost like ants, except they aren't climbing over each other."

Dan was curious about the conversation behind him, but couldn't turn to see the women, and he didn't want to ask Rigs if he knew what was going on; he didn't want the women to hear him. He would have to wait and talk to Rigs when they went shopping. He looked at his watch and began planning the last twenty minutes of the flight into Anchorage International Airport. When Dan caught sight of Willow, a small town below the plane, he flew south until he reached Cook Inlet. Then he adjusted his course toward the northern coast of Fire Island. When the plane was just north of the island, he turned east, and made radio contact with the airport. Luckily, there was a window of light air traffic, and Glacier Phoenix made a swift landing.

Rigs got out of the plane as soon as the engine stopped and reached back into the cabin to take Chyler's luggage, which she had retrieved from the back seat. Rigs helped Chyler to the tarmac and said, "I'll bring the luggage, you lead the way to the ticket counter."

"Thanks, Rigs."

"You're welcome, ma'am. You may call me Roy. I'm your porter for today's journey."

Chyler looked at Rigs and started to laugh as she moved toward the terminal. They walked about thirty yards, and as they approached the door, it swung open automatically.

Rigs followed Chyler into the terminal saying, "Huh, they got that door repaired. The last time I was here, I had to force it open from the inside and carry a drunk out to his snowmobile."

Chyler stopped to look around for the ticket counter and asked, "When were you here last? Why would you let a drunk drive a snowmobile?"

Rigs smiled, "Never been here before, Miss Skyze. I was just saying what Roy, the porter, might say. Roy would see that the drunk got home safely."

Chyler responded, still smiling, "You must be a very good teacher, you have a great imagination."

Chyler purchased her ticket and Rigs placed her luggage where it was tagged and moved to be loaded on the plane. Chyler turned to Rigs and said, "Thank you so much for helping me. Tell Dan thanks, also. I've enjoyed being with you gentlemen and the Olsons. I hope to see you again when I return." She reached up to Rigs and kissed him on the cheek.

Rigs gave Chyler a bear hug and handed her the fifty dollar bill. "Promise me you will get in touch with me when you get back. I'd like to see you again."

"What's the money for?" She quizzed.

"Well, Dan said to give it to you and say I wanted you to have some extra spending money, but I don't want to start our relationship with a fib. That's the money Dan charged Lisa to fly her here from Fairbanks. We wanted you to have it. Did you guys have a good talk?"

"We sure did, but I haven't forgiven her yet." Chyler grinned, "She's on probation."

"You are a smart woman, Chyler. Have a nice trip and good luck with your surgery."

"Thank you. Have fun shopping and have a safe flight back to Fairbanks. Bye."

"Bye, Chyler." Rigs watched Chyler move toward Gate 23 where she would pass through the metal detector and wait for boarding. He turned away and began looking for Dan.

As Rigs and Chyler moved to the terminal, Dan helped Lisa out of the plane and carried her blankets and suitcase to Gate 18, where the flight from Seattle was to arrive in twenty minutes. Dan had left Nomah in the plane while he helped Lisa with her belongings.

Lisa sat down to wait for her grandfather and said, "I'm sorry I lied, Dan. I hope you'll forgive me."

"Lisa, you and I know what happened, and it wasn't my fault, but I can't just erase what you told Chyler from my memory. Maybe in time I will let it go. Have a safe drive with your grandfather to Fairbanks. Keep your seatbelt buckled and your eyes on the road. Goodbye."

"Bye, Dan." Lisa watched Dan turn and walk away.

C H A P T E R   1 4

SURMOUNTING DIFFICULTIES

The Ivanov siblings had worked long hours on their salvation ship throughout the summer months. Luka had discovered the wing could be detached from the fuselage in two sections which made re-covering the wing fairly easy.

However, when planning to add new skin to the wing sections, Arina calculated the canvas from the truck covers was going to add too much weight to the plane. She came up with a solution: bed sheets would be used on the bottom of the wing and fuselage. The sheets were painted to make the material stronger and waterproof.

During July, while Rolan and Luka reassembled the engine and tested it, Arina checked the altimeter and verified that it was useless. Without an altimeter the escape to Alaska would be impossible, only God would guarantee safe passage across the sea, and the Ivanovs were not a reverent family. They were not atheists, but believed that in time of need, be it mental or physical, they must rely on themselves, not on an unseen, perhaps nonexistent almighty God, for deliverance. They believed God had more important things to do than intrude into the affairs of unworthy human beings, who could and should fend for themselves.

One option would be to make a mercury barometer, but it would not be sensitive enough, plus it would be bulky and not totally stable. A second option looked more promising. An altimeter from a World War II Japanese plane was on display at the technical school. Arina had seen the device when she had begun classes, but she had considered it to be an antique; except now, she had renewed interest in the object, even though it was labeled with Japanese characters; the translations would be in the library. She planned to swap the altimeter they removed from their plane with the one on display; she was positive nobody would notice. At first glance, they even looked the same. But there was no point in swapping them if the Japanese instrument didn't work. How was she going to find out? She had been thinking about it for a couple of days.

93

One evening in early August, Arina mentioned the altimeter problem to the family.

Ivan commented, "You are going to steal the instrument on display? It belongs to the school. I do not like that, Arina. We are not thieves."

"No, Papa. I want to exchange ours for theirs. It would not be stealing, really."

Rolan and Luka had been helping themselves to materials from the naval base for months, so Luka said, "What about us, Papa. We have been taking things from the base for a long time. Are Rolan and I thieves?"

Ivan looked at his sons and said, "Those things are going to waste. If they are not used, they will rust and become garbage. In my way of thinking, that is not stealing. Besides, we are a part of Russia, so those materials are things we have worked for; we own them."

Luka suggested. "I will ask Aleksey if he knows any of the evening workers at the technical school. Maybe we can make an evening visit to that display case."

Rolan gave Luka a slap in the back. "Hey, Luka, that is a good idea. What do we tell the custodian?"

Sofiya was alarmed, "Who is this Aleksey person? Does he know our secret?"

Luka explained, "He was a classmate of mine, Mama. He lets us have anything we want from the base. He even tells us where to find things, but he does not know what we are doing. He thinks we are using the materials to fix our boat."

Sofiya nodded, "That is good. I was afraid he might tip over the borscht."

Ivan grinned and said, "Dear, in English it is spill the beans."

Sofiya smiled and said, "Thank you," and patted Ivan's hand. "I will remember."

Rolan cleared his throat. "I have a plan," he said. "Arina and I will take our altimeter and ask the custodian to open the display case so we can compare the two units. If he is any kind of man, he will enjoy talking to Arina. She will move so the custodian is between us. I will suck on the input port at the back of the device and Arina can watch the dial to see if it moves. If she winks twice, I will switch the units. We will leave with the Japanese altimeter. Do you think my scheme might work?"

Luka asked, "What if the custodian is a woman?"

Rolan grinned, "That is easy; we will just trade places. I think I can distract most women. If she is a young woman, all the better. I will tell her how pretty she is."

"And what if she is a mature woman?" Ivan asked.

"I will ask her about her family or something else, like how beautiful she was when she was young lady."

Ivan commented, "You better watch out, Rolan. She could slap you."

Arina said, "We will try it, but Luka has to talk to Aleksey first."

Arina and Rolan paid the school a visit a week later. It was in the evening; most of the faculty and students had left the premises. Because there were few students still taking classes during the day and no more evening meetings, the school was nearly deserted at night, except for a few custodians. A young man, dressed in a light-blue uniform, let them in the building after they tapped on a side-door window, not far from the display case.

Arina wore a disguise that her mother had helped fashion. Sofiya had covered Arina's blond hair with a black wig from the old days. It was stored in a trunk in Ivan's and Sofiya's bedroom closet and should have been discarded long ago. Sofiya had kept it, but even she did not know why. Sofiya applied a brown birthmark near Arina's upper lip below her right nostril and had Arina apply red-orange lipstick sloppily. Arina wore a tight-fitting shirt unbuttoned half-way to her waist making her appear to be a hooker. Her nipples made projections in the cloth of her shirt.

The custodian, Yuri Baikal, was the same height as Arina, but looked to be in his early thirties. He was rather nice looking, his long black hair combed back from his face and glasses. Yuri looked more like an office worker than a custodian.

Arina asked, "Are you Yuri?"

"Da. You must be the people Aleksey mentioned." From that moment, he was totally absorbed with Arina, looking at her face and trying to glimpse behind her partially unbuttoned shirt. Her tight pants and high heels had completed the devious disguise.

He shook hands with Rolan but hardly looked at him, or the altimeter he carried. Yuri fumbled with the display-case lock as he watched Arina and answered her questions. The lock dropped to the floor, but Rolan retrieved it and handed it to Yuri, who repeatedly locked and unlocked it as he nervously stared at Arina while they talked.

Rolan did as they had planned. Arina winked twice. The broken altimeter was placed in the case and Rolan asked Yuri for the lock. Yuri held out the lock but couldn't pry his eyes from Arina. Rolan locked the display cabinet and joined Arina in conversation with Yuri. As they walked toward the door, Yuri asked Arina for her name and phone number.

"My name is Elena Sverdlov. This is my brother Vladimir." She gave Yuri the number of a math professor she had when she took differential equations two years earlier. He had moved to Moscow a year ago. "Thank you for talking with us, Yuri. The instrument we looked at is not the same as ours."

"I am sorry you were not able to find the information you needed. Maybe we will see each other another time. Yes?"

Arina said, "Goodbye, Yuri. Thank you for your assistance." She smiled and waved.

"Goodbye, Elena."

As they drove back home, Rolan commented, "My plan actually worked, Arina! Yuri could not keep from looking at you. You were fantastic!"

"Yuri is a nice man, but a little too introverted for me. I feel bad taking advantage of him like that. When we get to the United States, I will send him some stamps for his collection. He said he plays chess against the computer; level nine. That is very good. I have only gotten to level seven. He told me he has few friends, so I think we need not worry about him gossiping about me. Other young men might know my real name because of student talk. I hope he does not become suspicious."

"But you should not feel bad. He will enjoy thinking of you for a few days, maybe longer. His eyes were removing your clothes while I switched the instruments. I know what he was thinking. Tonight was best night of his whole life."

"You men are all the same, always thinking about sex."

"But Arina, someone has to be in the mood to make babies."

As Arina buttoned up her shirt, she commented, "Yes, my brother, but all the time?"

Rolan looked at Arina and shrugged, "I do not think we can help it, especially when a pretty woman makes it difficult to keep from staring because of the way she dresses."

They drove for a few minutes before Arina said, "Maybe you are correct. Look, we now have a working altimeter. I will translate the Japanese, make a reference table, and tape it to the instrument panel."

Rolan commented, "Do we need to calibrate it? I hope it is graduated in meters, not feet. Feet causes a problem."

"Oh, I am sure it will be in meters. Only the British and Americans use inches and feet. They are gradually changing to centimeters and meters, however, it seems the changeover is taking a long time. I will have to think about the calibration."

The next week brought overcast skies and four days of light blustery winds and sporadic rain showers. Luka and Rolan journeyed out to sea to fish every other day, fishing on only two of the rainy days. While her brothers were catching fish for the market, Arina spent hours thinking about the details of their flight to Alaska.

By the end of the second week of August, Arina had gone over and over the original plan to use the Maligin V to transport the plane to pack ice where they could take off.

She began to check the times that ice would start to form along the coastline, north of Provideniya where the secret inlet was located. On a visit to the library, Arina located a Japanese dictionary, so she could label the altimeter. She also found a tabulation of winter ice field locations contained in statistics from the local commercial airport.

As Arina studied the weather reports, she suddenly realized that the inlet would be frozen solid when they wanted to fly east. The Maligin V was not going to be able to transport the plane and the irregular coastal ice would prevent the plane from leaving the inlet for six months, starting in late October. She began to think of alternative ways to get the plane into the air during a snowstorm. It was time to discuss the situation with Rolan and Luka.

During dinner on the seventeenth of August, Arina brought up the problem the ice was going to cause. "I have thought of one way to overcome this problem. We will have to move the airplane to the top of the plateau and partially conceal it under the trees." She looked at all the faces of her family members; Sofiya was stunned and stared ahead silently. Ivan sighed and looked down at the napkin in his lap. Just as Ivan was about to comment, Luka stood up and went in the kitchen with his dirty dishes. When he returned to the table he was smiling.

"I have an idea. Let me tell you what I am thinking."

Rolan quipped, "This better be good."

Luka sat down and buttered a piece of bread. He took a bite and said, "The wing can be moved in two pieces, correct?" He looked at Arina and Rolan; they both nodded. "We have pulleys and enough cable and rope to pull the wing parts up to the top of the plateau. Arina will determine optimum positions of the pulleys. Rolan and I will make a triangular cart having three wheels to hold the wing, and we will hoist it to the top. We cannot pull the wing without wheels; it would be torn apart. Can we do it, Arina?"

She smiled, "Yes! I am sure of it."

Sofiya clapped her hands, glanced at Ivan, and said, "We have some smart children, yes?"

Ivan nodded, smiled, and replied, "I think so, Mama."

Rolan inquired, "What about the rest of the plane? Do we pull it up like the wing?"

"Sure. We will put a wheel on the tail so we will have another triangle. Then we will pull it up to the top. Will it work, Arina?" Luka looked questioningly at his sister, anticipating a positive response.

"Da. We must take out the gas and remove the propeller to make the fuselage lighter, and to prevent breakage or a fire. We must do this very soon; it is getting chilly at night now."

Ivan cleared his throat, drawing everyone's attention. "You have only six more weeks before ice begins to form along the shore to the north, then the boat will not carry you to the plane any longer, you will have to go over the land. How far is it to the airplane?"

Rolan answered. "Forty-five kilometers, Papa. I have been thinking about that. The entire ocean surface to the north does not freeze until mid-December, so Luka can take us near the inlet, and we can walk over the ice to land. It should not be too difficult. What do you think, Arina?"

"I think we can do that starting in November. We can camp for a few days and then Luka can bring us back home to get more supplies. We will meet him on the ice." She glanced at her brothers and said, "I wish we had radios." She thought for a moment and said, "Maybe not, someone might overhear us."

With both hands, Sofiya grabbed Ivan's arm, and asked Arina, "Is there a radio on the airplane? What if another plane tries to contact you? What will you do if it is a warplane? Would the United States Air Force shoot you down?"

"Oh, Mama, what a good question!" Arina had just written NO RADIO on her pad of concerns about the flight. Arina added, "The American pilots are not as dumb as Russian pilots. A small plane like ours would not be carrying a nuclear bomb."

Rolan was looking over Arina's shoulder at her list and suddenly said, "We must paint no radio on the sides of the airplane, in big letters any pilot can see."

"Good idea, Rolan." Arina made a fist and playfully hit Rolan on the shoulder. He quickly reached over and pulled her hair when she tried to move away. Arina giggled and said, "We all have some good ideas. This is becoming a real family project."

Luka had been listening and had become very quiet as he scanned the rest of the family.

"Do you think there are any Americans doing secret projects like this?"

Rolan chuckled, "So they can escape to Canada?"

CHAPTER 15

CHANGING LOCATION

Two days later, Rolan and Luka made another trip to the military base and acquired the materiel they needed to move the plane to the top of the plateau. It had rained the day before and everything, except the pulleys, which were on the machine shop floor, was wet. Instead of removing wheels from a baggage transfer cart, they loaded the whole cart onto the bed of the pickup. Luka reasoned they could use the bottom of the cart for building the triangular apparatus to move the wing.

The next morning, after a heavy fog lifted from the fjord, Arina and her brothers took a tent and enough provisions for a week and set out for the airplane. After reaching the inlet and unloading the boat, they ate a quick lunch. As the brothers built the wing cart, Arina secured three of the pulleys to the top of the rocky wall of the plateau. She attached a cable to the cart when Rolan and Luka finished construction. Combining the cables and ropes, there was little excess line for the brothers to grasp to begin moving the wing up the rough rocky incline.

Arina got in front of the cart, ready to guide the wheels over bumps and depressions in the rocks as Rolan and Luka began pulling on the rope.

After the wing had moved about three meters, Luka said, "Arina, this is easier than I expected. Yell if you cannot stay in front of the wing. We do not want to run over you, the wing might be damaged." Luka smiled at Rolan. Rolan laughed.

"Thank you for your concern, Luka. Let me know if any rocks roll down the hill and hit you in the head. We would not want to get any blood on the rocks. Oh, Luka, could you please throw me some gloves, I just broke a fingernail."

100

Rolan started laughing and yelled at Arina, "Just a minute, Arina. Luka will hold the rope while I get your gloves. Do you need a bandage?" He heard a muffled no thank you and ran over to the boat, returning with a pair of gloves that would fit Arina's smaller hands. "Where are you, Arina?" Out of sight, Arina had ducked under the wing to straighten the leading wheel of the cart. Rolan started up the incline and then tossed the gloves in front of the wing just as Arina's head popped up. One of the gloves bounced off the top of Arina's head. "Got you," he laughed.

"Thank you for the gloves, but that was not funny; you were just lucky. Why do you dummies always pick on me? You must be jealous. You had better watch out for rocks, too."

Rolan grinned and answered, "We pick on you because you are cute, and we love you."

Arina replied, "You are full of yak poop, Rolan."

It took about twenty minutes to get the wing to the top edge of the plateau. Luka and Rolan tied off the rope and climbed to the top to help Arina get the wing over the edge and positioned near the trees where the plane would be reassembled. The pulley-cart assembly was removed from the wing, taken down to the fuselage, and attached to the tailskid. Then the lifting procedure was repeated, this time more slowly because the fuselage was much heavier than the wing. Hoisting the fuselage to the edge of the plateau required nearly an hour of sweating and appropriate profanity from the brothers. It was necessary to use a lever to get the wheels out of deep ruts. Arina was able to free the wheels without help, but on occasion, frustration set in, and she uttered words that turned the air blue.

When the tail section was within five meters of the top, Arina signaled to her brothers to stop pulling on the rope; it was going to take a special procedure to get the fuselage over the edge onto firm ground without tearing the cloth covering off the bottom of the plane.

With the rope secured so the fuselage wouldn't roll back down the steep rocky terrain and crash, Rolan and Luka joined Arina at the top of the plateau. She sat looking at the body of the plane, hoping the cables and ropes wouldn't break.

She asked her brothers, "Have we got enough material to repair the bottom of the fuselage?"

Luka and Rolan glanced at each other, then at their sister. Luka said, "Sure, but if we need more sheets, we can take them from your bed at home."

Roland exhaled loudly, then said, "That is not a problem; that will just require a bandage if we scrape off some of the covering. We will put a piece of wood across the bottom of the plane behind the cabin, and then two beams from the ends of the wood to the skid; so we have a triangle under the fuselage. As we pull, the beams will support the plane and slide on the rocks at the edge of the plateau until the wheels touch. When the wheels touch, everything will roll up and over the edge. What do you think, Luka?"

Luka smiled, and slapped Rolan on the back, "Just what I was thinking, Rolan. We will pull from here. Let us turn the pulleys around and cut the friction on the rocks with a blanket. Maybe it will not be too difficult."

Two hours later, clouds were drifting in from the west and the wind had begun to blow in from the ocean. Everything was in place for the final pull to get the plane on top of the plateau. Arina had begun to worry that they might lose control of the plane.

"Rolan, Luka, the wind! We have to hurry; we might lose the plane."

Luka quickly answered back, "Is everyone ready?"

Arina was watching her brothers as they started pulling on the rope, when she heard a tearing sound and then a snap. She noticed the rope appeared to be slipping, but only a few centimeters. She yelled into the wind, "What happened? Is the rope all right?"

"Check the rope, Arina! See if it is breaking!"

Rolan had called to Arina, but she was already looking over the edge of the plateau to see what might have happened. She looked back at Luka and yelled, "One strand of the rope has broken, right here! Stop pulling!" She hurried to the loose end of the tow rope behind her brothers, grabbed it, and secured it to the tightly stretched rope between the tail and where the rope had begun to separate.

Out of breath, she gulped some air and tried to calm down. The wind had begun to blow slightly harder, the ocean breeze causing her hair to flutter back from her face. She was pulling on the rope she had just attached to the tow rope that wound through the pulleys. "Roland, take this rope and I will take your place with Luka, then we will continue pulling. The two ropes should hold the weight of the plane without breaking."

In fifteen minutes, the fuselage was on top of the plateau. The team dropped to the ground out of breath, relieved that the plane had not plunged down the hillside to the rocks below. After resting a few minutes, they removed the triangular beam support from beneath the plane and reattached the cart to the tail skid. Arina and Rolan pulled on the tail and Luka pushed from the nose until they reached the trees where the wing was waiting for its body. The wind was increasing in strength, preventing them from reattaching the wing to the fuselage without risking damages. They were afraid the wind would overturn the plane. They agreed that the wing would have to be remounted to the fuselage after the stormy weather had subsided.

Luka warned, "We had better stay here tonight, the water is getting very rough. In this storm, I do not trust our boat to get us safely home. We have to get the tent, our sleeping bags and some food from the boat. I prefer to do it now; in case the storm gets worse."

"We can use the cart," Arina contributed. "It will require only one trip. Luka, I will guide the cart down. Rolan will stay here and pull it up after it is loaded. Okay?"

Rolan grinned, "Good idea, Arina, Luka will have to get his feet wet. He must tie down the boat so it does not drift away."

"Not funny, Rolan. The only reason I will do it is because you got your feet wet once before. I am being generous, plus you are stronger than I am. You will enjoy pulling the loaded cart up the hill. We will be in your debt forever." Luka glanced at Arina and winked.

Arina laughed, "You morons are wasting valuable time! Get busy! Luka, start down the hill, and I will get the pulley system reset for the cart. I will join you in a few minutes."

Arina and Rolan fed the good end of the rope through the pulleys to avoid the splice where the rope had begun to separate, and then Arina started down the steep incline, occasionally freeing the wheels from cracks in the rocky slope.

Thirty minutes later the tent was erected, and they were moving their possessions to the inside, out of the drizzle. They had been working in the light rain for about ten minutes. The atmosphere to the east had become dark-blue-gray and as the sun began to dip below the horizon, the western sky was light-turquoise, and the bottoms of the clouds were a beautiful pink.

Luka asked, "What are we having for dinner, Arina?"

"I am having a sandwich I prepared last night and some tea. What are you having? I am not going to cook for you, my big brother. You are on your own, but you might get Rolan to cook for you."

Rolan announced, "I am having cheese, bread, and tea. I do not need to cook, either, but I will heat some water over a small fire."

"Okay, I get the idea. We are all on our own. Next time, I will bring my mother with me."

Rolan and Arina began to laugh, knowing how difficult it would be to get their mother to come to the countryside just to cook dinner for Luka. Their mother did not like to ride in the Maligin V.

Arina left the tent and gathered some dry brush from under the nearby trees. Rolan made a small fire pit under the outer edge of the trees downwind from the tent. Working together, in ten minutes they had a small fire burning, shielded from the wind by some rocks, weeds, and small tree limbs. As soon as their water had boiled, they yelled to Luka.

"Luka! You can use the fire; we are finished with it." Arina waited for Luka to answer, but she heard nothing. "Luka!" She tried to yell above the wind again, but still she heard no reply. She was sitting beside the fire, warming her hands with a mug of tea, as Rolan got up and looked in the tent.

"Luka is not here, Arina."

"What? Where did he go? I did not see him leave the tent."

"I have no idea, but we should build up the fire, it will be completely dark in a few minutes. Luka will be able to see the firelight reflecting off the trees."

The rain continued, but it had little, if any, effect on the fire once Arina and Rolan added more fuel from the dry floor of the little forest. They waited in the rain for Luka to return, trying to guess where he had gone.

"He must have gone back to the boat," mused Rolan.

"But why? He knows that would be dangerous in the dark. What if he slipped and tumbled down the rocks? If he got injured and was bleeding, we would not hear his calls for help. The wind and rain would muffle his voice."

A bright flash of light illuminated the top of the plateau. A clap of thunder followed in three seconds, which seemed to shake the ground. Wide eyed, Arina looked at Rolan and said, "Should we get away from the trees?"

"I think it is all right here, we are in a crater on the plateau; the treetops are almost below the rock surrounding the trees. I hope the rocks are better conductors than the trees."

Another flash occurred, then another, a split second later. The surroundings were revealed briefly, but long enough for Arina to see a figure approaching, dressed in yellow.

She pointed, "Look, Rolan. It must be Luka. He is wearing a long, yellow coat, clear to his knees."

Rolan looked into the darkness, but he couldn't see anything beyond the short range of the firelight. He waited for a five seconds, hoping for another lightning flash, but none came. "If it is Luka, he will be here in a few seconds." Rolan tossed several small, wet branches on the fire, which sizzled as the surface water fell into the flames, and then popped when the pitch and water, entombed in the wood, burst from confinement.

Arina heard a noise from behind her and spun around to see the gigantic yellow form standing a few meters away holding a canvas bag.

"Why are you two still out here in the rain? You should get in the tent."

"Luka! You scared us. Where did you go?"

"I went down to the boat, little sister. I got two raincoats, some fish, and a piece of metal so I can cook the fish over the fire. I see you built up the fire. I could see it easily from the top edge of the plateau."

"We lost track of you so we made the fire bigger so you could see where to go. It got dark so fast. I saw you over there a few minutes ago, but then you were gone in a flash, just like the lightning."

"Yes, Arina, I had to go to the bathroom—urgently," Luka chuckled. "Do you want me to cook you some fish? I have enough for all of us."

Arina giggled and said, "Did you wash your hands?"

After cooking some fish and boiling more water for tea, they went to the tent to eat. Arina sat in silence listening to her brothers talking about the storm. The rain would diminish in intensity, and then suddenly the sound of the drops striking the tent would increase so she couldn't hear what Luka and Rolan were saying. She only heard part of the conversation.

Rolan glanced at his sister and asked, "What do you think, Arina?"

"About what?"

"Luka just asked me what we should call the airplane."

"Oh. I did not hear; the rain was too noisy. I was just remembering something and trying to figure out where the thoughts came from. Maybe you and Luka can help me remember; I think it was when I was a little girl."

"How old were you?" Luka asked.

"I think five or six. Let me tell you what I was thinking: earlier when the rope was starting to break, I was looking down at our boat and the wind was blowing my hair back, I had a feeling like I had been here before."

"You mean a deja vu experience?" Rolan quizzed.

"Not like that, this really happened. I think it did, anyway. I remember a big bird and looking down at Papa's boat, but it was not the same as the Maligin V, and my hair was blowing in the wind."

Luka said, "Oh, I think I remember. We were all on the old wooden pier, before the new concrete one was constructed. I was about ten years old. You saw a big bird and mother said it was an albatross. Papa said it should not be this far north, and you wanted to help it get home. Papa said the hurricanes near Formosa might have caused it to fly from its home. He said that type of bird should never go farther north than Japan. I remember the wind was very strong that day and Mama had to hold onto your hand to keep you from being blown off the pier."

"So, Arina, do you want to call our plane Albatross?" Rolan asked.

"Maybe. Do you guys have any other suggestions?"

Luka commented, "I do. What was the name of the mythical bird of Egypt that rose from its ashes after burning in a fire?"

Arina answered immediately, "Phoenix. It is a constellation in the southern hemisphere.

Oh, I like that idea, Luka! Since our plane arose from ice, we can call it Ice Phoenix."

CHAPTER 16
DIMITRI SHOWS UP

"Rolan! Wake up! You are snoring. Turnover and close your mouth." Arina watched Rolan follow her commands; the snoring ceased. She pulled her arm from her sleeping bag and checked her watch. It was 5:17 a.m. and very quiet, except for the sounds of breathing. The storm had passed, but the morning was going to be cold until the sun burned off the haze along the coastline. She snuggled into her down-filled bag, zippered it up except for a few inches, and slept for nearly two more hours.

Rolan and Luka had gotten up at 7:00 a.m.; their normal time to start a day of fishing. They were trying to be quiet to let Arina sleep a little longer. A fire was started, and water was almost ready for tea. Arina woke up and heard talking about attaching the wing-halves to the fuselage. She pulled on a sweater and long pants, slipped into her heavy coat, and went into the trees for a few of minutes of privacy.

When she returned, Rolan asked, "What do we have to eat? Do we have anything besides cold fish and bread?"

Arina smiled. "I have four different colors of paint and two brushes. What color soup would you like?"

"No joking, Arina. Do we have anything else to eat?" Luka was being serious.

"Yes, my big brother. I put a dozen eggs in the cooler on the boat. When you got the fish, you should have noticed them. I guess you had your mind set on eating fish. Do you want to get them, or should I? If I get the eggs, you have to cook them."

Rolan chuckled, "Are they from albatross or phoenix?"

Luka added, "You must know, Rolan, the albatross's eggs are still in Japan and the phoenix's eggs are already cooked, but they are in the southern sky. The eggs in the cooler must be chicken eggs."

107

Arina commented, "Very funny, but logical reasoning. I will cook the eggs if you go get them. You need to check on the boat anyway—see if it is still there. I hope we don't have to walk home; forty-five kilometers is a long walk after eating fish, bread, and drinking tea—we will all lose weight."

Rolan patted his stomach and headed for the edge of the plateau. Just before he started down to the boat, he turned and yelled, "Build up the fire! I will be right back."

During breakfast, the team planned the day's activities. The brothers were going to mate the wing to the fuselage, and Arina was going to paint both sides of the green fuselage with the NO RADIO message in large white letters. Anyone that could comprehend English, would understand the brief information.

Arina had the message painted on one side and had started on the other side when Luka and Rolan completed attaching the wing to the fuselage. The boys watched Arina paint the R and then began talking with her about making the native rock surface of the plateau into a smoother runway. They had inspected enough of the plateau to think the sharp rock bumps would prevent the plane from reaching takeoff velocity or might puncture a tire.

"Okay, we need to take off into the wind to get more air speed over the wing and increase lift, so we will have to go either west or east; the direction of breezes, toward or away from the ocean. If we leave in the morning, when the ocean breeze is from the east, we have to take off toward the ocean." Arina looked at her brothers, and they nodded in agreement.

Rolan stated, "The ocean breezes are not steady, but we have the luck of being thirty-five meters above sea level. So, if we fly off the plateau edge, we can drop about thirty meters, gaining speed and lift before we skim over the ocean. If we don't have enough lift, then—." He looked at the others but didn't have to say anything.

Luka stated, "We must make the runway long enough to get the plane in the air before you leave the top of the plateau. We do not want you and the airplane to take a bath."

Arina laughed and commented, "The long runway would be a very good idea." She wrapped her paintbrush in a rag and started toward the edge of the plateau. "I have to go back down to our supplies for more white paint.

You guys figure out a path for the runway; a little more than 400 meters, while I get the paint." She backed toward the edge of the plateau watching her brothers talking and pointing in the distance, then walking side by side, one of them counting, as they began pacing off the length of the airstrip.

She turned at the edge of the plateau, grabbed the rope and began backing down the steep rock surface toward the Maligin V. When she reached the end of the rope, not far from the boat, she scanned the area for the paint cans, but couldn't see them. Rolan or Luka must have moved the paint onboard. She considered wading out to the boat and climbing in, rather than using the rowboat to move the required few meters. She bent down to see how cold the water was, swishing the water with her fingers, and uttered, "Hmm. Not too bad. I will wade."

She pulled off her boots and socks and rolled her pants up above her knees. As soon as she stepped into the water, she wished she had taken the rowboat; the water was much colder on her feet and ankles than it seemed on her fingers. She thought, "Too late, I will get the paint—and a towel to dry my feet." She grabbed the gunnel and swung her body over the side of the boat, sat down on the deck, and looked around. With no idea where the paint was, she moved towards the bow to the cabin area to check beneath the tool cabinet.

Arina ducked down to look into the shadows, squinting to try to recognize a reflection from the edges of a paint can. As she peered into the semidarkness, she heard the rumble of an engine. At first, she reasoned the boys were warming up the Ice Phoenix's engine, but she realized the noise from the plane would be very different, a lower pitch and fainter. Someone had come into the inlet! The droning had to be from a small boat; she hoped it was someone other than Dimitri. He would have many questions—but she had handled his inquisitions before. Her lies just had to be solid with evidence to back them up. As the engine noise grew louder, she peeked over the gunnel to see who it was.

She watched as the small boat cut its engine and drifted toward the Maligin V, causing the fishing boat to roll and pitch slightly. When the smaller boat was within ten meters, Arina could plainly see Dimitri and a crewman. She stood up, forced a smile, and waved. Scrambled thoughts were running through her mind, but she decided to let Dimitri do the talking, and she would respond logically, but perhaps untruthfully, keeping silent about the airplane.

"Hello, beautiful lady. What are you doing out here all alone?"

"I am not alone, Captain Dimitri. Rolan and Luka are up there." She pointed toward the edge of the plateau. "They will be back in a few minutes. They are exploring the area to find a better place for our smoke house, this place has a sign saying it is off limits."

"Yes, I see the sign put up by the military, but the soldiers are gone now, except for some maintenance and custodial troops, so perhaps it has no meaning. What is up above?"

"My brothers said a few trees, wildflowers, and many rocks." Arina smiled. "I was going to climb up there, but it is very steep, and I do not want to ruin my fingernails, or cut my legs on the sharp rocks. Luka said the climbing is dangerous. If I slip, I might get hurt."

Dimitri was scanning the rocky, interior walls of the inlet. His eyes locked on the cross where the remains of the American aviator and his dog were buried. "What is the cross for, my dear?"

"Oh! I was going to tell you the next time I saw you, Captain. We found a body of a Yupik man; he had washed up on the shoreline here. He was very decomposed, his skin very dark, nearly black, and bloated in places. I could not look, so Rolan and Luka searched him, but they found no identity papers. We buried him up there where we could dig in the dirt; everywhere else is too rocky. Do you want us to dig him up for you to examine? Luka said there wasn't much meat on his bones, and he smelled very bad."

The captain appeared to be mulling over Arina's description of the corpse. After a few seconds, he said, "No. That will not be necessary." Dimitri glanced around the immediate, limited shoreline, and saw the ashes from heating the water to liberate the airplane from the ice and asked, "You made a big fire here?"

"Oh! That was funny, Captain. We ignored the sign at first and built a small smoke house to test how it would work. When we lit the fire to try it out, Rolan threw the Yupik's clothing on the flames, and the fire got so big it set the entire structure aflame. We tried to put it out but had to give up. It was not a total loss though; we were warm for about one hour." Arina smiled and raised her arms into the air, wiggling her fingers. "We got heat and lots of smoke but burned down the little house and all the fish we were preparing. That was a sad day."

"You will not have smoked fish at your market?"

"Not this year, but we will have some next spring when the ice melts along the shoreline. We will build a new and better smoke house; one that we will not burn down."

"I will look forward to buying some smoked fish from your market. Will you be there?"

"I might be going to Moscow to study, but if not, I will be there. Will you come and see us?"

"Certainly, but now I will inspect your boat."

When Arina heard that, she looked away from Dimitri to locate where she could put her hands when she swung her body from the Maligin V into the water. She didn't want to be trapped with him; she had seen that look of lust in his eyes previously. She remembered what her father had said if she were ever attacked on the boat, "Yell in his face, kick him in the family jewels, and push him overboard." But this time, she did not want to make an enemy of Dimitri; he could ruin their plan for escape.

Dimitri spoke to his seaman, who stood up and held the boats together. Dimitri began to climb aboard the Maligin V, whose gunnels were about a meter higher than those of his little skiff. When he grabbed the side of the Maligin, Arina jumped over into the knee-deep water and waded ashore to get her socks and boots.

Dimitri was surprised by Arina's exit and said, "I was going to give you a friendship-hug, Arina." As he moved to climb overboard to follow her, they heard yelling from above. He looked up to the edge of the plateau to see two figures, the Ivanov brothers, and froze in place with one leg over the side of the boat.

Arina yelled back to Rolan and Luka, "It is Captain Dimitri. He wants to inspect our boat."

Luka yelled, "We will be right there, Arina. We have finished up here," Luka and Rolan began sliding and taking short, quick steps, to maintain their balance as they descended the steep incline. They ran a few paces, nearly stopped to keep from falling, and then forged ahead, down to the rough shoreline and their boat. They were out of breath when they reached Arina, who was sitting on the ground. She had dropped the bath towel in the boat, so she had put her socks on to dry her feet. She sat watching Dimitri who pretended to search the boat. Luka sat beside Arina and she whispered to him what she had told Dimitri.

Rolan was watching Dimitri, but glanced at Arina, who zippered her mouth so Rolan would not say anything to the captain.

Dimitri stood in the boat looking around the area and said, "Are you thinking of painting your boat?"

"You saw the cans of paint. Yes, we will paint the outside before long, but we need to get it out of the water first. I have a friend at the old base who will help us lift it with one of the cranes. Maybe I will talk with him next week."

In his right hand, Dimitri was holding the ice ax he had loaned Rolan and Luka, striking the palm of his left hand with it, he asked, "Do you need this any longer?"

Luka answered, "No, Captain. Thank you for letting us use it. It was useful when we took ice from that small berg you told us about. Next time we will be better prepared. Did you find any problems with our boat?"

"Nyet, everything is in good shape. I suggest that you not come up this way much longer; ocean ice will be forming soon. Your hull will not withstand pressure from the ice, you would be marooned or sunk. I would miss all three of you. Telling your parents you were lost at sea would be very difficult for me."

Arina had slipped on her boots and was standing between Luka and Rolan. She said, "Thank you for your concern, Captain. Are you sure you do not want us to dig up that dead Yupik we buried up there?" She pointed up the incline and said, "Do you have a shovel and a bag? It would not take long."

"Nyet. That will not be necessary. I must go now." Dimitri climbed into his miniature patrol boat and had the seaman start the engine. He pushed away from the Maligin V, sat down, and waved as the little engine propelled their boat across the inlet toward the channel to the sea.

The Ivanovs waved goodbye, and Arina said, "You saved me! You were just in time. Dimitri was after me to give me a hug, but I probably would have kneed him in the groin like Papa told me."

Luka commented, "If that fart had touched you, we would have to dig a bigger hole up there to bury two more bodies; his and that seaman's."

Rolan added, "They are probably not good swimmers, especially with clothes on. We could have drowned them and taken the bodies out to their boat. That way the inlet would not stink."

Arina laughed, "That is a good idea, but I came down here for some white paint. I didn't see it. Where did you put the can? Dimitri said he saw it."

C H A P T E R   1 7

SURPRISE VISITORS

As soon as they were sure Captain Dimitri had departed for good, the Ivanovs ascended the rocky inlet wall to the top. Back on top of the plateau, Rolan and Luka showed Arina the airstrip trail they had paced off. In order to avoid some large surface rocks, the pathway was not made exactly east-west, but Arina decided it was close enough for their requirements. There were several spots where some leveling would be required, and while the brothers began breaking up some of the smaller bumps with their hammer, Arina finished painting the message on the fuselage.

She put the lid on the can of paint and used the wet brush to dab over the broken rocks, which were darker than the surrounding, unbroken, weathered material. She was trying to make the airstrip difficult to spot from the air; the dark spots would form a straight trail across the plateau.

"What are you going to do with that old paint brush, Arina?" quizzed Luka.

"When we make our next fire, I will burn it. I don't want to waste any gasoline to clean it; besides, paint brushes are cheap at the base." Arina smiled.

Rolan laughed, and said, "There was a sale; a whole box free, so I took a box. They are in the back of our truck."

Luka took a rest from pounding rocks with the hammer, sat down with Rolan and Arina, and said, "We need to go back home and get more tools to make the airstrip. This hammer is not very useful. We need heavier equipment. As soon as we can, I think we need to make a test flight. What do you think, Arina? Do you want to be our test pilot?"

"Yes! I want to be the first to fly. I think you are correct. We need to test the plane and our runway. I will take off, fly around for a few minutes and then land. Everything must be in order before the weather gets bad. We need to measure how much gasoline the engine uses so we can determine how far we can fly on a tank of gas. Take the tent down, tether the plane, and cover it with the camouflage netting, then we can go home for a day."

After a home-cooked dinner with their parents, Arina, Luka, and Rolan spent the evening telling their parents about the difficulties getting the plane to the top of the plateau, the encounter with Dimitri, and their plans to make an airstrip.

When Ivan heard Arina tell about Dimitri coming aboard the boat, he pounded his fist on the table and said, "If that excuse for a man touches you, Arina, the fish will be eating little pieces of a Russian military officer."

Sofiya said, "Ivan! You are not serious. We have successfully avoided the military for many years; we do not want a bunch of uniforms sticking their noses in our business now. I have a better idea—we will poison his food and make him very sick, maybe kill him. I know how." She nodded her head and smiled. She looked around at her children and then asked, "Did anyone tip over—spill the beans?" She grinned, proud of remembering the American expression.

Arina chuckled and said, "No, Mama. We did not tell any secrets. No one knows about the airplane. I will test fly it in a day or two. We must be sure everything works, including the pilot, but I am not afraid."

Sofiya put her hands on Arina's shoulders and looked into her daughter's eyes. She spoke quietly, "Why not let one of the boys fly the plane first? They are stronger."

"I have taken that into account, Mama. We do not want to wreck the plane during the tests." She looked at her brothers with a half-grin and raised her eyebrows, expecting an argument. "I am the best pilot; Rolan and Luka are not quite as good, and flying does not require much strength." Arina grabbed Sofiya's hands tightly and said, "I will be careful; the flights will be short, but we must test our runway and the ability to land the plane before we have a bigger load and worse conditions."

Sofiya looked at Ivan for moral support, but Ivan could not criticize his daughter's reasoning. He stood up, wrapped his arms around both women, and said, "Arina will be fine, Mama. She is a very capable girl. She is always prepared for the worst or the best."

"Thank you, Papa. Now we have to plan what materials we will need for a longer stay with the airplane. We must make a runway that is not too bumpy. We cannot afford to puncture a tire."

Luka and Rolan were turned away from the table talking quietly, not paying attention to what the others were doing. Luka turned, looked at his sister, and said, "Arina, we have an idea—how we can fix the airstrip, but we will have to visit the military base one more time. This time we will just borrow the equipment."

Arina frowned and said, "What equipment? Don't we just need some hammers?"

"Yes, we do need some hammers, but we know where there is a jackhammer. It will be much faster than the small hammers we would have to use to break the rocks. It will fit in the back of our truck. After dinner, we will borrow it, wrap canvas over it, and put it on the boat after dark—no one will see it." Luka and Rolan looked at each other and smiled as if they had just solved all the world's problems.

Arina asked, "Is this jackhammer thing heavy?"

Roland answered, "About 100 kilos, maybe." He tilted his head and looked at Arina, "You could lift it. You can lift me, can you not?"

"Probably, but I do not want a hernia or hemorrhoids."

"Do not worry, Arina; Luka and I will do the lifting. You need to figure out how much gasoline we need to fill up the airplane's gas tank. Did you save the measurements when we recovered the wing?"

"Oh, I almost forgot. I put the notes in my jacket pocket. I'll get them." Arina went to the closet to get her jacket.

Luka added, "The jackhammer has a gasoline engine to supply air to the hammer. The hammer alone weighs about thirty kilos. We will lift the hammer and the air pump to the top of the plateau with ropes and pulleys, just like we did the airplane. We need gasoline for it, too."

Rolan looked over at Arina, who was calculating the size of the wing tank, and asked, "How much gasoline do we need for the airplane, Arina?"

Arina dropped her pencil, checked her calculations, and replied, "About forty-five liters, or about twelve US gallons. But we do not have to fill up the tank to test fly the plane. We should take one twenty-liter can of gas with us on the boat. That will not cause suspicion. Next time we go out to the plane, we can take another twenty liters. One more time and we should have the airstrip made and the plane fueled for the trip. I hope we will not have to worry about ice. How would we carry twenty liters of fuel across country?"

Luka and Rolan nodded their agreement. Luka said, "That is a good plan. I knew we had you around for a good reason—your brain is like a computer, but we do not have to program it."

Arina stood up, stretched, grinned, and said, "I know that. I am going to sleep in my soft bed. Sleeping in a bag on the hard ground is necessary, but not very comfortable. I will see you all in the morning. Good night."

Rolan called out, "Do not forget your stuffed bear; the one you call Dimitri."

Luka slapped Rolan's back and laughed, "Good one, Rolan."

When Arina woke up the next morning, the silence of the house bothered her. She normally heard talking, the sounds of dishes banging together, and smells from the kitchen, but not today. Everything was quiet. She slipped into her clothes, cracked her bedroom door, and peered out into the hallway. She listened for a moment, but could not detect a sound, and then went to the kitchen to say good morning to her mother.

"Hello! Mama?" She yelled, but no one was in the kitchen or dining room. Then she saw it: a note was on the dining room table. The message was written at 7:30 a.m. Arina looked at the wall clock; it was 8:35. The family had let her sleep in. Everyone had been gone for over an hour. The note said Rolan and Luka were fishing and the boys would be back for dinner. If Arina ran out of things to do or got bored, she could come down to the market. She might even see Dimitri; ha-ha.

Arina flipped over the paper and started making a list of things to include for the next trip to the airplane. A few items of clothing, a toothbrush, and feminine items topped the list. Planning for a variety of things to eat for three people for a week used up the remainder of the paper, but she was not finished. She turned the paper over and continued her list, writing around the edges of Sofiya's note. When she read the last few words about Dimitri again, she had to laugh. Except for her father, everyone was teasing her about Dimitri. She had to think of something so she could tease her brothers. Before she went to get groceries, she would clean the floors and dust the living room and the kitchen, saving her mom some time for relaxation in the evening. That should keep her mom from teasing her, but Rolan and Luka: that was another problem. She had to keep alert; something would surely come up.

After putting away the cleaning equipment, Arina put on her jacket and started for the door. She turned the knob and stopped. She had no money. The only capital she had was the money she had been saving for studying astronomy. But she had no choice, without the airstrip, she would never get away from Siberia. She could always work somewhere in the United States and earn more money. She could clean houses, work for McDonalds, or many other jobs. She decided quickly; she had to use some of her study funds.

She went to her bedroom, flipped over the study lamp, and tore open the envelope of money taped to the bottom recess of the iron lamp base. With half of her hard-earned money stuffed in her pocket, she locked the door and got on her mother's bicycle; it had rusty wire baskets straddling the rear wheel.

Ninety minutes later, Arina was back home unpacking the bicycle. She had purchased enough food for a week, as long as the boys did not eat like hungry bears. Her initial plan was to buy only essential items, but at the last minute, she decided to get a few snack foods to help relieve stress if they were cooped up in the tent due to the weather. It wouldn't be long before arctic winds would be blowing snow and sleet across the plateau and ice would begin forming along the Siberian coastline. Arina knew they must get the runway prepared before the inclement weather arrived. They had to test the airplane before it was too late. The plane would not survive the winter in the torturing cold arctic winds and snow.

Ivan and Sofiya came home from the market at 6:00 p.m. Arina had started dinner a half-hour earlier and had been waiting to hear the voices of Rolan and Luka, who were overdue. They usually got home before their parents, occasionally a little later. They would begin snacking and cracking jokes or playing basketball. She missed their teasing, even though it was sometimes annoying. She had grown up assuming that being the youngest and a girl, she had to suffer the disturbances to her peace of mind. She had concluded she would be a stronger person having such experiences. She often though perhaps that is why she loved astronomy; it was an escape from her everyday life. She imagined visiting far-off stars and planets, even other galaxies, millions of light years away. She loved the Star Trek movies.

Ivan kicked off his shoes, came in the kitchen, kissed the top of Arina's head, grabbed a beer, and without saying a word, sat down in front of the television set to watch the news. Sofiya joined Arina in the kitchen and gave her daughter a big hug. "Thank you for starting dinner, Arina. I will take a shower and wash off the smell of fish. Then I will help you. The boys are visiting the base; they will be home before long. They are getting a hammer."

"Okay, Mama. They might be a little later than you think. They have to take the jack hammer to the boat and load it, so we will be ready to leave in the morning.

The boys did arrive home later than Sofiya had expected by about an hour. They had to lower the air compressor with a crane; it was too heavy for Rolan and Luka to wrestle it into the Maligin V without the fear of causing damage to the boat. Rolan moved the boat and Luka drove the pickup to the end of the pier where they could make the transfer without being noticed. After covering the equipment and returning the boat to its normal location, they drove home for dinner. They smelled of fish and sweat, but were happy to have the proper equipment for constructing the airstrip stored on the Maligin V. Following a shower and a change of clothes, the brothers ate like tomorrow was their last day on earth.

Almost ready to leave Provideniya at eight in the morning, after all the other fishing craft had gone to sea, the three Ivanov siblings loaded the Maligin V with twenty liters of extra gasoline and all the food Arina had purchased the day before. They had watched the other fishing boats leave port and head south. The early autumn Siberian winds had begun, but not as fierce as they would become in winter. The early breezes were bearing frigid air that would eventually encompass the entire Chukchi Peninsula. Ocean ice would begin to form along the coastline, preventing the Ivanovs from entering the inlet by boat. There were at most, two more weeks to access the plane by sea.

As they made their way north to the inlet, Rolan pulled in several fish to supplement Arina's purchases. As the Maligin V chugged through the inlet entrance, Luka could feel the change in the wind, his cheeks began to tingle as they warmed up. The water inside the inlet was quiet, almost mirror-like, except for small ripples being generated by the boat. Luka scanned the shoreline looking for their usual spot to tie-up, marked by ashes. He noticed two big rocks near the edge of the water where they normally docked. At first, he thought the rocks had tumbled down from the steep rocky surface where they climbed to the top of the plateau, but when he squinted, trying to see more clearly, the rocks moved.

He pointed and yelled over the engine noise, "Arina, Rolan! We have company!"

Arina and Rolan were sitting together talking when they heard Luka's yell. They stood, steading themselves by grabbing the gunnels, and looked where Luka was pointing. Rolan retrieved the Ivanov's rifle and checked to make sure there was a round ready to fire. He was thinking, "Would we have to defend the plane?"

CHAPTER 18
CHANGE OF PLANS

Luka continued pointing toward the shoreline, worried by the presence of intruders. He had raised his voice thinking Arina and Rolan were not paying attention. "Take a look! Can you see them better than I can? I cannot tell who they are. Are they military?" The two figures, dressed in dark clothing were now standing, watching the Maligin V approach them. The larger of the two figures was holding a rifle above his head with his right hand, waving with his left.

Arina moved closer to the bow, shielded her eyes, then smiled, and waved to the two figures on the shore. She turned and said to Luka, "I know that girl; her name is Sue. She sells Yupik art at the commercial airport in Provideniya. The ivory carvings are very beautiful, but too expensive for me. Some of the Yupik artists that live on St. Lawrence Island cater to the American tourists. I don't know who the man is; maybe her brother or her husband. I am wondering why they are way out here."

Luka cut the engine, and the Maligin V drifted toward the shallows, the keel striking bottom about three meters from shore. Rolan grabbed the loose end of the mooring line, quickly coiled the rope, and tossed it to the man with the rifle who easily caught it with one hand. Rolan jumped from the boat, not quite making it to dry land; one foot splashing in the cold water. He reached for the mooring rope, and the stocky young man swung the line so Rolan could grab ahold. The two men tugged on the line and brought the boat a meter closer to shore. Rolan tied the rope to a metal post he and Luka had driven into a crack in the rocks when they had originally anchored the ice they had towed into the arctic lagoon.

Arina ran about half the length of the boat and jumped, clearing the ice-cold water by half a meter. She greeted the young lady, "Hello, Sue. Why are you out here so far from home?"

"Waqaa (Hello), Arina. We are looking for a way to get to St. Lawrence Island. My grandmother is sick. We want to see her before she leaves us. Is the airplane yours?"

"Yes, we own the airplane. We have been restoring it to fly again. It was encased in ice for many years. None of us has ever flown a plane. Luka and Rolan, my brothers, are fishermen, amongst other things," Arina said with a big grin.

"Oh! The Shaman was right! He told us to go north and we would find a way to fly to St. Lawrence Island. He said the sea animals told him of a large bird trapped in the pack ice. My brother and I believed he was just a crazy old man, but we decided to learn if he was right, so we set out across the land. We have travelled for three days." Sue paused, nodded to Luka and Rolan, and said, "I would like you to meet John, my husband. He is a hunter, and a fisherman, too."

After everyone had shaken hands and exchanged greetings, Arina said, "We have not tried to fly yet. We have to build a runway so we can take off without damaging anything. We have some equipment with us to help remove the rough spots in the rocks. I must tell you, only two people can ride in the airplane. I can only take one person to St. Lawrence Island. We do not want anyone to discover the airplane, so I will only make one trip."

Sue replied, "You will take me then. John can stay here, but we will help you with the runway. How long do you think it will be before we can leave?"

Arina shrugged her shoulders and said, "I do not know. We need to find out how much gasoline the plane uses; the tank is not very large. A round trip to St. Lawrence Island from here is about 150 kilometers, or ninety-five miles. That is what I remember from looking at maps in the library, but that is too far for testing the plane."

"How fast will the airplane go?" Sue inquired.

"We don't even know, Sue. We have to make a runway, fly a known distance, and keep track of the time; then we can figure it out."

John, who had been listening intently, commented, "You must be careful about flying around the coast, at least to the south; the government has helicopters that patrol regularly. This entire area is a military zone because it is so close to the United States. I am wondering why they have not discovered your airplane. If they knew you had a plane, they would take it from you. I am sure of that. I believe I can help you keep the plane a secret. I know how to hide in plain sight, at least from animals I hunt."

Sue looked at Arina and laughed. "Your brothers are so big; my John looks like their baby brother when they stand next to him." Then she looked up at Arina and said, "I look like your baby sister, but I believe I am older than you."

Arina was amused by Sue's comment; the Ivanovs were tall and blond, Sue and her husband were short and had nearly black hair, their faces round, and when they smiled, they looked like dolls; slits for eyes and arched black eyebrows, perfect for living in the far north.

Arina was very concerned about exposing the airplane to government observers patrolling the coast, looking for illegals coming across the sea from Alaska, but those trespassers usually came in the summer months during good weather. When they were caught without proper papers, their boats were confiscated, and the transgressors were returned to the United States after extensive questioning.

"We must all get busy." Arina asked Sue and John, "Can you help us take things up to the airplane?"

"Tell us what to do," Sue said enthusiastically.

Sue joined Arina on the boat and they prepared packs of food to be taken up the rocks to the plateau. They handed the packs to the men, who piled the food near the rope used for assisting the climb to the top. The women loaded the packs on their backs and climbed while the men rigged the pulley system to move the compressor and jack hammer up the rocky slope.

Forty-five minutes later, everything was on the plateau, including the twenty-liter can of gasoline.

As Luka and Rolan began setting up the jack hammer near a rocky area that needed to be modified, John walked around the plane, and then stood back and looked at the trees behind it. He walked over to Arina and asked, "Do you have an ax or a hatchet?"

"Yes, on the boat in the tool chest under the seat in the wheelhouse. Should I get it for you?"

"No, thank you. I will get it." John walked swiftly to the edge of the plateau, grabbed the rope, and disappeared from Arina's sight in a couple of seconds. She turned to Sue and asked, "Do you know what he is going to do?"

Sue raised her shoulders and answered, "I do not know, but whatever it is, it will be good. Everything he does turns out great, John is a cunning hunter."

Arina frowned and asked Sue, "What is he thinking about?" Several thoughts shot through Arina's mind; "John has a rifle. Would he use it and take the plane? If he did, Sue and John could go to St. Lawrence Island together. Would he kill Luka, Rolan, and me? But can they fly a plane?"

Sue replied, "It is not the hunt itself; it is the preparation. The kill is like the period of a sentence. You see, the words of a sentence are the preparation for the period. Just watch when he returns. You might be surprised." She beamed with confidence, and Arina tried to relax.

Ten minutes later, John was back at the plane with Ivanovs' ax. Using the ax handle as a measuring device, he determined the size of the stabilizer, walked over to the edge of the sparsely timbered forest, and began cutting down a small misshapen tree set behind and partially hidden between two larger evergreens. Out of breath from hacking near the ground at the dwarf tree, the almost barren of foliage neighbor of the adjacent fully-grown timbers, John dropped the ax, and squatted, looking up at his wife. He wiped the sweat from his forehead with his right wrist and said, "A few more cuts and then I want you ladies to help me."

As soon as the dwarf tree had been felled, and after using the ax to measure from the ground to the top of the wing, he went to the nearby trees and decided which of the lower limbs needed to be removed. John counted with his fingers as he looked up at the lowest branches above his head. He joined Sue and Arina, sat down beside Sue, grinned, and said, "Why did God make me so short?"

Sue answered, "He made you just the right size for me, dear husband. You are the perfect height." She looked at John, grinned, and said, "You do not have to be tall to make babies."

He smiled and gave Sue a hug, then he exclaimed, "I have it!" John suddenly jumped to his feet and went over to the felled tree and began to cut it into meter-long pieces. When he had made eight short logs, he stacked them in a pyramidal shape, took the ax, and mounted the structure. He removed three low branches from one tree and two from the adjacent tree, moved the short logs out of the way and said, "Time for you to help me, ladies."

Arina could see what John had accomplished, and as she got up, she pulled Sue to her feet. Arina could see John smiling; he realized Arina had recognized what he wanted to do. John lifted the tail of the plane and instructed the ladies to push on the landing gear. They turned the plane slightly and pushed it slowly back, so the wing was almost entirely hidden beneath the trees, the tail positioned over the short dwarf tree stump. Arina watched John approach her from the woods. She asked, "Is that all?"

"Not quite. We must paint the tail of the plane green and brown, so it looks like part of the trees. We also need to move the camouflage net from the wing to the nose of the plane to cover the windows and the propeller. We do not want any shiny surfaces to reflect light. The parts of the wing that stick out from under the tree limbs need to be painted so it looks like the ground. Do you have more paint?"

"What good ideas, John. We have more paint in the boat: brown, green, black, and white, so we should be able to make a green color similar to the trees, and shades of brown resembling the dirt and rocks. We have a box full of paintbrushes."

John nodded, welcoming the information, and then commented, "After we have painted the plane, we need to paint the ground where your brothers have broken up the rocks. We do not want a long straight mark across the rocks to be seen from the sky; it will be obvious to any pilot there is a landing strip running across the top of the plateau."

Suddenly, all was quiet, except for the rustling from the slight wind stirring the foliage of the grove of trees and shrubs that concealed the airplane from prying eyes. The generator had been shut off. Arina surmised that Luka and Rolan must have let the equipment run out of gasoline, but then she looked at her watch; it was time for lunch. Her brothers had exhausted their breakfast calories, probably sometime before they quit to eat. Arina watched Rolan and Luka walking around the edge of the trees toward the plane. They were both shaking their arms and wiggling their fingers as if they were trying to rid their appendages of bugs. She laughed and said, "You guys look like you have a disease and have no control of your arms."

Luka replied, "That air hammer causes our arms to feel like they do not belong to us any longer. It is a strange feeling."

Rolan quit shaking his arms, pointed at the plane, and said, "You have moved the airplane under the trees. Whose idea was that, Arina?

"John's. I think we did a good job, no? We are going to do some painting next." Arina smiled and continued, "Also, John is going to show us how to paint the runway so it will not be noticeable from the air. He has some very clever ideas that he learned from hunting."

"Well, Luka and I will be finished with the air-hammer in a few hours. Maybe you will be able to fly before the day is over, but now, we need something to eat. We are starving."

Following the food and an all too short rest, Sue, John, and Arina retrieved the painting supplies from the Maligin V and began artistic work on the plane's surfaces they imagined were visible from the air.

Rolan and Luka returned to the generator, filled the gas tank, and continued breaking up rocks and mounds of hardened earth, periodically checking to see they were following a relatively straight path.

As Arina and Sue followed John's instructions, painting irregular patches of green, brown, and black on exposed portions of the aircraft, Arina asked John, "Do you know of any locations, maybe small islands, within thirty kilometers? I need to know an accurate distance so I can calculate the speed of the plane and how far a full tank of fuel will take us."

John stood, reached into a zippered pocket inside his fur-lined coat, and withdrew a map which he unfolded and spread on the ground. He traced over the cloth from Provideniya to his estimate of their present location. He used his fingers like a divider and twisted his wrist to make an arc. "There!" He pointed at an island to the northwest about three kilometers from the coastline. "That is Mirokov Island. It is about . . ." He measured with his thumb and forefinger and compared the distance to the scale on the edge of the map, looked up at Arina and said, "twenty-three kilometers from here."

"Thank you, John. That will be perfect for my first flight. I just hope no one sees the plane."

John smiled and looked up from the map, "Little chance of that, Arina. Much of that area is already iced over. None of the fishing boats go there any longer and Dimitri does not want to get trapped in the ice. The only human beings that might see the plane would be native people fishing through the ice or those hunting bear. You should be safe from any eyes on land, and I think the helicopters are not coming this far north any longer. They mostly patrol Big Diomede, in the Bering Strait and to more southern waters. The stupid military is afraid a few people from the United States might steal some rocks from the Russian Federation." He slapped his thigh and started laughing.

Arina began to laugh and said, "Maybe they think some Russians will escape by boat to the United States." None of the Ivanovs had mentioned the purpose of resurrecting the airplane to Sue and John Slwooko. They let the Slwookos believe the plane was just a passing fancy and would be used for joy rides, or for seeking polar bears for tribal hunters, including John.

After Sue makes the trip to St. Lawrence Island, John was thinking Arina, or one of her brothers, could fly him over the ice pack to look for polar bears. John still did not realize the plane could not carry much weight in addition to the pilot and a passenger. If he were to land on the ice and kill a bear, he would have to return to the site with a sled to carry back the pelt and the majority of the meat. Finding the kill from the ice would present problems. John walked the area cleared of humps and sharp rocks and then went over to Rolan and Luka, who had just shut down the generator. He was glad the mechanical noises were gone; he relished the noises from birds and the ocean. They had forever been a part of his life.

Luka was shaking out his arms as John commented, "Looks good, Luka." John pointed to the western sky which was the color of dirty cotton, irregular horizontal gray streaks through thin white clouds. There was a cool wind, perhaps ten kilometers per hour, blowing from the northwest. "There is a storm coming tonight, we will have snow in the morning, but not too much—a few centimeters at most. I have seen clouds like those before."

Rolan pulled earplugs from his ears, grabbed the front of Luka's jacket, and said, "Did he say snow? If that is the case, Arina needs to get into the air before it comes. She will not be able to see the landing strip if it snows."

"John thinks it will snow later, and he likes the landing strip," Luka informed Rolan. "Put the gas from the generator in the plane and I will add the rest from the twenty liter container. That should give her about one-third of a tank. Do you think that is enough fuel for a test flight?"

Rolan replied, "That should be enough. Tell her to get ready. I will move the equipment out of the way."

Fifteen minutes had elapsed by the time Arina was sitting in the pilot's seat, going through the takeoff procedure she had memorized from the simulator. The brothers had put every available drop of gasoline in the tank, and Luka was standing in front of the plane ready to spin the prop.

Arina gave a thumbs up to Luka and he yanked the prop down, quickly stepping to the side. The engine coughed, the prop rotated a few times, and stopped. Frustration could be seen on Luka's face. Arina motioned for Luka to come over to talk to her.

Rolan could see Arina making a circular motion with her hands, and then Luka resumed his position at the nose of the plane. He watched Luka yank down on the prop and it began to spin slowly, then faster, the motor sprang to life, and the prop could no longer be seen, the loud noise of the engine roaring, as if a new life form had taken over the top of the plateau.

Luka joined Rolan and they gave each other a bear hug, stepped back and watched Arina taxi the plane up the slope, away from the trees, and out onto the landing strip near the edge of the plateau. The wings rocked up and down as the wheels encountered some uneven spots on the rocky surface of the plateau.

Luka was running toward the plane, motioning with his arm and yelling over the engine noise, "Come on, Rolan, we need to turn the plane around to face into the wind."

C H A P T E R   1 9
TEST FLIGHT

Sue and John watched the Ivanov brothers lift the tail off the ground and rotate the plane 180 degrees. Sue looked at her husband and laughed. She said, "It looks like a big toy, doesn't it? It does not seem like a person is inside. I wonder if the boys will push it down the airstrip."

John smiled and said, "I do not think so. Arina knows what to do." John hoped his assessment of Arina was correct and the little plane would speed across the plateau, rise gracefully into the air, turn northwest, and fly out of sight. He was not sure Rolan or Luka had looked at their watches to keep track of the time Arina was in the air, but he was watching the seconds, ready to note when the plane rose into the sky.

The brothers stepped out of the draft from the propeller, waved to Arina, and walked toward the Slwookos. They watched the diminutive, oddly painted plane as Arina brought the engine up to full speed and the little aircraft began to move, slowly at first, but gradually picking up speed. The tail came off the ground, and the plane, rolling forward on the two balloon tires, after travelling about two-hundred-fifty meters, seemed to lunge into the air. Feeling the flow of wind over its wings for the first time in over seventy years, the cloth-covered, strangely painted bird turned and headed northwest up the coast, gradually gaining altitude and speed.

Rolan said, "God, I love my sister," as tears formed in his eyes.

"Me, too. I have goose bumps all over. I have the takeoff time; I remembered to record it just when she lifted off. This is so great! I wish Mama and Papa could see it—Arina flying an airplane!" Luka looked at Rolan and realized they were both crying for joy for Arina and their aged, rebuilt airplane. The Slwookos and the Ivanovs hugged each other, realizing how important this first flight was. They were all celebrating, knowing that each of them had helped make the flight possible. Now, they had to wait nervously until Arina returned and landed safely.

Arina had been apprehensive and her jaw had been hurting as she gunned the engine and started the craft moving down the landing strip. She had been grinding her teeth together as Rolan and Luka turned the little airplane into the wind. Her thoughts were haunting, "Have I forgotten anything? Have I done everything correctly?" She could feel every bump of the wheels. The scraping sound of the tail skid vanished first, and when the low frequency rumbling noise of the wheels on the rocky surface of the plateau quickly faded away, she was certain the plane had risen into the air. Suddenly, the only noises were from the engine and the imagined beating of her heart. Her mental flight plan took over, just as her pondering during a mathematics exam was translated into marks on her test booklet.

She had zeroed the altimeter at takeoff and as the plane climbed, she took glances at the dial, watching the numbers increase until they reached 155 meters. She leveled off, adjusted the fuel to cruising speed, and began to relax, amazed at how the ground below looked. She saw ocean waves crashing against the rocky cliffs below as she left land behind, flying over open water. She had seen birds below, gliding along the coastline, riding currents of air above the cliffs. "Birds, you stay away from me," she said aloud.

Arina was intent on watching where she was going, but she looked away from the windscreen to see her watch. She had been in the air less than ten minutes when she saw her destination, Mirokov Island. A quick estimate of her air speed indicated she was moving about 140 kilometers per hour. She began a slow turn when the island was about a kilometer away. Ice Phoenix passed directly over the rocky, arctic, bird sanctuary at an altitude of 185 meters above the ocean. Now, it would be only a few minutes before she would be landing, the most difficult part of the flying procedure. Many things could go wrong when landing.

Her heart seemed to be pounding again, just like it had at takeoff, as she followed the coastline back to the landing strip. Afraid she would miss seeing it, run out of fuel, and crash where the rocks were more treacherous than the takeoff site, she had to believe in herself. Rolan and Luka would have to search for her if she crashed. What a terrible waste of time that would be. Then they would have to rebuild the airplane, their escape postponed for another year. Arina exhaled when she saw a grove of trees, but was it the right place? She took a deep breath, and saw the inlet, and the Maligin V below her. The boat looked like a toy in a sunken bathtub.

She banked the plane to the left, turned 270 degrees over the water, and lined up with the landing strip, which she could barely make out, extending across the plateau. She knew she had to contact the runway close to the edge of the plateau to prevent from running off the far end of the airstrip and damaging the plane. When she felt the wheels touch down, she let out another big sigh, not realizing she had been holding her breath since she had begun the turn to the approach.

She had adjusted the throttle so the engine was barely turning over when the breaks stopped the plane. Sitting with her eyes closed, her hands in her lap, fingers entwined, not knowing whether to cry because she was so relieved, or scream for joy, having made her first totally successful solo flight, it seemed like everything was a blur for several minutes, emotions cascading through her brain. As Arina realized she could relax, the flight was over, her teeth hurt. She made a mental note: "Next time I will get some gum to chew."

The next thing Arina was aware of from outside her flying cocoon was a rapid tapping on the cockpit door. She saw Rolan knocking on the side window and yelling at her, "We will turn the airplane around so you can taxi back to the trees."

As Luka and Rolan lifted the tail and swung the plane around, Arina looked at her watch, irritated with herself for not looking at the time when she approached the runway. She hoped one of the others had kept track of the elapsed time in the air. She was sure John had recorded her time; he knew how important it was for her to have that data, but maybe a brother had recorded her time in the air, also. Arina increased the propeller's rotations to taxi to the edge of the trees where she shut down the engine and popped the cabin door open.

Luka caught her as she stepped from the cockpit, kissed her on both cheeks, and swung her around, almost knocking Rolan to the ground. "You did it! Fantastic!" He held her by the shoulders and quizzed, "How was it? Was it fun?"

Arina staggered a bit, got her land-legs back, and answered, "I do not know, I was too scared to enjoy the flight. I am glad I went to the bathroom before I took off, though." She smiled, leaned against the plane, and watched as Rolan put his arms around her, and squeezed her in a bear hug. Then she was in his arms as he lifted her off the ground and twirled her around and around before putting her back down.

"Tell us all about it," he said as he kissed her eyelids.

"I will, but we must measure how much fuel was used, and how long the trip took. Did anyone record the time?" All three young men answered, "Yes." Arina said, "Wonderful. I will get my calculator. Rolan, Luka, please measure how much fuel was used—an estimate will do, and put the plane back under the trees."

She sat on the ground with Sue and John as they congratulated her. Using John's map, and the time she was in the air; the average of three measurements, Arina began to calculate her average speed. The Slwookos watched as Arina did the calculations.

John was the first to ask, "How fast did you go, Arina? It seemed you were not gone long. Are you sure you went to Mirokov Island?"

"My average speed was 135 kilometers per hour. It was the only island I could see. Ice is starting to form around it, mostly on the northern side, and I could see some birds. I am sure I went in the correct direction. The trip to the island seemed to take forever, but I experimented a little bit with the rudder and ailerons; I was very nervous, but the return was very fast, I only worried about missing the runway. Maybe the wind gave me a boost coming back," she said.

John commented, "I am sure the wind slowed you down going and speeded your return, but the wind is not much; less than ten kilometers per hour. I am very curious to know how much fuel you used."

Rolan and Luka heard John's comment as they returned from concealing the Ice Phoenix. Luka volunteered, "We guess fuel used is four liters, Arina. How far can the plane fly with full tank? We need enough gas to make round trip to St. Lawrence Island."

Arina rolled her eyes around for a second or two and replied, "Five-hundred-eighty kilometers; about three-hundred-sixty miles, and then we would run out of gasoline."

Sue spoke up, "That is a good distance. John said it is 150 kilometers to the island. How long would it take?"

"About one hour each way and half a tank of fuel, but it is dangerous. If we are forced to land on the water, we would die of exposure." Arina followed with, "We have no radio, no life raft, and there are no shipping lanes nearby, only an occasional small plane."

Sue looked at her husband and grimaced. John looked around, stood up, and said, "Let us think about it. We will talk at dinner time. Come, Sue, we need to put up our tent; it will be dark in another hour. It will be cold tonight."

When Luka heard John say tent, it was the cue for the Ivanovs to set up their tent and begin preparing dinner. As the Ivanovs and the Slwookos erected their shelters, they could feel the temperature dropping; John's earlier prediction of snow arriving during the night seemed more likely than it had earlier in the day when the sky was still blue, and the sun was shining. The nearly overcast atmosphere, the diminishing light as the sun neared the horizon, and the wind from the northwest increasing in velocity, portended the first snow-bearing storm of fall.

John and Rolan collected some of the rock debris generated from smoothing the airstrip and fashioned a fire pit between the two tents. The last time Luka had visited the military base at Provideniya, he had collected four one-meter-long pieces of reinforcing steel which he wanted to use for making a support for a frying pan. He set out for the Maligin V to retrieve the metal as the fire pit was being constructed. Sue and Arina collected combustibles for fires, piling the firewood under a nearby tree next to the airplane where empty paint cans and used paint brushes had been tossed. As soon as Luka returned and put the rebar in position, the ladies started a fire and cooked dinner.

After eating, Luka excused himself from the conversation and walked toward the edge of the plateau.

Arina looked at Rolan and said, "Where is Luka going? He should not go down to the boat now; it is getting dark. He will fall and get injured."

Rolan stood and said, "I will check. Stay here."

Arina smiled at Sue and John and said, "I am never sure what my brothers are up to, so I call them idiots, or morons, but they usually have good intentions. Oh, look, it is beginning to snow." A few snowflakes were beginning to reflect the light from the fire as they tumbled through the cold evening air. Arina watched Sue lean towards John and say, "You were right, John. It is snowing already. I love the snow." A flake fell on Arina's left eyelash and she blinked and laughed, making a vain attempt to brush away the already melted crystal. Then she heard singing: Rolan and Luka were chanting a beer song as they approached the campsite.

As the brothers approached the fire, Luka said, "Time to celebrate! We want to drink to our sister's successful flight. May she have many more." Rolan and Luka dropped to their knees next to the fire and handed out bottles of Ochakovo, a beer that was popularized during the 1980 Olympics.

Sue said something in her native language to John. He thought for a second and gave his beer to Luka, saying "Thank you, but we will share just one." He smiled and continued, "Small amount of beer makes us drunk. We are little people, not like you." Sue grabbed her husband's arm and laughed.

As they drank, they discussed the pros and cons of the flight to St. Lawrence Island. After they deliberated the hazards involved on the flight over the ocean, John said, "I do not want Sue to go in the small plane, is too dangerous, maybe a bigger one with two engines; maybe a plane that floats, so it can stay on top of the water."

Arina commented, "I think that is a good decision, John. I have been wondering what the shaman told you. Are you allowed to tell us?"

"Yes. He say polar bears tell him of bird trapped in ice like in egg. They hear noises like egg will crack and bird will come out. The bird is big so will take Sue to St. Lawrence Island. But bears did not say danger to fly over ocean. Bears not afraid, they swim in ocean very much. I am afraid to lose Sue. We will find another way."

"We understand. We would like to help. What is your biggest problem?" Arina questioned.

Sue was quick to answer, "Money," and then she laughed nervously. She took a deep breath, slowly exhaled and said, "We cannot afford the round trip ticket from Provideniya to the Savoonga landing strip for even one of us. I took a week off from work because business was so slow."

Arina said, "Maybe you can help us at the market and John can help my brothers with fishing. I will ask my parents. That should help you earn enough for you to fly to Savoonga within two weeks. If you need a place to stay, you could sleep at the market, if you do not mind the smell of fish."

Sue brushed the snowflakes from around her face that had gathered on her fur-lined parka, wiped tears from her eyes, and hugged Arina. "That would be wonderful! You are so kind."

Arina held Sue's hands and said, "I think we are all tired and should go to bed. We will talk more in the morning. Good night."

Sue joined John in their tent, stuck her childlike head out of the opening, and said, "Good night, everybody."

C H A P T E R   2 0
EXPANDING GROUP

The tiny snow crystals, almost like particles of dust, were falling at an angle, carried by the northwest breeze, which had increased significantly in velocity and muted blusters while everyone was getting settled for the night. The early snow, barely perceptible when contacting one's face, having fallen while they were eating, had melted upon striking the ground, but now the rocky surface of the plateau was beginning to turn white, the little warmth remaining in the surface rock had been extracted by the earlier sacrificial crystals. In the darkness, using her flashlight, Arina checked the fire to be sure it was extinguished, made certain the plane was secure, and crawled into the tent fastening the hooks on the interior flaps. She found her sleeping bag between those of Rolan and Luka, sat down, took off her boots and parka, put the flashlight next to the tent entrance, and slipped into her insulated bed. She shivered for a moment as her bedding warmed, and then whispered, "Are you guys still awake?"

Rolan didn't answer, but Luka mumbled, "Barely—good night, pretty pilot. Sleep well, and no farting."

Arina chuckled and answered, "Good night, handsome moron. No belching." She closed the sleeping bag over her head, except for a small opening for breathing what she hoped would be fresh air, but she wasn't sure what the tent's interior might smell like in the morning since they had all consumed beer. She hadn't slept in a tent with Rolan and Luka, except for one night, since they were children when farting and belching were funny.

As Arina relaxed, happy with the success of her maiden flight in Ice Phoenix, sporadic gusts of wind created a flutter of the tent walls, which reminded her of the sound of the Russian flag, flying high above her grade school, as it flapped in the wind. But now, years later, she pictured an American flag, its stars in a field of blue, like evening stars appearing as the sun was setting. She began attaching important names to the stars in

136

the flag: Polaris, Altair, Vega, and Deneb. As the flag continued to move in waves, the stars dancing from peaks to troughs, she tried to name the states represented by the stars sewn onto the flag: Alaska, Arizona, and California were counted with her fingers. Texas was the ninth, and last, name that came to her increasingly cloudy mind as she drifted off to sleep.

"Arina?"

Arina was flying high in the clouds, so high she could hear an angel speaking her name. She could not remember hearing a feminine voice call her name so clearly, but where was the angel? She looked all around but could not see through the opaque clouds. Then she felt the angel behind her, gently brushing against her shoulder with her wings.

"Arina?" The angel spoke louder and began to shake her shoulder. Arina opened her eyes and realized someone was poking her from outside the sleeping bag. She found the zipper and pulled it down so she could see the inside of the tent. Sue was sitting beside her on Rolan's sleeping bag, holding a mug of hot tea, the water vapor, like smoke, rising from the container.

"Good morning, Sue. Oh! It is light out. What time is it? Where are my brothers?"

"Good morning, Arina. It is 7:30. They are sitting beside the fire with John talking about getting more fuel for the airplane. John started a fire and your brothers joined us thirty minutes ago. Luka and Rolan wanted you to sleep a little longer after yesterday's excitement."

"I was dreaming. An angel spoke to me, saying my name. I was floating up high in puffy white clouds. It was so peaceful." Arina smiled. "I wonder if that is what heaven is like."

Sue was grinning and said, "John calls me his angel sometimes, so you are the second person to say that." Her voice was child-like. "If you want, I can be your angel, too."

Arina did not want to refuse the offer. To do so might insult Sue, so she said, "That would be nice. You would not be required to do anything; I will live a long life and do not expect I will need an angel for many years. However, could you be an angel right now and get me a mug of hot tea?" Arina laughed. Sue grinned, "One moment," and backed out of the tent. Arina quickly put on her shoes and parka and rolled up her sleeping bag before Sue returned with the steaming tea.

"Oh, thank you." Arina took the mug, warming her hands as she held the ceramic container for a few seconds, before sipping some of the fragrant solution. "What is in the tea, Sue? It gives the tea a wonderful taste."

Sue responded, "I do not know the English name, but it comes from dried wildflowers; the purple ones that grow around here during the summer; their six petals are a little bigger than the others'. There are only a few so I pick them to use during the cold winter months. They help keep away the runny nose, the headaches, and the coughing. The flowers with other colors do not work—most are very bitter, especially the white ones. The whites and yellows have only five petals."

Arina said, "You must keep your knowledge a secret as long as possible, Sue. If a drug company hears of it, they will get rich and the flowers will disappear forever."

When Arina exited the tent, she was surprised at the amount of snow that covered the ground. The five centimeter depth was twice the amount John had estimated would fall during the night. The women joined the men at the fire and sat down to eat breakfast.

Arina posed a question to the others, "Do you think we can takeoff in this amount of snow? I will not be able to see the landing strip on takeoff, and it will be even worse for the landing."

John answered first. "This snow should melt in a day or two, but in two or three weeks it will be October when the temperature will be below freezing all day long. Very small amounts of snow will melt until next spring. Do you still want to fly the plane this winter?"

Luka ignored John's question and added, "We can put the skis back on if the snow accumulates, but with the weight of the skis and Rolan in the plane, the runway will have to be longer—or we will have to build a catapult to start the plane moving so we will not run out of runway. We will not be able to depend on the propeller to get airborne with added weight and our short airstrip."

Rolan said, "No, a catapult would be too complicated. We need a rocket to assist us to takeoff, but I think I know how to mark the runway."

Luka could not believe what he had heard from his brother. "A rocket? Are you a cosmonaut cadet! That is one of the craziest ideas you have ever had! You must be making a joke! You have to get serious, Rolan."

Arina was waiting to answer John's question. She glanced at Luka and Rolan, thinking of taking them aside to discuss whether to share their secret with the Slwookos, but she decided to react on her own volition. She raised her eyebrows, took a deep breath, and started telling Sue and John the reason they had rebuilt the airplane. As she began to divulge their intentions, John interrupted excitedly.

"You are going to fly to Alaska. Is that not correct?"

Arina was alarmed. John's comment almost took her breath away. She could not deny what John had said, but Sue and John must be sworn to secrecy or the plan might have no chance of success. She stood, took a step toward John, caught between wanting to threaten him if he divulged their secret and complimenting him for being perceptive. She smiled, and said, "How did you know?"

John smiled and looked at Sue. "See, you did not believe me." He glanced at all the Ivanovs and answered Arina, "You wanted to know how far the plane could fly and you are still going to fill the tank with gasoline, although it is getting too late in the year to do much flying. I figured you were going to go to the United States. Last night I told Sue what I was thinking, but she said I was talking like a shaman." John stood up, rubbed his legs, and stomped his feet. Luka was convinced that John was going to perform a native dance, but John explained that he had been sitting in one position too long.

Rolan poked the fire with a stick and said, "Well, you are correct. Arina and I want to fly to Alaska. After we get there, we will figure a way to bring the rest of the family."

Sue jumped up, grabbed John's left arm with both hands, and began to jump up and down excitedly. "Oh! I want to go, too."

Arina sat down next to Rolan and sighed, dropped her lower jaw, tipped her head back, and almost cussed. She closed her eyes and kept quiet; not wanting to complicate the relationship between the two families. All she could think of was that now they would have to figure a way to get five more people out of Russia instead of only three more.

Rolan leaned over and whispered to Arina, "I hope we do not have to take their whole tribe."

Luka had not heard the whispers, but his reaction was to say sarcastically, "I think we should start selling tickets."

Arina, annoyed by her older brother's uncouth comment, swatted the air at Luka and said, "Hush. Let us all work together and figure out a way to move to Alaska."

Sue and John sat quietly for a few seconds, not knowing how to interpret Luka's remark. Then John, wanting to make a positive contribution, said, "I think we should lengthen the runway first and get all the tools and parts ready in case the skis are necessary. If the snow does not get much deeper by the day you leave, we do not have to attach the skis. But if you want to land on snow, we should mount the skis."

Luka stood and addressed the others, "Logical thinking, John. Come on, Rolan, help me get the air-hammer ready. Sue and John can move the snow away from the rocks after Arina marks off the distance—one hundred meters should be enough."

Rolan and Luka siphoned gas from the airplane to the compressor while the others marked the current runway with sticks in the snow and moved snow to expose the runway every fifty meters. Arina located the start of the old landing strip and paced off another 100 meters, then she joined Sue and John who had started pushing snow to the sides of the soon to be lengthened runway. When they had moved about one third of the snow, the sun came out. Sue dropped to her knees beside Arina and said a Yupik prayer which Arina could not completely understand. She would have to ask Sue about some of the words in order to appreciate the meaning.

"Sue, can you please tell me about your prayer?"

Sue responded to the question saying, "I thanked the ruler of the heavens for removing the clouds so the sun could melt the snow. Then the snow water will return to the sea to make waves and keep the ocean animals healthy. The Shaman will tell the sea animals the snow is being given back to them so they can supply us with more food, clothing, and ivory. With the snow gone, we can return to Provideniya the same way we came."

Arina said, "Perhaps I should thank the ruler of the heavens for the stars provided for me to study." She smiled and put her arm around the diminutive Sue's shoulders. Just as she started to say something else to Sue, the air-hammer began to break up the rocks, creating enough noise to mask all her words. Rather than yelling, she gave up trying to talk, pushed back the hood of her parka, lay back, and made a snow angel after feeling the warming rays of the sun on her face.

Sue joined Arina making snow angels. Sue made several angels around Arina's and said, "You are the big angel in charge of the little ones." The two women laughed, enjoying their antics, got up from the snow, brushed themselves off, and ran back to the tents where the air-hammer noise was diminished by distance and muffled by the trees.

Sue said, "What were you going to tell me, Arina?"

"I wanted to tell you that you and John can ride back home with us in the boat. You do not need to walk all that distance."

"Oh, thank you. I did not want to ask about riding in your boat since we had already asked you to fly me to St. Lawrence Island. We do not want to impose on your family. I should have asked you about going to America before I got so excited. I think your brothers do not like the idea."

Arina thought for a minute about the situation. If they did not include Sue and John in their plans, the Slwookos could sabotage the entire plan just by telling someone else about the scheme, but Arina did not want to mention that the Ivanovs were worried about the Slwookos using their knowledge of the plan as a mode of blackmail. Arina had to find out from Sue if there were any other relatives that might have to be included in the escape plot.

She asked Sue, "Are you and John the only part of your family here on the Chukchi Peninsula?"

Sue smiled, pleased that Arina was asking about her family. "No. John's uncle, aunt, and two cousins live up north in Uelen. His aunt is a teacher, his uncle is a hunter and a tribe elder. They are very happy to live there. My family lives on St. Lawrence Island, in Savoonga. That is where my grandmother is, not far from the airstrip. My family and others make the ivory carvings I sell at the airport. John's parents live on the island in Gambell. His father is a mechanic at the airstrip."

"What about your family, Arina? Where do your grandparents live?"

"I do not know exactly, but they live in western Russia near or in Moscow. We have been so far away; I have never met them. Mother says my babushka is a fine cook."

Arina lied, she couldn't answer truthfully. She wasn't sure whether they were still alive or had passed, and she did not know where they might reside, if they were still living. The names of her relatives would have no meaning to her; as a little girl, she had seen pictures of them, but could not remember their names. All she knew was that her present name was Ivanov, but she, Luka, and Rolan had no knowledge of their real surnames, including their mother's. Until her parents had recently divulged their secret, Arina had believed her father's parents bore the name Ivanov and they lived in Moscow. As a young child, she had been told that her maternal grandparents, the Fedotovs were deceased. They had lived in Sochi, but a black shroud hid the true roots of the Ivanov family tree. Arina began to plan an investigation of her grandparents to be conducted after the Ivanov family got to America, beyond the reach of the Russian authorities. She could only hope for a positive outcome.

CHAPTER 21

SCRIMMAGES

As the Slwookos and the Ivanovs were preparing to flee Russia, American football had garnered the enthusiasm of many high school students in Fairbanks, Alaska. However, the students' worries were nothing like those of their western neighbors' across the sea. The students never considered the government would shoot them for what they were doing.

The east-side Mammoths had lost their first game of the season to cross-town rivals by ten points. The west-side Caribous had out-scored the Mammoths in the last quarter by two touchdowns, otherwise Rig's team would have won. The Mammoths could not bring down the opposing quarterback in the pocket. Their defense was picked apart with accurate passing and off-tackle keepers.

Dan had gone to the game and watched critically. After the game, Rigs came over to the Newcombs' to let off some steam.

Hank had gone over to the Olsons' to be with Beverly as she watched LD. Ann was attending an EMT meeting in Anchorage and wouldn't be back until Monday. Rigs popped the cap off a beer as he and Dan sat in the kitchen talking. "Goddamn it, Dan. I can't get that kid to listen to me."

Dan laughed, took a swig of beer, burped, and asked, "Which one? I saw a number of mistakes during the last quarter."

"The Linton kid. The one I told you about. His dad's the lawyer and played ball years ago. Hey, I wonder if he knows your dad, in addition to his knowledge of your dad's probation."

Dan sat thinking for a minute and then said, "I could knock him on his ass a few times and tell him what he's doing wrong. He outweighs me, but if I pancake him, maybe he'll listen to some coaching."

"That would be great! Come to the practice field Monday at four o'clock. I'll get you a set of pads. We'll have to keep you out of eyesight of the coach, or we might get in trouble, but I think it's worth the risk. The coach will be working with the offensive backs at the other end of the field while we work with the linemen about sixty yards away. We have a scrimmage planned for Tuesday."

"Okay, I'll be there, but I can only come on Monday. I have to fly to Galena on Tuesday to take care of Chyler's uncle and deliver mail for the next two weeks. Dad and I will change places after that time for another two week period. That will get us into early November."

Monday morning, Dan and Nomah drove the company pickup to Fairbanks International at nine a.m. and returned to the duplex with Ann. Bev was feeding LD and having coffee as she read the Sunday paper. Bev was still in her pajamas as was the toddler. Larry was picking up Holey-Oats one at a time from the highchair tray and popping them into his mouth and chewing. When Ann and Dan entered the house, the two-year-old got excited, forgot to chew, and inhaled a Holey-Oat. In a split second, Larry began to cry. Ann, Bev, and Dan clustered around the two-year-old, wondering what had happened.

Ann took him in her arms, flipped him upside-down, and patted his back. He coughed and a large blob of saliva mixed with partially chewed cereal, resembling lumpy patching plaster, splattered on the linoleum floor. Ann transferred Larry to Dan, who held him at arms-length, head up, not wanting any further eruptions transferred to his clothes. The little guy had stopped crying and Beverly had begun laughing, observing the combination of Dan's frown and LD's red face, tears rolling down his cheeks. Ann stepped into the kitchen and returned with some water for her son and a wet rag to clean the floor. LD appeared a little bewildered at first, but then looked at Dan and smiled. Larry blinked his eyes, twisted his body, pointed at the floor and said, "Uh-oh."

Dan wiped LD's tears with his fingers, smiled back and said, "Hey little buddy, are you all right now?"

Watching Ann wiping up the floor, Larry said, "Uh-huh."

Dan lowered him to the floor and the two-year-old ran to his mother with his arms outstretched. He needed the comfort and security of his mommy's hug. Ann left the rag on the floor and scooped LD up, saying, "God, you're getting heavy, Larry Daniel. I think Admiral Mills is putting lead in those Holey-Oats. I'm sure glad they dissolve in saliva." She looked at Dan, laughed, and said, "I've got to check on the ingredients to see if lead or other heavy metals are in the Holey-Oats." She hugged her little boy and asked, "Better now?" LD nodded.

Dan smiled and said, "I thought he was putting on weight. We'd better keep him out of the sun, he's growing like a weed. Well, I'd better get back to the shop. Max or Dad might need the truck. I'll see you later." Dan kissed Ann and LD and waved to Bev as he went out the door.

Thinking Dan had forgotten about him, Nomah barked when he saw Dan exit Olsons' half of the duplex. Dan hustled to the pickup, climbed in, scratched Nomah behind the ears, and drove to the shop. When Dan entered the store, Max and Hank were talking about buying new GPS systems for the planes. Hank's plane possessed a GPS, but Glacier Phoenix had never had a Global Positioning System installed. Dan poured himself a mug of coffee and joined the other men at the sales counter. He looked over Hank's shoulder at a catalog the two men were studying.

"What are we looking at?"

Hank said, "These GPS units have seven-inch touch screens and are $900 each. They can be mounted in the plane in several ways and can be removed for movement away from the plane—in case the pilot wants to move by foot or ride in another vehicle."

"Sounds good to me, Dad. When will they be here?"

"Within a week. I'll order them today from Anchorage. I'll bring you one next Monday when I fly the mail to you in Galena. You can learn to use it while you're sitting around waiting for something to deliver."

Max spoke up, "You guys want a burger for lunch? I'm placing an order. It'll be here in twenty minutes."

Dan replied, "Okay. A chocolate shake, too."

"Same here, Max, and get a pile of fries," added Hank. "Dan has ketchup upstairs in his little refrigerator."

Almost exactly twenty minutes later, a Caribou-Burger delivery truck pulled up outside and a kid jumped out with three containers. Max gave the kid a twenty and said, "Keep the change; put some of it in the bank, you need to go to college."

Before Dan had finished his burger, his cell phone rang. It was Ann's ring, a hospital paging tone. As he stood to extract the phone from his pocket, he said, "I wonder what Ann wants; maybe she's planning dinner. Hi, Ann."

"It's Beverly, Dan. Come home right now. Josh Springer is yelling and banging on the front door. I'm in the bedroom with Larry."

"Be right there, Dad. Dial 911! Send them to Olsons'. Let's go Nomah. Ann needs us!"

Nomah jumped to his feet and was out the door and at the pickup as soon as Dan opened the shop door. Dan opened the passenger door and Nomah jumped in. Dan was in the driver's seat a couple of seconds later starting the engine and stepping on the throttle. He went through one red light and then another before he heard a police siren behind him. He was three blocks away from the duplex before he saw a police cruiser in the rear-view mirror. At fifty miles per hour, Dan was at the duplex in less than twenty seconds. He slammed on the breaks and skidded through the gravel parking lot coming to a stop ten yards from Olsons' front door. There was a man pounding on Ann's door, yelling. "Goddamn it, Ann. Let me see my kid! You bitch!"

Dan didn't let Nomah out of the truck, but when Dan bounded from the driver's seat, Nomah followed. Dan was so pissed at the man at the door, he grabbed the figure around the waist, threw him to the ground, and forced him on his stomach. Dan straddled him, pinning him to the ground, cinched his left arm around Josh Springer's neck, and tightened his wrist and bicep against Josh's carotid artery. Josh squirmed, tried for a few seconds to pull Dan's arm from his neck, and yelled, "Who the hell are you?" Then Josh went limp, no match for Dan's strength and knowledge of how to render an aggressor unconscious without causing permanent damage.

With Josh subdued, Dan called out to Ann, "You can come out Ann, he's unconscious."

When Ann opened the door, she was holding a twenty-two pistol at her side in her right hand. Two police officers, with guns drawn approached the duplex. One officer yelled, "Drop the gun and step away from the body, both of you!"

Nomah stood next to Josh's limp body growling, ready to sink his fangs into Josh's arms and legs. The other cop yelled out, "Call the dog off or I'll have to shoot it."

Dan reacted immediately, "Nomah! Heel!" Nomah relaxed and moved next to Dan and sat down, staring at the man on the ground, and then watching the officers. Ann had bent down and put the gun on the concrete porch next to the front door. Josh rolled over, surprising the policemen, who apparently considered the man on the ground to have been shot and perhaps dead.

The officer who had ordered Nomah away from Josh said, "Hey, I know you. You're Dan Newcomb. I sat beside you in Miss McClellan's senior English class."

Dan frowned and then looked closely at the officer. "Oh! I remember you, too, but you had long hair and you've put on some weight. I didn't know you were a policeman, Mike."

Officer Mike Newelson said, "What's going on here, Dan?"

"The guy on the ground is my fiancée's ex-husband. He's not supposed to have any contact with Ann or the child. He was beating on the door and yelling obscenities. He wanted to see his son. I put him to sleep by cutting off the blood to his brain with a choke hold. He'll be all right in a few minutes."

Mike looked at Ann and said, "You're his ex?"

"That's right, officer. When Josh started pounding on the door, I had my mom call Dan and 911. Dan got here before you officers showed up."

Another police car drove into the parking area and two more policemen joined the first two officers. As Dan and Mike continued talking, Mike picked up the twenty-two pistol, unloaded it, and handed it to Dan. Mike's partner, Gerry Pattenburgur, talked with the officers from the second car explaining what had happened. They had responded to the 911 call, five minutes late. Since they were no longer needed, they drove away.

Josh Springer was handcuffed and escorted to the back seat of the cruiser by Officer Newelson, who returned to talk with Dan. Ann invited everyone inside and gave the police some coffee. Bev tip-toed out of the bedroom, closed the door, and joined the others at the dining room table.

Mike took the last sip of his coffee and said, "I have to issue you a ticket for speeding, Dan. You were eight miles an hour over the limit. The limit in town is twenty-five, you know."

Mike was smiling as he wrote out the ticket, had Dan sign it, and tore off a copy for Dan. "It's going to cost you about twelve bucks."

Dan took the ticket and shook hand with both officers. As Mike went out the door, Dan tapped Mike on the shoulder and said, "Thanks, Mike. I owe you one."

Mike stopped, turned to Dan and said, "Just remember, pal, you're not flying a plane on city streets." Both Dan and Mike laughed, and Dan said, "I hope I don't see you again today, but thanks for showing up so quickly."

"You bet. I'm amazed that I couldn't catch you after you went through two red lights. I'll have to ask our mechanic for a tune-up," he smiled. "I'm glad no one was hurt. We'll send Mr. Springer back home with a warning to stay out of Alaska."

Dan stayed with the Olsons for about an hour making sure everyone had calmed down before he and Nomah returned to the shop in the pickup at a speed slightly below the limit. When he entered the shop, both Hank and Max were waiting on customers, but they surveyed Dan with quizzical looks on their faces. Dan tossed the truck keys on the sales counter and went upstairs to sit quietly for a few minutes, thinking about what he would have done to Josh Springer had any of the Olsons been harmed. Dan worried as he considered that it would have only taken him ten seconds to kill Springer. Would he lose control, or would he maintain his cool if one of his loves were hurt? Dan knew one thing for sure. If Ann, LD, Beverly, or Nomah were attacked, he would lose control, and probably kill the assailant. He knew that Hank would do the same.

Nomah jumped on the bed beside Dan and put his head in Dan's lap. Nomah seemed to know when Dan wanted to take a time-out to clear his mind. Nomah's eyes were on Dan's face. Dan scratched Nomah behind the ears and said, "Good boy, Nomah. Have I forgotten something? Are we supposed to be somewhere?" Dan suddenly remembered the practice session at the football field, stood up and said, "Thank you, Buddy. I almost forgot about helping Rigs. Let's go downstairs and tell Max and Hank what happened, then we'll go to the school."

Dan felt as if he had been sleeping as he descended the steps to the ground floor of the shop. The customers were gone, and Dan told Max and Hank about the confrontation with Josh Springer. Though Dan had been speeding, twenty-five miles per hour over the city limit, his high school friend had let him off with a minimal speeding ticket and didn't cite him for running two red lights.

Hank inquired, "So what happened to Ann's ex?"

"Yah, they should pants him on Main Street and not give him any clothes until he leaves the state." Max thought his suggestion was apropos and started chuckling, thinking about the humiliation Josh would suffer. He would certainly never return to Fairbanks and would probably never set foot in Alaska again. Josh Springer might never leave the security of Boise.

Dan smiled and asked, "Do either of you need the pickup? I need to go to the high school to assist Rigs. I'll be gone for about an hour."

Hank and Max shook their heads and Max said, "No. Go ahead and take the truck. We'll survive for an hour. If it starts to snow, you'd better bring it back right away."

"Thanks. C'mon, Nomah, Rigs needs some help on the practice field."

When Dan arrived at the field, the entire team was already practicing, and as Rigs had said, the linemen were at one end and the backs were eighty yards away at the other extreme of the practice area. Dan told Nomah to stay in the back of the pickup. Dan spotted Rigs and walked up behind him.

"Hi, Rigs. What can I help you with?"

Rigs frowned and said, "You're a little late, Bud. We can't get you in pads now."

"Sorry, Rigs. Something came up. I'll tell you about it later. I don't need pads; I can do what I wanted to in my civvies."

"You sure?"

"Yah, I'm okay this way."

"Okay, I'm the QB and you're my offensive lineman. Hey, eighty-nine—Linton, you rush me. See if you can get by my friend."

"Coach, he's in street clothes. I might hurt him."

Dan smiled and said, "Don't worry, kid. I might hurt you."

Rigs called signals and Tobe tried to get to him, but Dan was too quick and knocked the Linton boy on his butt.

"Hey, mister, what do you weigh?"

Dan answered, matter-of-factly, "196. How about you?"

Tobe got up, straightening his pads, and said, "220."

"Okay, Tobe. You have to hit me lower and move your feet;

you're too slow. A faster, smaller man will beat you every time. Let's try it again."

The second time was almost as bad as the first. Dan drove the Linton kid sideways about five yards, removing him from the play.

As they walked back to Rigs, Tobe asked, "Who are you, anyway?"

Dan stuck out his hand and said, "Dan Newcomb. I played ball with your coach about six years ago."

"No shit? You're Dan Newcomb? Glad to meet you. You're a legend."

Number eighty-nine shook hands with Dan and said, "I've got to tell my dad who I met today."

"I'm going to tell my dad who I knocked on his ass today. Mr. Linton, listen to your coach; you can learn from him. Mr. Riggins is a good coach. Well, I've got to get back to work. Good luck for the rest of the season. Nice meeting you, Tobe."

"Yeah, you too. Thanks for the advice, dude."

CHAPTER 22

MORE CONSTRUCTION

Lengthening of the airstrip completed, Rolan was steering the Maligin V out of the inlet and into choppy seas. Luka and John were preparing to do some fishing and the women were sitting together quietly at the stern grasping the railing. Arina was gazing to the east across the dark blue-green water thinking of landing Ice Phoenix in the safety of Alaska.

"What do you see, Arina?"

"I see my future." Arina grinned and said, "Maybe a trip to Mars. What do you see?"

"I see a big smile on my grandmother's face. She will be so happy to see me again."

She looked at Arina, smiled, and they began talking about how three Ivanovs and two Slwookos would cross the ocean ice from Siberia to Alaska. Arina looked west and could see from the familiar rocky shore that the boat was halfway back to Provideniya.

"How will we go across the ice, Arina? The sea will not be completely covered with ice and the water is freezing cold. If we fell into the water, we would die very quickly."

"Yes, Sue. I have been thinking about that for several days now. I have an idea, but I have to draw some diagrams so Luka, Rolan, and John can help me construct an ice-traveler. I'll show you what I am thinking about. You can help, too." Arina extracted a small notebook from inside her parka and leaned back against the stern bench cushion. She pulled a short stub of a pencil from her pocket and began to draw.

Sue watched as a shallow, flat-bottom boat with sled runners emerged from the pencil tip. When a propeller appeared, mounted above the boat, Sue smiled and said, "I am beginning to like your idea, Arina. You are very clever—like my John. I am worried about the boat tipping over sideways, though."

151

"That is easy to prevent, Sue. We will put outrigger pods on both sides—like the south sea islanders have on their canoes, but I have to figure out where to get a propeller and a small engine to turn it. Rolan and Luka will know where to get those things. I have been thinking of using a six-blade ventilation fan from one of the old military buildings."

Luka and John had each caught a salmon and John additionally pulled in a perch, which was unusual because perch were normally found at much greater depths. Luka took over the steering of the boat and Rolan joined the women.

"What have you ladies been talking about? I see Arina has her idea pad out; what has she been calculating, Sue?"

Sue broke into a smile and replied, "Not calculating, Rolan—drawing the motorized iceboat so we can travel to Alaska over the frozen sea. A fan will blow us across the ice and water. The boat will not sink in the ocean."

"Let me see what you have imagined, Arina." Rolan almost lost his balance as the boat lurched. He dropped to the bench beside Arina and reached for the pad.

Arina moved the pad away and said, "Not yet, let me finish my sketch. I will show you in a minute. Just be patient." She turned so Rolan could not see the markings. After completing her design, she gave him the pad and said, "It is not to scale; we will work that out later. We will have to estimate the total weight of the boat and the people so we can tell how high to make the sides."

Rolan examined the diagram, smiled at Arina, returned the pad, and commented enthusiastically, "I know where we can get a fan blade, but we will need to get a light-weight engine. Maybe Luka or John have ideas. We will figure it out at home. I like your idea, little sister."

"Thank you, Rolan, but where can we construct it? It will be too big to transport on the Maligin V."

"We will take the components and assemble them in the inlet, but we will have to get things together quickly, ice will begin forming along the shoreline soon. We have a week to get it built, so all of us will have to contribute." Rolan looked at Sue and she nodded in agreement.

The men stowed the fishing gear and Luka began moving the Maligin V closer toward shore, the mountainous terrain had begun to cast long shadows across the sea and the temperature had noticeably dropped during the last hour's journey homeward. As they approached the fjord leading to Provideniya, they could hear the warning buoys, but could barely see them as they entered the harbor. The city was in the shade of the hills rising up from the edge of the buildings, squeezed between the waterfront and the steep western elevations.

Luka guided the boat into its moorage; the dock lights, although not yet necessary, were already burning brightly, fully illuminating the concrete pier and the other fishing vessels in the waning daylight. By the time the crew of five would reach the Ivanov residence, the majority of the city streets would be dark. The government had not invested in many streetlights except in the waterfront area, where twenty-four hour activity proceeded when cargo was being processed, or ships, especially military, were taking on fuel.

The Ivanovs helped the Slwookos transfer their two packs of belongings to the top of the pier where the Ivanov pickup sat empty, awaiting the group's return from the airplane. Arina, Sue and John rode in the cab and Luka and Rolan climbed in back with the fish. Arina drove slowly down the pier, turned left, and began the normal route past the old military barracks, the empty, three-story, concrete buildings, devoid of lights.

The black windows and lack of street lighting made Sue shudder; the two cold-looking buildings seemed to be haunted. She reached out to John and grabbed his hands, and said, "This place looks like the spirits of dead people live here. It makes me shiver." As she looked at the empty buildings, she saw puffs of vapor in her peripheral vision coming from the back of the pickup. "How much farther, Arina?"

"We are almost home—another two-hundred meters. I can see the lights at our complex." A large truck, going in the opposite direction, had only one headlamp, and passed very closely to the pickup. It surprised Arina and she swerved to avoid a collision with the rear of the vehicle as it seemed to move abruptly toward the pickup. She wondered if the driver was drunk and why such a large truck was in the residential area of Provideniya.

Before Arina could completely stop in front of the two-story complex, housing four families, she felt the truck shake as Rolan and Luka jumped to the ground. They always vaulted from the truck when she pulled into the parking area. They told her she stopped so slowly, they lost valuable time enjoying an after-work beer, so they wanted to get into the house and relax as soon as possible. She usually chided them saying they had already relaxed all day, so what was the rush?

Arina beeped the horn to let her parents know they were home, and within ten seconds the outside door light came on, the door opened, and Ivan stepped out. He was surprised to find five people unloading the pickup. He stepped back inside when he noted it had begun to snow and returned wearing a parka. When inside, he had mentioned to Sofiya there were five more for dinner.

"Any catch?" Ivan asked, vapor rising from his wet hair and from his mouth when he spoke and exhaled into the cold night air. He had taken a shower to wash off the smell of fish after spending the entire day at the market. Sofiya had been preparing dinner for two, but had suddenly changed plans, hastily getting ready for seven.

Rolan answered, "Three fish, two people, but we only eat the fish." He laughed and introduced Sue and John to his father. Ivan helped lug all the belongings into the house, carrying the Slwookos' packs into Arina's bedroom. Arina followed Ivan and moved her things out of sight and cleared off the bureau top so Sue and John had a place for their things. She stripped the bed and remade it with fresh linen, moving her things temporarily into the boys' room. She would be sleeping on the sofa.

Sue and John were somewhat restrained during dinner, encountering a different fare than usual, and not wanting to violate any rules of etiquette of their Russian hosts. However, following dinner, they declined the offers of beer and vodka, but shared a glass of wine.

The Ivanovs and the Slwookos gathered in the living room to discuss Arina's proposal for building a vehicle, able to contain five people, capable of crossing the ocean ice.

Arina stated, "I must know how much each of you weigh fully dressed for the voyage and the weight of anything you will be taking with you, but remember, you must not take much with you. It is not a pleasure cruise."

Ivan commented, "I suggest we all make a list of items we want to take. Let Arina decide if we can take those things. She will determine how much each item weighs. She has told me she will have to have the weight of the engine, the amount of fuel, and the weight of the boat."

John raised his hand and Ivan called on him. "I think the inside bottom of the boat should be covered with Styrofoam to insulate us from the cold metal of the boat. I do not think it will add much weight."

Luka was listening intently and asked, "Arina, how big will the boat be?"

Arina looked at Luka and answered with uncertainty in her voice. "I think about two meters wide and three meters in length—just big enough for five people huddled together to keep from freezing. There will not be a heater."

Luka frowned and quizzed, "How will we steer it?"

"Well, there are two ways: you can turn the runners if you are on ice, but that will not work in the water, so I think we will have to have a rudder like on an airplane. I do not like the runners, the steering mechanism would be difficult to make. The rudder should be easy to construct."

Luka agreed and said, "We need a small, light, but powerful motor to turn the fan blades. I cannot think of such a motor, can you, Rolan?"

Rolan thought for a few seconds. "No." He turned and looked at John. "Do you know of such a motor, John?"

John shook his head, looking a little dejected.

"I know of such an engine and I think I can get it tomorrow." Ivan's voice boomed with enthusiasm.

Sofiya was surprised by Ivan's comment. She inquired, "Where can you get such a thing, dear?"

Ivan grinned and glanced at his wife, "You know, Sofiya, the Fin."

Arina jumped to her feet and did a fist pump. "Yes! He runs the skiing areas in the hills west of the city. His wife's name is Ida. Is that not correct, Mama?"

"Yes. I do not care for her; she is a bit snooty. She thinks she is a world class skier, but I bet I could beat her on a downhill race. I have better balance. Her husband seems nice, though."

Ivan wanted to laugh at Sofiya's comments, but he decided not to. He said, "Yes, Anders Calonius is a nice guy and his Ida is nice looking, but not as pretty as your mother."

Luka, Rolan, and Arina laughed and Arina quickly remarked, "Saved from certain death, Papa." Everyone laughed, including Sue and John.

Ivan offered some background information, "Anders told me about a week ago that he had purchased another, almost new, snowmobile for people wanting to ski in the back country, away from the traditional ski runs. One of his old machines is broken. I think I can get the old one for a five percent interest in our business."

Sofiya was disappointed and said, "No, that is too much, Ivan."

Ivan stepped behind Sofiya, placing his hands on her shoulders, leaned down, and said, "We will be here only two more months and then he can have the entire business; it will be worthless to us. We will be gone."

Sofiya turned her head, looked up at Ivan, and smiled, "Oh! I forgot about that. I still do not know if our plan is going to work, so I do not spend time thinking about all the things that could go wrong. But I hope nothing goes bad." She looked at Arina and asked, "Did you fly the airplane?"

"Yes, Mama, It was wonderful, but I did not realize it until after I landed. I was scared most of the time flying alone. It will be different when Rolan goes with me." Arina smiled, recounted her solo flight for her parents, and then said, "We must get all the materials for the iceboat quickly, return to the inlet, and build the experimental craft. Can you get the motor for us tomorrow, Papa?"

Ivan winked at Sofiya and said, "We were thinking of going up to the ski lodge for a day to visit with Anders and Ida. We will go tomorrow—but we need the truck. Can you get some things at the base without the truck?"

Luka answered confidently, "No doubt. We will locate items, get them ready to transport, and take them to the boat with the pickup in the evening when it is dark. All five of us will find all that we will need—I am sure."

Sofiya clapped her hands and said, "Okay! Time for bed. Tomorrow will be a long day, we must get our rest. Is the snow still dropping?"

CHAPTER 23

ACQUISITIONS

Breakfast began at six o'clock. Ivan was frying potatoes and Sofiya was slicing black bread. After putting a pound of butter on the table, she started melting cheese to pour over the potatoes and was spooning caviar onto plates ringing the circular dining table. Arina started coffee and placed a pile of napkins at the center of the table beside a metal pan filled with knives, forks, and spoons.

When everyone had finished eating, Ivan announced, "Sofiya and I will take you young people to the military base before we go to Anders' ski lodge to get the motor. If you finish your work early, you will have to walk home. However, we will try to return before it gets dark. If you are not here, I will get you at the same place I drop you off. How does that sound?"

"Okay, Papa. After spending all day outside and in those unheated buildings, we will have to warm up before recovering the materials we find. After dinner we will go back to the base in the dark. Listen, everyone. Take something to eat with you, like bread and cheese, or bread stuffed with butter. It is getting chilly these days; the high temperature is the freezing point of water. Do not run out of energy. We do not need any sickness."

Sofiya chimed in with, "I have some chocolate that I was saving for the holidays, but I will give it to Sue to guard, so you men do not eat it all at once." She smiled, went into the kitchen and returned with a small bag, which she handed to Sue. Sofiya whispered to Sue, "Everyone gets some, but Luka and Rolan last, or they will eat it all. Put it in your pocket—out of sight. It should not melt."

As the Ivanovs and the Slwookos were climbing into the back of the pickup, Arina pushed her hair from her face, grabbed Rolan's arm when she sat down, and asked, "Do you have some tools?"

157

"Silly girl. You are sitting on them in the toolbox underneath your skinny butt. You still think Luka and I are morons?"

"No. I have reevaluated. You have moved up a notch to idiots. I am gaining more confidence in you all the time. You might get to normal intelligence soon."

Rolan said, "Thank you for the promotion," and kissed her forehead.

When everyone was in the pickup, Arina tapped on the cab and her father began driving the truck toward the military base. The pickup moved slowly through the fog for about ten minutes, gradually slowed, and stopped next to the machine shop area, the best place to find useful equipment.

John jumped out of the pickup and helped Sue drop to the ground. Arina vaulted to the ground ahead of Rolan and waited for Luka to hand her the toolbox. Rolan helped her set the heavy box on the ground and watched Luka drop to the ground. When everyone was out of the truck bed, Ivan lowered the window, leaned his head out and said, "Good luck—see you when we return."

Luka led the way to the big sliding doors and pushed them enough to slide through into the enormous metal building. He was carrying a length of rope, as was John, and Rolan had the toolbox. He looked up into the lofty heights of the building, fully fifteen meters or more above the ground, and pointed, "That is what we are after."

Everyone looked up past the beams supporting the roof and saw a six-bladed fan in a housing near the peak of the roof. Sue was the first to react vocally with, "Oh! How will we get that thing down?"

Luka replied, "We just need the fan blades, not the motor. How would you, John, like to go up there and tie a rope on the fan?"

"This is one time that I am glad to be short." John quipped. He smiled at Sue and sat down on the floor.

"Sorry, John, but you have been selected to get the fan. Rolan and I will hoist you up there so you can tie a rope around the blade and lower it. You must do it since you are the lightest of the men. I do not think Sue would have the strength to undue the bolts while hanging in the air. It might be too scary for her, also."

John grinned and said resignedly, "Now I wish I was both short and fat, too heavy to be flying up there held by a rope. Is there any way to get the fan from the roof?"

Luka replied, "We would have to remove the weather cap above the fan; it would take too long. Don't worry, John. Rolan and I both know how to tie sailor's knots that will not slip. We will hold you up there while you free the fan and then let you down."

"What are you people doing here?" A man, dressed in a green Army parka, black trousers, and black army boots, had squeezed through the opening of the large shop doors and had yelled out. Surprised, everyone turned to see who had yelled.

Luka said quietly, nearly whispering, "It is Aleksey, our old friend. Do not worry, I will handle this." Luka waved to Aleksey and yelled, "Aleksey! I have not seen you in some time. I thought you were on night duty."

"Oh! It is you, Luka. I did not recognize you at first. The Army changed my work schedule to daylight hours; they said I was not getting enough vitamin D. I remember your brother; who are these other people?" Aleksey walked up to Luka and shook hands, nodded to Rolan, and looked at Arina and Sue, and gave John a glance before shifting his eyes back to Arina. "Is this your beautiful sister I have heard about?"

"Aleksey, do not let her hear such things. She will be even more difficult to live with, but yes, this is my sister, Arina, and our friends, Sue and John Slwookos. This is Aleksey Karpov, everybody. We have come to get that fan from the ceiling."

"The fan? What will you do with the fan?"

Luka was ready with a fictitious story. "We are building an ice crushing machine driven by wind power. We just want the propeller part, not the motor. Is it hooked up to the power?"

"Nyet. The breakers have all been taken; no power to this building exists. If you want, you can cut the wires with no worry." Aleksey looked up at the metal rafters. "How are you getting up there?"

"John is going to stand on my shoulders," Luka grinned.

Aleksey laughed. "You joke much. I have idea. I notice you have ropes. I will get twine and we will toss a bolt, tied to the twine, over the roof support. Then you can pull the rope over the metal beam and hoist your friend up to the fan. What do you think?"

Luka smiled, slapped Aleksey on the back, and replied, "What a good idea, Aleksey. You have solved our problem."

"I get the twine, come right back."

"We have fishing line, Aleksey. Stay here, you can help lift John up there."

Rolan opened the toolbox and extracted a 100-meter spool of fishing line. John had picked up a bolt about ten centimeters long and tied the line to it. After unrolling most of the line from the roll, he gave the bolt to Luka. Luka closed his fingers around the spool and threw the bolt overhand at the fan, but the bolt ricocheted off the fan and fell back to the floor. Sue and Arina had stepped back from beneath the fan with their hands over their heads for protection.

Rolan said, "Let me try, Luka, I have better aim." Rolan threw the bolt, but it was short of the target and fell to the floor. Everyone booed him and he said, "Hey! That is harder than it looks. John, would you like to try?"

John put the spool into his pocket, measured off about one meter of line from the bolt and began swinging the bolt in a vertical circle. On the fourth revolution, he released the line and the bolt shot up, slowing as it approached its peak, but struck the roof and ricocheted over a beam supporting the fan.

Both women screamed, "Yeah!" as they clapped their hands. Arina said, "Good job, John, a perfect throw. Sue rushed over and gave John a hug.

Luka and Rolan were not smiling, but both Ivanov men congratulated John on his accurate throw. Luka tied the fishing line to the end of the rope and began pulling, raising the rope toward the fan. As soon as the rope was hanging from its center, Luka fashioned three loops: one for John's waist and two smaller ones for his legs.

John put the larger loop around his stomach and stepped into the other two, but Luka stopped him and commented, "John, you have the knots for the small loops on the wrong side of your body. When we lift you, your family jewels will be crushed. Put the knots behind you under your butt, unless of course, you do not want any children."

Sue reacted, "Yes, John, please do as Luka said," then she giggled.

Luka had Rolan give John two adjustable gap wrenches, which he put in his pants' pockets. Then he removed his parka, but kept his gloves handy, tucked in his belt. The big building was cold, but John knew the parka was going to interfere with his flexibility. He didn't think he would be up in the rafters very long, the shorter the time the better.

Luka inquired, "Ready, John?" John nodded, and Luka, Rolan, and Aleksey began pulling on the rope simultaneously. John slowly went into the air, about a meter at a time. John was holding the rope with both hands, unsure of what he was going to do high in the air held by a single rope, but after rising about halfway to the top, he quit looking down, relaxed, and held on to the hemp line with one hand, as he leaned back and observed the fan's assemblage.

The fan blade was secured to the motor shaft with two bolts, in opposition to each other. There was no way he could reach the shaft locking bolts, his arms were too short, so he would have to detach the fan motor and blade from the surrounding metal cylinder. He had to remove eight bolts and severe the wires to the motor.

When John was within reach of the first pair of bolts, he yelled down, "Stop pulling while I remove some bolts." He undid two bolts from one brace holding the fan and tossed them to the ground away from the others. He pulled himself a quarter of the way around the fan structure and removed two more bolts, but there were four more bolts that he couldn't reach. They were more than a meter beyond his outstretched arms, hands, and wrenches. He hung there for about fifteen seconds without moving, as he looked for a way to access the other fasteners.

Luka observed, talking to Rolan and Aleksey, "This is taking longer than I believed it would. We are going to get tired holding the rope. Can we tie it to the truck over in the corner?"

Rolan replied, "Good idea, Luka."

The three men, while keeping tension on the rope, slowly walked to the massive truck and tied the rope to the front bumper and returned to where the women were standing. Luka noticed Sue was biting her upper lip as she watched her husband dangling from the solitary rope with no one holding it. He could imagine her worrying that John might fall, surely dying on impact with the concrete floor. Luka watched Sue wringing her hands and walking around, only occasionally looking up to make sure John was all right. After her husband had not moved for a period of time, Sue yelled, "Are you all right, John?"

John answered immediately, "Yes. I am thinking."

Everyone laughed, relieving the tension that had developed when they had noticed John's lack of movement.

"I need another line to lower the fan. Do we have another rope?"

Luka answered, "No. That is the only line we brought. We have another rope in the pickup, but that is up in the mountains. Damn, we should have thought of that when we got out of the truck."

"I will get rope for you," Aleksey volunteered. "Back in few minutes." He walked a few steps, then ran for the door and vanished into the fog.

John yelled down, "I need slack in the rope—two meters."

Luka glanced at Rolan and shrugged, not knowing why John wanted to be lowered two meters. "Come on, Rolan, help me do what he wants."

Luka grabbed the rope to hold John's weight and Rolan untied the rope from the truck. They let out about two meters of rope and retied the line to the truck. Luka yelled up to John, "How is that?"

"Wait a minute, I will see." John began swinging like a pendulum and suddenly grabbed the fan support on the opposite side, swung his legs over the metal structure, and was hanging upside down.

Sue screamed, "John! What are you doing? You will fall!"

Very calmly, John replied, "Do not worry, my legs are strong. Now, Luka, untie the rope so I can pull it up."

Luka could tell what John was doing, so he removed the rope from the truck bumper, and watched the rope go up toward the roof like a snake. He then explained to the others what John was going to do. As they watched, John moved the rope to the other side of the fan where he was holding on and dropped it back to the ground. Luka and Rolan retied the rope, after removing the two meters of slack. Luka suggested to Arina that she involve Sue in a search for pulleys, belts, angle iron, and bolts for holding the ice-mobile structure together.

The women began exploring the clutter on the floor, picking up objects, and throwing most of the items aside. They piled the useful parts next to the truck where the rope was tied, keeping John from falling. Aleksey returned with a large roll of yellow-nylon line and gave it to Luka.

John had seen what Aleksey had brought back and yelled down from above, "I will need to tie the fan to the nylon line now, only two bolts are holding it."

Luka yelled back, "Tie yourself to the metal beams and pull up the rope as before. I will attach the nylon rope to the hemp line, and you can pull up the nylon. Secure the nylon to the fan, toss it over one of the support beams and drop it down to us. Rolan and I will lower the fan. Make sure you severe the power wires before you remove the bolts."

Ten minutes later, John stood on the ground with one foot on the fan, smiling like he had just killed a polar bear. When John had descended and was back on the ground, Sue rushed over to him, gave him a hug, and helped him into his parka. He ran around in circles, pumping his legs, for about ten seconds to try to warm up. Everyone congratulated John for successfully completing the dangerous job.

With the apparatus on the floor, the motor was quickly removed from the fan blade and discarded. When Rolan tossed the old electric motor through the open window of the half-demolished truck, it bounced on the seat and fell to the floor of the cab. Aleksey coiled the nylon line and asked if he could help them find anything else. Luka said no, thanked him for his assistance, and when he said he had to complete his rounds, Luka asked him to have some bread and cheese. He thanked them but declined until Luka mentioned the chocolate. He stayed for another ten minutes for bread and cheese. Two large pieces of chocolate were his reward. Sue gave him her share.

The five-person crew scoured the work benches and found a plentiful supply of bolts, lock washers, and nuts to use for assembling the frame to hold the fan blade. A small locked room at the rear of the building drew the women's attention, thinking it was a bathroom. Sue pointed out the lock to Arina who summoned Rolan. He inspected the padlock, picked up two screwdrivers from a work bench and pried the lock open. The little room smelled like tires but was stocked with metric v-belts and pulleys, just the objects on Arina's list needed to run the fan blade from the motor Ivan and Sofiya were trying to obtain.

The Ivanovs and the Slwookos had been in the machine shop for over two hours, although it seemed much longer. Watching and worrying about John had made everyone nervous, and the cold was beginning to fray everyone's patience. But they had accumulated most of the items Arina had recorded in her design notebook. There were two more items on her list of must-haves: fifteen meters of angle iron and a container to serve as the boat hull. She expected the angle iron to be the easier to obtain, there were supplies of metal dispersed throughout the base. Arina showed the remaining items on her list to everyone and they dispersed to all corners of the facility to search. They were to return in thirty minutes to report their findings.

Ivan and Sofiya drove for nearly forty-five minutes before reaching the Fin's skiing area. The road was not improved, and the pickup didn't have the guts it had when new, but the 500 meter climb in altitude had to be made slowly anyway. There were a number of switchbacks and long gradual rises before they arrived at a gravel parking lot in front of a reasonably large resort building.

The single story structure had a sign on the green metal roof. This was Angels' Haven. The red-brown vertical siding was rough-cut, which made it feel like a mountain cabin, but there were no trees in sight. About thirty meters in length, with a stone chimney at either end, the resort center had smoke issuing from one chimney. A half-dozen small cabins, randomly placed, not far from the main lodge, were connected by gravel pathways. The resort was not like one would see near a large population area, but the cabins had been freshly painted and looked modern. Each cabin had a metal chimney and a stack of wood outside.

When Sofiya saw the little buildings, she gasped, "Oh, my. Ivan, the color of the cabins looks like the inside of baby Arina's dirty diapers."

Ivan smiled as he tried to think of something to say that wasn't too nasty. "Now, be nice, Sofie, but if this is Angels' Haven, the angels must be blind from birth." Ivan turned off the engine and they sat for a moment surveying the resort from the pickup. "There is not enough snow for skiing, only a few centimeters. Hopefully, Anders and Ida are here. Come on, we should go in, say hello, and try to be nice in spite of Ida's comments."

When they opened the door to the lodge, a bell rang, and Ida appeared from a doorway behind a small registration desk. She was wiping her hands on her apron and she said, "Welcome to Angels' Haven. May I assist you?" She suddenly recognized Ivan and Sofiya and exclaimed, "Oh! It is nice to see the Ivanovs. What brings you way out here?"

Ivan asked, "Is Anders available? I have a question for him."

"He is chopping wood for the cabins, but he should be in for a sandwich in a few minutes. Wait by the fire, I have some things to do in the kitchen. I will join you in a few minutes." She turned and scurried back through the doorway, apparently leading to the kitchen.

Ivan and Sofiya walked over to the large river-rock fireplace and stood in front of the fire warming their hands. Sofiya turned around with her back to the fire and noticed something above the mantel at the other end of the building. She reached out, grabbed Ivan's parka, and whispered excitedly, "Look, Ivan, a propeller!"

Ivan turned, looked around the big room, but did not see where Sofiya was looking. "Where? I do not see a propeller."

"Give me your hand and stick out your index finger."

Sofiya took Ivan's hand and pointed it above the mantel at the opposite end of the lobby.

"Wow! Good eyes, Sofie." He smiled and stated, "I will ask Anders if we can buy it for Arina's birthday. You know she has much interest in aviation."

"Does she?" Sofie laughed. "But we have no money."

"Ah, but we do, Sofie. We have a fish market—another five percent should do it. We should see if the propeller is damaged." Ivan put his arm around Sofiya, and they walked toward the other end of the lobby, their attention and eyes focused on the two-bladed, wooden propeller.

"Hello, Sofiya! Hello, Ivan! It is nice to see you. Did you come to ski?" Anders laughed heartily, knowing that the Ivanovs knew there was too little snow for skiing.

Ivan answered, "No, we have come to buy your old snowmobile. Will you sell it to us?"

"What would you do with that piece of junk? It is worthless, the drive mechanism is broken and is too expensive to fix. You know I bought a new machine."

"Yes, I remember you telling me about that. But my boys need a motor to make a machine for breaking large pieces of ice to keep the catch cold on the way back from fishing. Can you help us? How much do you want for it?"

Anders began to think. He motioned for Ivan and Sofiya to follow and sit by the fire. As they walked the length of the lodge, Ivan noticed that

Anders was a smaller man than he had originally thought. The Fin removed his parka, tossed it over the back of a large overstuffed chair, took a poker, stirred the coals, and added two more logs to the fire. Sparks flew up when the logs landed on the glowing red-orange coals between the artistically crafted andirons. Anders seemed to have lost some weight, looking thin, not filling out his six-foot frame as before. Maybe he had been sick, but Ivan had heard nothing of Anders being ill.

Anders inquired, "How is the fishing business, my friend?"

Ivan pondered briefly and decided to make his business sound more lucrative than it really was, in order to get Anders to accept ten percent of the business as payment for the snowmobile and the propeller. "It is doing fine. We are making enough to support five, and a little more for luxury items. Almost every month we buy something new for the house. How is your ski business?"

"Fortunately, the American tourists have helped the seasonal businesses here. I have been taking them on tourist outings during the off season. It has been good for me; I have replaced much fat with good hard muscle. I have lost six kilos of body fat. But, if we do not get more snow this winter, I might have to sell the business." Anders sat back in his chair and took a deep breath, then exhaled slowly. "Ida has been working very hard, too, she painted everything, both inside and outside walls of the cabins."

Ivan decided to make Anders a proposal. "I will give you ten percent stake in my business for the broken snowmobile and the propeller on the wall over there." He pointed his right hand toward the other end of the building.

"What would you want with old propeller? It is from Chinese airplane of World War II." Anders frowned as he looked at Ivan and then Sofiya.

Without any hesitation, Ivan replied, "My daughter's birthday— you know Arina—is coming soon. She loves everything about old airplanes. I want to make a surprise. She will be twenty-one."

Anders looked at Sofiya for assurance, thinking it was strange to give a young lady such a gift, especially for her twenty-first birthday. He assumed that a young lady would want pretty clothes or some jewelry; Ida would. If he gave Ida such a present, she would leave him, but what did he know of modern girls?

Sofiya could see that Anders was confused. She commented, "Arina studies physics and she asked us about the wind power of a propeller the other day. We did not know how to answer her question. We told her to ask a professor at the technical institute. She always does experiments; she wants to study in Moscow."

"Well, all right. I will do that. We will make up a paper for all of us to sign. It will be our contract. Ten percent of your business will be paid to us each month." Anders, Ivan, and Sofiya stood up and they all shook hands. Anders called Ida into the lobby and explained the deal. Ida got tea for everyone while Anders and Ivan wrote up a contract. After signing the document, the two couples enjoyed tea and black bread coated with a thick layer of butter.

Ivan and Anders struggled to get the snowmobile in the back of the pickup, but after ten minutes of straining muscles and distorting their vocal cords with cuss words, they secured the machine in the truck. Anders retrieved the propeller from above the mantel and slid it in beside the defunct snowmobile. While the men loaded the truck, Ida and Sofiya worked in the kitchen preparing loaves of bread to feed the snowboarders that would be showing up before the end of the week. Fifteen centimeters of snow had been forecast for the next twenty-four to thirty-six hours, but the Fin said they would need about a thirty centimeters for good skiing.

On the way home, Sofiya and Ivan discussed their visit to the ski lodge. Ivan was humming a Russian song from the 1980s as he drove slowly down the winding roads, slippery in spots where the snow had melted and then refrozen forming small spots of black ice. Ivan could not risk having an accident and potentially losing their precious cargo.

Sofiya commented, "They were dressed in Austrian clothes, Ivan. I thought they would ask us to polka with them." She giggled. "But Ida was nice to me—first time that I can remember. Maybe they need help with their finances after all. In a few months, they will have two businesses, but neither will make them rich. They will have to hire someone to fish for them though, Anders and Ida do not know a sardine from a salmon. Also, they should have fresh fish for skiers."

An hour later, the old pickup rolled into the military base where the young people had been dropped off to gather equipment. The first thing Ivan noticed was a pile of junk sitting beside the road and then he saw Luka and Arina standing beside it talking. When the breaks squeaked upon stopping, Luka, Rolan, and Arina converged on the back of the pickup. Ivan shut off the engine and got out of the cab.

"Look what we brought you. What do you think?"

Sue and John had been sitting on the ground and were the last to see the propeller.

John ran his hands over the smooth surface of the airplane propeller and said, "Do I have to put the fan blade back?"

Everyone except Ivan laughed; he wasn't aware of the effort John had made getting the fan blade from the ceiling of the building. Rolan grabbed John by the neck and shoulder, grinned, and said, "You are a very funny man, John, but you are not an engineer. We will test both propellers and see which is most efficient. Your efforts were not wasted."

Ivan looked at the objects on the ground and commented, "Put what you can in the back of the truck, and we will return for another load. Luka and Rolan: come with me and your mother to help me unload the snowmobile; it is very heavy. Then Luka or Rolan will return to get the rest of you and the remainder of your junk. Do not be afraid of the dark."

Arina's arms fell to her sides, she stomped her feet, and said, "Papa! We are not babies!"

Ivan laughed and replied, "You still do not know when I tease. Relax, everyone. One of my boys will return in thirty minutes. We will celebrate today's achievements with a big meal when you get back home. Stay warm!"

CHAPTER 24

THE ICEBOAT

The Ivanovs and the Slwookos had maintained the secrecy of the camouflaged airplane throughout construction of the iceboat. The team had assembled the various segments of the craft on the pier where the Maligin V was moored, and as each of the components was finished, it was transported on the Maligin V to the inlet. When observers on the pier asked what was being built, the crew answered, "Equipment for next year's fishing season." No one but the crew would have any notion the various segments were being fashioned into a vehicle to transport five people across both freezing cold water and sea ice.

However, the final two trips of the Maligin V, transporting the support structures for the outriggers, were difficult. Ice was beginning to seal the opening to the inlet and the fishing boat had to be moored at the shoreline nearly a kilometer south of the semi-concealed channel to the assembly area. Fortunately, the components, though awkward to carry by hand, could be packed overland across the plateau. Once the parts were hauled to the top of the plateau, lugged to the airstrip, and lowered with ropes to the construction site, they were secured in place with bolts.

The iceboat was always referred to as the boat, so anyone overhearing the crew would assume they were talking about the Maligin V, but there were few people, other than the crew, on the docks on these late fall days. Most of the fishing boats had been taken out of the water for inspection, repair, and to avoid being trapped in harbor ice. What fishing was taking place was being done by anglers on the pier, who would occasionally amble by, stop and watch construction for a few minutes, turn and walk away thinking of their own lives and duties.

During the first day of construction, Sue sat and watched, occasionally helping by going for something, such as food, extra bolts, or a tool. Arina, noticing Sue's lack of involvement in construction, sat down beside Sue and said, "How would you like to be a spy?"

Sue's eyelids opened wide and a smile broke out on her face. She answered, "Oh! I've always wanted to be a spy. Who do I spy on?"

Arina whispered, "Are you working at the airport again soon?"

"Yes, I go back tomorrow for three hours in the afternoon. Then I will help your mother at the market until quitting time."

"You must watch for the mail delivery at the airport and record when the mail arrives, and if possible, where the letters came from. Can you do that for me for a week? It is very important."

Sue, full of enthusiasm, her eyes twinkling, said, "Oh, yes. Is that all of my assignment?"

Arina grinned and replied, "If you can read the postmarks, write them down so we know how long it takes a letter to get here from its source. But, be careful, do not let anyone know what you are doing."

"Okay. I will start tomorrow."

Halfway through the fabrication process, one of the fixtures of the Provideniya community, a long time fisherman and renowned storyteller, stopped to observe what the crew was building. He watched very closely as the metal parts of the support structure for the propeller and motor were bolted together. Though it was near freezing on the pier, the old man, Anatoli Pirogov, unbuttoned his parka, and squatted next to Rolan. "I know what you are building," he said confidently with his raspy voice almost at whisper level.

Rolan, a little surprised initially, looked at the bearded old fisherman, and asked, "What do you think, will it work?" Rolan looked closely at the wrinkled, weathered face beside him wondering if the elderly man had really figured out what they were constructing.

The gravelly voice inquired, "Why do you want to climb above your deck so far? Will you be able to see schools at greater distance?"

Rolan relaxed and replied, "We want to see other boats before they are upon us, like Dimitri investigating our boat, and other fishing boats looking for where our best yields are. How did you know what we are building, old timer?"

"I have a fine eye for detail. I have been able to figure things out always, like puzzles. Good luck, young man." He stood up, tried to straighten his spine, turned and walked off shifting his weight from one foot to the other as he became more erect. As he shuffled off, he waved his arm, either in disgust, or as a goodbye; Rolan could not tell which.

Arina had calculated all the dimensions of the components, including the positions of bolt holes, so the parts would fit perfectly when assembled on site. The main hull of the boat was made from a shallow mixing vessel, about one-third meter high, which possessed one curved side oriented to be the bow of the craft. The propeller, motor, and gas tank were mounted a meter behind and above the stern with supports attached to the hull and to the two outriggers, which were also mounted behind the stern. The outriggers were made from an empty 200-liter barrel cut in half with curved pieces of bow added to one end to allow a more streamlined flow through water. Polished metal runners were added beneath the half-barrels and below the main hull.

Luka and Rolan had dismantled the broken snowmobile and recovered the gas tank and the motor, which was adapted to turn the propeller to push the iceboat across the sea ice and open water when necessary. They had tried to use the fan blade early on, but when it was turned fast enough to push the iceboat, the blades began to separate from the hub. Fortunately, the propeller Ivan purchased passed all trial tests. By the time the craft was completely assembled, the inlet was nearly half frozen over.

The inaugural launch took place with John and Luka piloting the odd-looking craft around the inlet. The boat had been sitting half-in and half-out of the water. It took Rolan, Luka, John, and Arina to push the craft into the water over the rough shoreline ice. Since Rolan and Arina would never be riding in the iceboat, Luka and John carried out all the testing. The speed of the boat over clear ice was estimated at thirty kilometers per hour and in water, about one-third that value. But it was difficult for Luka to even guess the speed on clear pack ice, because only a circular portion of inlet water was frozen along the shoreline, and some of that ice had been melted and refrozen daily, forming a very rough ring of inlet ice about ten meters wide.

Not wanting to risk discovery, the fledgling engineers kept the new boat inlet-bound and covered until it was time to leave Siberia. When the boat was out on the open sea, loaded with provisions and five travelers, the actual capabilities of the craft would be discovered. John recommended the interior of the boat be covered with Styrofoam to insulate human bodies from the metal surface that was in contact with the ice-cold water. Styrofoam was obtained from a wall in one of the military dormitories. The iceboat was ready for travel.

CHAPTER 25

EMIGRATION

The inevitable severe winter high winds and blizzard conditions in Eastern Siberia were overdue. Few storms had come to the Chukchi Sea, the Bering Strait, or the edges of the coastal land masses on the west and the east of the ocean water, but continual sub-zero temperatures had fostered the accumulation of cap ice. The Siberian Eskimos to the west and the Alaskan Eskimos to the east had enjoyed these relatively mild atmospheric conditions for the first two weeks of November, experiencing late September and early October weather for nearly seven weeks. The mild weather had to end before long.

Meteorologists in the United States, able to foresee the birth of major winter storms, aided by satellites and the most up-to-date barometric equipment, began to observe the conditions that signaled blizzards and the accompanying large scale Arctic winds. Small plane cautions of the impending assault of foul weather had been broadcast after the tenth of November.

Following the first week of November, and final testing of the iceboat, the crew returned home for supplies. Rolan and Arina packed for staying at the airplane until departure. That last day in Provideniya for her two younger children was especially difficult for Sofiya.

Sofiya was very quiet that morning. She had tossed and turned all night, thinking of losing two of her children during their dangerous flight to Alaska during a snowstorm. The feelings of fear she had encountered years ago, when she and Ivan had run away, returned. The future could not be predicted, but she had great confidence in her children's abilities to deal with the unexpected. She kept telling herself that they will be all right, but she still thought that something could go wrong, and she might never see them again.

Since Sofiya had not slept, or at least felt she had not rested, she decided to get up an hour early to begin preparing breakfast and checking the quantity of food that was packed for Arina and Rolan. She suddenly remembered, "Oh, I have forgotten Luka and John. They will need food until the plane leaves for the United States." She set about to double the amount of food she had already packed. She thought keeping busy would keep tears from her eyes, but she was wrong. Each time she finished preparing a sandwich, she would reach for a kitchen towel to wipe her eyes.

When Ivan joined Sofiya in the kitchen, she put down what she was doing and walked over to him. She needed a hug and reassurance that everything would go well. When his arms circled her and pulled her close, the tears began to flow continuously. She cried openly. Sofiya heard his words, but they could not erase the overwhelming fear of losing two of her wonderful children.

She heard Ivan tell her to hold her emotions together so they both would appear strong when they waved goodbye to Rolan and Arina. Her crying began to subside when Ivan mentioned the letter. When they received the letter containing the code, she would know Arina and Rolan were safe and waiting for them in Alaska. The instructions in the code would signal the end of the years of worry that someday a representative of the government would appear at their door and arrest them. Sofiya had always felt relatively safe with Ivan as long as they were so far away from Moscow, but the whiff of fear had forever been there, like a piece of clothing misplaced and forgotten in a closet, to be discovered at an unexpected moment when looking for something else.

Arina had stirred when she heard her mother begin work in the kitchen, but she just turned over and sank back into oblivion. It seemed only a moment later when she heard her father's deep voice, a whispering from far away. It was too soon to get up, she did not hear Rolan or Luka. If they were up, she would have to join them for breakfast. She turned once more, pulled the pillow over her ears, and drifted away.

"Arina! Time to get your butt out of bed. We have to go to the airplane today."

"Go away, Rolan. I want to sleep. You are not an angel."

"What are you talking about? I am the devil, dear sister. You must get up. We will have to hike to the plane from the beach two kilometers south of the inlet. Maligin V is not an icebreaker."

"Is Luka up?"

Rolan shook his head, began to walk away, and said, "Yes! Get up! I will fly the plane without you, if you do not get up."

Arina sat up immediately, opened her eyes wide, and said, "What? You would leave me here after all I have done?" She looked around, but no one else was in the room. She could hear Rolan talking with Luka in the kitchen. Her dream had been so vivid! She heard her mother's voice, "Arina, time to get up. Rolan and Luka are talking about the code. We need you to make sure everything is right."

She answered, "Okay, I am up—just a minute." She pulled on her clothes, rushed into the bathroom, brushed her teeth, quickly combed and brushed her hair, and darted from the bathroom down the hall toward the kitchen. She hesitated and sauntered into the room, smiling, trying not to show that she was out of breath.

She sat beside Luka, who had pulled out a chair for her, and grabbed a piece of black bread smeared with butter. As she began chewing, she looked at the list of codes Luka had written down in order that any of the Ivanovs or Slwookos could translate a message from Arina and Rolan. She scanned the meanings of the numbers and the order of appearance of them in the message and gave the list back to Luka.

"That is correct. We will send you a message from Nome, Fairbanks, or Anchorage as soon as we can. I hope it will come before January, but we will have to figure out a way to meet you on the ice." She drank some coffee, set her mug down, and said, "Papa, are Sue and John up yet?"

Ivan responded, "John said they were packing his bags. They will be here in a minute."

As soon as John and Sue joined the others for breakfast, the total plan was discussed. Sue had to work three hours daily at the commercial airport and then would get a ride to the fish market to help the elder Ivanovs. John and Luka were to travel with Arina and Rolan to the plane and return to Provideniya after the plane took off. Once a week John and Luka would make the trek to the iceboat to be sure it was in working order. When the two families received the letter, they would journey to the iceboat, and make their way across the icecap to Alaska.

Each of the four going to the plane carried a pack weighing about twenty kilograms.

After shaking hands and giving big hugs and kisses, they climbed into the back of the pickup and Ivan drove them to the pier. As soon as the four boarded the Maligin V, they waved to Ivan who said, "Good luck, Arina and Rolan, we will be waiting your letter." Arina wiped the tears from her eyes and yelled, "Papa, take care of Mama. She gets very emotional. Tell her we will see her soon." Arina was not sure her father heard all she said as the boat moved away from the dock out into the light fog in the harbor. As the pier vanished into the fog, Arina's mind was set on saying goodbye to Provideniya; she hoped to never return.

Rolan and Arina were staying with the airplane continuously now, waiting for their chance to fly, but their patience was wearing thin. Every day Luka spun the prop, started the engine for a few minutes, then shut down the motor and topped off the wing tank. Every day Arina asked John for good news. "When will the weather change so we can be on our journey?" John watched the winds, the clouds, and the ice forming along the shores. On the third Wednesday of November, John entered the tent late in the evening, sat down on his sleeping bag, took a deep breath, and said, "I have been watching the northern lights, I believe you will go in the next twenty-four to thirty-six hours. I have seen these conditions before. There is a warm humid breeze coming from the south; when it hits the Arctic cold front that is coming, I expect we will have much snow—maybe snow for several days."

The Ivanovs looked at each other, smiled, and exchanged high-fives. Arina crawled on her knees to John and gave him a big hug. "Thank you, John. A large amount of snow arriving will be the best event we have had since we found the plane. In the morning we must determine if we need skis on the plane."

It was snowing heavily the next morning, the wind had picked up and drifts had formed against the tent and the wheels of the plane. Arina inspected the plane, kicked snow away from the wheels, and announced that skis would be necessary for takeoff. As soon as the team had eaten, they began to attach the skis. Lacking finger dexterity, they found it was very difficult to work with gloves, so a tag-team was set up so each person would work for five minutes, warm their nearly frozen fingers and palms over the fire, and then enter the tent to drink some warm water. Another pair of hands would take their place and resume working. With two people working at all times, the normal thirty-minute job took over an hour. The snow measured over fifteen centimeters in depth when the plane was ready.

When the Ivanovs were in the tent, John carried a bag of powdered charcoal, walked the length of the airstrip, and marked the runway so it could be easily seen in the snow. He placed a mark 100 meters shy of the plateau edge, the agreed on distance to save the plane. If the plane had not become airborne at that point, the plane would have to turn off the runway, or crash into the rocks or ocean below.

Luka checked Arina's and Rolan's packs to make sure nothing had been forgotten. Luka added another half-kilo of cheese to each pack before he laced them shut. As Arina and Rolan ran a last check of their clothing and belongings they were carrying, John and Luka loaded the bags of provisions onto the plane behind the seats. Luka returned to the tent, stuck his head in, and asked, "Are you ready?"

Arina and Rolan glanced at each other and simultaneously answered, "We are ready."

They put on their gloves, crawled out of the tent and hugged Luka and John. Arina said, "We will see you before long. Thank you for all you have done." The two fliers trudged through the snow, leaning slightly into the wind, and made their way to the plane with Luka following close behind.

John watched for a moment and then ran to the plane as Arina and Rolan were closing the cabin doors. He yelled to Arina just before she shut her door, "I put my best rifle behind the seat on the floor. There is also a small bag of ammunition attached to the trigger guard. Good luck!" Arina smiled and gave a thumbs-up sign to John.

John moved away from the plane as Luka swung the propeller. The engine coughed but did not start. Luka tried a second time and the engine took hold and idled for about thirty seconds before Arina increased engine speed and the plane began to move slowly at first, but then began moving away from the trees, slipping through the snow, and picking up speed. She guided the plane the length of the airstrip, swung the plane around into the wind, and increased the engine speed to near red-line. Ice Phoenix shuddered as the power of the engine urged the skis forward into the snow, the plane accelerating, bumping at first, but gradually moving smoothly.

Arina felt as if they were going too slow to ever get off the plateau in the remaining distance of the airstrip, but Ice Phoenix began to skip across the snow, gathering speed. She used the rudder to keep from deviating from the marks John had made. The 100-meter marker was approaching, and she could feel the plane trying to lift above the snow. The marker passed beneath them, but Arina had faith that the plane they had worked so hard to rebuild, was going to get off the ground before they ran out of airstrip.

But Arina was wrong. Ice Phoenix began to drop off the edge of the plateau, gradually dropping into the inlet. Arina pointed the nose up and the plane barely cleared the rocks near the inlet opening and began to rise into the air above the partially ice-covered Bering Sea. The Ice Phoenix and her human cargo were finally on their way to Alaska.

Back at the airstrip, Luka and John had thought everything was lost when the plane dropped from sight, the engine noise vanishing. But a second later, they heard the roar of the engine and watched Ice Phoenix climb into the snow-filled sky. They let out whoops of joy, grabbed each other in a bear hug, and watched the little plane quickly disappear into the opaque atmosphere.

Luka was smiling when he looked at John and said, "When the plane dropped below the plateau, I was convinced I would have to tell my parents that Arina and Rolan were dead. I did not know Arina had such guts."

John replied, "I did not know what to think when the plane went past the 100-meter mark and did not try to stop. Then the plane disappeared, the sound faded, but suddenly the plane reappeared, roaring like a she polar bear defending her cubs. I will tell Sue about this. She will be so thrilled!" John smiled at Luka as he rubbed his gloved hands together and said, "We have to clean everything up here, take it to the boat, and get back to Provideniya with the news. Your parents will be pleased."

"Mother will be singing and humming again, John. For the last week she has been very quiet, worrying about Arina and Rolan flying the plane to Alaska. I think she was afraid it was not going to work." Luka paused for a moment and then continued, "I hope they do not have trouble flying in the snow." Luka took a last look across the sea where the plane had disappeared in the falling snow; the engine could no longer be heard, the snow sliding off his parka in tiny avalanches. The nearly complete quiet felt strange, Arina and Rolan had always been around to talk to, but now he had to get used to working with John; their success travelling across the ice was going to require close cooperation. He was not worried; it was just going to be different. He moved toward the tent, his footsteps crunching in the snow, his breath forming clouds of vapor dispersing into the air, filled with tiny snowflakes penetrating the Chukchi atmosphere.

C H A P T E R   2 6

INSIDE ICE PHOENIX

Arina slumped against the back cushion of the pilot's chair, took a deep breath, and exhaled. She asked herself why she did not have some gum. After her first flight, she was going to get some gum, but in the excitement of the preparation of the iceboat, she had forgotten. Her neck and teeth hurt from clenching her jaw during takeoff, so she began working her jaw open and closed to loosen up her muscles. It was time for her to relax somewhat and settle into flying.

She felt Rolan's hand patting her on the shoulder and heard his words, "Fantastic job, Arina. You saved us. Now we will land in Alaska! Wow! I had visions of us crashing at the bottom of the inlet. I almost peed my pants."

Arina watched the altimeter as the plane slowly gained altitude to fifteen meters. She had adjusted the meter to zero at takeoff, so they were now about fifty meters above the ocean. Ice Phoenix was handling much differently than when she had made her solo flight. The drag from and the weight of the skis, and the extra weight of Rolan and the provisions had been almost too much of a load for the little plane to lift into the air from their short runway, but they had made it. They were on their way to the United States.

Now for the direction. Magnetic north was about fifteen degrees south of the geographic North Pole so for the Ice Phoenix to travel directly east, the plane would have to fly northeast, and a small correction had to be made for the wind. But the wind was variable, and they had no visible points of reference, so Arina was guessing at the adjustment. Hopefully they would get out of the snowstorm before long and see something on the ground they could recognize. She was going to begin to worry about striking a mountain after being in the air for an hour. They would have to risk being seen by radar and gain altitude to avoid mountains.

Arina realized the 100-meter failsafe marker had been a big mistake. When they had decided to mark the runway at 100 meters, it was to give enough distance to stop if they were using wheels, not skis. In the excitement of readying their supplies, and filling up the gas tank, they had all overlooked the situation of stopping the plane when using skis. But, she had felt the plane was nearly off the ground when they passed that last-ditch marker, so she could not slow down; if she had tried to stop, they would have tumbled over the edge of the plateau and crashed thirty-five meters below on the rocks or on the inlet ice.

As Arina thought of their close approach to crashing, she realized another factor had contributed to boosting the plane into the air; the wind was entering the inlet and rising against the plateau. If it hadn't been for the wind, they would not have made it. She looked at the altimeter and realized they could not gain more altitude. They could not risk being detected by Russian radar until they were beyond the territorial limits or about twenty kilometers away from land. That meant they could not gain altitude until they had been in the air around ten minutes.

Arina glanced at her watch. They had been flying for just over four minutes, but it had seemed much longer. She could feel Rolan looking at her but she could not look away from the front of the plane.

Rolan spoke up, "I think we should fly farther north, Arina."

"Why is that? We will burn more fuel and we will not know where we are if we make too many adjustments to our course."

"I have been wondering what to do if we have to land on the ocean—we would die. The ocean is only partly covered with ice. We would crash and sink very quickly, but if we travel farther north, the ocean is completely frozen. We could land and cross over the ice by foot. We have enough food for two weeks, if we conserve, and we have John's gun. I am a good shot; I could shoot a bear."

Arina thought for a few moments and replied, "Okay. You have a good argument. I will fly directly north for thirty minutes and then resume our present course." She altered the direction of the plane and was aware how the wind affected the flight; the sound of the engine was different. The headwind was slowing the plane somewhat, but it gave the plane some added lift.

"Rolan, I am going to tell you our directions since we took off. Please write them down. We will record the compass headings and the time at that orientation. Record it in my notepad. It's in my right hand pocket. Then you can estimate where we are on the map. I think we are still in Russian air space."

She glanced at her watch. Time was moving so slowly. They had been in the air nine minutes, but it seemed like an hour. They had changed course and were not going east now, they were moving north, still not over international waters. Arina worried that the plane would be detected by radar and they would be shot down by a Russian fighter. The Russian military would assume the plane was from the United States and it would be destroyed, no questions asked. She had to assume they would not go down where the ice only partially covered the sea. Arina changed course back to flying east.

Rolan was watching the compass as he was recording the information Arina was giving him and he could feel the plane banking to the right. He frowned and looked at Arina's determined expression.

"What are you doing? We will die if we land on the ocean water."

"Yes, we will die if a fighter shoots us down, also. As soon as we are over international waters, I will turn north again. It will only take a few minutes."

"Okay, Arina, I guess you are right. I wondered if you were going crazy on me."

Arina laughed and slapped Rolan's knee. "I am fine, Rolan. Remember, you are the moron."

Both Rolan and Arina were tiring of the lack of visibility; the snow was omnipresent, their nerves ready to snap. They strained to see through the snow; the whiteout conditions were very unsettling to the novice pilots, but Arina was grateful that the snow was not sticking to the windshield. Relying on the altimeter and the compass with no visual reference points had finally claimed their toll on Arina. Her thinking seemed to fluctuate from one way to die to another. She checked her watch again, and after three more minutes, Ice Phoenix began to climb slowly until the altimeter read 200 meters.

Rolan was again surprised. "What are you doing now, Arina? You want the radar to see us?"

"I have been thinking about that. We are in a storm and much of our plane is made of wood and cloth, not metal. I do not think the radar can see us under these conditions."

Rolan considered what Arina had said about the radar and realized she could be right. Then he commented, "You might be correct. We are too far from Russian territory to worry about their radar and planes, but now we must worry about the Americans. I think their radar is better than Russian radar because they have stealth fighters and bombers. Perhaps they can see planes that have the stealth technology. When a new weapon is made, a countermeasure is developed."

The radar screens at Elmendorf Air Force Base had begun to pick up a tiny, sporadic flicker off the coast somewhat south of the Arctic Circle, but the signal was so erratic, it was assumed to be a computer glitch. The computers had not yet calculated a trajectory from the intermittent signal, apparently system noise, so no alarm had been triggered.

Arina still worried about the altitude. She had dropped radar from her thinking and was now considering only achieving enough distance above the ground to avoid striking a mountain.

In her studies of the Alaskan coastline, Arina had not seen mountains higher than 1,400 meters marked on the maps, so she tilted the nose of Ice Phoenix up and climbed to 1,500 meters. She decided the 1,500-meter elevation should provide a safe clearance. She checked the fuel gauge and it indicated they had used more than one-third of their fuel, which meant they had travelled approximately 180 kilometers or a little more than 100 miles, if they had gone in a straight line.

Rolan asked, "Do you think we are over the land yet?"

Arina mulled over what they had done since taking off and answered, "Probably, but I would not bet our lives on it. I think we should keep flying until we are almost out of fuel. If we crash, there would be little chance for a fire to burn us or the plane. What do you think?"

Rolan looked at his watch and bit his lips together. "We have been flying for one-hour-seventeen minutes, but we went north part of the time and fought the wind some, too. I have to agree with you, keep on flying. What would you have done if I said we should try to land?"

"Well, my brother, I value your opinion, but in this case, I would continue flying. If you have finished writing, put the pad and pencil back in my pocket. I do not want to lose them."

They sat in silence for another fifteen minutes before Arina commented, "I believe we are coming out of the snow."

Rolan reacted with some excitement. "Hey! That is the best thing that has happened since we got off the plateau and cleared the inlet. If we can see where we are going, we can follow the map. We will not worry about running into mountains."

Frank Nayokpuk was walking along the seawall with his dog, Ulik, when they heard a plane approaching from the west. Frank new the mail would not be coming to Shishmaref for two more days and the mail plane would not be approaching from the west. He had met the new bush pilot, Dan Newcomb, the week before, so he knew the schedule. Dan and his father had taken over for the previous pilot, Ralph Stutz, who had retired and moved to Florida to live with his daughter's family. He had laughed when he mentioned that now he had to worry about hurricanes.

Frank had been carving ivory continuously for three hours and needed a break from the intricate detailing. He had to get out of his shop for some real exercise to clear his lungs, and get circulation going in his legs. Sitting was bad for his health—he was already taking a blood-thinner. His four-legged companion, Ulik, loved to be out in the snow watching the water from the seawall for seals and walrus. But today, Ulik knew they were just out for exercise, Frank had left his rifle at home.

"Some dumb pilot, huh? What's he doing out on a day like this—barely ten yards of visibility? He'd better have enough altitude to clear Devil Mountain; course that won't take much, only 800 feet. Looks like snow's letting up some."

The five-six, fifty-nine-year-old Frank stood on the concrete seawall looking below into the cold, dark-green water. He watched tiny floating islands of snow develop, rocking back and forth, and then melt into the darkness, returning to their source. Normally at this time of year, ice should be covering the Chukchi Sea to the west and Shishmaref Inlet to the east. Global warming had begun to change conditions along the coast significantly. The move of the town of Shishmaref was going to be expensive, but it had to be done. As Frank aged, he had become used to changes in his life.

He cleared his throat and said, "Let's go back, Ulik. I'll get to work, and you can take a nap." Ulik turned around, barked, and ran ahead of his master—just out of sight, but waited for Frank to catch up. As Frank began retracing his footsteps, returning to his home, the noise of the plane's engine gradually faded into the snowy eastern sky. Frank wondered what fools were in the plane and what their destination was. As he sat down at his workbench, he shook his head, and put the sounds of the plane out of his mind. He had work to do.

The pixels on the radar screen at Elmendorf had begun to show an indistinct pattern, resembling dots and dashes of Morse code, as an object creeped parallel to the Arctic Circle. A low level alert was issued as the unidentified object rose to 4,000 feet above sea level. Captain Ezra Hillane asked, "What's that signal?"

Technician Benjamin Walker answered, "Looks like a small plane, Sir. It's very slow—about eighty miles per hour at 4,000 feet."

Another tech, James Kincade, announced, "Too early for Santa Claus, Sir." He glanced at his buddy, Ben, who smiled and pulled his head down between his raised shoulders trying to hide from Kincade's comment.

Stone faced Captain Hillane didn't smile. "Funny, Kincade. Who do we have up there today?"

Walker looked at a chart and said, "Captain Sieberns: Polar Bear 2, Sir—F-22."

Hillane instructed, "Have PB-2 take a look. It may be a light plane in trouble; its velocity is abnormally low. If it goes down, we'll have a hunt on our hands. I'm guessing it must be thirty below out there. I'd hate to call for a search. Keep tabs on that signal, airmen."

Polar Bear 2 was at 10,000 feet, approximately 2,500 feet above the clouds, cruising at 550 knots over the Air Force Landing Strip, Cape Lisburne, near Wevok. PB-2 was headed to Point Barrow, Alaska, to the northeast for lunch when Captain Sieberns' radio came alive with instructions to investigate the radar signal that had appeared on the screen at Elmendorf, in Anchorage, 850 miles to the southeast.

Staying above the clouds, the F-22 changed heading and accelerated, reaching the radar position sent from Anchorage in less than ten minutes. The snow below seemed to be breaking up, so PB-2 began descending and decelerating so Captain Sieberns could take a visual scan of the area: nothing had appeared on his radar.

Arina and Rolan were tiring of the white-out conditions, but their mood was changing as they began to clear the snow. Rolan looked down, catching brief glimpses of land when there were occasional voids in the flurries.

Rolan announced excitedly, "We are over the land, Arina."

"What do you see?"

"Snow covered hills to the north and rivers below. They look like snakes on a white blanket."

Arina looked at Rolan for a moment as she was thinking of a plan, and said, "Okay, I am going to fly in a circle to see if there are any roads or cities." She banked to the right and began to fly a loop while watching the compass. "Tell me if you see anything, Rolan."

Rolan smiled and saluted, "Do not worry, my captain. I will report to you any findings."

Arina chuckled, "Try not to act like a moron, Rolan, even if you are one."

Captain Sieberns was nearly on top of the position now. A blip appeared on his screen and it looked like the object was taking evasive action. He was 500 feet above the signal, so he dropped suddenly, to surprise his prey. The surprise, however, occurring simultaneously for both pilots, was an almost head-on collision. When Sieberns saw the little plane, it was almost too late, but he veered to the left and cut across the path of the Piper Cub.

Unfortunately, when the jet slashed across in front of Ice Phoenix, Arina lost control of the defenseless plane in the wash from the jet aircraft. She was shocked by the sudden massive shape appearing in front of her. Arina jerked back on the stick in an attempt to avoid striking the large silver object. The close, violent turbulence from the fighter caused the little plane to nosedive, even though the control surfaces should have caused the plane to climb. Arina fought to get control back, but it was too late, by the time she was able to regain horizontal flight, they were too close to a hill. Although the plane was climbing, it was too late to avoid clipping the hill with the landing gear, and a collision was imminent.

She yelled as she braced herself, "Hang on, we are crashing!"

C H A P T E R 2 7
RESCUE

Dan had waited for the snow to let up before he took off from Galena with the mail to Bornite, Kobuk, and Shungnak, all three towns about 145 miles directly north of Galena. Although there were landing strips near each town, he was only stopping at Shungnak Landing Strip. After dropping the mail pouches off, he grabbed a cup of coffee, gassed up, and headed for Selawik, half-an-hour west, to pick up mail going south.

It was early in the afternoon when he set Glacier Phoenix down at the Selawik Landing Strip. Dirk Stevens, another bush pilot, was walking toward his plane when Dan landed. Dirk nodded to Dan and mentioned he was on his way to Noorvik, farther west by about thirty-five miles.

"Good to see you, Dan. It just quit snowin' 'bout twenty minutes back. I'm headed out to Noorvik and on to Kotzebue. I've got some hurry-up deliveries to make. Back early tomorra'."

"How's the wife?"

Five-eight, heavily bearded Dirk ran his fingers through his long dark-brown hair, tightened up his parka, and replied, "She's hunkered down next to the stove; eight months pregnant. Be our third."

"Are you flying to Fairbanks for the delivery?"

"Nah. There's a midwife in Bornite. She'll help out."

"All right but let me know if you need a nurse. I can get one here in less than three hours."

"Thanks, Dan. See ya later."

"Take care, Dirk." Dan waved as Dirk climbed in the cockpit of his canary-yellow deHavilland Beaver and pulled the door closed. For a minute, Dan watched Dirk takeoff, wiggle his wings, and zoom off to the west. Then he picked up the outgoing mail; five letters to Fairbanks and a small package addressed to Seattle.

Nomah wanted out of the cockpit, but Dan didn't want to stay out in the cold any longer than necessary, so he said, "No, big guy, we've got to get back to Galena to meet Dad and get this mail on its way." He had to push Nomah back from the cockpit door before he could get in the pilot's seat. He inserted the mail into a pouch Beverly had made that hung on the adjacent seat, gunned the engine, and swung Glacier Phoenix facing into the slight breeze and took off.

Back in the air, Dan banked to the left, turned ninety degrees, and climbed to 4,000 feet, headed toward the Selawik Hills, a bit over thirty miles away. After five minutes in the air, thirteen miles south of Selawik, a message came over the radio. At first, he was a bit startled; he had no clue that someone had Glacier Phoenix under observation. A Captain Sieberns was addressing the pilot just east of Selawik Lake at 4,000 feet. Dan realized the message was for him, no one else was in the vicinity, but he couldn't see another plane. Where was Captain Sieberns?

Dan spoke into his radio, "Where are you, Captain?"

The answer surprised Dan. "I'm in an F-22 at 8,000 feet—twelve o'clock high. I just passed a small plane—looked like an old Piper Cub. We almost collided, and I watched it go down. The wash from my plane shook the little one out of the air. It appears the Piper clipped the side of the hill just west of the Mangoak River and crashed. "Can you take a look? I'd appreciate it. Let me know if you need assistance. What is your designation?"

"I'm Dan Newcomb—N9101AK."

"Okay, Mr. Newcomb, I'm Polar Bear 2. I'll stay around for about thirty minutes before I have to hightail it. Are you alone?"

"No, my dog is with me. He's better than another human. I'll contact you ASAP, Captain. I'll start a search in about seven to eight minutes. If I see them, I'll land and go to the wreckage on foot. N9101AK out."

Dan followed the Mangoak River until he reasoned he was near the location Captain Sieberns had described. At 4,000 feet, he couldn't see any disturbance in the snow along the steep hill to his right, so he flew past the hill, circled and came back from the south, descending to the same elevation as the summit. He slowed, dropped another 300 feet, and circled the rounded peak going counterclockwise at 3,000 feet, a little below the summit.

"Damn, that plane has to be here somewhere. Can you see anyone, Nomah?"

Nomah's ears perked up and he looked out, then returned a look to Dan and whined.

"Nothing? Everything is white, except for those steep rocky walls and parts of the river. I'm going down closer to the ground in that valley where the river starts. Maybe the plane glided away from these hills before it went down."

Dan dropped to 1,500 feet and slowed to eighty miles per hour. Now he was less than 500 feet above the ground, but he was able to see more of the undulations in the terrain.

"See anything, Nomah?"

Nomah stood in the seat and barked—he had seen something! Nomah looked at Dan and barked again, so Dan flew north, downstream, turned back, and retraced his previous route, peering out his window to the left as they flew south. He saw a figure waving both arms overhead. Dan wigwagged the wings to signal the individual on the ground that he had been seen, but Dan still couldn't see the plane. Now, he had to find a place to land. While looking for a site to set Glacier Phoenix down, Dan radioed PB-2 and told Captain Sieberns that one survivor had been found, that N9101AK was landing, and he would walk to the survivor, although he hadn't yet found the wreckage.

Dan found a probable landing site along the Mangoak River about a mile north of the location of the crash survivor, but at approximately the same elevation. Dan made two low-level passes before setting Glacier Phoenix down along the riverbank. The landing was a little bumpy, but the plane wasn't damaged. As Nomah was bundled in his dog parka and boots, Dan planned what he needed to carry on the mile-long trek. He wanted to move fast, so he left his rifle in the plane, carrying his serrated knife as his only weapon. He wasn't worried about bears; they were in hibernation. With his first-aid kit and two rolled-up blankets strapped to his back, he closed the cabin door and set out with Nomah. They followed the riverbank, gradually ascending the valley between the two prominent hills.

When Dan and Nomah left the plane, the air temperature was minus ten degrees Fahrenheit. Fortunately, the snow from the recent storm had dropped only six inches of powder and the climb was not very difficult except for a ledge where a small waterfall, a couple of feet in height, was beginning to freeze over. Nomah took the lead. Dan had to smile as he watched his companion high-stepping through the snow. The banks of the river, though covered with snow, were mostly gravel, with occasional small boulders which could be discerned by lumps in the blanket of white.

After a half-hour of Dan's footsteps crunching through the snow, occasionally breaking through thin ice along the riverbank, Nomah barked and ran ahead. Dan looked upstream about 100 yards and saw a man standing with a rifle, ready to fire.

Dan yelled, "Don't worry, he's my dog. He won't bite. He's here to help." Dan watched Nomah approach the man and sniff his legs. The stranger looked down at Nomah, let the gun drop in the snow, knelt, and encircled Nomah with his arms. Dan was puffing a little when he reached the stranger, having hurried when he glimpsed the man pointing a rifle at Nomah.

The man tried to stand, but was unsteady, so sank back to one knee on the ground. Dan could see confusion in his eyes when he got closer. The man was bigger than Rigs; even though he was not standing, he was an imposing figure, broad shoulders and like Rigs, looked like an NFL lineman.

Dan inquired, "Are you the pilot of the small plane that went down?"

"No. I am the passenger. My sister is the pilot. She got hurt. I show you."

Dan was correct, when the man stood, he was a half-foot taller than Dan. "What is your name? Mine is Dan."

"Rolan Ivanov. My sister is Arina. I think she has broken bones. We need help to hospital. Will your plane—" Rolan looked at Nomah and continued, "carry four people?"

"I can take five passengers. Don't worry, there's plenty of room. I don't see your plane."

Rolan motioned for Dan to follow as he stepped ahead around a large boulder that invaded the right-hand side of the stream. Rolan disappeared momentarily but waited for Dan around the next turn of the narrow creek.

Dan caught up to Rolan and saw the plane, landing gear missing, and the right half of the wing bent, partly under water, the left half being tilted into the air by another large boulder midstream. Dan recognized immediately how he missed seeing the plane from the air; the tail was painted greenish-black, nearly the color of a boulder, and the wing was painted in very effective camouflage colors.

A woman's anxious voice issued from the plane. "Rolan! Are you there?"

Rolan answered without hesitation, "Yes, Arina, we have help—a pilot and his big dog."

Dan had already waded into the water, only about six inches deep, after breaking through the thin layer of ice, and flung the cabin door open on the pilot's side. The back of the pilot's chair was broken and the young woman, Arina, looked cold and pale. Her right leg was folded beneath her and her left hand was bent at nearly thirty degrees to her forearm. Dan stripped off the medical pack and two blankets and wrapped Arina as best he could.

"We have to get you out of here. I'm going to give you a shot of morphine, so you won't feel pain. I will set your broken wrist and put a splint on it, then we will work on your leg. Do you understand?"

Arina opened her eyes to a slit, raised her head barely an inch, nodded, and then closed her eyes and let her head fall back.

Dan instructed, "Rolan, come here, on the other side of the cabin."

Rolan splashed into the stream and jerked the cabin door open. "What do you want done?"

"Can you remove that door?"

Rolan looked at the door, grabbed it with both hands, and replied, "Yes. Now?"

"Not yet. Ask your sister if she is allergic to morphine."

"Morphine?"

Dan had to explain. "A drug from a plant native to Turkey; from opium."

Rolan nodded and said, "Oh, I know that." He took Arina's right hand in his and asked quietly in Russian if she was allergic to morphine. Arina shook her head and leaned back with her eyes closed.

Dan took his serrated knife from his leg sheath and said to Rolan, "I have to cut her parka so I can see all of her arm. Okay?"

Rolan nodded that he understood, and said, "Big knife."

Dan sliced open Arina's parka from the wrist to the shoulder with a quick maneuver that surprised Rolan.

Rolan commented, "You are good with that very sharp knife."

Dan took the bottle of morphine sulfate solution from the medical kit, prepared the syringe, and injected the drug into Arina's arm just below her shoulder.

Rolan was watching intently and said, "How you know that?"

"My girlfriend is an emergency medical technician. She helps people who have medical problems. I take her in my plane to her patients and observe what she does. It's fascinating."

"Oh, nurse," Rolan nodded.

"Okay, Rolan, I want you to wrap this knife with tape so it will not cut. We will use it as a splint to hold your sister's arm steady." Dan gave Rolan a roll of tape so the sharp edge of the blade could be covered. As Dan observed Rolan's work, he quizzed, "How long have you been in Alaska, Rolan?"

Rolan stopped wrapping and glanced at his watch. "About four hours."

"Really? Where did you come from, Canada?"

"Canada? No—Siberia. We come during the snowing." Rolan finished wrapping the knife and handed to Dan. "Is okay?"

"Yes. Now we have to straighten your sister's arm. You will have to hold her shoulder so I can get the bone back in the correct position. Let's hurry, my feet are freezing."

It only took a minute to set Arina's arm. Afterwards, Rolan gently lifted her out of the cockpit and carried her to shore. Dan had kicked most of the snow away so it would not get the blankets wet. Dan straightened Arina's leg and felt the bones. Nothing appeared to be broken, but he believed she probably had a bad ligament strain or tear in her knee. That would have to be addressed in a hospital. They wrapped Arina in the blankets to keep her warm.

Dan took off his boots and dried his feet, as did Rolan. A survey of the area gave no hope for anything but the airplane to burn. Dan said, "Can you get that door now, Rolan?"

Rolan slipped on his boots without socks and waded back into the water, grabbed the passenger door and ripped it off the little plane as if he were separating two perforated postage stamps. While holding the cabin door in his left hand, Rolan reached into the cockpit, grabbed two backpacks and John's rifle, and returned to the riverbank joining Arina and Dan. Nomah was lying next to Arina.

Dan checked the rifle to be sure it wasn't loaded and used it as a splint to hold Arina's leg in a fixed position. Following Dan's instructions, Rolan tied the two backpacks together. The passenger side door was used as a stretcher to carry Arina the mile to Glacier Phoenix, Rolan on one side and Dan on the other. Nomah carried the two backpacks fastened to his dog vest like saddlebags. Because of some slight stumbling and a few minutes rest at the half-way point, it took them close to forty minutes to reach the plane.

C H A P T E R   2 8

BACK TO FAIRBANKS

Dan and Rolan put Arina on the back seats so she could lie down. She was still drowsy from the morphine, but when the plane was in the air headed toward Galena, about fifty minutes away, she asked, "Are you flying the plane, Rolan? Be careful, do not crash."

Rolan and Dan looked at each other and grinned, realizing that Arina was still under the influence of the drug, but Rolan said, "We are in a different plane, Arina, with another pilot. His name is Dan. He has a big dog, Nomah, a German shepherd."

Arina replied, "Oh, a German. Can we trust him? I cannot move my leg, Rolan."

"Please sleep, Arina. We are going to a good place. You will like it."

"Okay. See you tomorrow."

Rolan smiled and shook his head, knowing Arina was not able to entirely comprehend what was happening. Rolan opened his backpack and withdrew a large brick of cheese and broke off two good sized pieces and offered one to Dan.

"Thank you. I haven't eaten since breakfast."

Rolan said, "I did not eat much this morning, I was very nervous."

Dan finished the cheese and said, "We are at 4,000 feet. I am going to call my father and have him fly my girlfriend to Galena. She will look after your sister until we can get her to the hospital in Fairbanks." Dan radioed Hank, in Fairbanks, and explained the situation.

"Where is Galena?" Rolan asked.

"It's about 240 miles east of Nome and about two hours west of Fairbanks." Dan looked at Rolan and sensed that Rolan was not familiar with distances in miles, so he made a quick estimate. "Galena is 380 kilometers east of Nome and about 510 kilometers from Fairbanks. My plane's speed is about 260 kilometers an hour."

194

Rolan nodded that he understood and noted, "That is twice the speed of our airplane."

"So, you are from Siberia. Where did you live and how did you get the little Piper Cub airplane?"

Rolan and Dan talked about the rebuilding of the Piper Cub after the Ivanovs recovered it from the ice. Rolan told about life in Provideniya, Luka's and his fishing adventures, and the families left behind. Dan's questions kept Rolan talking for almost the entire trip to Galena. While talking to Rolan, Dan realized that if he flew to Ruby, about forty-seven miles east of Galena, help for Arina would be obtained about fifteen minutes sooner than originally planned.

He called Hank and changed the meeting place to Ruby Landing Strip, on the southern bank of the Yukon River. In the following ten minutes, both men were silent. Rolan had explained everything except the iceboat to Dan, and was growing weary, both in body and mind; Dan was trying to digest all the information about the Ivanov brother and sister team and their desperate flight across the Bering Sea, only to be knocked out of the air by accident, tangling with a modern jet fighter. Had the two planes actually collided, Rolan and Arina would surely have been killed. As Dan was preparing to land, Rolan had just begun to explain the construction of the iceboat but hadn't mentioned the rest of the Ivanov family.

When Glacier Phoenix arrived in Ruby, everyone remained in the warm cabin. There was no reason to expose themselves to near-zero degree temperatures until necessary. Rolan leaned over the seats and talked with Arina. She was thirsty, so Rolan gave her water and half a sandwich, which she attempted to eat, but after taking a few small bites, she handed it back to Rolan.

Arina had become more lucid and had disclosed that both her arm and leg hurt, but not too bad, so Dan decided to give her an aspirin, not wanting to administer another dose of morphine. He would wait and let Ann take care of further medication.

They had been waiting in the plane for about ten minutes when a plane arrived from the east. At first glance, Dan had thought it was Hank's plane, but it couldn't be, he wouldn't be arriving for another half hour. As he watched the Cessna taxi and stop next to Glacier Phoenix, he recognized it was Hank's plane. Hank, smiling, was waving to Dan. As soon as the prop stopped, Dan got out and walked toward the plane.

Expecting Ann to be in the cabin, Dan was startled to see a man moving around, apparently gathering some medical equipment from behind the front seats.

Hank stepped to the ground, raised his parka's hood, and walked briskly to greet Dan. They gave each other a hug and Hank explained, "I had to leave Ann in Eureka. She had an emergency call to assist with a birth. Fortunately, this gentleman, Rick Leisell, was waiting for a ride back to Fairbanks, so he came with me. He's an EMT—just like Ann, but not as pretty." Hank laughed.

Dan turned his back to the wind and said, "Okay, Dad. I'm going to take Rick, my injured passenger, and Nomah, and head for home. My other passenger, Rolan, will fly back with you. He's got quite a story to tell. I'll let Rolan know what we're going to do, and you tell Rick to transfer to my plane. We'll meet at International. I'll call ahead for an ambulance. Let's do it. I'm getting cold out here."

Dan shook hands with Rick and helped him move his medical bags into Glacier Phoenix.

Rolan had gotten out with Nomah and was waiting beside the plane but didn't ask what was happening; he just watched. Dan ushered Rolan over to Hank's plane and introduced the two men, the wind blowing clouds of vapor from everyone's breath. Dan shut the cabin door after Rolan had gotten in Hank's plane and rushed back to help Nomah jump into Glacier Phoenix. Dan signaled Hank to take off, and as soon as Hank and Rolan were in the air, Dan took off and followed his father's plane to Fairbanks.

During the forty minute trip to Fairbanks, Rick examined Arina's broken arm and was satisfied with Dan's realignment of the broken ulna. He replaced the knife with a normal splint and rewrapped the cut open parka over Arina's arm. As he worked, Arina asked, "Where is Rolan?"

"He's on the other plane, on the way to Fairbanks."

"Oh. Are you the German?"

Rick was puzzled by the question. "No. I'm an American; a medical technician."

"I cannot move my leg."

"I know. It was injured when the plane crashed. It is being held steady so you can't move it. We will fix it when we get to Fairbanks—at the hospital."

Arina gave a slight nod, sighed, and closed her eyes.

Rick had found it difficult to evaluate Arina's leg injury in the cabin, but since she wasn't suffering great pain, Rick decided to let the hospital staff do the investigation. After he completed checking Arina's blood pressure and pulse, he sat behind Dan on the seats in front of Arina.

Rick started a conversation, "You did a good job with the broken arm, Dan. That's a hell of a knife. Where'd you get that?"

"Thanks. I made the knife when I was in Oregon; it comes in handy sometimes."

"I'll bet. It looks like you could cut down small trees with it."

Dan laughed, thinking about the knife's use in Oregon.

"Your father said you are Ann's fiancé. You're a lucky man. She's smart and good looking—kind of a rare combination."

"You got that right. She keeps me on my toes. We both like to tease. Where did you meet Ann?"

"We are in the same EMT class at the hospital in Anchorage. There are twenty of us that have meetings every two months, mostly about new or updated procedures."

Rolan sat quietly beside Hank for a few minutes, as if in a cloud, not being able to focus his eyes on anything, hoping Arina would be all right. If someone was to have gotten hurt, he wished he had been the one, not his pretty, smart, young sister. He was mad at himself for not being able to help her when she was lying broken in that sorry little airplane. All he had done was to wave at a plane as it passed overhead. But now she was in good hands; there was something about Dan he felt but could not explain. Dan possessed a strength that was like his father's; he just knew what to do in an emergency.

"Well, young man, are you feeling all right?"

Rolan came out of drifting in a cloud when he heard the deep voice of the pilot beside him. He thought, "What is his name? Hank?"

"Yes, Sir. My leg hurts some. I think it is bruised, and my feet are cold."

"Take your feet out of those boots and wrap them in a blanket. There's a blanket behind you on the seat."

Rolan followed Hank's instructions, then began looking around the cockpit. The seats were cushioned, covered in leather, and he marveled at the differences between the instrument panel of Ice Phoenix and the more modern, larger Cessna. He asked, "What do you call this airplane?"

It hadn't occurred to Hank to give his plane a name other than the official designation. He grinned and said, "Second Chance."

Rolan had to ask, "Where is First Chance?"

"I flew it into the side of a mountain. I imagine it is buried in snow, along with two bodies."

Rolan looked closely at Hank's face, wondering if the older man was joking. Hank's lack of expression showed that he was dead serious. Rolan, feeling a bit uneasy, thought a minute, and asked, "Should I worry?"

"Nothing to worry about, Rolan, unless you threaten my family."

Rolan grinned, "Not to worry, Mr. Newcomb. I am—how you say?—a teddy bear."

When approaching the airport in Fairbanks, N9101AK was given clearance to land immediately. Hank and Rolan had to circle the international airport for five minutes while a commercial jet landed. When Rolan reached the tarmac, he rushed over to Dan's plane and watched the ambulance crew transfer Arina from the plane. He grabbed the backpacks and the rifle from Dan's plane and wanted to ride with Arina, but an airport security officer stopped him. Rolan was not allowed to carry the rifle at either the airport or the hospital.

Hank had anticipated the problem with the gun and caught up to Rolan just as he was being detained. "Hey, Rolan. I told you I'd buy that gun from you for two hundred dollars. Here's the money." Hank fished his wallet from his trousers and counted out $200 in twenties and fifties. Hank saw the puzzled look on Rolan's face and winked. Rolan smiled, gave Hank the gun, and stuffed the money in his pants' pocket. Hank watched Rolan climb into the ambulance with Arina and said, "We'll come to the hospital after we move our planes. It won't be long. Tell the hospital that the Newcombs will take care of the expenses; they know who we are."

As the ambulance door closed, Rolan said, "Thank you, Mr. Newcomb. We have some questions for you and Dan."

Hank waved at the back of the ambulance as it pulled away from the planes heading for Old Airport Way and east to the hospital. Hank stored Rolan's rifle in his plane and then met with Dan, who had helped Rick take medical equipment to his Ranger. Hank planned on borrowing a car to drive to the hospital to assist Rolan and Arina while Dan used the company truck to deliver the outgoing mail to the post office. After flying his plane to their private airstrip, and taking Nomah home, Dan was going to join Hank at the medical facility.

"Dad, it'll take me about forty-five minutes before I can get to the hospital. The admitting people will probably need a signature before they do anything. I'll help Rolan and Arina with the medical expenses; tell them for me."

Hank grinned and said, "I told Rolan to give our name when they asked who was going to pay for treatment. I don't imagine any problems; those accountants know we're good for it—as long as they don't charge the normal rates. Otherwise, they will have to contact our lawyers."

"Our lawyers?"

"Yah. You know—when it gets really cold outside, they're the ones with the wool blankets and everyone else gets a blanket of snow."

Dan snickered, "Good one, Dad."

Hank grinned and replied, "It just came to me—made it up myself. When I was alone in the Yukon, I thought of a lot of jokes, but I've forgotten most of them. I don't think any of those jokes had to do with lawyers, though. They were about the weather, animals and me."

C H A P T E R   2 9
FAMILY PLANS

An hour later, Dan was walking in the main entrance of Seward Memorial Hospital. He stopped at the admissions desk and asked for Arina Ivanov's room, but was told she was having an MRI taken of her knee. She would be back in her room in fifteen minutes.

The young receptionist said, "Mr. Newcomb, her brother is waiting in her room. You could talk with him if you like. He is in 411; take the elevator on the right, number two."

"Thank you—," his eyes flashed across her name tag, "Joan." He wondered how she knew his name; maybe Ann knew her. The elevator was empty, and he watched the floor numbers flash as the sterile box, capacity 4,200 pounds, rose to the fourth floor. The red number four appearing on the wall panel and a ding were simultaneous. A final floor adjustment took place and the door slid open. Across from the elevator were restrooms and a wall directory displayed the room numbers to the left and right. Dan turned left, and found room 411, about halfway down the hall. The door was open.

Dan hesitated for a moment and then entered to find Rolan slouched in a chair with his head against the wall, his legs extended across the floor nearly to the bed. It was a two person room, but only one bed was prepared. The bottom portion of the walls, simulating a wainscoting, was beige in color and the top a cream tint. He hesitated to say anything; Rolan looked like he was asleep.

Rolan broke the silence, "Hello, Dan. Arina is having her knee explored. Doctor says he might have to cut her, but only a small scar."

"I thought you were asleep. I didn't want to wake you." Dan grabbed the chair next to the other bed, moved it next to Rolan, and sat down. Rolan looked like he had been drained of energy; starting the day worrying about being caught leaving Siberia, then worrying about crashing into a mountain, and finally worrying about getting help for his sister had worn him out. Given an opportunity, he could probably sleep soundly for twenty-four hours.

"I worry about Arina. I have no control. I try to keep her safe. I am disappointed."

Dan responded, "The accident was not your fault. I noticed you had painted on your plane that you had no radio, so no one could talk to you when you were in the snowstorm. Come with me and get something to eat downstairs in the cafeteria. They said fifteen minutes for the MRI, but that was optimistic. It's been longer than that."

The two men exited the elevator and walked to the front desk. Dan asked the receptionist, "Can you tell us if Arina Ivanov is in surgery?"

"No, Mr. Newcomb, but I can tell a family member." She smiled, looked at Rolan, and said, "She will be back in her room at 4:45 p.m. They are repairing her leg."

Dan quizzed, "How do you know me? Have we met before?"

Joan smiled and said, "I was a sophomore when you were a senior. I was at all your football games. I had a crush on you." She smiled again and held up her left hand, sporting a small diamond wedding ring. "I got over it—I'm happily married now. I know Ann, too. You are a lucky man."

Dan grinned and replied, "Thank you, Joan." The clock behind Joan read 4:17, so they had about half-an-hour to eat before returning to room 411. Dan suggested some menu items for Rolan to try, and as they ate, Dan brought up something he had been thinking about ever since he had found the downed airplane.

"Do you have more family in Siberia, Rolan?"

Rolan swallowed hard and washed his spaghetti and meatballs down with a-half-glass of milk before answering. "Yes. Mother, father, and brother, Luka—still in Provideniya."

"How did they feel when you and Arina wanted to leave?"

"They help us to get ready. Mother pack food for us. Before we go, we build iceboat so they can come to America—we think in January. We send them a letter, in code, so they know where to go, but no one else knows. We need to find how to help them."

"So, you have three more family members that are coming in an iceboat. I can't land on the ice. Let me think about it, maybe I can help."

"That would be good, Dan. Thank you. But there are five more people"

"Five? Who are the others?"

"A couple helped us with the plane and the boat: Sue and John Slwookos. They have relations on St. Lawrence Island and need to see grandmother before she dies." Rolan checked his watch and noted, "Time to see Arina."

Dan had already paid for the food, so they rode the elevator back to the fourth floor. There were three nurses, one burley male and two females, assisting the transfer of Arina from the gurney to her bed. She looked like she had been hit by a car, her left arm was in a cast and her right leg was in a brace from her thigh to her ankle, her knee bandaged, but she was talking to the nurses. The male nurse and one of the female nurses left the room and Rolan walked over to Arina, leaned over the bed, and kissed her forehead.

"How are you, Arina?"

She smiled, "Oh, I feel wonderful."

The nurse looked at Dan and said, "We gave her something for the pain—makes her happy for a while. When it wears off, we'll give her something else. We don't want to get her hooked on anything. I'll be back in thirty minutes to check on her."

"Thank you, nurse. We'll use the call button if necessary."

Arina, still smiling, looked at Dan and asked, "Are you the German?"

Rolan burst out laughing and put his hand on Arina's shoulder. "Arina, there was no German. This is Dan, the pilot that rescued us. His dog is a German shepherd."

Arina frowned and replied, "No German? I am confused. Tell me how you found us, Dan."

Dan related the entire day's activities, including Captain Sieberns' radio message about the near collision. Dan was standing next to the bed by the time he finished the story. Arina reached out with her right hand, grasped Dan's left hand and pulled him closer.

"Thank you, Dan, for saving us. Are you married?"

Rolan laughed again and stated, "Arina looks for an American husband too soon."

Dan smiled and replied, "I'm engaged to Ann Olson. We plan on getting married in December. I'm sure you will meet my fiancée. She will have many questions for you. She has a little boy; he will be interested in your cast." Dan stepped back thinking he had said too much.

Arina asked, "Will the police come for us?"

"Don't worry about the police, they don't handle these things. You will probably be granted a temporary visa. Do you have any relatives in the United States?"

Rolan hastily answered, "No."

Dan wasn't sure Rolan's answer was the truth, or whether he was trying to hide something. His quick answer could be interpreted either way.

Arina, however, had become very quiet. Dan was watching her eyes move around the room as if searching for something. He could almost hear gears turning in her pretty head. He watched as she pointed at a wall plate next to her bed and asked, "Is that for the Internet?"

Dan hadn't paid attention to the wall plug; this was the first time he had been in a patient's room. He glanced at it and answered, "Yes. Would you like me to get you a computer?"

"Please, if it is not much trouble. I have an idea, but it might be just wishful thinking."

Dan turned and walked briskly toward the hallway, and as he left the room, he said, "I'll be right back." He went to the nurse's station, but none of the computers were portable, and besides, the hospital computers were only connected to the hospital network. He placed a call on his cell phone and asked Rigs to bring his computer and a connector for the Internet to the hospital, room 411. Rigs was a little grumpy. He had just started eating, but he said he would be right over, he was only ten minutes away.

As Dan reentered Arina's room, Rolan was asking Arina to tell him why she wanted a computer. Arina said, "If it doesn't work, I don't want you to call me a moron, okay?"

Rolan grinned and replied, "You know I am the moron; you are the brain."

Arina looked at Dan and asked, disappointedly, "No computer?"

"Not yet. There is one coming in a few minutes, and a boyfriend for you, also."

"Oh, you know someone that is not married or engaged. What is his name?"

"Roy Riggins. He's a high school math and physics teacher. I call him Rigs, we used to play football together."

Arina smiled at Dan and said, "This Rigs sounds interesting. Is he a big man?"

Dan looked at and pointed at Rolan, "About Rolan's size, but not quite as tall." Dan heard footsteps in the hallway and Rigs came hesitantly into the room carrying a laptop. "Speak of the devil," Dan grinned and continued, "Hi, Rigs. I'd like you to meet Arina and Rolan Ivanov."

Arina sat up straighter, straightened her gown, and smoothed the blanket covering her legs. Rolan had stood and they shook hands, but Rigs had hardly glanced at Rolan, he was transfixed by the girl in the bed. All Rigs could say was, "Holy cow!" He couldn't seem to move, his feet seemed glued to the floor, but he repeated, "Holy cow."

"Calm down, Rigs. Arina just wants to use your computer."

Arina was starting to giggle. She extended her good arm toward Rigs and he handed her the laptop. She opened the computer and watched the screen as the computer booted. Thirty seconds later, she looked up at Rigs and said, "How do I get on the Internet, please."

Immediately, Rigs offered, "I'll show you." In order to see the display, he leaned over the bed next to Arina. He took her hand in his and showed her what to do on the touch-screen.

"Oh! So easy. Can you sit beside me?" She patted the bed, displaying a coquettish smile, encouraging Rigs to sit beside her.

Rigs was only too happy to join this ravishing young woman in bed, even though it was a hospital bed, and she was a patient. He had never been this close to a beauty pageant contestant or a Playboy Bunny; Arina qualified as either. All he had done was a simple thing, he had brought a computer to a hospital room.

Arina was trying to type, but with only one hand, she found it difficult, so she asked Rigs if he could enter what she told him.

Rigs was happy to accommodate and typed 1987 European Basketball Champions. He watched Arina move the cursor to team photos and list of players. She then selected USSR and a full screen image appeared.

"Rolan! Look! A picture of Papa when he was playing basketball!"

Rolan took the computer and studied the faces, locating his father's image in 1987, when Ivan was twenty years old.

Arina almost ripped the computer away from Rolan saying, "Please!" She squinted and studied the list of names matched with the photos and said, "Our name is Petroff, not Ivanov! Papa is Oleg Petroff!"

"Oh, thank you, Mr. Rigs." She tried to put her left arm around Rigs but realized the cast would prevent her from giving him a hug. She reached out with her light hand and squeezed his hand.

"Call me Roy, Arina. Rigs is my nick name from high school. You need to tell me why you didn't know your real name. Is it a long story?"

"No, it is a short story, but you need to help me more with the computer. Okay?"

"Sure. What can I do for you?"

"Please type in 1986 Russian Basketball Champions."

A list of items appeared on the flat-screen and Arina selected a newspaper article with a photo and list of names, all in Russian. She glanced at the photo to make sure her father was in the picture and then she began to read the article, scanning with her finger. She moved to the second page and continued reading. Rolan watched Arina's eye movements as she read rapidly through the Cyrillic write up. Rigs looked at Rolan and he shrugged and shook his head, indicating he didn't know what she was looking for.

"There! I found it!" Arina squealed with delight. "Look, Rolan, our grandma's and grandpa's names are Akilina and Sergei. This is so wonderful! I cannot believe it! I want to kiss someone. Roy, please kiss me."

Rigs didn't have time to get embarrassed or even think about it. He kissed Arina and she returned the kiss for an even longer time, much longer, than the first one. He felt like thanking her.

Rolan was also happy about the information they had found, but he thought to himself, "Why was Arina acting like a twelve-year-old? She was kissing this stranger who had been in the same room with them for less than ten minutes. What was she thinking? Maybe it was a result of all the medication she had been given. Why was she being so aggressive?"

Dan was watching the unusual display of affection, but he thought maybe it was a Russian thing. Maybe kissing wasn't such a big deal in Siberia. He began to wonder if Arina had loose morals, but maybe the drugs contributed to her actions. He lacked experience dealing with different cultures. Not many of the world's social behaviors were represented in Afghanistan, Oregon, and Alaska.

Arina sat in bed beaming with satisfaction about the names she had uncovered. Now for the biggest search of all. She looked at Rigs and commented, "I am sorry to have embarrassed you."

Rigs felt a little uncomfortable, but he wasn't sorry about the kissing. "You surprised me, Arina, but you are a good kisser. I haven't had much practice recently."

Arina smiled and replied, "Me either. My brothers scare off all the boys that want to go out with me. Please help me with one more computer search. Type in Akilina and Sergei Petroff."

Forty-one responses came up on the screen, ten at a time. Arina began scanning through the listings, but not until the third grouping of ten did she find an exact match for the names and spellings. She selected the item and it returned an address in the United States.

"Oh! Could it be? These people are the correct age." She looked at Dan and asked, "Do you know where Gresham, Oregon is?"

Dan moved so he could see the screen and said, after reading the address, "I don't believe it. I know where that is, I lived a few miles from there for six months." He looked at Arina and smiled, but she didn't smile back. Dan had seen that look before. He closed the computer and said, "Rigs, get off the bed, she's going to be sick."

Rigs slid off the edge of the bed just in time. Arina leaned forward and vomited all over the blanket covering her. Rigs called out, "Nurse! Cleanup on aisle 411." Rigs pulled the Internet connection from the wall and stepped back as a matronly nurse came rushing into the room.

"All of you! Out! This girl is not feeling well; too much excitement for one person in a day." Two more women suddenly appeared at the door: a nurse, younger and taller than the first, and a young lady, a little chubby, dressed in a blue uniform, carrying a mop and pail. "We don't need a mop, Vera, please get the linen cart. We have to give this young woman a change of clothes and bedding; I'll wash her face and hands. You men go away. Visitation is over for today; come back tomorrow—in the afternoon."

Marion Andrews, acting like a sergeant disguised as a nurse, had sent the visitors on their way. Rolan and Dan took the company truck, and Rigs met them at the duplex.

CHAPTER 30
PLANNING FOR THE IVANOVS

When the men arrived at the duplex, Beverly invited everyone over for dinner. Dan introduced Rolan to Bev, LD, and Ann, who had gotten back from Eureka around 4:30. Rolan had been adopted by the little boy and they were involved in a complex interaction on the floor in front of the TV. Rolan would build a toy castle on the floor with building blocks and LD would knock it down with his toy truck and laugh hilariously.

Rigs was holding a beer he had been nursing for a few minutes, and joined Dan, who was observing LD and Rolan. "Dan, if you had told me how gorgeous Arina was, I would have been there in about three minutes. What a knock-out! On a scale from one to ten, she's got to be an eleven."

"Look, Rigs, if I had told you what she looked like you would have probably had an accident driving to the hospital, and then we wouldn't have had a computer. I think that kiss happened because she was full of drugs. She must have been up there with the Northern Lights. I wouldn't give it much meaning if I were you. Besides, don't you like Chyler?"

"Geez, Dan, you always rain on my dogsled run." Both men laughed and Dan went to the kitchen to talk with Ann and get a beer. Rigs sat down to watch the news, or at least listen to it; Rolan was blocking the screen as he played with Larry.

During dinner, everyone had questions for Rolan, and in order to eat anything, he had to talk with his mouth full. He described how the Ivanov family and the two Slwookos had constructed an iceboat for moving across ice and water in the Bering and the Chukchi Seas. He explained how Arina was going to send a coded message so they would know when to leave Siberia in the boat. Rolan was still embarrassed by the way Arina had acted at the hospital. He said several times that Arina had never taken drugs before.

Ann asked, "Dan, did they say what medication they had given her?"

Dan replied, "The nurse I talked to said they gave her a happy pill, but she didn't give us the medical name for the drug."

Ann grinned, "Oh, tomorrow she won't remember anything she did today. The happy pill seems to erase most of recent memory or doesn't allow the brain to store much new input."

Dan remarked, "She found out the names of her father's parents; they live in Oregon, not far from the cabin where I lived. Did you write the names down or do you remember them, Rolan?"

"I have in the notebook. Arina has little book just like this." He held up a little black pad with a plastic cover.

Dan spoke with some confidence, "Since you and Arina have relatives in the US, there shouldn't be any problems getting visas."

Beverly asked Rolan, "Would you like to call them and talk on the phone?"

Rolan acted a bit uncomfortable, he hesitated a moment and said, "Maybe Arina should do that. She is better to talk to people. But thank you. I am too sleepy."

Rolan was given Dan's room for the night and Dan took the sofa. Hank left for Galena in the morning carrying a large sack of mail. Dan had called Max and found that business had been very slow the last couple of days. Dan wasn't needed at the shop; however, he would be called if necessary. Rolan and Dan spent the morning shopping; Rolan's only clothes were the things he was wearing.

Ann had talked with Hank before he flew off with the mail. He had told her to use her credit cards and he would reimburse her for anything she bought for Arina. Ann took a woman's magazine and went to the hospital to visit with Arina while the men were hunting for bargains in the downtown area. The two women looked at the fashions in the magazine and Ann marked Arina's likes and dislikes. During the hour with Arina, who admitted she did not remember much of the day before, except for the plane crash and the German, Ann explained that the Ivanov's real family name was discovered, and that her father's parents lived in Oregon. Unfortunately, Ann had not heard the names from Rolan, and if she had, she might not have remembered them. Arina would have to wait until the afternoon for the information, when Rolan and Dan would return to the hospital.

After the hospital patients had finished lunch and normal visitation hours had resumed, Rolan and Dan entered room 411. Arina was holding the channel selector, gazing at the television above the doorway as she scanned through the numerous channels. Rolan was wearing a new shirt, which Arina noticed immediately.

"Hello, Arina. How are you feeling today?" Rolan quizzed.

"Rolan, you have a new shirt. You have been shopping." She looked at Dan and said, "Who is this young man, the German?"

Rolan and Dan both smiled, having had this conversation the day before. Dan approached the bed and introduced himself, explaining about Nomah, and how he found them.

Arina's eyes shifted back to Rolan and she asked excitedly, "Tell me about the names, Rolan. Ann Olson was here and told me we found out our real family name, Papa's first name, and his parents' names."

Rolan explained how she had found the names, assisted by Roy Riggins. He didn't mention the kissing; he felt it was unnecessary to embarrass Arina after she had broken her arm and had knee surgery. After she had fully recovered, he would tell her how she had acted; maybe after the next time she called him a moron.

Dan asked Arina if she would like to phone her grandparents, now that she knew where they lived. Arina talked with Rolan for a minute before answering.

She responded, "Yes. I would like that. They will be very surprised, but before we do that, I want to think of what I will say to them. I do not believe they know Rolan and I exist."

While Arina put her thoughts together, Dan searched the Gresham, Oregon, white pages and found the number for Sergei and Akilina Petroff. He showed the number to Rolan who wrote it in his little notebook. Dan glanced at Arina and she nodded that she was ready. He gave her the phone and Rolan pointed at the number he had recorded.

Arina was able to hold the phone in her left hand and dial with the right, but as she dialed the number, Dan could see her hands were shaking. When the phone rang the first time, she pressed the speaker phone button so everyone could hear what was said.

After the third ring, Arina said, "They are not home." She looked disappointed and started to hang up, but a voice suddenly came from the phone.

"Hello."

"Is this the Sergei and Akilina Petroff home?"

There was a pause before the female voice said, "Yes. Can I help you?"

Arina smiled at Dan and Rolan and said, "I am your granddaughter, Arina Petroff, calling from Fairbanks, Alaska."

"I have no grandchildren. My son disappeared many years ago. He is dead."

"No, Grandma. He is alive and lives in Provideniya, Siberia. His name is Oleg, correct?"

The voice on the phone stuttered, "Y-Yes," and suddenly changed to sobbing. A few seconds passed, and then an agitated, resonant, male voice said, "Who is this? Why do you say these things?"

Arina had tears in her eyes now, but she repeated what she had said previously, and the man said, "Oh, my God! We were sure Oleg had died. He just disappeared. The government would not tell us what happened. How did you find us? How did you get to Alaska?"

Arina began talking in Russian and Dan could no longer follow what was said. They talked for several minutes before Rolan spoke into the phone, explaining he was the middle grandchild, Luka was still at home with Oleg and Sofiya.

The male voice changed back to English and said, "We are coming to Fairbanks. We will call this number when we have the trip arranged. It will be about a week, maybe ten days to two weeks. Thank you so much for calling, Arina. Tell your American friends thank you. We will see you before too long. Good-bye."

Arina was crying now, but was able to choke out, "Good-bye, Grandpapa." She sat quietly for a few seconds, looked up at Dan, smiled, and handed him the phone. Rolan was sitting on the edge of the bed next to Arina when the conversation in Russian had begun, and when Rolan had heard his grandfather's voice, he put his arm around Arina's shoulders. He wiped his eyes with the palm of his other hand. They were both moved by what they had heard. They had always believed they would never know any of their grandparents.

Rolan spoke excitedly to Arina, "Did you hear that voice? It sounded much like Papa's."

Dan had tears in his eyes, too. The emotions from both ends of the phone connection had caused a resurfacing of his feelings when Hank had reappeared from the remote areas of the Yukon. The emotions from the discovery that members of their families were not lost forever had surfaced and were overwhelming.

Dan was thinking ahead and commented, "We have to find a place for you to live. There will be nine of you for a short time. I think your friends will want to go to St. Lawrence Island, but we still need to find a house large enough for the Petroff family for maybe a month. Then, you will probably move to Oregon to keep your family together. You will be able to find jobs in the Portland area."

Arina said, "But Dan, we have no money and I cannot work."

Dan smiled and nodded, "Yes, I've been thinking about that. You could be a tutor at the high school or the university—probably at the university. I don't think the high school pays for tutoring. Because you were piloting the airplane, do you know anything about math or physics?"

Rolan laughed loudly. "Dan, Arina knows more about math and physics than any of the professors at the technical school in Provideniya. She is a brain."

"That's great! Rigs can take you over to the university and get you an interview with some of the professors; maybe someone will hire you—to work on their research."

Arina was frowning. "Who is this Rigs?" she asked.

"Oh, that's right, you don't remember. He brought us a computer yesterday so we could find your grandparents on the Internet. He will be here after school is out for the day—after 3:30. He teaches math and physics at the high school, and—he is not married." Dan smiled, thinking of what Arina had her mind stuck on the day before.

Arina looked at Dan quizzically, not catching on to his last comment.

Rolan asked, "But what can I do? There is no ocean here to fish."

"Rolan, my good man, you will work for my uncle, my father, and me at our repair shop. You know all about motors, correct?"

When Arina heard what Dan said, she snickered, putting her hand to her mouth. "Rolan is an expert with motors—all kinds. He can fix anything."

"All right, that settles that problem. We have jobs for you, but we need to find you a large house." Dan thought for a moment and continued, "I have a friend who might loan us a house. I will call him this evening. Oh, yes, something else. Wouldn't it be nice to have your parents and brother here when your grandparents arrive from Oregon?"

Arina responded, "Rolan and I have talked about that, but we do not think it is possible.

They cannot cross the sea in the little boat, it was made to only get them away from the mainland, not all the way to Alaska." Arina gave a heavy sigh and looked at Rolan, who had his hands folded across his chest, his head tilted forward, looking at the floor.

Dan sensed their frustration and suddenly considered that his former commanding officer, Captain Harwood, might be able to pull a few strings. Dan smiled, and trying to give them some hope, said, "I have some friends who might help us. I will call one of them tonight after I arrange for a place for you to stay when you get out of the hospital."

Arina, with tears in her eyes, reacted, "You are so nice, Dan. Why do you do these things for us? We are strangers."

Dan grinned and replied, "I guess I have a weakness for pretty girls, and their brother, who can fix motors."

Rolan smiled and said, "Am I not handsome, too?"

Arina gave Rolan a menacing look and shot back, "Rolan, Dan likes women and you are a man and a moron. Remember?" She laughed and told Dan, "Not long ago he was promoted from idiot."

Dan chuckled and asked, "Does Luka keep you two from fighting? I've always wondered what it would be like to have a brother or sister, now I know."

"We are having jokes, Dan. I love Arina; she is my little sister, but she is dumb blond."

Dan nodded and replied, "Yes, I saw how carefully you lifted her from the wreckage of the plane. I knew you were very close, but your comments surprise me sometimes."

Arina grinned and commented, "You will get used to our Russian family humor."

A nurse appeared pushing a stainless steel cart, the top shelf covered with equipment. Laura Barnes, RN, was on her name tag. She checked Arina's ID on her wrist and said, "This is for you, Arina, so we don't have to keep giving you pain medication. It is a cooling cuff for your knee, ice and compression therapy. I'll hook you up and you can adjust it by yourself. We hope to get you out of bed tomorrow evening, on crutches, of course. In two days, you can go home."

Arina frowned as she studied the apparatus. The RN told Rolan and Dan to move to the hall for a couple of minutes. Mrs. Barnes folded back the blanket and began removing the knee brace. It only took a couple of minutes to get the cooling/compression cuff in place and attached to the cold water pump. Laura showed Arina how to operate the pump, picked up the brace, and left the room. As she walked away from the room, she said, "You can go back in now."

Dan waited in the hall, checked his watch, and made a call to Rigs, who would have been between fifth and sixth periods. "Hey, Rigs, when you come to the hospital, bring the highest level math and physics books you have. I want you to evaluate Arina's competence before I take her for an interview at the university."

"Okay, be right over. I'll send my last period physics class to the library with a problem set—due tomorrow. That'll keep all eight of 'em busy. Fifteen minutes. Bye."

Arina was experimenting with the temperature controller when Dan reentered the room. Rolan had his hand over the cuff, feeling the temperature of the cold water circulating around Arina's knee. Arina looked up and said, "Feels good," and smiled.

Dan noticed Rigs was right on time, maybe a hair late, but he walked into the room carrying two thick textbooks. He was introduced to Arina by Dan, who explained that Rigs was going to ask her some technical questions. Neither Dan nor Rolan made any reference to the kissing during their previous meeting. Dan excused himself, saying he would return the next day with information about their living arrangements. He didn't want to raise false hopes, so Dan skipped mentioning the possibility of assistance from military contacts.

At the shop, Dan talked with Max about having Rolan help out. Max was agreeable as long as the job wasn't permanent. After Dan looked over the mail to be flown to Galena, he headed home to talk with Ann, Beverly, and Larry Daniel. Ann had to go to a meeting at the hospital and would miss dinner, so Dan asked Bev to bring LD over for dinner at their house. Hank and Dan would rack their brains for ideas for dinner, probably settling on pizza and beer, except for the little boy. He would get regular, wholesome food and a tiny slice of pizza.

Rigs and Rolan arrived a few minutes after six o'clock. The pizza had already been ordered. While Rolan was showering, Dan talked with Rigs.

"What's the diagnosis of Arina's abilities, Rigs?"

"I can't believe it, Dan. She is way beyond anything in those books, and they are graduate level texts. I'll bet her IQ is off the charts; her abilities are almost scary. She was pointing out all the errors in the books I had. The professors at the university are going to be surprised—maybe envious."

"Thanks for the evaluation. I'll take her over to the Physics Department first. They might be able to use her on one of their research projects."

That evening, Dan called his friend, Stu Graves, who owned the property where their landing strip was located. After the third ring, Dan recognized Stu's rough voice.

"Yeah?"

"Hi, Stu. This is Dan Newcomb. I have a quest... "

Stu interrupted, "Hey, Dan. I was going to call you tomorrow. I'm lookin' for someone to watch after my spread while I'm in Texas meetin' with investors. I'll be gone 'til Christmas."

"I have some people that would work out perfectly, Stu. It's a Russian family—just here from Siberia. They need a place to stay for a month or so."

"Russians? You trust 'em?"

"Yep! They're good people, looking for a new start."

"Sounds like we got a deal. Bring 'em out and we'll draw up a contract."

"How do I find your place, Stu?"

"Take Route 3 to Ester. There's a sign at the post office pointing to my place. Ya can't miss it; it's a big house—made a logs—green metal ruff."

"Thanks, Stu. It will be a couple of days; one of them has a bum knee; she can't travel right now."

"Okay. I'll be here a waitin'. I'm stackin' up my firewood. I'll be leaving for Dallas next week. See ya, Daniel."

Dan went in the living room to talk with Rolan, but Rigs and Rolan were playing chess, so he just sat and watched, waiting for an opportunity to tell Rolan he had found the Petroffs a house. As the game progressed, both men were studying the board intensely, but little change in positions had been made for nearly ten minutes. Dan went into his room and made another call.

Dan was calling San Diego, an hour ahead of Alaskan time. It was 9:07 in southern California when the phone rang. Dan heard two rings and then a woman's voice, "Hello, Harwood residence."

"Hello, Mrs. Harwood. Is the Captain in? This is Dan Newcomb."

The female voice said, "Yes, I'll call him." Dan could hear, "Lee, it's for you. He said it's Dan Newcomb."

In less than five seconds, Dan heard, "Hello, soldier. How's it going?"

"Fine, Sir. How are you?"

"Washington's got me doing the same old crap, son. How can I help you?"

"I do need some help, but I don't know if you can swing it. Let me tell you a story."

Dan related Arina's and Rolan's flight to Alaska and their desire to bring the rest of their family and two friends to Alaska. Dan had talked for about five minutes before Harwood asked,

"How soon do you think the Petroffs will be ready to take their boat across the ice?"

"Well, Sir, it will take about a week to get a letter to them in Provideniya and another day for them to get to the boat and start across the ice."

"Hmm. Dan, I'll have to work on it. I'll call you back as soon as I can get the mission planned. It might take a couple of days to grease some palms, but I'll see what I can do."

"Thanks, Captain. Let me know if I can ever help you."

"I'll do that. Take care, Dan. Talk to you later."

"Bye, Sir. Thank you."

CHAPTER 31
MISSIONS

Friday was overcast, but Dan was to fly to Galena with the mail early in the morning and return before noon. Average daylight times for November in Fairbanks were less than eight hours, so early risers woke up to dark skies. Rolan was sleeping soundly so Dan cooked a couple of eggs, some bacon, and ate some pancakes smothered in real butter and maple syrup. At a quarter to seven, he tapped on Ann's door. She had asked him to say goodbye when he left, but there was a problem, he couldn't take the truck; Rolan needed it to get to work.

As Ann was opening the door, rubbing her right eye with her fist, she smiled, and said, "I'll bet you need a ride. I'll get my coat and the car keys and be right with you. Come in, it's only two degrees outside. I don't want you to freeze anything." She grinned as she pulled on her boots, slipped into her parka, and grabbed the keys from the peg next to the door. "Let's go, Daniel."

"Wait a minute!" Dan grabbed her around the waist and kissed her, smiled, and said, "I was afraid to kiss you outside—our lips might get stuck together. Then you'd have to go with me. It would be difficult to fly until we thawed out."

Ann laughed and replied, "That wouldn't take long, would it? You know, you're always a little goofy after you have pancakes—must be a spike in your blood sugar. Hmm, I believe I taste maple syrup."

It took about ten minutes to get to the airstrip; snow still remained in some low spots along the unimproved road to the airstrip, but the tires weren't slipping. Few lights illuminated the roadway. Ann dropped off Dan and drove back to the duplex. The city streets were clear of snow and traffic appeared to be normal for an early Friday morning.

The approaching weekend with two days' relaxation in warm surroundings was normally anticipated, but not for Ann. Saturday, she was on call, and Sunday, she was going to help Dan get Arina and Rolan

217

settled at Stu Graves' ranch house. She wondered if his cabin was going to be a dump. She had seen Stu a couple of times and he resembled a partially shaved bear wearing overalls, although a bear might smell better. But Dan had said Stu was a nice guy; you had to get to know him. Dan once mentioned he wanted to take Stu to a car wash and give him a bath, but then Dan laughed, saying all the dirt might clog the sewers.

When Ann returned to the duplex, Beverly was getting breakfast and Rolan had been invited over. Rolan was talking to LD, telling the two-year-old the Russian words for items on the table. LD would say, "No," and then say the English word when he knew it. When LD tried to say the Russian words, Rolan laughed and said, "Good try!" Ann was thinking Rolan would make a good babysitter. Not a bad idea; LD would learn a second language.

Rolan went to work and Ann helped Bev clean both sides of the duplex. Dan got back from Galena at eleven-thirty, just in time for lunch. He had transferred the mail to Hank's plane, had a cup of coffee and a doughnut, told Hank about contacting Captain Harwood, and flew back to Fairbanks. The round-trip had taken just under four hours.

After having lunch with Beverly, Ann and Dan took LD to the hospital to meet Arina. Ann took two sweaters, two pairs of pants, and a new, red parka for Arina to look at. Unfortunately, Arina was not able to try on the clothing, the cast and the knee brace presented obstructions. They were confident she could get the parka on, but she would have to be standing, so they would wait 'til Sunday. She would begin walking, with the assistance of nurses, Saturday morning.

Arina was pleased with the new clothes, and thanked Ann profusely, but she was more interested in LD. He tried to climb on the bed, so Dan placed him beside Arina so he could see the cast and the strange object on her right knee. He had to touch the cast and the cuff, and when he found the cuff was cold, he wanted Arina to take it off. Ann explained to the toddler that the cuff was to make Arina's knee better. Arina said something to LD in Russian and he reacted with "No!" Arina was surprised, so she repeated her words in English and LD smiled.

Dan told Arina about Stu Graves' log cabin outside of town and she and Rolan would be taken there on Sunday. She would be able to get around on crutches and would also have a wheelchair, rented for a month from a medical supply company.

LD was getting bored and starting to slap at Arina's cast, so Dan put him down and he walked over to Ann, who asked, "Do you want to go home?" LD nodded, walked to the chair where his coat was piled, pulled it off the chair, and dragged it across the floor to Ann.

"Well, I guess we know where we're going," Ann smiled. "I had hoped he would have lasted a little longer, but we'll see you again on Sunday, Arina."

Ann was getting her parka when a nearly bald man, about sixty years old, appeared at the doorway to room 411. A little taller than Dan, wearing glasses, a red-plaid shirt, and khaki pants, he sported a large silver-and-gold belt buckle in the shape of a bear.

He leaned into the room and inquired, "Miss Petroff?"

Arina frowned and answered, "Yes?"

The man stepped into the room and approached the bed, extending his right hand. "I'm Professor James Wheaton from the university. A friend of yours, Roy Riggins, told me I should come and see you about working for me on my atmospheric research projects. Do you mind if I take a few minutes?"

"I do not mind, Professor. These are my friends, Dan, Ann, and LD."

The professor shook hands with Ann and Dan and he got on one knee and shook hands with LD. "It's nice meeting you. Are you leaving? I don't want to run you off."

Dan said, "We were just leaving; the little guy is getting tired. We probably won't understand anything you talk about anyway, so we'll take off now. It was nice meeting you, Professor. We'll see you tomorrow, Arina." Dan picked up LD and they left the room.

Arina smiled, gave them a little wave, said "Bye," and asked the professor to sit down.

Max began receiving customers' calls at seven o'clock Saturday morning. Dan, Rolan, and Max were kept busy all day at the shop. Customers were frantic, they had to have things fixed for Thanksgiving, which was the following Thursday. Without Rolan's able assistance, Max and Dan would have been overwhelmed.

While the men were busy with repairs, Mona Conley, Bev, Ann, and LD went shopping to buy everything they needed for Thanksgiving. Bev used Hank's credit card, but limited expenses to those absolutely necessary for eleven people. She had estimated LD as only half that of an adult, but Ann reminded her about Rolan, who would probably eat enough for one and a half adults. They would spend Thanksgiving at the Conley's, the only house large enough to accommodate all members of four families.

Sunday started slowly; the north wind brought a wind chill of minus eighteen degrees. No one but the old-timers wanted to go outside unless they absolutely had to. It was one of those days that Dan had once described as being unable to hear what someone else was saying; the words froze in the air. By noon the wind had lessened somewhat, and activity began to increase throughout the city.

Early that afternoon, Arina was given a ride around the hospital in a wheelchair, and after she was used to sitting and motion, she was given crutches and escorted up and down the halls with a nurse on each side. The first journey was slow and clumsy, but the second transit down the hallway was much easier; she had gotten into the rhythm of moving with the aid of crutches. She surprised her nurses by adjusting to being ambulatory so quickly. Ann had called the hospital and asked about Arina and found the doctors had discharged her after the nurses and a physical therapist had given her instructions. She was waiting to be picked up.

Ann took Bev's car and drove to the hospital; Dan and Rolan followed in the company pickup. Arina, with help from the nurses, had dressed in new clothing Ann had brought to the hospital. The sweater was loose enough to fit over the cast and the knee brace was placed over her pants. Near the entrance, Arina was sitting in a wheelchair reading papers from a file folder when the team arrived, her new parka was on the bench beside her. She could feel the cold through the windows and could see the condensation of moisture from exhaled air as people approached the building.

She saw Rolan first, then Ann and Dan. When they entered the building, she smiled and asked, "What took you so long?"

Rolan grinned and answered, "I had to get army to come for you, dear sister. I found pilot, nurse, and I am chauffeur, Lady Arina. Shall we go?"

Arina stood up and reached for her parka, but Rolan grabbed her arm to make sure she didn't fall. Dan picked up the parka and helped her into it as Rolan steadied her.

Dan stated, "Okay, Ann and you will follow Rolan and me. We are going to your new home. Don't be surprised if it is a messy little cabin. We will help you clean it up. Let's go."

It took nearly fifteen minutes to arrive at Ester and another five to find Stu Graves' cabin. When they arrived at a substantial log structure two-stories-high with a highly pitched roof, surrounded by a covered deck, Dan stopped the pickup, got out, and walked over to Ann's car. He had watched Ann park a few feet to the right of his truck; engine running. Dan leaned toward Ann's window, which she had lowered about an inch, and said, "I'm going to ask for directions. I'll be right back."

Ann quickly put the window up and the two women waited, watching Dan climb the stairs to the front of the chateau. Using the knocker, a metal moose head casting, Dan rapped twice on the large front door. A moment later, the door opened, and Dan stepped into the building. In less than a minute, he reappeared, descended the steps, and jogged over to Ann's vehicle.

She lowered her window and said, "Where do we go from here?"

Dan was nearly laughing, "I don't believe it, but Stu lives here."

Ann's eyes widened and her jaw dropped in surprise, "Really?"

"Yeah! I'll get Rolan to carry Arina up the stairs, you and I will get the wheelchair. Stu said to come on in."

The interior of the home was beautiful, not short of fantastic, it was fantastic. The great room had a massive fireplace of river rock with a mantel at least twelve feet wide and a foot deep. It was a log, roughly cut with a chainsaw, sanded, and coated with varnish so the surface looked like it was covered in glass.

When Ann stepped inside, she was in heaven. She gazed around and exclaimed, "Wow!"

Rolan and Arina were dumbstruck, all they could do was look around and point to the furniture and highly-polished hardwood flooring. They had never been exposed to such a home, and they suddenly realized they were going to live there. It was far beyond their imaginations. Now they knew what it was like to have fine things in the United States.

Rolan commented, "Listen, Arina! The music of Tchaikovsky!"

A booming voice from the second floor said, "Welcome to my home. Please make yourselves comfortable. Take off your coats. Dan, there is a large closet to the right of the front door. Is it warm enough for you? Can I get you something to drink, or eat?"

Stu Graves descended the steps to the living room and walked toward his guests. Even taller than Rolan, he extended his hand and introduced himself to Arina and Rolan, having met Ann and Dan before. If Ann had walked past Stu on the street, she wouldn't have recognized him. He was clean shaven and dressed in a white dress shirt and a mahogany-brown tie, brown slacks, and brown shoes. He looked like a banker or the head of a chain of large department stores.

Dan was still somewhat shocked, having encountered the transformed Stu a few minutes before the others. He was wondering about the dramatic changes that had occurred. Stu was speaking as an educated, highly intelligent man, not as an unkempt, uneducated, swearing gold miner.

Stu had recognized the surprise exhibited by Ann when he came down from the balcony. He began explaining, "I have a master's degree in theater arts, so I am acting when I do a job such as gold mining. Your expressions tell me that I have done a good job. Maybe someday I will get an award." He laughed heartily and said, "Come on, I'll show you around—upstairs first."

Rolan picked up Arina and carried her to the balcony. Ann handed her the crutches and they all followed Stu as he showed them the bedrooms and study. The media station in the study had shelves sporting a large collection of CDs, all sorted by artist, given a number and listed on a computer at his desk. Swan Lake was playing, so he showed them how to run the system to select other Tchaikovsky music. He had put Swan Lake on after Dan had come to the front door. He picked up a remote and shut off the music.

The library was stocked with numerous books, and he admitted to have only read a small number of them. He confessed to having an eclectic taste in books, when an idea came to mind, he would order books, but sometimes never get around to reading them, the idea remaining fallow for an indefinite time.

The master bedroom had a fireplace, a wet bar, a walk-in closet, and a large spa-like bathroom. The shower was enormous with plenty of room for bathing the physique of a pro-football lineman, which accurately described Stu.

The ground floor was full of treasures, from an African safari to Native American weapons and beaded clothing. Another fifteen minutes and the tour was complete. Stu went outside with Rolan and showed him the fireplace wood, the emergency generator, and the pickup they could use while Stu was away. When Stu and Rolan reentered the house, Stu sat down with them and said, "I will be leaving in the morning and you will be on your own. You may investigate and use anything—just don't burn the house down. You'll have to buy some groceries and if any bills show up, just toss them on my desk in the study; I'll take care of those things when I return. I'll be gone at least four weeks. Are there any questions?"

Arina and Rolan looked at each other, back at Stu, and then shook their heads. Arina said, "Thank you very much Mr. Graves. We will take care of your things as if they were our own—we will be very careful. Oh, there is one question, sir. Do we get a key?"

Stu reached into his pocket and pulled out some loose keys. He selected two of them and gave one to Arina and one to Rolan and then commented, "The pickup key is in the ignition—I leave it there all the time. No one will steal it; it's not worth anything. Will you be staying the night?"

Arina answered, "We have all our things at Dan's home. We will come back tomorrow."

"Okay. You youngsters have fun here and don't worry about anything. Enjoy your stay." Stu looked at Arina and Rolan and said, "It was nice meeting you—and seeing you and Ann again, Dan."

Dan stood and shook hands with Stu and thanked him for everything. Just as they were walking toward the door, Dan's phone rang.

"Hello? Oh, it's you, Captain." Dan listened and said, "Just a minute, Sir. I'll get a pen and paper."

Stu fished a pen from his shirt pocket, handed it to Dan, and motioned toward the entrance table where there was a pad of paper.

"All right, Sir, give me the information." Ann watched Dan write down a series of numbers which meant nothing to her. She looked at the others with a frown and shrugged her shoulders, not knowing what was transpiring.

"Thank you, Captain. I owe you. Goodbye."

As soon as Dan got off the phone, he informed the others, "That was my old commanding officer, Captain Harwood. He has arranged for your family to be picked up, Arina."

Arina grabbed Rolan and they hugged each other. Arina wiped tears from her eyes and exclaimed, "That is wonderful!" Arina gave Ann a hug, too, and then Arina turned to Dan and asked, "When can we mail the letter?"

Dan was smiling and said, "You write the letter tonight. I will fly it to Nome tomorrow."

CHAPTER 32

CELEBRATIONS

That evening, Arina and Rolan composed a letter to their parents, containing the geographic position and time for the rescue of the Petroffs and the Slwookos. It was addressed to Arina and Rolan Ivanov, as they had planned before they left for Alaska. If one of the two had been injured, they would send the letter addressed to the uninjured one, but Arina didn't want her parents to worry, so she indicated that both of them were fine.

But left-handed Arina could not actually write the letter, her arm was in a cast, her fingers held too rigidly to manipulate a pen or pencil, so Rolan wrote what Arina dictated. Rolan wrote a return address on the letter, a real location in Nome that Dan had gotten from a map of the city. Dan was going to Galena to relieve Hank the next day, Monday. Dan would carry the letter to Nome and drop it in the outgoing mail at the post office after affixing the appropriate stamps.

The morning after Arina and Rolan had prepared the letter, Ivan, back in Provideniya, had begun to worry. Daily walks to the postal station in Provideniya were taken to check their box for mail from Alaska. Deep down, he knew it was too soon to expect any mail to arrive so soon, but Sofiya had encouraged him to investigate to lessen their anxieties. Actually, he longed to make the journey to be the first to see evidence that his younger children's flight had been successful. His greatest desire was to see both their names on the address. He had no idea that the letter was on its way to St. Lawrence Island and from the island to the mainland and Provideniya.

Ivan noticed he was being watched at the station on the second day's journey to pick up the mail. He had dialed the combination lock: right to two, left past two to thirty-two, and right to twenty. He extracted three envelopes, but none was the one he was watching for.

As he glanced at the envelopes, he noticed a reflection from the window of an adjacent box; a man, partly hidden by another bank of mailboxes, seemed to be watching him.

He closed his box and spun the dial, put the mail into his shirt pocket beneath his sweater, and buttoned his heavy parka. The man stepped back from view as Ivan turned away from his box and began moving toward the door. Since Ivan had matured, he had never been afraid of another man. Ivan stood over two meters in height and weighed 118 kilos. As he passed the corner of the other bank of boxes, he stepped to the side, turned, and grabbed the man's coat under his chin with both hands, and lifted him off the ground, pushing the figure up against the wall of boxes.

"Why are you watching me?" he asked menacingly.

"Oh! Hello, Mr. Ivanov. I did not see you." It was that little military shit, Dimitri, obviously lying.

When Ivan realized who it was, he dropped Dimitri to the ground and straightened the man's rumpled clothing. "Sorry, Captain, I thought you were someone else."

"Do not worry, Mr. Ivanov. How are your young people in Moscow? I have always liked them. How is your daughter?"

Ivan wanted to tell Dimitri he was too old and ugly to interest Arina and to stay away from her or he would suffer the repercussions of a protective father and her brothers, but Arina was now out of reach of this turd, and Ivan did not want to irritate Dimitri. A mad military man could retaliate with ruthless measures. Ivan smiled and answered, "We have not heard from them yet. They went to Vladivostok to take the train all the way to Moscow. It will take at least a week, maybe longer, before we hear from them. Perhaps they will send a postcard from one of the train stops."

"I have always wanted to ask you, my friend, did you ever play basketball?"

"No, Captain. When I was a youngster, I was not coordinated, so I studied most of the time. I liked mathematics and chemistry. Mendeleev was from Tobolsk. Did you know that?"

Dimitri shook his head. "No. I never met him. Where did you go to school?"

Ivan almost laughed. Mendeleev devised the periodic table and died in 1907, but Ivan let it go. He didn't want to embarrass Dimitri. Ivan almost said where he had gone to school, but he remembered his birthplace on his most recent papers, and said, "A private school in the outskirts of Tobolsk; my father worked in the oil industry." He figured it would take Dimitri many days to check his story, so he was not worrying about telling lies. By the time Dimitri found out that Ivan had never attended school in Tobolsk, all of the Ivanovs would be in Alaska; at least that is what he hoped.

"It has been enjoyable talking to you, Captain, but I have to get to work. Maybe I will see you some other time. Good day, Sir."

Ivan turned to go through the door, and he heard Dimitri say, "Tell your daughter hello for me."

"Yes, I will do that," Ivan answered. Ivan walked to the market thinking Dimitri must have become suspicious of the Ivanovs, and the next time Ivan saw his daughter, they would laugh about Dimitri and his vain attempts to attract Arina's interest. From now on, Ivan would be on the alert for Dimitri, or some other government stooge, watching from the shadows.

When he reached the market, everyone was waiting to see the mail. He told of his meeting with Dimitri and how all five of the travelers must take some rides on the Maligin V to establish a routine set of behaviors. Tomorrow, they would all go for an hour's trip outside of the harbor to the south to fish, or make it appear that is what they are doing. They would place a sign in the window of the market saying they will open at two in the afternoon instead of the normal one o'clock time. Every other day, they would repeat the behavior until the letter arrived. Then some adjustments to the routine might be made until they would be off to cross the sea.

As they watched the calendar, the days seemed to drag by, but the trips in the Maligin V helped break the monotony and they brought back a few fish. Sue was not able to go on the second trip; she had to be at the airport to sell ivory carvings. That was her primary job and she did not want to change that part of her routine. On the twenty-eighth of November, Sofiya noted that it was Thanksgiving in America, November 27, so they celebrated with a thanksgiving of their own, thankful, not just for what they had, but for the future to be within their grasp. If everything went as planned, they would be leaving Siberia very soon and starting a new life in the United States.

With help from Beverly and Ann, Mona Conley had begun preparing a special Thanksgiving meal, beginning by baking breads and rolls on the twenty-fifth. Arina went shopping with Mona and was surprised to find the wide selection of cheeses available. Among other things, Mona bought cheese and butter, in larger than normal quantities, suggested by Arina.

After Dan returned from Galena on Wednesday, he drove to Stu's house to talk to Rolan and Arina. He was curious to see if they had adjusted to living in a mansion and he wanted to tell them when and where he had mailed their letter to Provideniya. The postal clerk in Nome mentioned that the mail would reach its destination within a week, just as Arina and Rolan had said. Dan also wanted to be sure the Petroffs knew they were invited for Thanksgiving at the Conleys'.

"Thank you for mailing our letter, Dan. Mona told us to come over in the early afternoon for the Thanksgiving feast. We will be there."

"You're welcome. There is one more thing I need to tell you, Arina."

Arina looked concerned and asked, "What? Should we know something about the manners?"

Dan grinned and replied, "The Conleys have two boys and they will be staring at you all day. A pretty girl is like candy they want but can't have."

Arina smiled and then began to laugh. "I understand. I will not encourage them."

"Okay, I'll see both of you tomorrow. Bye." As Dan got into the truck, he smiled as he imagined how Duke and Earl were going to react when Arina came to the Conleys' home for Thanksgiving. He was predicting that something embarrassing was bound to happen, and it would be very funny. On the way home, Dan delivered the mail from Galena to the main post office.

Thursday morning was a busy time for Mona and Beverly, they had prepared a dinner like never before, primarily in honor of Arina and Rolan; it was their first American Thanksgiving, and the older ladies wanted everyone to remember it. The ladies wanted Hank to propose a toast, so they suggested what he might say, but what he actually said was much more stimulating and powerful. Dan had never been so proud of his father and when Hank concluded his thoughts, there was complete silence—and then everyone applauded. When the clapping started, accompanied by some bravos, the sudden noise scared Larry Daniel and he started to cry.

Arina stood, her eyes full of tears, went over to Hank, and hugged him, then she turned toward everyone else and thanked them for a wonderful Thanksgiving and for all they had done to make Rolan's and her adjustments to the United States so smooth.

Rolan was not to be left out. He stood, raised his glass of wine and said, "Arina has said more than I could, but I must also give you my thanks." He stood there, a little embarrassed, and then after taking a gulp of wine, followed with, "The wine is very good—and the company, too."

CHAPTER 33
TRIP TO THE INLET

The week following Thanksgiving passed quickly for the Petroff brother and sister in Alaska. Arina began working for Professor Wheaton at the computer center on Monday, the first of December, interpreting the results of complex mathematical modeling of atmospheric disturbances related to sunspot activity. Rolan drove Arina to the campus in the morning, worked all day at the repair shop, and picked her up on campus in the evening to return to Stu's chateau for dinner and a night of relaxation.

Arina was totally absorbed in her work and brought some of it home so she would stay busy, spending less time worrying about her parents, Luka, and the Slwookos making their way across the frozen sea. They were to leave the coast of Siberia on the fifth of December and cross the International Dateline at ten o'clock in the morning, arriving a few minutes later on the 4th of December in United States waters at one in the afternoon, where they were to be picked up and flown to Nome. Dan and Hank were going to fly to Nome in the morning of the fourth and wait for them to be delivered by the Coast Guard. Then they would fly the Petroffs and the Slwookos to Fairbanks.

It was December 3, and as usual, Ivan arrived at the postal station in the early morning. The building was dark except for the entryway, where a single bulb hung down from the ceiling, and the yellowish hallway lights illuminated the mailboxes. Ivan removed his gloves, cupped his hands, and blew on his fingers to warm them. He looked through the little glass window on box 452 where there was one envelope, face down. Was this the letter from Arina and Rolan?

He hurried to open the mailbox but made a mistake with the combination and had to start over. His fingers trembled as he carefully turned the dial pointing at the numbers. With the door open, he pulled out the envelope with his big fingers and turned it over. It was the letter!

Both names were on the address, so he knew Rolan and Arina were safe. He decided to let Sofiya open the letter, so he folded the envelope, slipped it into his pants pocket, and turned to leave the post office. As he approached the foyer, he suddenly remembered, in his excitement, he had not shut the mailbox. He retraced his steps, pushed the mailbox door shut, heard the click, and spun the dial. He pushed open the heavy door and went into the cold and jammed his hands to the bottoms of his pockets.

Sofiya was watching through the front window, wondering if today would be the day for the letter to arrive. When she saw Ivan on his way home, she moved beside the door, ready to open it to get Ivan in from the cold. She watched as Ivan, several meters from the door, smiled and reached into his pocket, pulling out a folded envelope, waving it as he approached the door.

As soon as the door was open, she asked excitedly, "Is that the letter?"

"Yes. It has a United States stamp and is addressed to Arina and Rolan. They are both all right."

"But, Ivan, what does it say?"

"Here, you open it." Ivan gave the envelope to Sofiya, who tore it open and looked intently at the writing.

"This is Rolan's writing. Arina must have hurt her left hand or she would have written it. I hope she is all right."

"She must be, or the letter would not have been addressed to both of them." Ivan called out, "Luka! Come look at the letter. You know the code better than we do."

Luka hurried from his bedroom in his stocking feet, with one hand holding up his pants, and reached for the letter. He squinted in the dimly lit room and slowly read the note. He stood looking at the paper for a moment and said, "We have to leave early on the fifth of December. I will show John the position where we will be met on the ice. Both of us should know where we are to be." He gave the letter to Ivan, finished sticking his shirt into his pants, and buckled his belt. "Oh, I just remembered. I must return a book to instructor Gamov before we leave. I will do that tomorrow."

The evening before leaving Provideniya for the last time, Sofiya was cleaning up the kitchen, getting ready for the next, and last, morning in the home she, Ivan, and their three children had occupied for the last twelve years. She rinsed the washcloth and hung it up to dry just as she had done thousands of times before. She leaned against the counter next to the sink and sighed, looking around at all the familiar objects residing on the walls and counter tops. She reached toward the thermometer next to the window and then quickly pulled her hand back, remembering what Ivan had said: "Do not take anything unnecessary. Leave all but the clothes you are wearing on the trip and the food." That little thermometer had been a part of every kitchen since before the birth of Luka, twenty-five years ago. As Sofiya began preparing lunches for the trip, she thought to herself, "I wish I could tell Mrs. Glinka that she can have all my things, but I must not even leave her a note."

Ivan joined her in the kitchen and asked, "What can I help you with, Sofiya?"

She looked at Ivan and asked, "How many sandwiches should I prepare? How long will we be on the ice?" She appeared a bit apprehensive; she held the knife tightly in one hand and the loaf of bread in the other but had not yet attempted to slice it. "I do not want to worry, Ivan, but I cannot help it. We are leaving our entire life behind."

"I think two for each man and one for each woman; eight in all. We should not be on the ice more than a few hours if everything goes as planned." He smiled reassuringly and continued, "If I know Arina, she will have taken care of everything—leaving nothing to chance. Luka and I will take care of you. Do not worry. But we will need something strong to drink. I will make some strong tea early in the morning. We will take it in those insulated army bottles. Luka said there is some climbing, so take us something for quick energy."

"Can I take my new blouse? I have not worn it yet."

Ivan knew Arina had given the blouse to Sofiya. It was special. He answered quickly, "Yes, but don't carry it like baggage, put it on and wear it under your sweater. Tell Sue she can only take her regular clothes. She will have to leave everything else; no extra baggage."

Sofiya was trying to be upbeat and smiled slightly at Ivan. "Can I leave a note about the market for the Fins? They do not know anything about the fishing. Will they find the boat?"

Ivan could tell Sofiya had forced a smile. "I am sorry, Sofiya. We cannot leave any notes. They will have to figure things out for themselves. We will leave the boat on shore not far from the iceboat, maybe they will find it. If not, some fisherman will find it and return it to Provideniya. Everyone around here knows our boat. We do not want to help anyone look for us. We want it to look like we are coming back after our outing along the coast."

He gave Sofiya a hug and said, "If you do not need my help, I will get ready for bed. I have talked to Luka and John about tomorrow. Do not take much more time in the kitchen—we need to get some rest tonight. We must go to the Maligin V at two o'clock in the morning."

Sofiya extended her arm across the bedding to see if Ivan was there, but all she felt was cool blankets; Ivan was already up, he had been for some time. She blinked her eyes and looked at the clock: one-eleven in the morning—time to get ready for travelling. There was no time for slippers, she left them beside the bed, pulled on two pairs of woolen socks, her ski pants, her new blouse and a heavy sweater. When she got to the kitchen, Ivan was cracking eggs, had started tea, and had placed a brick of cheese on the counter.

Ivan said, "Good morning," as he leaned down to kiss her cheek.

"Good morning. You got up early," she replied, as she tried to get her arms around his waist for a hug.

"Yes, I could not sleep. I have been worrying about the iceboat. I hope it is strong enough for five people. Maybe the ice will be smooth, and we will make good time."

Sofiya began slicing cheese for breakfast and snacks, and said, "It is too late to worry, dear. I am sure your children made a good boat."

Ivan laughed, "Ah, they are my children if something might go wrong, they are your children if they do something great."

Sofiya laughed in return, "You scoundrel! You know what I mean. Are the others up?"

"They are getting their things in piles in the other room. As soon as we eat, we will drive to the Maligin V."

Luka was the only one to say much as they ate, warning the ladies about the climb from the shore to the top of the plateau. The Maligin V would be abandoned at the shoreline. John and Sue listened, but were not concerned; they had made many such climbs before, but only once in the dark. Sofiya was not worried about herself, but she was a little uneasy about Ivan and Luka because of their size. She imagined they were going to be a bit clumsy.

After piling the dirty dishes in the sink, Sofiya joined the others in the living room as they donned their outdoor clothing and stuffed extra socks into their pockets. Each traveler carried a bag of food, but nothing else, except for Ivan, who also carried two canisters of hot tea, and John, who had a rifle, and in addition, a small leather pouch filled with cartridges attached to his waist. They climbed into the truck and began the cold, dark drive through the deserted city streets to the pier. As they approached the last turn to the dock, a delivery truck passed them leaving the pier. Ivan had to shield his eyes from the bright truck lights. Two hundred meters later, Ivan stopped, turned off the engine, and left the key in the ignition. He had decided the previous evening that anyone wanting the truck was welcome to it.

As soon as they were in the Maligin V, Luka started the engine and piloted the boat out of the harbor and into the ocean, turning to port and following the coast northward. Without much light except from the nearly full moon, Luka and Ivan relied on the sounds of the surf and adjusted to keep from grounding the boat. They traveled for nearly two hours shadowing the rocky coastline before encountering continuous ocean ice, making travel by boat impossible. Having beached the Maligin V, they climbed the rocky slope to the top of the plateau where they rested for a few minutes while having cookies and tea, before setting off across the almost barren tableland.

John took the lead, setting a pace both women could follow without undue effort, followed by Sue, Ivan, Sofiya, and Luka. Snowy areas were avoided for fear of turning ankles on hidden rocks and voids beneath the white covering. After two hours of monotonous hiking across the rock-strewn landscape, they stopped for a ten-minute break.

Sofiya asked, "How much longer, John? I am getting tired; my legs are sore."

John climbed a nearby rock outcropping and, after shielding his eyes and scanning to the north, answered, "I think about an hour more; about four kilometers. But we must continue to move; if your legs cool off, they might cramp. Then Ivan and Luka would have to carry you." John looked back at Sue; she smiled and nodded; she was ready to go. John turned north and resumed his previous pace, angling toward the coastline into a slight breeze.

Luka was the first to notice familiar territory. Thirty-five minutes after their last stop for rest, he could see the tops of the trees where the plane had been concealed. He yelled ahead to Sofiya and Ivan, "We are almost there, I recognize this area: ten more minutes."

John yelled back at the others, "Luka is correct, we will be at the iceboat in fifteen minutes, but we still have to climb down to sea level."

Sofiya wondered if she were the only one desiring to be in the boat, resting her tired legs, and skimming across the ice. It had been so many years since she had trained as a world-class athlete, she had forgotten the feelings, both mental and physical, of those long days of training her muscles to remember how to react during competition on that ten-centimeter-wide balance beam. Fortunately, those days were in the distant past.

They arrived at the edge of the plateau and looked down onto the completely frozen inlet. Just as Sofiya was about to ask where the iceboat was, she began to recognize the structure, though indistinct, of the boat that Luka had sketched, quite effectively camouflaged with netting and difficult to perceive in the shadows of the inlet walls.

Luka had picked up a length of rope from beneath the trees and made a loop in one end. He threw the line over the edge of the plateau and said, "You first, Papa. John and I will hold you."

Ivan showed no reluctance, turning his back to the dark inlet's open air and backing down the incline to the bottom. When he reached bottom, he gave a slight tug on the rope. Sofiya began descending, much faster than Ivan had. She had less weight to lower and she was confident that, if she slipped, Ivan would catch her. Sue followed before Sofiya had reached the bottom, and when Sue yelled up from below, John disappeared over the edge into the darkness of the inlet as Luka braced himself to hold the rope.

"Okay, Luka. Be careful, go slowly." John had yelled from below, knowing no one was holding the rope for his friend.

Luka decided to go down the slope with his stomach near the rocky surface. In case he began to slide he could drop his body quickly to arrest the uncontrolled movement, but he slipped slightly only once, causing him to hold his breath for a moment, but reached the others without a scratch. With everyone safely at the bottom of the inlet, Luka looked above his head and said, "Look up into the sky, the northern lights are beautiful." The green curtains were dancing, almost as if a stage performance had ended and the cast was bustling behind the curtains, brushing into the drapes, getting into position for a group bow, to acknowledge applause from the theater audience.

Suddenly, there was a moving light that caused them to squint to see who was holding the source. John said, "Do not be surprised, I brought us a secret weapon. It is a small diode lamp that I bought at the tourist counter at the airport. I thought we might need it if we had no moonlight. "

Sofiya commented, "The light scared me for a moment. I pictured Dimitri discovering our plan and arresting us. He would take us to prison."

John turned off the light and was apologetic. "I guess I should have mentioned it, but if the light was used too soon, I feared the batteries would run out. Then we would have no light but the moon for travelling on the ice. Clouds might end our trip too early."

Luka spoke up, "We need to get the netting off the boat and get the engine started. John, lead the way with your light so we do not fall."

The netting was not removed with ease. It was larger than the boat and had sagged into the water and frozen. Using his lamp, John found the hammer and chipped the ice away from the edge of the boat, freeing the netting and the boat from the ice covering the surface of the inlet. John yelled at Luka to flip the propeller. As he had done with the airplane, Luka gave the propeller a giant tug. The engine coughed but did not start, the prop had rotated only once. "Try again!" John yelled after making some adjustments to the engine.

Sofiya yelled, "You be careful, Luka!" She grabbed Sue's arm and squeezed. Sue reached over and held onto Sofiya's parka.

This time, the engine started, slowly at first, and then the propeller rotated faster and faster until the blades were only a blur in the dim light from John's little lamp. John yelled above the whine of the engine, "Get in ladies!"

Luka guided Sofiya and Sue onto the ice at the port side of the boat where they walked gingerly across the ice to the craft, climbed in, and sat down. Luka told Ivan to get on the starboard side of the boat and push when John revved the engine. Luka got into position on the port side and motioned to John. John gave full power to the engine and, with the push assisting, the boat climbed from the water onto the ice and began to slide slowly forward. Luka yelled at his father, "Get in, Papa. We are going to America!"

CHAPTER 34
RUSSIA SAYS NO

John was at the bow of the boat watching the frozen surface, making slight adjustments with the rudder, guiding the boat over the inlet ice. When they arrived at the opening to the sea, the ice had formed ridges which the boat would have to transit. John slowed the craft and then stopped, the engine idling. "Luka, we cannot slide over this ice, we will have to break it up with the hammers." The ridges poked up from the surrounding ice about twenty-centimeters and extended horizontally for three-to-four meters.

Luka and Ivan stepped from the boat armed with hammers and they crushed the irregular ice jutting above the surrounding, nearly flat, frozen surface. In ten minutes, the job was completed, and the men climbed back in the boat. John revved the engine and the boat slipped and bumped over the rough ice onto smoother pack ice and continued eastward across the frozen sea.

With the moon beginning to drop below the horizon, John slowed the iceboat. He was having difficulty seeing an unhindered path and did not want to plunge off the ice into water, fearing difficulties of getting back onto the ice. Several times he turned the boat taking a zig-zag path and circling to avoid dark areas where the ice was thin or nonexistent. But after thirty-five minutes on the ice, he noticed the sky to the east was growing lighter. The sun would soon rise, enabling him to see ahead more clearly than with only moonlight and his diode lamp.

Ten more minutes of easy passage covering an appreciable distance across the ice was giving the entire party confidence in the success of their escape from the militarized coast of Siberia. Luka was the first to become aware of a thumping sound. Thinking it was coming from the boat, he slid forward, tapped John's left shoulder, and said, "I think the engine is breaking apart—slow down; we can listen to the noise."

John slowed the propeller and turned to look back at Luka, but what he saw in the air behind Luka was a helicopter—a Russian helicopter approaching from the west. He pointed into the sky and Luka looked back, realizing the noise was not from their engine, but from the military aircraft. The aircraft moved slowly toward the iceboat, but when within about 100 meters, it stopped, and hovered. John could see the side door of the helicopter slide open and a man kneeling, pointing a rifle in the direction of the iceboat. Three shots rang out and ice chips flew into the air about ten meters from the boat.

A few seconds passed before a voice was heard from a loudspeaker. "You are all under arrest! Turn your craft around and return the way you came. That is an order!"

Luka recognized the voice; it was Captain Dimitri Ulisnilov.

Ivan also recognized Dimitri's voice and cussed. He looked at John and Luka and asked, "What do we do, Luka? Do we go back? Will they shoot us?"

John answered quickly. "The helicopter is not moving toward us. I think we are on the United States' side of the date line."

Luka realized John was correct, but if Dimitri shot them and sank the iceboat there would be no trace of the five people. No one except Dimitri and his crew would ever know what happened.

Sue and Sofiya spoke almost simultaneously, "What is that noise?"

John cut the engine and they all listened. A rumbling noise was coming from the south and all of a sudden, a jet fighter streaked across the sky about a kilometer to the east. It was an American fighter, and as it shot by, it wagged its wings. As they watched it disappear to the north, they yelled excitedly. Luka recognized the plane as an F-22. He had seen such a plane when doing simulations at the technical school.

Luka laughed and remarked, "I do not think Dimitri will be shooting at us any longer."

They heard the aircraft returning, but at a greater distance this time. There was a moment of silence, followed by a loud boom that occurred just after the plane passed them going south. When they heard the boom, everyone ducked, thinking it was the noise from a projectile hitting the ice nearby.

John picked up his rifle and as he held the gun above his head in defiance of the order from the Russian helicopter, he yelled, "A sonic boom! The plane just went faster than sound. I think the pilot was warning the Russian helicopter to leave us alone."

As the Slwookos and the Ivanovs watched, the Russian helicopter landed, and two men began walking toward the iceboat. Ivan said, "Everyone get down behind the boat. John, get ready to do some shooting."

Sue said, "I do not see a gun. Maybe they just want to talk."

Sofiya agreed, "I think Dimitri wants to tell us something. Maybe we should listen. What do you think, Ivan?"

"Yes, we will listen to that fool and then send him on his way. He has nothing to offer us."

When Dimitri and a soldier were about ten meters away, they stopped. Dimitri looked at each passenger of the iceboat and said, "You have left a militarized zone without authorization. You must return with us to talk with the authorities. There will be a fine and imprisonment if you do not come with us." He looked straight at Ivan and said, "I know your name. It is not Ivan Ivanov, it is Oleg Petroff, and your wife is Lidiya Bardzecki. You ran away from the Olympic training center long ago. The Russian Olympic Committee wants to talk with you."

Ivan walked toward the two men and said, "You have no authority or ability to take us back."

Dimitri raised his voice, "Oh, but I do. If you do not return with me, your children in Moscow will suffer. The authorities are looking for them as we speak."

Ivan began laughing. Sofiya and Luka joined in the laughter.

Dimitri frowned and asked, "Why do you laugh? Do you not realize your children are in danger? They will go to prison until you report to the authorities."

Ivan grinned and said, "Arina and Rolan are not in danger; they are in the United States. We are on our way to meet them in Alaska. Go back to your helicopter and fly away, unless you want to meet the authorities from the United States. I am sure they can find a prison cell for you."

Dimitri did not know what to say, but he was startled at what he saw beyond the iceboat. The pack ice was beginning to crack and lifting out of the water. He stepped back five more meters and watched in disbelief as a pipe-like object rose above the ice and then the ice fell away from the periscope and conning tower of a United States submarine.

The Petroffs and the Slwookos were just as surprised as Dimitri was, but they watched with smiles on their faces as four sailors from the submarine, two of them armed, began to walk across the ice toward the iceboat. The sailors were from the United States Navy, led by Lieutenant Darrel Walker.

The lieutenant introduced his men, himself, and then said, "The Coast Guard is sending two helicopters to take you back to Nome. We are just here to make sure nothing goes wrong. In fact, I think I hear them now." He looked toward the southeast and two orange, white, and black helicopters were arriving. They circled the submarine and landed on the ice south of the iceboat and shut off their rotors. The sailors escorted the Petroffs and the Slwookos to the Coast Guard craft and helped them board the choppers. When the doors were closed, the Navy men saluted the Coast Guard aircraft and began walking toward the iceboat.

One of the Coast Guard crewmen made sure the passengers' seatbelts were fastened and after all was ready, the pilot restarted the engine. Ivan watched from the helicopter as two of the sailors climbed into the iceboat, stayed momentarily, and then began running across the ice toward the conning tower sticking above the surface of the pack ice. As the two Coast Guard aircraft rose from the ice and moved away from the iceboat, Ivan saw a flash of light, and as a cloud of smoke drifted away to the west, the iceboat was gone, a ten-meter-wide hole had appeared in the ice. Ivan could do nothing but smile. He looked out the window to see Dimitri's helicopter diminishing in size as it flew west toward Siberia. Ivan continued to smile as he pointed the middle finger of his right hand in the direction of Dimitri's aircraft.

An hour later, the two Coast Guard helicopters arrived at the Nome airport about two minutes apart. Dan and Hank were waiting in the terminal having coffee and donuts and watched the Guard helicopters land.

Hank commented as they saw the cabin doors slide open and crewmen began helping the passengers deplane. "I guess we don't have to worry about them having too much luggage. I don't see any luggage at all. Let's go meet our passengers."

Dan stuffed the last third of his second donut into his mouth, washed it down with coffee and got to his feet. "C'mon, Nomah, we have to say hello to some people from Siberia."

Nomah followed Dan and Hank onto the tarmac. The new arrivals were standing together looking around as if they were lost. Hank and Dan walked with Nomah between them and greeted the newcomers.

Hank spoke to Ivan, "Should I call you Ivan or Oleg? Your daughter told me your original name."

Ivan grinned, "Either one, I spent about half my life with each name."

After Hank and Dan introduced themselves, Ivan introduced Luka, Sofiya, and the Slwookos.

Hank asked, "Have you eaten since this morning?"

"Not since about ten hours, except for some snacks." Ivan replied.

Sofiya pulled at Ivan's coat and whispered something. Ivan looked at Hank and said, "Is my daughter all right? Why she did not write the letter?"

Dan explained what had happened to Rolan and Arina and that they were waiting for them in Fairbanks, three and a half hours away. Then Dan said, "You need to eat before we take you to Fairbanks."

Sofiya stuttered, her voice hardly audible, "B-But we have no money."

Hank grinned and said, "Don't you worry about that, Dan and I have money. You don't need any. Let's go inside and get you a meal. You'll all feel better after you eat something."

Two tables were moved so everyone could be seated together. Hank and Dan helped the new arrivals order, and while they waited for their meals, they visited the restrooms.

Sofiya and Sue returned quickly and were talking with Dan and Hank as the men were in the men's room. The women were marveling about the cleanliness of the ladies' room.

After the men rejoined them at the table, John said, "Sue and I wonder. Could we go to Savoonga on St. Lawrence Island; our family is there. We do not know anyone in Fairbanks."

Hank and Dan looked at each other and said, "Sure." Hank said, "Let's get you two tickets to Savoonga: it's only forty-five minutes from here."

Sue frowned and asked, "Can't you take us? I think you are good pilots."

"No, little lady. We don't have the right plane for ocean flight." He pointed outside and commented, "Those planes are the ones to take. They fly there every day; it's a quick trip. They have good pilots and planes. They never have any trouble." Hank smiled and got up from the table. "I'll get you some tickets. Any luggage besides that rifle?"

John replied, staring at his rifle, "No, we left everything we had behind. I gave my other gun to Rolan when they left in the airplane. It was newer than this one, but they both shoot good."

Dan heard John mention the other rifle and said, "I have your other rifle in our shop, John. Here is one of our business cards. Send me your address and I will ship the gun to you."

John grinned, looked at Sue, and back at Dan. "Thank you. I will sell this one to get us a few dollars."

"C'mon, John, let's get those tickets." Hank escorted John and Sue to the ticket counter and returned a few minutes later with the Slwookos.

Sue, with tears in her eyes, thanked the Ivanovs for the exciting trip out of Siberia. She hugged Sofiya, Ivan, and Luka, and wished them a happy life with Arina and Rolan in Fairbanks.

She shook hands with Hank and Dan, as did John, but John could only utter a single good-bye to everyone, his voice cracking.

Ivan, Sofiya, and Luka thanked the Slwookos for their assistance at the market, with the airplane, and the iceboat, and especially for steering it across the ice.

John grasped Sue's right hand and said, "We must go now. We hope to see you again." He ushered her outside to the aircraft going to St. Lawrence Island; the next flight was planned at daylight the next day, they had to go now. As they disappeared into the plane, John leaned out and waved. The cabin door was sealed, the props began to rotate faster, and the plane taxied onto the runway, halted momentarily and then began moving down the runway headed to Savoonga so Sue could visit with her grandmother.

CHAPTER 35
REUNION

It was almost five o'clock and getting dark when the Newcombs' planes left Nome headed for Fairbanks. Hank took the Ivanovs and began the three-and-one-half-hour trip. Dan and Nomah had taken off first to get a few minutes head start. They were going to deliver mail to Galena and then fly to Fairbanks for the Ivanovs' reunion at Stu Graves' home.

Luka sat closest to Hank and they began talking about how the brothers found the Piper Cub plane and the effort that went into its reconstruction. Fifteen minutes had passed when Hank asked, "Did you learn to fly?"

There was no answer, so Hank asked again, "Did you learn to fly, Luka?"

Hank checked his altitude and speed, glanced at the fuel gauge, and looked over at Luka. He was sound asleep. He looked very relaxed, his breathing was slow and steady. Hank took off his headset and listened to the snoring from behind the pilot's seat. He grinned and estimated the Ivanovs had been on the ice about three hours, had spent an hour on the Coast Guard helicopters, and another hour in Nome. After little sleep the night before, and travelling five hours worrying about being caught on the way to their iceboat, Hank understood why the family members had fallen asleep; they were worn out.

He watched for the signs of the towns below, having flown this route many times before, each small patch of lights had its particular signature providing landmarks that were easy to follow. Hank didn't need any navigation help. He hadn't even bothered to look at the compass on the trip home. When the Fairbanks' lights came into view, Hank received a message from Dan, saying that he was about fifteen minutes out.

Hank answered back, "You must be right behind me, I'm only ten minutes out myself. My passengers are all asleep."

Dan said, "I called Mona and asked her to call Ann to see if she can pick us up. I've called Rigs and Max. I wanted to make sure we'll have transportation for everyone."

Earlier in the day, Max had received a call from the airport. It was about eleven o'clock when the phone rang in the shop.

"Hello, Conley and Newcomb Repairs: Max speaking."

"I need talk to Arina; I am her grandfather. We are here."

Max knew Dan was expecting a call from the Gresham Petroffs but didn't think they could call until after the seventh of December. "One moment please." He put down the phone and ran to the back door. Rolan had gone into the shop's boneyard to find a piece of metal for a repair. Max flung open the door and yelled, "Rolan! There's a phone call for Arina—it's your grandfather. I think your grandparents are in Fairbanks."

Rolan dropped two pieces of metal he had picked up and ran for the phone.

"This is Rolan. Arina is at work at the computer center. Where are you?"

"We are at big airport: Alaska Airways, flight 113 from Seattle. We wait for you. Good-bye."

Rolan shrugged his shoulders, looked at the phone, and said, "He hung up. They are waiting for us to pick them up. What should I do? I do not know if they can get in pickup."

Max responding quickly, "Don't worry. We'll get the family car, pick them up, and take them to your place. Let's close early for lunch. Put the sign up—back at 1:00 p.m."

Max and Rolan drove the Conleys' SUV to the main entrance of the airport to meet Akilina and Sergei. The elder Petroffs were sitting on large suitcases inside the automatic doors watching people come and go. They had done their homework about the December weather in Fairbanks and were dressed warmly. Rolan had gone ahead to locate the Petroffs while Max waited in the parking area for Rolan's signal that he had found them. Rolan signaled Max to drive closer to the entranceway. Max jumped out and loaded the luggage as Rolan assisted the elder Petroffs into the back seat. Rolan briefly introduced his newly discovered relatives to Max, who welcomed them to Alaska.

Other than the few words in English used during the introductions, the three Petroffs spoke in Russian. Though Max could not understand a word, he listened to the grandparents' queries and was amused by the short answers given by Rolan. The conversation sounded much like the Conleys' exchanges at the dinner table, the boys nearly always giving short replies to Max and Mona, rarely initiating questions or making observations of their own.

When Max drove into the parking area at the computer center, Rolan ran into the building, and a minute later, Arina was walking from the building with the assistance of crutches and steadied by Rolan. Sergei got out of the car and helped Arina get into the back seat so she would be sitting between her grandparents. An animated conversation began in the back seat, with occasional contributions from Rolan, who sat sideways without fastening the seatbelt. Arina had started talking in English, but she quickly shifted to Russian, and as Max drove toward Stu Graves' home, he could hear some English mixed with Russian.

As Max pulled into the log cabin parking lot, he heard Arina laughing. He turned off the engine, and Rolan joined him to help everyone out of the rear seat. Rolan grabbed the baggage and they made their way into Stu's luxurious cabin.

Arina thanked Max for the taxi service and she explained why she had been laughing.

"My grandparents said that Rolan had found a good driver. Rolan had told them he had a good job so they thought he had hired the car and driver. I told them you were his boss and we were riding in your car. They were embarrassed and said they would apologize to you. I told them you did not understand Russian, so an apology was not necessary. Is that not correct?"

Max grinned and said, "That is correct, Arina. Say, do you want to have lunch here? That would prevent some driving around. You still have to work this afternoon, don't you?"

"Yes, we will eat here. You can join us. I do not have work this afternoon. My boss told me to take care of my grandparents and come back tomorrow."

"Okay. Rolan doesn't have to work today, either, but I will need him tomorrow. This afternoon you and Rolan get your grandparents unpacked and familiar with the house. I'll call you as soon as I hear from Hank or Dan, but I don't think they will be back until evening. You will have a nice surprise for the rest of your family."

Max worked alone all afternoon and didn't get home until seven o'clock. He had called Mona at six o'clock to tell her he would be late and would pick up pizza on the way home. Just as the Conleys were sitting down to eat, the phone rang. Max shook his head and thought, "Not another call! Can't people call during business hours?"

Mona grabbed the phone and answered, "Hello. Oh! Hi, Dan. Where are you?"

"Dad and I are about an hour out. Dad's got the Petroffs. Nomah and I are following about five minutes behind. Can you please call Arina and tell her we will be there around nine o'clock?"

"Will do. See you soon. Bye." Mona checked her watch. It was 7:28 p.m. It had been dark for over two hours and the temperature was dropping rapidly. She hoped Hank and Dan didn't have any problems touching down at their landing strip. The landing lights out there weren't very bright, but they had landed there many times—though mostly during daylight hours. Dan had put lights, in the shape of an arrow, on top of the Quonset building indicating the direction of the landing strip and Hank had put three lights perpendicular to the landing strip at both ends. The marker lights came on automatically during the nighttime hours but could be controlled from the planes if necessary.

Max, Rigs, and Ann had arrived at the landing strip within ten minutes of each other. Rigs had arrived at eight-fifteen p.m. By eight-thirty they were waiting together in Max's SUV when Hank arrived and taxied off the strip next to the Quonset building to allow Dan free access to the runway. Hank and Max transferred the Petroffs to Max's car after introductions were made. Hank told Max to go ahead and take his passengers to Stu's cabin, the rest of them would follow in a few minutes. As Max drove away from the landing strip, Dan landed, gave Ann a hug and a kiss, and secured his plane. Hank rode with Rigs and Dan drove Ann's car with Ann and Nomah as passengers.

Arina was anticipating the arrival of her family and had planned a surprise for her parents, especially for her father. She watched out the window, waiting for headlights to come down the road to the cabin. When

Max's SUV pulled into the parking area, Arina said excitedly, "They're here! Grandma and Grandpa, please go in the kitchen. As soon as the excitement is over here, I will send Papa into the kitchen. You will surprise him there." She looked at her grandparents and said, "I hope no one has a heart attack."

With their hearts pounding, as if trying to escape from their chests, Rolan and Arina, smiling from ear to ear, waited behind the giant front door to welcome their parents and Luka. Arina could hear footsteps on the deck approaching the door, and when there was a knock, she swung the door open and ran into her mother's arms. Both women began crying and Rolan, Luka, and Ivan had a three-way bear hug, followed with handshakes and pats on each other's backs. While the excitement at the front door was taking place, Ann, Rigs, Dan, Hank, and Nomah were climbing the stairs to the deck and the front door.

The Ivanov family moved into the living room and sat down, everyone trying to talk at the same time. Rolan stood up from the sofa and motioned to Dan for everyone on the deck to come into the house. Dan took over with the introductions of Ann, Rigs, and Nomah. As the conversations began to subside, Arina said, "Papa, I want you to help me get some drinks for our friends. Follow me into the kitchen."

Arina grabbed her father's arm and began pulling him toward the kitchen's swinging doors. Ivan put his arm around Arina and helped her move the five meters across the family room. Rolan had motioned for everyone to be quiet, and as they realized something was going to happen, a hush came over the living room.

A woman's shriek could be heard coming from behind the kitchen doors, followed by loud laughter. Ivan burst from the kitchen holding his mother in his arms, his father following closely behind with Arina. Ivan put his mother, Akilina, down and she began kissing him and wiping tears from his cheeks. His father, Sergei, gave Ivan a big bear hug and said loudly, "This is my son! It has been twenty-eight years! All this time we thought he was dead. He has wonderful family and many friends. This is wonderful Christmas for us."

Arina called to Ann and waved for her to come and help in the kitchen. In a few minutes, everyone had drinks, bread, and cheese. Sergei was going around to all the men saying, "Have you met my granddaughter? She is very beautiful, no?"

When he came to Dan, Dan agreed and said, "I have a fiancée, she is very beautiful, too. Her name is Ann. She is the one helping with the refreshments."

"You are not married?" asked Sergei.

"Not yet. We are planning a Christmas wedding."

Sergei held up his right hand holding a beer. "Ah, we give you Russian wedding. Everybody will come. You have done much for our family, we give you wedding of your dreams."

Dan and Ann were smiling at each other, arm in arm. Dan said, "That would be very nice of you, but it isn't necessary. We were just going to have a small wedding. We both have jobs so we can't take much time off."

Ivan and Sofiya joined Sergei and Akilina in their attempt to persuade Dan and Ann to let them take care of the wedding. Sofiya said, "We would like to get married again and this would be our opportunity. When we married long ago, it was in an office where we signed some papers. We would like to have a ceremony. Would you let us share your wedding?"

Dan grinned, looked at Ann, and she nodded, smiling, and said, "Let's do it, Dan. Let's see if Mom and Hank want to get married, too. We'll have three marriages. It'll be fun!"

Life was hectic the weeks following the Petroff family reunion. Chyler returned from Seattle having undergone facial reconstruction surgery. Although she was healing quickly, it would be several months before her facial expressions were nearly symmetrical. Rigs was on Christmas break until after New Year's and he accompanied Chyler home to Galena in Hank's plane. After Hank transferred the mail to Dan's plane, Chyler and Rigs convinced her uncle Jack to join them on their return flight to Fairbanks for Christmas and the weddings. Chyler was going to be in the weddings, serving as a bride's maid with Arina. In addition, she was going to help all three ladies with their clothes.

Stu Graves returned from Texas in great spirits. He had found four investors: each had invested $75,000 for five percent interests in his gold mine. Now he was playing the waiting game; mining couldn't begin until spring when the ground thawed. He was very gracious and was going to let the Petroffs stay in his home until they could arrange for travel to Portland, Oregon. Dan and Hank gave Stu a key to the shop where he could live until the Petroffs were gone.

Twelve days before Christmas, the Petroffs invited everyone for dinner. When Stu heard about the weddings planned, he asked Dan, "Do you have a commissioner or minister?"

The talking at the extended dining table suddenly ceased, no one could miss hearing Stu's booming voice. Dan looked at Ann and she shook her head. None of the ladies had considered hiring a minister. They had assumed either Dan or Hank had taken care of it. Hank shook his head, too, and said, "I didn't even think about it, sorry."

Stu smiled and announced, "There is nothing to worry about, folks. Among other things, I am an ordained minister. I understand the Petroffs are just reaffirming their vows; they do not need a certificate. Do you two couples have marriage certificates?" He looked at Hank, Beverly, Dan, and Ann, expecting affirmation.

Dan and Hank answered in unison, "No."

"All right. You still have time to apply at court. You will need my name and address for the certificate. I will get the appropriate forms for my participation. What time is the ceremony?"

Beverly spoke up, "Two o'clock on Christmas Day—if that is okay with you."

"That is fine with me. I will program the sound system to start at 2:00 pm, unless you have other arrangements for music. Will there be any more guests?"

Beverly looked around the room, counted heads, and answered, "Your music will be fine, and everyone here is expected, unless you have someone coming. Oh, Mrs. Riggins might come, and I almost forgot Mona, Max, and their boys."

Stu glanced around the room, apparently counting heads. "I just wanted to know so I can order a cake big enough and have plenty of champagne. Oh! My fee is one dollar."

Stu began to laugh and said, "Is that too much? Well, I'll pay for the cake and booze. It will be a first for me, two marriages at the same time plus a reaffirmation of vows. It will be something to celebrate!"

Stu had erected a twelve-foot evergreen tree in the great room of his home the week before Christmas, and throughout the week, the Petroffs and visitors had been adding decorations and gifts. Early Christmas Day, guests and principals began to arrive at 7:00 a.m. bearing more gifts and food. The weddings took place just as planned. Following the vows, the certificates were signed and witnessed. A big buffet table was loaded with a great variety of food. Cake and champagne were present in abundance.

Wedding gifts were combined with Christmas presents under the tree, but the wedding gifts far outnumbered the presents. Stu donned a Santa's hat and handed out items to everyone. Hank and Dan gave Stu a battery-operated, digital-scale to weigh gold accurately. When all the gifts had been distributed, Stu went upstairs and reprogrammed the stereo to play Christmas music. After he had rejoined the group around the tree, Ivan stood and walked over to the tree and began looking under the boughs. No one knew he was looking for a present for Sofiya.

Ivan passed behind the tree, and when he reappeared, he held a small package in his massive hands. Hank asked, "What have you got there, Ivan? Something Stu didn't see?"

"Yes. This was hidden out of sight under the limbs. It is for Sofiya."

Sofiya was surprised and scolded, "We decided not to trade gifts, Ivan. We do not have any money to waste." There was silence as Ivan presented Sofiya with a small box wrapped in red paper and tied with a white ribbon.

"I did not spend any money, my dear."

Sofiya shook the box and listened for a rattle, but there was none. She smiled, lay the package in her lap, and looked around at everyone.

Beverly said, "Open it, Sofiya. Show us what it is."

Sofiya removed the ribbon carefully and folded back the red paper to reveal a small, white, rectangular box. Sofiya expected to see a handkerchief, or a pretty scarf, but what she saw made her begin to cry. It was the little thermometer from her kitchen that she had gotten when they were married, twenty-seven years ago.

She couldn't speak, tears were cascading down her cheeks. She stood and ran the few steps to Ivan and threw her arms around him. He lifted her off the floor, hugged her, and said,

"I knew the thermometer was something special; I could not leave it behind. We will start our new life together with an old friend that reminds us of all the years we have had together. Now you can kiss me, and please do not cry any more. It is Christmas."

BOOKS BY THE AUTHOR INCLUDE:

Glacier Fires and Ornaments of Value
Missing Notes, Hidden Talents, and Other Stories
Wolves' Hollow Murders
Detour in Oregon
An Iceberg's Gift
The Lighthouse Library
The Lighthouse Fire
The Niffits
The Kuiper Belt Deception
The Antarctic Deception
A Professor's Affair
The Kidnapping of Megan Isaacs
The Bitterroot Diamonds
The Bitterroot Fire
The Twig Lady & A Crystal for Charity
The Distant Lighthouse

ACKNOWLEDGMENTS:

Thanks to Bob Griswold and Barbara Schroeder for proof reading and to Alain Douchinsky for her great assistance in editing.